SPARK'S EUROPE

'[Spark] has a receptive and wholly distinctive genius'
A.N. WILSON

'Spark is a natural, a paradigm of that rare sort of
artist from whom work of the highest quality flows as
elementally as a current through a circuit' *NEW YORKER*

'I consider Muriel Spark to be the most gifted and innovative
British novelist of her generation' DAVID LODGE

'A profoundly serious comic writer whose wit advances,
never undermines or diminishes, her ideas'
NEW YORK TIMES BOOK REVIEW

'Reading a blast of her prose every morning is a far more
restorative way to start a day than a shot of espresso'
DAILY TELEGRAPH

'Delightful, laced with wry and witty observations'
DAILY MAIL

ALSO BY MURIEL SPARK

Muriel Spark

SPARK'S EUROPE

CANONGATE
Edinburgh · London

This Canons edition published in Great Britain in 2016
by Canongate Books Ltd, 14 High Street, Edinburgh EH1 1TE

www.canongate.tv

1

Not to Disturb © 1971 Copyright Administration Ltd
The Takeover © 1976 Copyright Administration Ltd
The Only Problem © 1984 Copyright Administration Ltd

British Library Cataloguing-in-Publication Data
A catalogue record for this book is available on
request from the British Library.

ISBN 978 1 78211 765 0

Typeset in Sabon MT by Canongate Books Ltd

Printed and bound in Great Britain by Clays Ltd, St Ives plc.

CONTENTS

CONTENTS

NOT to DISTURB

I

THE OTHER SERVANTS FALL SILENT as Lister enters the room.

'Their life,' says Lister, 'a general mist of error. Their death, a hideous storm of terror. – I quote from *The Duchess of Malfi* by John Webster, an English dramatist of old.'

'When you say a thing is not impossible, that isn't quite as if to say it's possible,' says Eleanor who, although younger than Lister, is his aunt. She is taking off her outdoor clothes. 'Only technically is the not impossible, possible.'

'We are not discussing possibilities today,' Lister says. 'Today we speak of facts. This is not the time for inconsequential talk.'

'Of facts accomplished,' says Pablo the handyman.

Eleanor hangs her winter coat on a hanger.

'The whole of Geneva will be talking,' she says.

'What about him in the attic?' says Heloise, the youngest maid whose hands fold over her round stomach as she speaks. The stomach moves of its own accord and she pats it. 'What about him in the attic?' she says. 'Shall we let him loose?'

Eleanor looks at the girl's stomach. 'You better get out of the way when the journalists come,' she says. 'Never mind him in the attic. They'll be making inquiries of you. Wanting to know.'

'Oh,' says Heloise, holding her stomach. 'It's the quickening. I could faint.' But she stands tall, placid and unfainting, gazing out of the window of the servants' sitting-room.

3

'He was a very fine man in his way. The whole of Geneva got a great surprise.'

'Will get a surprise,' Eleanor says.

'Let us not split hairs,' says Lister, 'between the past, present and future tenses. I am agog for word from the porter's lodge. They should be arriving. Watch from the window.' And to the pregnant maid he says, 'Have you got out all the luggage?'

'Pablo has packed his bags already,' says Heloise, swivelling her big eyes over to the handyman with a slight turn of her body.

'Sensible,' says Lister.

'Pablo is the father,' Heloise declares, patting her stomach which quivers under her apron.

'I wouldn't be so sure of that,' Lister says. 'And neither would you.'

'Well it isn't the Baron,' says Heloise.

'No, it isn't the Baron,' says Lister.

'It isn't the Baron, that's for sure,' says Eleanor.

'The poor late Baron,' says Heloise.

'Precisely,' says Lister. 'He'll be turning up soon. In the Buick, I should imagine.'

Eleanor is putting on an apron. 'Where's my carrot juice? Go and ask Monsieur Clovis for my carrot juice. My eyes have improved since I went on carrot juice.'

'Clovis is busy with his contract,' Lister says. 'He left it rather late. I made mine with *Stern* and *Paris-Match* over a month ago. Now of course there's still the movie deal to consider, but you want to play it cool. Don't forget. Play it cool and sell to the highest bidder.'

Clovis looks up, irritably, from his papers. 'France, Germany, Italy, bid high. But don't forget in the long run that English is the higher-income language. We ought to coordinate on that point.' He continues his scrutiny of documents.

'Surely Monsieur Clovis is going to prepare a meal to-night, isn't he?' says Eleanor. She goes through the door to the kitchen. 'Clovis!' she calls. 'Don't forget my carrot juice, will you?'

'Quiet!' says Clovis. 'I'm reading the small print. The small print in a contract is the important part. You can get your own damn carrot juice. There's carrots in the vegetable store and there's the blender in front of you. You all get your own supper tonight.'

'What about them?'

'They won't be needing supper.'

Lister stands in the doorway, now, watching his young aunt routing among the vegetables for a few carrots which she presses between her fingers disapprovingly.

'Supper, never again,' says Lister. 'For them, supper no more.'

'These carrots are soft,' says Eleanor. 'Heloise doesn't know how to market. She's out of place in a house this style.'

'The poor Baroness used to like her,' says Clovis, looking up from the table where he is sitting studying the fine print. 'The poor Baroness could see no wrong in Heloise.'

'I see no wrong in her, either,' Eleanor says. 'I only say she doesn't know how to buy carrots.'

Heloise comes to join them at the kitchen door.

'It's quickening,' she informs Clovis.

'Well it isn't my fault,' says the chef.

'Nor me neither, Heloise,' says Lister severely. 'I always took precautions the times I went with you.'

'It's Pablo,' says the girl, 'I could swear to it. Pablo's the father.'

'It could have been one of the visitors,' Lister says.

Clovis looks up from his papers, spread out as they are on the kitchen table. 'The visitors never got Heloise, never.'

'There were one or two,' says Heloise, reflectively. 'But it's day and night with Pablo when he's in the mood. After breakfast, even.' She looks at her stomach as if to discern by a kind of X-ray eye who the father truly might be. 'There was a visitor or two,' she says. 'I must say, there did happen to be a visitor or two about the time I caught on. Either a visitor of the Baroness or a visitor of the Baron.'

'We have serious business on hand tonight, my girl, so shut up,' says the chef. 'We have business to discuss and plenty to do. Quite a vigil. Has anybody arrived yet?'

'Eleanor, I say keep a look out of the window,' Lister orders his aunt. 'You never know when someone might leave their car out on the road and slip in. They're careless down at the lodge.'

Eleanor cranes her neck towards the window, still feeling the soft carrots with a contemptuous touch. 'Here comes Hadrian; it's only Hadrian coming up the drive. These carrots are past it. Terrible carrots.'

The footsteps crunch to the back of the house. Hadrian the assistant chef comes in with a briefcase under his arm.

'Did you get out my cabin trunk?' he asks Heloise.

'It's too big, in my condition.'

'Well get Pablo to fetch it, quick. I'm going to start my packing.'

'What about him in the attic?' says Heloise. 'We better take him up his supper or he might create or take one of his turns.'

'Of course he'll get his supper. It's early yet.'

'Suppose the Baron wants his dinner?'

'Of course he expected his dinner,' Lister says. 'But as things turned out he didn't live to eat it. He'll be arriving soon.'

'There might be an unexpected turn of events,' says Eleanor.

'There was sure to be something unexpected,' says Lister. 'But what's done is about to be done and the future has come to pass. My memoirs up to the funeral are as a matter of fact more or less complete. At all events, it's out of our hands. I place the event at about three a.m. so prepare to stay awake.'

'I would say six o'clock tomorrow morning. Right on the squeak of dawn,' says Heloise.

'You might well be right,' says Lister. 'Women in your condition are unusually intuitive.'

'How it kicks!' says Heloise with her hand on her stomach. 'Do you know something? I have a craving for grapes. Do we have any grapes? A great craving. Should I get a tray ready for him in the attic?'

'Rather early,' says Lister looking at the big moon-faced kitchen clock. 'It's only ten past six. Get your clothes packed.'

The large windowed wall of the servants' hall looks out on a gravelled courtyard and beyond that, the cold mountains, already lost in the early darkening of autumn.

A dark green, small car has parked here by the side entrance. The servants watch. Two women sit inside, one at the wheel and one in the back seat. They do not speak. A tall person has just left the other front seat and has come round to the front door.

Lister waits for the bell to ring and when it does he goes to open the door:

A long-locked young man, fair, wearing a remarkable white fur coat which makes his pink skin somewhat radiant. The coat reaches to his boots.

Lister acknowledges by a slight smile, in which he uses his mouth only, that he recognizes the caller well from previous visits. 'Sir?' says Lister.

'The Baroness,' says the young man, in the quiet voice of one who does not wish to spend much of it.

'She is not at home. Will you wait, sir?' Lister stands aside to make way at the door.

'Yes, she's expecting me. Is the Baron in?' sounds the low voice of the young man.

'We expect him back for dinner, sir. He should be in short-ly.'

Lister takes the white fur coat glancing at the quality and kind of mink, and at its lining and label as he does so. Lister, with the coat over his arm, turns to the left, crosses the oval hall, followed by the young man. Lister treads across the *trompe-l'œil* chequered paving of the hall and the young man follows. He wears a coat of deep blue satin with darker blue watered silk lapels, trousers of dark blue velvet, a pale mauve satin shirt with a very large high collar and a white cravat fixed with an amethyst pin. Lister opens a door and stands aside. The young man, as he enters, says politely to Lister, 'In the left-hand outer pocket, this time, Lister.'

'Thank you, sir,' says Lister, as he withdraws. He closes the door again and crosses the oval hall to another door. He opens it, hangs the white mink coat gently on one of a long line of coat-hangers which are placed expectantly in order on a carved rack. Lister then feels in the outer left-hand pocket of the coat, withdraws a fat, squat, brown envelope, opens it with a forefinger, half-pulls out a bundle of bank-notes, calculates them with his eyes, stuffs them back into the envelope, and places the envelope in one of his own pockets, somewhere beneath his white jacket, at heart-level. Lister looks at himself in the glass above the wash-basin and looks away. He arranges the neat unused hand-towels with the crested 'K' even more neatly, and leaves the cloak-room.

The other servants fall silent as Lister returns.

'Number One,' says Lister. 'He walked to his death most gingerly.'

'Sex,' muses Heloise.

Lister shudders, 'The forbidden word,' he says. 'Let me not hear you say it again.'

'It's Victor Passerat, waiting there in the library,' says Heloise.

'Mister Fair-locks,' says Eleanor, looking at the carrot juice which she has prepared with the blender.

'I never went with him,' says Heloise. 'I had the chance, though.'

'Didn't we all?' says Pablo.

'Speak for yourself,' says Clovis.

'Less talk,' says Lister.

'Victor Passerat isn't the dad,' says Heloise.

'He'd never have had it in him,' says Pablo.

'Are you aware,' says Eleanor to her nephew, 'that two ladies are waiting outside in the car that brought the visitor?'

Lister glances towards the window but next he goes to a large cupboard and, drawing up a chair, mounts it. He carefully, one by one, removes the neat jars of preserved fruit that are stacked there, ginger in gin, cherries in cognac, apple and pineapple, marmalades of several types, some of them capped and bottled with a home-made look, others, according to their shapes and labels, fetched in from as far as Fortnum and Mason in London and Charles's in New York. All these Lister carefully places on a side-table, assisted by Eleanor and watched by the others in a grave silence evidently due to the occasion. Lister removes a plank shelf, now bare of bottles. At the back of the cupboard is a wall-safe, the lock of which Lister slowly and respectfully opens, although not yet the door. He demands a pen, and while waiting for Hadrian the assistant cook to fetch it, he takes the envelope from his inner pocket, and counts the bank-notes in full view of the rest.

'Small change,' he says, 'compared with what is to come, or has already come, according as one's philosophy is temporal or eternal. To all intents and purposes, they're already dead although as a matter of banal fact, the night's business has still to accomplish itself.'

'Lister's in good vein tonight,' says Clovis, who has left the perusal of his contract to join the group. Meanwhile Hadrian returns, handing up the simple ballpoint pen to Lister.

Upstairs the shutters bang.

'The wind is high tonight,' Lister says. 'We might not hear the shots.' He takes the pen and marks a sum on the envelope, followed by the date. He then opens wide the safe which is neatly stacked with various envelopes and boxes, some of metal, some of leather. He places the new package among the rest, closes the safe, replaces the wooden shelf, and, assisted by Eleanor and Heloise, puts the preserve-bottles back in their places. He descends from his chair, hands the chair to Hadrian, closes the cupboard door, and goes to the window. 'Yes,' he says, 'two ladies waiting in the car, as well they might. Good night, ladies. Good night, sweet, sweet, ladies.'

'Why did they pull up round the side instead of waiting in the drive?' says Heloise.

'The answer,' says Lister, 'is that they know their place. They had the courage to accompany their kinsman on his errand, but at the last little moment, lacked the style which alone was necessary to save him. The Baron will arrive, and not see them, not inquire. Likewise the Baroness. No sense, for all their millions.'

'With all that in there alone,' says Heloise, still contemplating the closed cupboard wherein lies the wall-safe of treasure, 'we could buy the Montreux Palace Hotel.'

'Who needs the Montreux Palace?' says Hadrian.

'Think big,' says Pablo the handyman, patting her around the belly.

'How it kicks!' she says.

'How like,' says Lister, 'the death wish is to the life-urge! How urgently does an overwhelming obsession with life lead to suicide! Really, it's best to be half-awake and half-aware. That is the happiest stage.'

'The Baron Klopstocks were obsessed with sex,' says Eleanor. She is setting places at the long servants' table.

'Sex is not to be mentioned,' Lister says. 'To do so would be to belittle their activities. On their sphere sex is nothing but an overdose of life. They will die of it, or rather, to all intents and purposes, have died. We treat of spontaneous combustion. One remove from sex, as in Henry James, an English American who travelled.'

'They die of violence,' says Clovis who has transferred to the butler's desk his papers and the contract and documents he has been studying closely for the past three-quarters of an hour. He sits with his back to the others, looks half over his shoulders. 'To be precise, it is of violence that they shortly die.'

'Clovis,' says Eleanor, 'would you mind giving an eye to the oven?'

'Where's my assistant?' says Clovis.

'Hadrian has gone down to the lodge,' says Eleanor. 'Gone to borrow a couple of eggs. Him in the attic hasn't had his supper yet.'

'No eggs in the house?' says Clovis.

'There was too much else to arrange today,' says Eleanor as she places five tiny silver bowls of salt at regular intervals along the table, carefully measuring the distance with her eye. 'No marketing done.'

'Things have gone to rack and ruin,' says Lister, 'now that the crisis has arrived. This house hitherto was run like the solar system.'

'Cook your own damn dinner,' says Clovis, bending closely over his documents.

'Don't you want any?' says Heloise. 'I'll eat your share if you like, Clovis. I'm eating for two.'

Clovis bangs down his fist, drops his pen, goes across to the large white complicated cooking stove, studies the regulator, turns the dial, opens the stove door, and while looking inside, with the other hand snaps his finger. Heloise runs with a cloth and a spoon and places them in Clovis's hand. Protecting his hand with the cloth Clovis partly pulls out a casserole dish. He hooks up the lid with the handle of the spoon, peers in, sniffs, replaces the lid, shoves the dish back and closes the oven door. Again, he turns the dial of the regulator. Then with the spoon-handle, he lifts the lids from the two pots which are simmering on top of the stove. He glances inside each and replaces the lids.

'Fifteen minutes more for the casserole. In seven minutes you move the pots aside. We sit down at half-past seven if we're lucky and they don't decide to dine before they die.'

'No they won't eat,' says Lister. 'We can have our dinner in peace while they get on with the job.'

From somewhere far away at the top of the house comes a howl and a clatter.

'I'll have a vodka and tonic,' says Clovis, as he passes through the big kitchen and returns to his papers at the butler's desk.

'Very good,' says Lister, looking round. 'Any more orders?'

'Nothing for me. I had my carrot juice. I couldn't stomach a sherry, not tonight,' says Eleanor.

'Nerves,' says Lister, and has started to leave the kitchen when the house-telephone rings. He returns to answer it.

12

'Lister here,' he says, and listens briefly while something in the telephone crackles into the room. 'Very good,' he then says into the telephone and hangs up. 'The Baron,' says he, 'has arrived.'

The Baron's great car moves away from the porter's lodge while the porter closes the gates behind it. It slightly swerves to avoid Hadrian who is walking up the drive.

The porter, returning to the lodge, finds his wife hanging up the house-telephone in the cold hall. 'Lister sounds like himself,' she tells her husband.

'What the hell do you expect him to sound like?' says the porter. 'How should he sound?'

'He was no different from usual,' she says. 'Oh, I feel terrible.'

'Nothing's going to happen, dear,' he says, suddenly hugging her. 'Nothing at all.'

'I can feel it in the air, like electricity,' she says. He takes her arm, urging her into the warm sitting-room. She is young and small. She looks as if she were steady of mind but she says, 'I think I am going mad.'

'Clara!' says the porter. 'Clara!'

She says, 'Last night I had a terrible dream.'

Cecil Klopstock, the Baron, has arrived at his door, thin and wavering. The door is open and Lister stands by it.

'The Baroness?' says the Baron, passively departing from his coat which slides over Lister's arm.

'No, sir, she hasn't arrived. Mr Passerat is waiting.'

'When did he come?'

'About half-past six, sir.'

'Anyone with him?'

'Two women in the car. They're waiting outside.'

13

'Let them wait,' says the Baron and goes towards the library, across the black and white paving of the hall. He hesitates, half-turns, then says, 'I'll wash in here,' evidently referring to a wash-room adjoining the library.

'I thought it best,' Lister says as he enters the servants' sitting-room, 'to tell him about those two women waiting outside, perceiving as I did from his manner that he had already noticed them. – "Anyone with Mr Passerat?" he said with his eye to me. "Yes, sir," I said, "two ladies. They are waiting in the car." Why he asked me that redundant question I'll never know.'

'He was testing you out,' says Hadrian who is whisking two eggs in a bowl.

'Yes, that's what I think, too,' says Lister. 'I feel wounded. I opened the door of the library. Passerat got up. The Baron said "Good evening, Victor" and Passerat said "Good evening." Whereupon, being unwanted, I respectfully withdrew. *Sic transit gloria mundi.*'

'They will be sitting down having a drink,' says Pablo who has cleaned himself up and is now regarding his hair from a distance in the oval looking-glass. This way and that he turns his head, with its hair shiny-black.

'Didn't he ask for more ice?' says Eleanor. 'They never have enough ice.'

'They have plenty of ice in the drinks cupboard. I filled the ice-box, myself, and put more on refrigeration this afternoon when you were all busy with your telephoning and personal arrangements,' Lister says. 'They have ice. All they need now is the Baroness.'

'Oh, she'll come, don't worry,' says Clovis, stacking his papers neatly.

'I wish she'd hurry,' says Heloise, as she slumps in a puffy cretonned armchair. 'I want to eat my dinner in peace.'

Hadrian has prepared a tray on which he has placed a dish of scrambled eggs, a plate of thin toasted buttered bread, a large cup and saucer and a silver thermos-container of some beverage. Eleanor, with vague movements, leaves her table-setting to place on the tray a knife, a fork and a spoon; then she covers the toast and the eggs with silver plate-covers.

'What are you doing?' says Hadrian, grabbing the knife and fork off the tray. 'What's come over you?'

'Oh, I forgot,' says Eleanor. 'I've been in a state all day.' She replaces the knife and fork with one large spoon.

Lister goes to the house-telephone, lifts the receiver and presses a button. Presently the instrument wheezes. 'Supper on its way up to him in the attic,' says Lister. 'Yours will follow later.'

The instrument wheezes again.

'We'll keep you informed,' says Lister. 'All you have to do is stay there till we tell you not to.' He hangs up. 'Sister Barton is worried,' he says. 'Him in the attic is full of style this evening and likely to worsen as the night draws on. Another case of intuition.'

Hadrian takes the tray in his hands and as he leaves the room he asks, 'Shall I tell Sister Barton to call the doctor?'

'Leave it to Sister Barton,' says Lister, gloomily, with his eyes on other thoughts. 'Leave it to her.'

Heloise says, 'I can manage him in the attic myself, if it comes to that. I've always been good to him in the attic.'

'You better get some sleep after you've had your supper, my girl,' says Clovis. 'You've got a big night ahead. The reporters will be here in the morning if not before.'

'It might not take place till six-ish in the morning,' says Heloise. 'Once they start arguing it could drag on all night. I'm intuitive, as Mr Lister says, and – '

'Only as regards your condition,' says Lister. 'Normally, you are not a bit intuitive. You're thick, normally. It's merely that in your condition the Id tends to predominate over the Ego.'

'I have to be humoured,' says Heloise, shutting her eyes. 'Why can't I have some grapes?'

'Give her some grapes,' says Pablo.

'Not before dinner,' says Clovis.

'Clara!' says Theo the porter. 'Clara!'

'It's only that I'm burning with desire to ask them what's going on up at the house tonight,' she says.

'Come back here. Come right back, darling,' he says, drawing her into the sitting-room where the fire glows and flares behind the fender. 'Desire,' he says.

'Theo!' she says.

'You and your nightmares,' Theo says. He shuts the door of the sitting-room and sits beside her on the sofa, absent-mindedly plucking her thigh while he stares at the dancing fire. 'You and your dreams.'

Clara says, 'There's nothing in it for us. We were better off at the Ritz in Madrid.'

'Now, now. We're doing better here. We're doing much better here. Lister is very generous. Lister is very, very generous.' Theo picks up the poker and turns a coal on the fire, making it flare, while Clara swings her legs up on to the sofa. 'Theo,' she says, 'did I tell you Hadrian came down here to borrow a couple of eggs?'

'And what else, Clara,' says Theo. 'What else?'

'Nothing,' she says. 'Just the eggs.'

'I can't turn my back but he's down here,' says Theo. 'I'll report him to the Baron tomorrow morning.' He goes to draw the window-curtains. 'And Clovis,' he says, 'for not keeping an eye on him.' Theo returns to the sofa.

Clara screams 'No, no, I've changed my mind,' and pushes him away. She ties up her cord-trimmed dressing-gown.

'Not so much of it, Clara,' says Theo. 'All this yes-no. I could have the Baroness if I want. Any minute of the hour. Any hour of the day.'

'Oh, it's you that makes me dream these terrible things, Theo,' she says. 'When you talk like that, on and on about the Baroness, with her grey hair. You should be ashamed.'

'She's got grey hair all places,' Theo says, 'from all accounts.'

'If I was a man,' says Clara, 'I'd be sick at the thought.'

'Well, from all accounts, I'd sooner sleep with her than a dead policeman,' says Theo.

'Hark, there's a car on the road. It must be her,' says Clara. But Theo is not harking. She plucks at his elastic braces and says, 'A disgrace that they didn't have an egg in the house for the idiot-boy's supper. Something must be happening up there. I've felt it all week, haven't you, Theo?'

Theo has no words, his breath being concentrated by now on Clara alone. She says, 'And there's the car drawing up, Theo – it's stopped at the gate. Theo, you'd better go.'

He draws back from his wife for the split second which it takes him to say, 'Shut up.'

'I can hear the honking at the gate,' she says in a loud voice – 'Don't you hear her sounding the horn? All week in my dreams I've heard the honking at the gate.' Theo grunts.

The car honks twice and Theo now puts on his coat and pulls himself together with the dignity of a man who does one thing at a time in due order. He goes to the hall, takes the keys from the table drawer and walks forth into the damp air to open the gate beyond which a modest cream coupé is honking still.

It pulls up at the porter's lodge after it has been admitted. The square-faced woman at the wheel is the only occupant.

She lets down the window and says, cheerfully, 'How are you, Theo?'

'Very well, thanks, Madam. Sorry to keep you waiting, Madam. There was a question of eggs for the poor gentleman in the attic, his supper.'

She smiles charmingly from under her great fur hat.

'Everything goes wrong when I'm away, doesn't it? And how is Clara, is she enjoying this little house?'

'Oh yes, Madam, we're very happy in this job,' says Theo. 'We're settling in nicely.'

'You'll get used to our ways, Theo.'

'Well, Madam, we've had plenty of experience behind us, Clara and me. So we've shaken down here nicely.' He shivers, standing in the cold night, bareheaded in his porter's uniform.

'Your *rapport* with the servants – is that all right?' gently inquires the Baroness.

Theo hesitates, then opens his mouth to speak. But the Baroness puts in, 'Your relationship with them? You get on all right with them?'

'Oh yes, Madam. Perfectly, Madam. Thanks.' He steps back a little pace, as if only too ready to withdraw quickly into the warm cottage.

The Baroness makes no move to put her thick-gloved hand on the wheel. She says, 'I'm so very glad. Among servants of such mixed nationalities, it's very difficult sometimes to achieve harmony. Indeed, we're one of the few places in the country that has a decent-sized staff. I don't know what the Baron and I would do without you all.'

Theo crosses his arms and clutches each opposite sleeve of his coat just below the shoulders, like an isolated body quivering in its own icy sphere. He says, 'You'll be glad to get in the house tonight, Madam. Wind coming across the lake.'

'You must be feeling the cold,' she says, and starts up the car.

'Good night, Madam.'

'Good night.'

He backs into the porchway of the cottage, then quickly turns to push open the door. In the hall he lifts the house-telephone and waits for a few seconds, still shivering, till it comes alive. 'The Baroness,' he says, then. 'Just arrived. Anybody else expected?'

The speaker from the kitchen at the big house says something briefly and clicks off. 'What?' says Theo to the dead instrument. Then he hangs up, runs out of the front door and closes the big gates. He returns as rapidly to the warm sitting-room where Clara is lying dreamily on the sofa, one arm draped along its back and another drooping over the edge. 'You waiting for the photographer?' says Theo.

'What was all that talk?' Clara says.

'Shivering out there. She was in her car, of course, didn't feel it. On and on. Asked after you. She says, are we happy here?'

Pablo has got into the little cream coupé and driven it away from the front of the house as soon as Lister has helped the Baroness out of it, taken her parcels, banged shut the car door, and followed her up the steps and into the hall.

'Here,' she says, pulling off her big fur hat in front of the hall mirror. Lister takes it while she roughs up her curly grey hair. She slips off her tweed coat, picks up her handbag and says, 'Where's everyone?'

'The Baron is in the library, Madam, with Mr Passerat.'

'Good,' she says, and gives another hand to her hair. Then she pulls at her skirt, thick at the waist and hips, and says, 'Tell Irene I'll be up to change in half-an-hour.'

'Irene's off tonight, Madam.'

'Heloise, is she here?'

19

'Yes, Madam.'

'Still working? Is she fit and well?'

'Oh, she's all right, Madam. I'll tell her to go and prepare for you.'

'Only if she's feeling up to it,' says the Baroness. 'I think the world of Heloise,' she says, stumping heavily to the library door which she opens before Lister can reach it, pausing before she enters to turn to Lister while the voices within suddenly stop. 'Lister,' she says, standing in the doorway. 'Theo and Clara – they have to go. I'm so very sorry but I need the little house for one of my cousins. We don't really need a porter. I leave it to you, Lister.'

'Well, Madam, it's a delicate matter at the moment. They won't be expecting this.'

'I know, I know. Arrange something to make it easy, Lister. The Baron and I would be so grateful.' Then she throws open the door somewhat dramatically and walks in, while the two men get up from the grey leather armchairs. Lister waits in the room, by the door.

'Nothing, thanks, Lister,' says the Baron. 'We have everything here for the moment.' He waves towards the drinks cupboard in a preoccupied way. The Baroness flops into a sofa while Lister, about to leave the room, is halted by the Baron's afterthought – 'Lister, if anyone calls, we aren't on any account to be disturbed.' The Baron looks at the ormolu and blue enamelled clock, and then at his own wristwatch. 'We don't want to be disturbed by anyone whomsoever.' Lister moves his lips and head compliantly and leaves.

'They haunt the house,' says Lister, 'like insubstantial bodies, while still alive. I think we have a long wait in front of us.' He takes his place at the head of the table. 'He said on no account to disturb them. "Not to be disturbed, Lister." You should have seen the look on her face. My mind floats about, catching at phantoms and I think of the look on her face. I am bound to ventilate this impression or I won't digest my supper.'

'Not a bad woman,' says Pablo.

'She likes to keep grace and favour in her own hands,' Lister says, 'and leave disagreeable matters to others. "The couple at the lodge has to go, Lister," she said, "I rely on you to tell them. I need the lodge for my cousins," or was it "my cousin"? – one, two, three, I don't know. The point is she wants the lodge for them.'

'How many cousins can she possibly have?' says Eleanor, looking at the clean prongs of her fork, for some reason, before making them coincide with a morsel of veal. 'And all the secretaries besides.'

'Cousins uncountable, secretaries perhaps fewer,' says Lister, 'if only she had survived to enjoy them. As it is the lodge will probably be vacated anyhow. No need for me to speak to the poor silly couple.'

'You never know,' says Heloise.

'Listen! – I hear a noise,' says Pablo.

'The shutters banging upstairs,' says Hadrian.

'No, it's him in the attic, throwing his supper plates around,' Heloise says.

'It wasn't plates, it was a banging,' Pablo says. 'There it goes. Listen.'

'Eat on,' says Clovis. 'It's only the couple of ladies in the car again. They're getting impatient.'

'Why don't they ring?' says Lister as he listens to the thumping on the back door.

'I disconnected the back door bell,' Clovis says. 'We need our meal in peace. Since I was goaded to do most of the cooking it's my say that goes. Nobody leaves the table before their supper's over.'

'Suppose one of them in the library rings for us?' Eleanor says.

Lister reaches out for his wine-glass and sips from it. The banging at the door continues. Clovis says, 'It's doubtful if they will call us, now. However, we must no longer respond, it would be out of the question. To put it squarely, as I say in my memoir, the eternal triangle has come full circle.'

'They've as good as gone to Kingdom Come,' says Lister. 'However, it is I who decides whether or not we answer any summons, hypothetical or otherwise.'

'It's Lister who decides,' says his aunt Eleanor.

II

IT IS TEN-THIRTY AT NIGHT. Lister has changed his clothes and so has his young aunt, Eleanor. They walk hand-in-hand up the swirling great staircase with its filigree of Regency wrought-iron banisters, imported in their time as were so many other appointments of the house. Lister flicks on the light and opens the folding doors of the Klopstocks' long drawing-room, allowing Eleanor to pass before him into the vastness with its curtains looped along the row of French windows. Outside is a balustrade and beyond that the night. The parquet glitters obliquely, not having been trodden on today. The blue and shrimp-pink of the carpet, the pinks and browns of the tap-estried chairs, the little tables, the scrolled flat desk and the porcelain vases are spread around Lister and Eleanor, as they enter the room, like standing waiters on the arrival of the first guests at an official reception. A porcelain snow-white lamb, artfully woolly, sleeps peacefully on the mantelpiece where the Baron placed it eleven years ago when the house was built and his precious goods brought in. The Adam mantelpiece at one end of the room came through the Swiss customs along with the rest as did the twin mantelpiece in the ante-room at the other end. Eleanor, wearing a grey woollen dress and carrying a black bag, sits down gracefully on a wide, upholstered chair and leans her arms on a small table, toying with the pink-blond carnation she herself arranged freshly this morning.

She looks about thirty-four. Her nephew, Lister, well advanced into his mid-forties. He wears a dark business suit with a white shirt and a dull red tie. They could be anybody, and more conceivably could be the master and mistress of the house just returned at this time of night from a trip to a city – Paris or even Geneva – or just about to leave for an airport, a night flight. Eleanor's hair is short, curled and dull. Lister's gleams with dark life. Their faces are long and similar. Lister sits opposite Eleanor and looks at a part of the wall that is covered with miniature portraits. Many objects in this large room are on a miniature scale. There are no large pictures, such as would fit it. The Monet is one of the smaller scale, and so is the Goya. So too are a group of what appear to be family portraits, so that it seems as if the inclination towards the miniature is either a trait descending throughout a few generations to their present owner, or else these little portraits have been cleverly copied, more recently, from some more probable larger originals. Ornamental keys, enamelled snuff-boxes and bright coins stand by on the small tables.

Lister looks away from the wall, and straight at Eleanor. 'My dear,' he says.

She says, 'I hear their voices.'

'They are still alive,' says Lister. 'I'm sure of that. It hasn't happened yet.'

'It's going to happen,' she says.

'Oh, my dear, it's inevitable.' He takes a cigarette from the long silver box and lights it with the table lighter. Then he raises a finger for silence, as if Eleanor had been making a noise, which she had not. 'Listen!' he says. 'They're arguing in high tone. Eleanor, you're right!'

Eleanor takes from her bag a long steel nail-file, gets up, goes to a corner of the carpet, raises it, kneels, then with the file dislodges a loose piece of parquet.

'Softly and swiftly, my love.'

She looks up. 'Don't be so smart. This isn't the time to lark about.' She bends to dislodge another, and moving backward a little, knee by knee, leans forward on her elbows and places her ear to the planks of dusty common wood beneath the parquet.

'Eleanor, it isn't worthy of you,' he says. 'You look like a parlour maid. A minute ago you didn't.'

She listens hard, looking upward through space to the high ceiling as if in a trance. Every little while a wave of indistinct voices from below reaches the drawing-room, one shrill, another shrill, then all together, excited. From a floor above, somebody bangs and the sound is repeated, with voices and a scuffle. Eleanor raises her head and says, exasperated, 'With him in the attic barking again and banging, and you carrying on, it's impossible to hear properly what's being said below. Why didn't Sister Barton give him his injection?'

'I don't know,' he says, leaning back with his cigarette. 'I'm sure I advised her to. This parquet flooring once belonged to a foreign king. He had to flee his throne. He took the parquet of his palace with him, also the door-knobs. Royalty always do, when they have to leave. They take everything, like stage-companies who need their props. With royalty, of course, it all is largely a matter of stage production. And lighting. Royalty are very careful about their setting and their lighting. As is the Pope. The Baron resembled royalty and the Pope in that respect at least. Parquet flooring and door-handles. The Baron bought them all in a lot with the house when the old king passed away. They definitely came from the royal palace.'

'All I heard from down there,' says Eleanor, putting the oblongs of palace parquet back in place and rising, while she folds back the carpet over them, 'was something like "You said . . . "

25

– "No you did not. I said . . . " – "No, you did say . . . " – "When in hell did I say . . . " That means they're going over it all, Lister. It could take all night.'

'Heloise said it could be around six in the morning,' Lister remarks as Eleanor stands flicking her skirt against the strange event that it has gathered fluff or dust. 'Not,' he says, 'that I normally take any interest in Heloise's words. But she's in an interesting condition. They get good at guessing when they're in that state.'

Eleanor is back in her chair again. Down at the back door there is a noise loud enough to reach this quiet room. A banging. A demand. At the same time, at the front door the bell shrills.

'I hope someone answers that door before the Baroness gets it in her head to go and answer it herself,' says Eleanor. 'Any break in the meeting might distract them from the quarrel and side-track the climax, wouldn't you think?'

'The Baron said not to disturb,' says Lister, 'as if to say, nobody leaves the room till we've had a clarification, let the tension mount as it may. And that's final. She'll never leave the library.'

'Well, they must be getting hungry. They've had nothing to eat.'

'Let them eat cake,' says Lister, and he adds,

'Think, in this battered Caravanserai
Whose doorways are alternate Night and Day,
How Sultan after Sultan with his Pomp
Abode his Hour or two, and went his way.'

Eleanor says, 'It's true they've had some important visitors.'

'The adjective "battered",' Lister says, looking round the quiet expanse of drawing-room, 'I apply in the elastic sense.

Also "caravanserai" I use loosely. The house is more like a Swiss hotel, which you may be sure it will become. But endless caravans, so to speak, have most certainly come and gone here, they have come, they have stopped over, they have gone. I'm fairly to the point. It will make a fine hotel. Put different furniture into it, and you have a hotel.'

'Lister,' she says, 'you're always so wonderful. There could never be anyone else in my life.'

He says, rising to approach her, 'Aunt to me though you are, would you marry me outside the Book of Common Prayer?'

She says, 'I have my scruples and I'm proud of them.'

He says, 'In France an aunt may marry a nephew.'

'No, Lister, I stand by the Table of Kindred and Affinity. I don't want to get heated at this moment, on this night, Lister. You're starting me off. The press and the police are coming, and there are only sixty-four shopping days to Christmas.'

'I was only suggesting,' he says. 'I'm only giving you a little thought for when all this is over.'

'It's going too far. You have to keep your unreasonable demands within bounds. I'm old-fashioned beyond my years. One thought at a time is what I like.'

'Let's go down,' says Lister, 'and see what the servants are up to.'

As they come down the staircase voices rebound from the library. Lister and Eleanor continue silently and, turning into the servants' hall, Lister stops and looks at the library door. 'What were they doing anyway, amongst us, on the crust of this tender earth?' he says. 'What were they doing here?'

The other servants fall silent. 'What are they doing here, anyway in this world?'

Heloise, pink and white of skin, fresh from her little sleep, says, 'Doing their own thing.'

'They haven't finished it yet,' says Clovis. 'I'm getting anxious. Listen to their voices.'

'There must have been some good in them,' Eleanor says. 'They couldn't have been all bad.'

'Oh, I agree. They did wrong well. And they were good for a purpose so long as they lasted,' Lister says. 'As paper cups are suitable for occasions, you use them and throw them away. Who brought that fur coat in here?' He points to a white mink coat draped over a chair.

'It looks a dream on me,' Heloise says. 'It doesn't meet at the front, but afterwards it will.'

'You'd better put it back. Victor Passerat's been seen in it,' Lister says. 'The police will inquire.'

Heloise takes away the coat and says, as she goes, 'I'll get it in the end. Somehow I feel I'll get it in the end.'

'She might well be right,' Lister says. 'Her foresight runs high at this moment. Who were those people banging at the back door and ringing at the front?'

'The girls in the car, demanding what's happened to their friend, Passerat,' Hadrian says. 'I told them that he was with the Baron and Baroness and they were not to be disturbed. They said they had an appointment. One of them's a masseuse that I haven't seen before.'

'And the other?' says Lister.

'The other didn't say. I didn't ask.'

'You did right,' Lister says. 'They don't come into the story.'

Outside are the sounds of the lake-water lapping on the jetty and of the mountain-wind in the grandiose trees. The couple in the car are separated, one in the front, one in the back seat, each lolling under a rug. They seem to be sleeping but every now and then one of them moves, one of them speaks, and again their heads bend and the blankets move over their crouched uneasy shoulders. The lights from the house and from the distant drive touch on their movements.

They both start upright as another car, dark and large, pulls up. A lithe, leather-coated young man sprints out and approaches the couple. They are scrambling out of their car now.

'We can't get in the house,' says the one from the front seat. 'They won't open the door, even. We've been here over three hours, waiting for our friend.'

'What friend? What do you want?' says the lithe young man, impatiently jangling a bunch of keys. 'I'm the secretary, Mr Samuel. Tell me what you want.'

The other friend of Victor Passerat replies, 'Victor Passerat. We're waiting for him. It's serious. He had an appointment with the Baroness and with the Baron, and – '

'Just a minute,' says Mr Samuel, looking closely at the second friend, 'just a minute. You sound like a man.'

'I am a man.'

'All right. I thought you were a girl.'

'That's only my clothes. My friend here's a woman. I'm Alex – she's a masseuse.'

'My name's Anne,' states the masseuse, stockily regarding Mr Samuel's bunch of keys. 'Do you have the keys to the house?'

'I certainly do,' says Mr Samuel.

'Well, we want to know what's going on,' says the woman.

'We're worried, quite frankly,' says her young friend.

Mr Samuel places a gentle hand on the shoulders of each. 'Don't you think,' he says, 'that it would be more advisable for you to go away and let nature take its course? Go away, quietly and without fuss; just go away and play the piano, or something. Take a soothing nightcap, both of you, and forget about Passerat.'

From an upper room comes a sound like a human bark followed by an owl-screech.

Anne the masseuse adds a further cry to the night. 'Open that door,' she screams and running to the back door beats her heavy shoulder against it, banging with her fists as well.

Mr Samuel winds his way to her with pleasant-mannered authority. 'That was only the invalid,' he says. 'The nurse has probably bitten his finger again. You would do the same, I'm sure, if one of your patients attempted to place his hand over your mouth for some reason.'

Anne's friend, Alex, calls out, 'Come on back in the car, Anne. It might be dangerous.'

Mr Samuel is touching her elbow, urging her back to their small car. 'There's nothing in it for you,' he is saying. 'Go home and forget it.'

The masseuse is large but she appears to have very little moral resistance. She starts to cry, with huge baby-sobs, while her companion, Alex, his square bony face framed in a silk head-scarf and his eyes pleadingly laden with make-up under finely shaped eyebrows, puts out a bony hand to touch her face. 'Come back in the car, Anne,' he says, giving Mr Samuel a look of hurt umbrage.

Anne turns on Mr Samuel. 'Who made you the secretary?' she says. 'Victor Passerat has been secretary since June.'

'Please,' says Mr Samuel. 'I didn't say he wasn't secretary. I only say I'm the secretary in residence. There are I don't know how many secretaries. Victor is only one of the many and it's only just unfortunate that this appointment between him and the Baron Klopstocks should keep you hanging around outside the house on a cold night. Just go home. Put on a record.'

'Is everything going to be all right?' Anne says. Alex has got into the car waiting for her. Anne gets in and puts her hands on the wheel without certainty. She looks at Alex as if for guidance. Meanwhile Mr Samuel has flicked himself in a graceful and preoccupied way to the back door of the house and now selects a key.

The couple in the car stare after him and he gives them one more glance; he lets himself in and quietly closes the door upon them. They drive off, then, up the long avenue, round the winding drive, past the lawns which in summer lie luminously green and spread on the one hand towards the swimming-pool in its very blue basin, and on the other towards the lily-pond, the animal-shaped yews, the fountains and the sunken rose garden. Behind them, and beyond the darkness, twinkles the back of the house – a few slits of light peppering its whole length – and behind that again, in the further darkness, the sloping terraces leading to the Lake of Geneva where the boats are moored and the water stretches across to the mountain shore. The little dark green car, leaving it all behind, reaches the lodge. Anne sounds the horn. Theo, wrapped up, now, in a heavy coat, stands evidently forewarned; he unlocks the gate and swings it wide.

When they have reached the main road and are off, he goes indoors; there he writes down the number of their car on a scribbling block which he has set out ready in the hall.

His wife stands by in her cord-trimmed dressing-gown. 'Why are you doing that?' she says.

'I don't know, Clara. But seeing I've been told to expect an all-night spell of duty without any relief-man, I've been taking a note of all numbers. I don't know, Clara, I really don't know why.' He tears off the sheet and crumples it, tossing it on the sitting-room fire.

'What's wrong with the relief-men tonight?' Clara says. 'Where's Conrad, where's Bernard, where's Jean-Albert, where's Stephen? Why don't they send Pablo, what's he doing with them up there at the house? My sleep is terrible, how can I sleep?'

'I'm a simple man,' says Theo, 'and your dreams give me the jitters, but setting all that aside I smell a crisis. The Baroness hasn't been playing the game, and that's about it. Why did she let herself go to rack and ruin? They say she was a fine-looking woman a year ago. Lovely specimen.'

'She used to keep her hair frosted or blond-streaked,' Clara whispers. 'She shouldn't have let go her shape. Why did she suddenly start to go natural? She must have started to be sincere with someone.'

'Don't be frightened, Clara. Don't be afraid.'

'It's true what I say, Theo. She changed all of a sudden. I showed you her in the magazines in her ski-outfit. Wasn't she magnificent?'

'Go to bed, Clara. I say, go up to bed, dear.'

'Can't I have the wireless on for company?'

'All right. Keep it low. We aren't supposed to be here to enjoy ourselves, you know.'

Theo steps forth from his doorway as another car approaches the gate, flicking its large headlights.

The chauffeur puts his head out while Theo opens the gate, but Theo speaks first, apparently recognizing the occupant of the back seat.

'His Excellency, Prince Eugene,' Theo says, respectfully.

The chauffeur's mouth smiles a little, his eyes drooping, perhaps with boredom, perhaps with tiredness.

'I'm pretty sure they're not at home. Were they expecting his Excellency?' Theo says.

'Yes,' says the visitor from the depths of the back seat.

'I'll just call the house,' says Theo and returns to the lodge.

'Drive on,' says Prince Eugene to his driver. 'Don't wait for him and all that rot. I said to Klopstock I'd look in after dinner and I'm looking in after dinner. He should have told his porter to expect me.' As he speaks, the car is already off on its meander towards the house.

Lister is waiting at the door. He runs down the steps towards the big car as the driver gets out to open the door for the prince.

'The Baron and Baroness are not at home,' Lister says.

Prince Eugene has got out and looks at Lister. 'Who are you?' he says.

'Excuse me, your Excellency, that I'm in my off-duty clothes,' Lister says. 'I'm Lister, the butler.'

'You look like a Secretary of State.'

'Thank you, sir,' says Lister.

'It isn't a compliment,' says the prince. 'What do you mean, they're not at home? I saw the Baron this morning and he asked me to drop in after dinner. They're expecting me.' He mounts the steps, Lister following him, and enters the house.

In the hall he nods towards the library door from where the sound of voices come. 'Go and tell them I'm here.' He starts to unbutton his coat.

'Your Excellency, I have orders that they are not to be disturbed.' Lister edges round so that his back is turned to the library door, as if protecting it. He adds, 'The door is locked from the inside.'

'What's going on?'

'A meeting, sir, with one of the secretaries. It has already lasted some hours and is likely to continue far into the night.'

The prince, plump, with pale cheeks, refrains from taking off his coat as he says, 'Whose secretary is it, his or hers?'

'The gentleman in question is the one who's been secretary to both, sir, for the past five months, nearly.'

'Almighty God, I'd better get out of here!' says Prince Eugene.

'I would do that, sir,' Lister says, leading the way to the front door.

'The Baron seemed all right this morning,' says the Prince on the threshold. 'He'd just got back from Paris.'

'I imagine there have been telephone conversations throughout the afternoon, sir.'

'He didn't seem to be expecting any trouble.'

'None of them did, your Excellency. They were not prepared for it. They have placed themselves, unfortunately, within the realm of predestination.'

'You talk like a Secretary of State to the Vatican.'

'Thank you, sir.'

'It isn't a compliment.' The Prince, buttoning up his coat, passes out into the night air through the door which Lister is holding open for him. Before descending the steps to his car, he says, 'Lister, do you expect something to happen?'

'We do, sir. The domestic staff is prepared.'

'Lister, in case of investigations no need, you understand, to mention my visit tonight. It is quite a casual neighbourly visit. Not relevant.'

'Of course, your Excellency.'

'By the way, I'm not an Excellency, I'm a Highness.'

'Your Highness.'

'A domestic staff as large and efficient as yourselves is hard to come by. Quite exceptional in Switzerland. How did the Baron do it?'

'Money,' says Lister.

The voices, indistinguishable but excited, wave over to them from the library.

'I need a butler,' says his Highness. He takes out a card and gives it to Lister. Jerking his head towards the library door he says, 'When it's all over, if you need a place, come to me. I would be glad of some of the other servants, too.'

'I doubt if we shall be looking for further employment, sir, but I thank you deeply for your offer.' Lister puts the card in a note-case which he has brought out of his vest pocket.

'And his cook? That excellent chef? Will he be free?'

'He, too, has his plans, your Excellency.'

'There will of course be a scandal. He must have paid you all very well for your services.'

'For our silence, sir.'

Upstairs a voice growls and the shutters bang.

'That's him in the attic,' says Prince Eugene.

'A sad case, sir.'

'He inherits everything.'

'How, sir? He's a connection of the Baroness through her first marriage. A cousin of the first husband. I think the Baron could hardly bequeath a vast estate to him, poor thing in the attic. The Baron is succeeded by a brother in Brazil.'

'The one in Brazil is the youngest. The one in the attic is next in line – no relation to her at all.'

'That,' said Lister, 'I did not know.'

'Few people know it. Don't tell anyone I said so. Klopstock would kill me. Would have killed me.'

'Well, it makes no difference to us, sir, who gets the fortune. Our fortunes lie in other directions.'

'A great pity. I would have taken on the cook. An excellent cook. What's his name?'

'Clovis, sir.'

'Oh, yes, Clovis.'

'But he will be giving up his profession, I dare say.'

'A waste of talent.' The prince gets into his car and is driven away from the scene.

Mr Samuel has taken off his leather coat and is sitting in the large pantry office which gives off from the servants' hall, looking through a file of papers. He leans back in his chair, dressed in a black turtle-necked sweater and black corduroy trousers. The door is open behind him and the large window in front of him is black and shiny with blurs of light from the courtyard, like a faulty television screen. A car draws up to the back door. Mr Samuel says over his shoulder to the servants in the room beyond, 'Here's Mr McGuire, let him in.'

'He has the keys,' says Heloise.

'Show a little courtesy,' says Mr Samuel.

'I hear Lister coming,' says Eleanor.

Mr Samuel then gets up and comes into the servants' sitting-room. From the passage leading to the front of the house comes Lister, while from the back door a key is successfully playing with the lock.

Lister stops to listen. 'Who is this?'

'Mr McGuire,' says Mr Samuel. 'I asked him to come and join us. I might need a hand with the data. I hope that's all right.'

'You should have mentioned it to me first,' said Lister. 'You should have phoned me, Mr Samuel. However, I have no objection. As it happens I need Mr McGuire's services.'

A man now appears from the back door. He seems slightly older than Mr Samuel, with a weathered and freckled face. 'How's everything? How's everybody?' he says.

'Good evening, Mr McGuire,' says Lister.

'Make yourself at home,' says Clovis.

'Good evening, thanks. I'm a bit hungry,' says Mr McGuire.

'Secretaries get their own meals,' says Clovis.

'I've come flat out direct from Paris.'

'Heat him up something, Clovis,' Lister says.

'Leave it to me,' says Eleanor, rising from her chair with ostentatious meekness.

'Mr Samuel, Mr McGuire,' says Lister, 'are you here for a limited time, or do you intend to wait?'

Mr McGuire says, 'I'd like to see the Baron, actually.'

'Out of the question,' says Mr Samuel.

'Not to be disturbed,' says Lister.

'Then what have I come all this way for?' says Mr McGuire, pulling off his sheepskin coat in a resigned way.

'To hold Mr Samuel's hand,' says Pablo.

'I'll see the Baron in the morning. I have to talk to him,' says Mr McGuire.

'Too late,' says Lister. 'The Baron is no more.'

'I can hear his voice. What d'you mean?'

'Let us not strain after vulgar chronology,' says Lister. 'I have work for you.'

'There's veal stew,' Eleanor calls out from the kitchen.

'Blanquette,' says Clovis, 'de veau.' He puts a hand to his head and closes his eyes as one tormented by a long and fruitless effort to instruct.

'Do you have a cigarette handy?' says Heloise.

'There's a lot of noise,' says Mr McGuire, jerking his head to indicate the front part of the house. 'It fairly penetrates. Who's the company tonight?'

'Hadrian,' says Lister, taking a chair, 'give a hand to Eleanor. Tell her I'd be obliged for a cup of coffee.'

'When I was a boy of fourteen,' says Lister, 'I decided to leave England.'

Mr McGuire reaches down and stops the tape-recorder. 'Start again,' he says. 'Make it more colloquial, Lister. Don't say "a boy of fourteen", say "a boy, fourteen", like that, Lister.'

They sit alone in Lister's large bedroom. They each occupy an armchair of deep, olive-green soft leather which, ageless and unworn, seems almost certainly to have come from another part of the house, probably the library, in the course of some complete refurnishing. A thick grey carpet covers the whole floor. Lister's bed is narrow but spectacular with a well-preserved bushy bear-like fur cover which he might have acquired independently or which might have once covered the knees of an earlier Klopstock while crossing a winter landscape by car, and which, anyway, looks as if importance is attached to it; indeed, it is certain that everything in the room, including Mr McGuire, is there by the approval of Lister only.

Between the two men, on the floor, is a heavily built tape-recorder in an open case with a handle. It is attached by a long snaky cord to an electric plug beside the bed. The two magnetic bobbins, of the 18-centimetre size, have come to a standstill at Mr McGuire's touch of the stop-switch; the bobbins not being entirely equal in their content of tape it can be assessed that half-an-hour of something has already been recorded at some previous time.

Lister says, 'Style can be left to the journalists, Mr McGuire. This is only a preliminary press handout. The inside story is something else – it's an exclusive, and we've made our plans for the exclusive. All we need now is something for the general press to go on when they start to question us, you see.'

'Take my advice, Lister,' says Mr McGuire, 'and give it a conversational touch.'

'Whose conversational touch – mine or the journalists'?'

'Theirs,' says Mr McGuire.

'Turn on the machine,' says Lister.

Mr McGuire does so, and the bobbins go spinning.

'When I was a boy, fourteen,' says Lister, 'I decided to leave England. There was a bit of trouble over me having to do with Eleanor under the grand piano, she being my aunt and only nine. Dating from that traumatic experience, Eleanor conceived an inverted avuncular fixation, which is to say that she followed me up when she turned fourteen and – '

'It isn't right,' says Mr McGuire, turning off the machine.

'It isn't true, but that's not to say it isn't right,' Lister says. 'Now, Mr McGuire, my boy, we haven't got all night to waste. I want you to take a short statement of similar tone from Eleanor and one from Heloise. The others can take care of themselves. After that we have to pose for the photographs.' Lister bends down, turns on the machine, and continues. 'My father,' he says, 'was a valet in that house, a good position. It was Watham Grange, Leicestershire, under the grand piano. I worked in France. When Eleanor joined me I worked in a restaurant that was owned by a Greek in Amsterdam. Then we started in private families and now I've been butler with the Klopstocks here in Switzerland for over five years. But to sum up I really left England because of the climate – wet.' Lister turns off the switch and stares at the tape-recorder.

Mr McGuire says, 'Won't they want something about the Klopstocks?'

Lister says, impatiently, 'I am thinking.' Presently he turns on the recorder again, meanwhile glancing at his watch. 'The death of the Baron and Baroness has been a very great shock to us all. It was the last thing we expected. We heard no shots, naturally, since our quarters are quite isolated from the residential domain. And of course, in these large houses, the wind does make a lot of noise. The shutters upstairs are somewhat loose and in fact we were to have them seen to tomorrow afternoon.'

Mr McGuire halts the machine. 'I thought you were going to say that him in the attic makes so much noise that you mistook one of his fits for the shots being fired.'

'I've changed my mind,' Lister says.

'Why?' says Mr McGuire.

Lister closes his eyes with impatience while Mr McGuire switches on again. The bobbins whirl. 'The Baron gave orders that they were not to be disturbed,' Lister says.

'What's next?' says Mr McGuire.

'Play it back, Mr McGuire, please.'

Mr McGuire sets the reels in reverse, concentratedly stopping their motion a short distance from the beginning. 'It would be about here,' he says, 'that your bit begins.' He turns it on. The machine emits two long, dramatic sighs followed by a woman's voice – 'I climbed Mount Atlas alone every year on May Day and sacrificed a garland of bay leaves to Apollo. At last, one year he descended from his fiery chariot –'

Mr McGuire has turned off, and has manipulated the machine to run further forward silently.

'That must be the last of your Klopstock soundtracks,' Lister says.

'Yes, it is the last.'

'You should have used fresh reels for us. We don't want to be mixed up with what Apollo did.'

'I'll remove that bit of the tape before we start making copies. Leave it to me,' says Mr McGuire, getting up to unplug the machine.

'What is to emerge must emerge,' says Lister, standing, watching, while Mr McGuire packs the wire into place and fastens the lid on the tape-recorder. He lifts it and follows Lister out of the room. 'It's a heavy machine,' he says, 'to carry from place to place.'

They descend the stairs to the first landing of the servants' wing. Here, Lister leads the way to the grand staircase, followed after a little hesitation by Mr McGuire who has first seemed inclined to continue down the back stairs.

'I hear no voices,' Lister says as he descends, looking down the well of the great staircase to the black and white paving below. 'The books are silent.'

They have reached the ground floor. Mr McGuire stands with his heavy load while Lister approaches the library door.

He waits, turns the handle, pressing gently; the door does not give.

'Locked,' says Lister, turning away, 'and silent. Let's proceed,' he says, leading the way to the servants' quarters. 'There remain a good many things to be accomplished and still more chaos effectively to organize.'

III

'IT MUST HAVE HAPPENED QUICK. I wonder if they felt anything?' says Heloise. 'Maybe they still feel something. One of them could linger.'

Lister says, 'I can't forbear to ask, does a flame feel pain?'

'Lister and young Pablo,' says Mr Samuel who is moving round the servants' room with his camera, 'stand closer together. Lister, put your hand on the chair.'

Lister puts his hand on Pablo's shoulder.

'Why are you doing that? It doesn't look good,' says Mr Samuel.

'Leave it to Lister,' says Eleanor at the same time that Lister says, 'I'm consoling him.'

'Then Pablo must look inconsolable,' says Mr Samuel. 'It's a good idea in itself.'

'Look inconsolable, Pablo,' says Lister. 'Think of some disconsolate idea such as your being in Victor Passerat's shoes.'

The camera clicks quietly, like a well-reared machine. Mr Samuel moves a few steps then clicks from another angle. He then moves a lamp and says, 'Look this way,' pointing a finger to a place in the air.

'Pablo smiled the second time,' says Eleanor. 'You want to be careful.'

'Mr Samuel knows that the negatives are mine,' Lister says, 'don't you, Mr Samuel.'

'Yes,' says Mr Samuel.

'Where is that wreath?' Lister says. 'Where's our floral tribute?'

'On the floor in my room,' says Heloise.

'Go and fetch it.'

'I'm too tired.'

'I'll go,' says Hadrian, going. As he opens the door a long howl comes from above.

'Sister Barton failed to give him his injection tonight,' says Lister, 'and I wonder why.'

'Sister Barton is upset. She didn't touch her supper,' says Clovis.

'She's suffering from fear, quite a thrilling emotion,' says Lister. 'People love it.'

'I sent up cold chicken breast and lettuce cut into shreds the Swiss way, which she imagines in her inexperienced little heart to be the right way,' Clovis murmurs. He is standing with one hand on the belt that encircles his narrow hips. Several gold medallions hang from chains on his chest. Mr Samuel's camera trains upon him, as he seems to expect it to do. He lowers his lids. 'Good,' says Mr Samuel, moving round to Heloise.

'Head and shoulders only,' says Lister at the same time as he answers a buzz on the house-telephone. 'Him?' says Lister into the telephone. 'Why?' The answer fairly prolonged and intelligible apparently to Lister, is otherwise that of a bronchial and aged raven, penetrating the room, until Lister says, 'All right, all right,' and hangs up. Then he turns and says, 'We've got the Reverend on our hands. He's come on his motor-bike from Geneva. Sister Barton has summoned him to soothe her patient.'

'I smell treason,' says Eleanor.

'How do you mean?' Lister says. 'She always has been an outsider, so treason isn't the word.'

'Well, she's a bitch,' says Heloise.

'Here he is,' says Lister, as the sound of a motor approaches. 'Pablo, open the door.'

Pablo goes to the back door but the sound of the motor recedes round the house towards the front. 'He's gone to the front door,' Lister says. 'I'd better go myself.'

He passes Pablo, saying, 'Front door, front door, leave it to me,' and, crossing the black and white squares of the hall, admits the Reverend.

'Good evening, Lister. I thought you'd be in bed,' says the white-haired Reverend who carries a woollen cap in his hand.

'No, Reverend,' says Lister, 'none of us is in bed.'

'Oh well, I came to the front thinking you were in bed. The light's on in the library, I thought the Baron might let me in.' He looks up the staircase. 'He sounds quiet, now. Has he gone to sleep? Sister Barton called me urgently.'

'Sister Barton did wrong to bring you out, Reverend, but I must say I'm relieved to see you, and it just occurs to me after all, she may have done right.'

'Your riddles, Lister.' The Reverend is tall, skinny and wavering. He takes off his thick sheepskin coat. He wears a clerical collar and dark grey suit. He is quite aged, seeming to give out a certain life-force which perhaps only derives from the frailty of his appearance combined with his clear ability to come out on a windy night on a motor-bicycle.

He nods towards the library door. 'Is the Baron alone? – I know it's late but I'd like to pop in and have a word with him before going on upstairs. I've many times sat up later talking to the Baron.' The Reverend is already at the library door, waiting for Lister merely to knock and announce him.

'They are a party of three,' says Lister. 'I have orders from the Baron, I'm sorry, Reverend, that they are not to be disturbed. Not on any account.'

The Reverend, happily breathing the centrally heated air of the hall, sighs and then cocks his head slightly with sudden intelligence, his eyes bird-like. 'I don't hear anybody. Are you sure that he has company?'

'Quite sure,' says Lister moving away, sideways, backwards, indicating decisively the pathway that the Reverend must take. 'Come in with us, Reverend, and warm up. A hot drink. Whisky and water. Something warm. I would like to talk to you personally, Reverend, before you see Sister Barton.'

'Where? Oh, yes.' The Reverend's eyes are losing their previous thread of reasoning and lead him in the precise footsteps of Lister's polished shoes.

'Good evening, I have something here,' the Reverend says to the assembled room, putting his hand in his pocket, as Lister leads him in. 'Before I forget.' He brings out a small press-cutting and puts it on a ledge of the television table, sitting down near it. He feels in his inside coat pocket and pulls out his spectacles.

'Good evening, Reverend,' and, 'Nice to see you, Reverend,' say Heloise and Pablo respectively while Hadrian comes in bearing, platterwise under an airy cloud of cellophane, a large round flower-arrangement that looks as if it began as a wreath of laurel-leaves and was filled in according to taste with various rings of colour – red roses, double daffodils, white lilies, an inner ring of orange roses, and finally, at the bull's eye, a tight bunch of violets.

The sight seems to recall something to the Reverend. He moves his long bones to the process of getting up and says, 'He hasn't died, has he?'

'The Reverend means him in the attic,' says Heloise.

Eleanor says, 'I'll put them under the shower and give them a slight spray. Keep them fresh.'

Lister, while assisting the Reverend to relax back into the seat, says, 'We're having our photographs taken, Reverend.'

'Oh!' says the Reverend. 'Oh, I see,' and, plainly, he is practised at habituating himself swiftly and without fuss to newer and younger notions however odd or untimely. He seems to be considering this as he warms to the room. Mr Samuel brings his camera round and clicks at the pensive head, the loose and helpless hands of the Reverend. 'Good,' says Lister, bringing an elegant silver-cupped glass of softly steaming whisky on a tray from the kitchen, and stirring it with a long spoon. 'Do another,' he says to Mr Samuel, standing back meantime, withholding the glass from the Reverend who has begun to stretch out his hand to receive it. The camera clicks smoothly upon the gesture of benediction. Then the Reverend gets his hot toddy.

'Good evening – or rather it's good morning, isn't it, Reverend?' says Mr McGuire who comes in from the pantry office with his heavy tape-machine. 'This is a pleasure,' says Mr McGuire.

'Mr McGuire – good evening. I was in bed and the phone rings. Sister Barton is asking for me. It's urgent, she says, he's screaming. So here I am. Now I don't hear a sound. Everyone's gone to sleep. What are the Klopstocks up to, there in the library?'

Mr McGuire says, 'I really don't know. They're not to be disturbed.'

'The Klopstocks and Victor Passerat,' says Heloise.

'Heloise, it is not relevant who the guest is,' says Lister. 'It might be anybody.'

Pablo has returned with Eleanor from the bathroom quarters where they have left the funeral flowers. He sits on the arm of Heloise's chair. The Reverend looks at the couple and reaches out for the newspaper cutting. He puts on his glasses.

'I brought this along,' he says. And again looks at the couple. He looks at the scrap of paper and looks hard at Pablo. 'I cut it out of the *Daily American* for the Baron to read. It is quite relevant to the practices that go on in this house, and now I'm here and I see the Baron is busy, it seems to me that I can read it to whom it may concern.' He looks at Pablo.

'Let's have it,' says Pablo, leaning nearer to Heloise. She strokes her belly which moves involuntarily from time to time. Lister, seated at the table, silently points to the tape-machine and looks at Mr McGuire.

Mr McGuire heaves the machine on to the table while Lister says, 'I don't quite gather all this, Reverend. Would you mind explaining again?'

Mr McGuire is plugging his wire into the wall.

The Reverend now looks over his glasses at the tape-recorder. 'What's that?' he says.

'It's the new electronic food-blender,' says Lister. 'We're all computerized these days, Reverend. The personal touch is gone. We simply programme the meals.'

'Yes, oh yes.' The Reverend suddenly looks sleepy. His head droops with his eyelids, and his hands with the newspaper cutting held in them move jerkily a fragment lower.

'Reverend, you were explaining about the newspaper item,' Lister says, drawing on a cigarette. 'Naturally, we are all receptive to any precepts you may have to cast before us, real swine that we are, we have gone astray like sheep. Every one his own way, numbered among the goats. Normally – '

'Yes, sex,' says the Reverend, wakeful again. He looks at Pablo, then at Heloise, then back to the cutting.

Lister says, 'Normally it isn't a topic that we discuss between these four walls.'

'You have to be frank about it. No point concealing the facts,' says the Reverend severely.

Lister raises a finger and the discs of the machine begin to spin.

The Reverend says, 'I brought this for Cecil and Cathy Klopstock to see. I think it might have something in it to help them with their problems. I hope it will help you with yours, every one of you.' Then he reads, ' "New anti-sex drug" – that's the headline. "Edinburgh, Scotland – Medical science has come up with a drug that keeps sex offenders under control, a doctor has reported to the Royal Medico-Psychological Association. The head of Edinburgh trials of the German drug told association members of the case of the 40-year-old man who had sexually assaulted a number of girls. The man had a history of indecent exposure, homosexual activity and a need for sex daily. But, three weeks on the new drug, cyproterone acetate, damped down his urges, the expert said. Three other subjects were given the drug. All the men reported being happier." And so on, and so on. Well,' says the Reverend.

Lister raises a finger and the machine stops. 'You have given out an interesting statement, Reverend,' says Lister. 'It should be heard and seen by all as a comment on many things that have been going on under this roof.'

'That's what I thought,' says the Reverend gloomily, putting away the press-cutting in his pocket. 'I'd better go home,' he says, then.

'The wind has died down,' says Hadrian.

'He should spend the night here,' says Eleanor. 'He can't go all the way back to Geneva on that bike.'

'Quite frankly, I got out of bed,' says the Reverend. 'Go and tell Klopstock I'm here.'

'They are not to be disturbed. I had strict orders.'

'I hope they aren't carrying on in the library. In the library. What time is it?'

'Just past quarter to three,' says Lister.

'I should be in bed. You should all be in bed. Why did you bring me all this way?'

Lister goes to the house-phone, lifts the receiver, and presses a button. He waits. He presses again, leaving his finger on it for some minutes. At last comes a windy answer.

'Sister Barton,' says Lister into the phone. 'Why did you bring the Reverend all this way?'

The Reverend says immediately, 'Oh, yes, of course, my poor boy upstairs,' while Lister listens patiently.

The Reverend is creaking himself out of his chair. Clovis, who has been sitting with his arms folded and his little mouth shut tight, jumps to help him.

Lister is heard to say, 'There was no need,' and replaces the phone.

Lister says to the Reverend, 'Sister Barton says that him in the attic needed you, but now he's gone to sleep.'

At that moment a long wail comes from the top of the house, winding its way down the well of the stairs, followed then by another, winding through all the banisters and seeping into the servants' hall. 'She's woken him up,' says Hadrian. 'That's what she's done.'

'It's deliberate,' says Eleanor. 'She wants to bother the Reverend, that's all.'

'I wonder why?' says Clovis. 'What's her trend?'

'Take me up,' says the Reverend.

Heloise has gone to bed. She is propped up with pillows, drinking tea. At the foot of her bed, sitting on either side, are Pablo the handyman and Hadrian the assistant cook, both of them as absolutely young as Heloise.

'I really could sleep,' she says. 'I really feel like another nap.'

'No,' says Pablo. 'Lister wants us all to be suffering from shock when the police arrive. Lack of sleep has the same effect, Lister says.'

'I could act a state of shock at any time, and besides there's my condition.' She yawns, balancing her cup of tea in her left hand while covering her mouth with her right. 'Lister's wonderful,' she says.

'Terrific,' says Hadrian.

'Marvellous,' says Pablo. 'I never saw such a sense of timing.'

From the floor above comes the noise of a sharp clap, followed by another and another.

'It sounds like guns going off,' says Heloise.

'Well it isn't,' says Pablo. 'It's shutters. The wind must be rising again. I loosed those shutters really good, didn't I?'

'Let's put on a record,' says Hadrian. He slides off the bed and goes to the gramophone, to choose a record, first turning them this way and that, his sharp eyesight quickly discerning the details printed on either side of the disc, even though that part of the room is dim, the only light being that by Heloise's bed.

From above the shutters make further reports, followed by a more subdued clatter from a window below. Hadrian puts on a record and sets it going. The noise fills the room for an instant until Hadrian turns down the volume.

Then, while Heloise lights a cigarette, the two boys dance to the rock music. Heloise puts her tea-cup on the table by her bed. She takes a comb from a fringed satchel which is lying on the bed and a hand-mirror from her bedside table. She lays them on the bed while she loosens her hair which has been pulled back, ponytail style. Then she holds up the glass and begins to comb, swinging her shoulder a little in time to the rock vibrations, her tongue tapping the beat against her teeth. The boys dance, facing each other and swinging, their feet moving always in the same small area of shiny pinewood flooring.

Heloise's room is furnished much like that of a young daughter of the house. Posters, slogans and pin-up photographs cover part of the walls. The furniture is low-built with straight lines, and upholstered with dark red, black and yellow stuff. A white woolly rug lies askew before a desk piled with coloured magazines and crayons and some boxes of various medicines. The boys' feet just miss the rug as they continue to dance.

Heloise says, 'She didn't drink much, I'll say that for her.' She stubs out her cigarette.

Pablo stops dancing. He says, 'You're thinking thoughts, Heloise.'

Hadrian, who continues dancing by himself, says, 'Heloise, relate.'

'What do you mean, I don't relate?' she says.

'When you relate you don't ask what you mean. There's such a thing as a trend.'

'Who do you think you are, you – Chairman Mao?'

Pablo starts dancing again. The record ends. He turns it over and puts on the other side.

'Clovis is all right, too,' Heloise says. 'I'll miss Clovis.'

Pablo says, 'He could stay with us. Why shouldn't he stay with us?'

'Clovis can stay with us,' says Hadrian.

'The Baroness was natural,' says Heloise. 'I'll say that. Why shouldn't she be photographed and filmed in the nude?'

Hadrian stops dancing. 'You know what?' he says. 'Sorry for Victor Passerat I am not. Neither alive nor dead.'

'Nor me,' says Heloise.

'He had a kind of something,' Pablo says, jerking his arms as he rocks.

'I know,' says Hadrian. 'But it didn't correspond.'

'Funny that it had to be him,' says Heloise.

Pablo says, 'It could have been one of the others.'

Hadrian says, 'But she decided on him. She got hooked on him.'

'It was inevitable,' says Heloise.

'It could have been someone else,' Pablo says. 'Anyone could have made his mistake.'

'There's such a thing as a trend,' Hadrian says. 'If he was hooked on the Baron he should have coordinated.'

'Well he didn't coordinate,' says Heloise, putting her looking-glass back on the table, then lighting a cigarette.

They stop talking for a while. Heloise smokes her cigarette, languidly regarding the dance. When the music ends, the young men together silently choose another record and put it on. First Hadrian, then Pablo, start once more to dance, bobbing and swaying as if blown by a current which fuses out from the beat of the music.

After a while, Heloise says, 'I like Mr McGuire.'

'The finest sound-track man in the business. He coordinates,' says Hadrian.

'Very professional, though,' says Pablo. 'That kind of puts a division, doesn't it?'

'Mr McGuire and Mr Samuel,' says Hadrian, 'are in a class by themselves. You can't judge against them just because they made a success. They're a great team.'

'They went to prison for it,' Hadrian says.

'Is that true?' Pablo says, and simultaneously Heloise says, 'Did they? When was that?'

'Yes, when they started the business six, seven years ago. Mr Samuel told me a lot about it,' Hadrian says, stopping his long spell of dancing without any sign of having spent energy. 'Mr Samuel told me,' he says, 'that they were doing it

52

for small money. If you do a thing for peanuts you get caught for a crime. You have to do it privately for big money like everything else.'

Pablo stops dancing and sits on the bed.

'How did they do it before?' he says.

'It was the same technique. Mr Samuel did the photography and Mr McGuire did the sound-track. They put code ads in the papers. They got a lot of responses.'

'A lovely technique, they have,' Heloise says. 'I must say I liked it when they did me with Irene and Lister. Mr McGuire kept saying, "Speak out your fantasies", like that. I didn't know what the hell to say, I thought he meant a fairy story, so I started with Little Red Riding Hood, and Mr McGuire said "That's great, Heloise! You're great!" So I went on with Little Red Riding Hood and Lister and Irene changed sides. They joined in with Red Riding Hood. Lister was terrific as the grandmother when he ate me up. You can see in the film that I had a good time. Then Irene got eaten up by Lister's understudy. Mr Samuel is an artist, I'll say that, his perspectives coalesce.'

Hadrian says, 'Eleanor always does her Princess bit. You can't get her to do anything else.'

'Too old to change,' Pablo says, 'but she does it good. I like the Princess and the Pea where she can't sleep on her bed. You should always do your own thing in a simulation. It all works in. The Baroness shows up good doing the nun in the Congo with Eleanor doing the Princess bit. Puss in Boots is a big bore.'

'I can do the nun in the Congo,' says Heloise.

'So can I,' says Pablo. 'I like it.'

'Goldilocks and the three bears is best,' says Heloise. 'They got the idea of fairy stories from me. It was my idea, or anyway, it just came to me.'

'Are your health and security cards stamped up to date?' Pablo says.

'I don't think so,' says Hadrian.

'Mine aren't,' says Heloise. 'I meant to remind the Baroness.'

'Lister would have seen to it if it had mattered,' Hadrian says. 'Obviously, it doesn't matter.' He takes up another record, looks at it, says, 'The Far Fetchers. Not bad,' and puts it on while Heloise says, 'Anything goes for me.' The boys are dancing now. Heloise says, 'She went to finishing school in Lausanne and learnt to eat an orange with a little knife and fork without ever touching the orange.'

'Who?' says Pablo.

'The Baroness.'

The young men dance on.

'There must be fog coming up on the lake,' says Heloise. 'I can see it in the room already. It gets through the double windows, even, doesn't it?'

Pablo begins to sing to the music. He sings: ' "Pablo, the Baroness wishes to see you." – Knock, knock, "Come in, Pablo." – "Good morning, Madam, anything I can do, Madam?" – "Pablo, the shutters upstairs, they bang so much. I think they must be loose." – "Right away, Madam." – "See you later, then." – "See you at the party, Baroness." '

'See you at the party,' sings Hadrian.

'Don't make so much noise,' says Heloise. 'Lister's busy upstairs with the Reverend and Miss Barton.'

'There's something going on up there,' Hadrian says, stopping still as the music ends.

'Lister can adjust whatever it is. Lister never disparates, he symmetrizes,' Heloise says and lights a cigarette.

Pablo goes to the window and looks out at the fog. 'Lister's got equibalance,' he says, 'and what's more, he pertains.'

'Definitely,' says Hadrian.

Mr Samuel is sitting in a big chair looking through a bound typescript and Mr McGuire is looking over his shoulder.

Clovis sits at a round table which is covered with blue velvet. His elbows are on the table and his chin rests gloomily on his hands.

'It's a winner,' says Mr Samuel. 'Congratulations, Clovis.'

'It has a great deal of scope,' says Mr McGuire.

Clovis raises then lowers his eyebrows. His look of gloom does not change, his elbows remain still.

'A first-rate movie script,' says Mr Samuel. 'Some of the scenes are beyond belief. Only an authority on the subject could have pieced it together.'

'The lines are terrific,' says Mr McGuire, running his fingers fondly over his tape-recorder which lies closed on the table. 'You edited those tapes perfectly, Clovis.'

Clovis remains mute.

Mr Samuel says, 'That's a good idea to open with, where you build up the Baroness like an identikit, when the police are looking for the motive and they put an eye here and a nose there. Very visual, Clovis.'

'I'm waiting to hear,' Clovis says. 'We should have heard. Yesterday was the deadline.'

'We'll hear,' says Mr Samuel. 'Don't worry. The motion picture industry is a very funny thing.'

'The serialization's come through,' says Clovis, moving his right elbow from his chin in order to tap his hand on a bulky file which lies on the table. 'That contract's safe.'

'The film's in our pocket,' says Mr McGuire. 'Our only problem is the casting. You have to have everyone younger than they really are. If Hadrian plays Lister, Pablo could play Hadrian.'

'It's just that I wonder if they'll give Pablo the part.'

'They'll have to,' says Mr McGuire.

'Eleanor can play the Baroness. The same shots as I've got, she only needs to follow the original film and dialogue,' says Mr Samuel.

'I'm worried about Pablo,' says Clovis.

'He's very photogenic,' says Mr Samuel.

They fall silent as Lister enters the room followed by the Reverend.

'Where is Eleanor?' says Lister.

'Not here,' says Clovis.

'Give the Reverend a nice drink,' says Lister, going over to the house-phone.

'No, I should be in bed,' says the Reverend. 'I have to get up in the morning to see about the wedding.'

'I'm sorry, Reverend, but we shall probably have an urgent mission for you in this house tonight arising out of Sister Barton's request. You really must stay.'

'You must stay, Reverend,' says Mr McGuire. 'We'll make you comfortable.'

Lister has lifted the receiver and has pressed a button. He stands waiting for a reply which does not come. He presses another button, speaking meanwhile over his shoulder to those in the room. 'Sister Barton,' he says, 'has asked the Reverend to perform a marriage service. She wants to marry him in the attic, who apparently assents so far as one can gather.' Having got no answer from the phone he presses another button and meanwhile says to the others, 'I've managed to dissuade the Reverend from such an irregular action at the present moment.'

'She's out of her mind,' says Mr Samuel. 'Off her head,' says Mr McGuire. And now Lister has got an answer on the phone. 'Eleanor,' he says into the speaker, 'Any news? Any luck?'

The answer whistles briefly. From outside the house comes a clap of thunder. Lister says into the speaker, 'Be thorough, my dear,' and hangs up.

'A storm in the distance coming over,' says Mr McGuire.

Clovis brings a glass of hot whisky to the Reverend who is sitting dazedly on the sofa. The Reverend takes the drink, and places it on the table by his side, with his fingers playing gently on the glass. He begins to hum a hymn-tune, then he nods with sleep, opening his eyes suddenly when a crackle of thunder passes the house, and letting them drop again when the noise is past.

The house-telephone rings. Lister answers it and it hisses back through its wind-pipe.

'Irene?' Lister says. 'Yes, of course let her in. Use your common sense.' He hangs up. 'That porter,' he says to all in the room, 'is a humbug.'

The house-phone rings again. Lister takes the instrument off the hook very slowly, says into the speaker, 'Lister here,' and trains his ear on the garrulous sirocco that forces its way down the narrow flue of the phone. Meanwhile a car draws up at the back. A window can be heard opening above and Heloise's voice calls 'Hi, Irene' into the stormy night. Mr Samuel, who is peering out of the window, turns back to the room and says, 'Irene in the Mini-Morris.'

The house-phone in Lister's hand gives a brief gusty sigh. Lister says, 'Darling, did you find the files locked or unlocked?'

The phone crackles amok while a double crash of thunder beats the sky above the roof. A long wail comes from the top of the house and from another level upstairs comes an intermittent beat of music. The back door rattles, admits footsteps and clicks shut. Lister at the phone listens on.

'Then be careful,' he says at last, 'not to lock them again. Leave everything as you found it. Take the copies and put the papers back. And hurry, my love. There is no cause for alarm –

> But at my back I always hear
> Time's wingèd chariot hurrying near – '

A tall skinny chinless girl with bright black eyes has come into the servants' room meanwhile.

Lister puts down the phone and says to her,

> 'And yonder all before us lie
> Deserts of vast eternity. –

Where have you been all night, Irene?'

'It was my evening off,' says Irene, removing her leather, lambskin-lined driving gloves.

'Evening off,' says Lister. 'What kind of an hour is this to return to the Château Klopstock?'

'I got caught in the storm,' she says. 'Good evening, Reverend. What a pleasure!'

The Reverend opens his eyes, sits up, lets his eyes wander round the room, then, seeing his drink he takes it up and sips it.

'Too strong,' he says. 'I'd like a cup of tea before I go.'

'Listen to the storm, Reverend. You can't go all that way back to Geneva on your motor-bike tonight,' says Lister.

'Out of the question,' says Irene.

The outside telephone rings, piercing the warm room.

Lister says to Clovis, 'Answer it. If it's a cousin wanting to talk to the Baron Klopstocks they are not to be disturbed. Who else could it be at this hour except a cousin?'

Clovis is at the switchboard of the outside telephone, in the pantry office. The Geneva exchange is speaking audibly in French. Mr Samuel and Mr McGuire stand behind Clovis.

Clovis responds, then putting his hand over the speaker he says to them. 'It's for me, from the United States.'

58

'It's no doubt about the film,' Lister says. 'They should have telephoned yesterday. But it's still yesterday over there. They always ring in the middle of the night from the United States of America. They think that because they are five hours back we also are five hours back. Irene, go up and fetch Heloise and the boys. Bring them down here, we have things to discuss.'

Irene goes and Lister once more takes up the house-phone, presses a button and waits for the hum. 'Eleanor, are you coming?' he says. The house-phone gives vent as before, while thunder smacks at the windows and Clovis can be heard from the pantry office chatting joyfully to the United States. Lister says at length into the house-phone speaker, 'Good, it's just what we need. Bring it down, love, bring it down at once. Put back the originals, and leave unlocked what you found unlocked and locked what was locked.'

Clovis has come to the room again, followed by Messrs McGuire and Samuel. The Reverend sleeps. Clovis smiles. 'It's all tied up,' he says, 'and Pablo's getting the part of Hadrian, too.'

IV

'AT A QUARTER PAST SEVEN, while the sky whitens,' says
Lister, 'we all, with the exception of Mr Samuel and Mr
McGuire, shall go up to our rooms, change into our smart
working-day uniforms, and at eight or thereabouts we blun-
der downstairs to call the police and interview the journalists
who will already have arrived, or be arriving. Mr Samuel and
Mr McGuire will be in bed, but in the course of the breaking
open of the library door by the police, they too will float
down the staircase, surprised, and wearing their bath-robes
or something seemly. We will by then have put the Reverend
to bed and he can sleep on through the fuss until, and if,
wakened by the police. He in the attic and Sister Barton will
be back in their quarters. They – '

'Why should they be out of their quarters during the
night?' Heloise says.

'Let me prophesy,' Lister says. 'My forecasts are only ap-
proximate, as are Heloise's intuitions.'

'Let Lister speak,' says Eleanor.

The storm has moved away from the vicinity and can be
heard in the distance batting among the mountain-tops like
African drums.

Clovis says, 'We've got nothing to hide. We're innocent.'

'Well, we are crimeless,' Lister says. 'To continue with the
plans. Heloise, you are pregnant.'

60

The house-telephone rings. Eleanor lifts it up and bends an ear to its bronchial story. Heloise laughs.

'All right, let them come inside the gates. But don't let them out again,' Eleanor says, and puts down the phone. She says to Lister, 'That's Victor Passerat's two friends. They are threatening to call the police if we won't produce Passerat.'

'Here they come,' says Hadrian, at the window, and presently a car bumps up the drive. Presently again, a banging at the back door.

'Let them in,' says Lister. 'Bring them in here.'

'That's right,' says Clovis. 'Better straighten things out.'

Mr Samuel goes out to the back door and returns followed by Anne the masseuse and her friend, Alex. They stand staring at the assembled household. They look from Eleanor to the dozing Reverend, they look at laughing Heloise, at Pablo and at long-legged Irene and Lister.

'I understand you want to use the telephone,' Lister says. He waves towards the pantry office. 'Well there it is.'

'We want Victor,' says Anne.

'He is in the library with the Baron and the Baroness. They're not to be disturbed. Strict orders.'

'I feel afraid for Victor,' says Alex.

'Why not ring the police as you've suggested?' says Lister waving again towards the pantry office. 'The telephone's in there. We are having a busy night waiting up for the Baron and the Baroness.'

'I'd rather keep the police out of it,' Anne says.

'Yes, I dare say. What sort of reward are you hoping for, large or small?'

'Victor's our friend. We know Cathy Klopstock, too,' says Anne.

Heloise says, 'Why don't you call the police and tell them you've got those tape-recordings and films ready in your car, so that Victor and the Baroness can do a deal with the Baron, and then clear out? – Threats of exposure.'

Eleanor says, 'Don't be crude and literal, Heloise. This has been a tiring night. I wish you had bought some decent carrots for my juice.'

'You have to be frank with these types,' Heloise says.

'They don't connect,' says Pablo.

'Come on, let's go,' says Anne to Alex, whose eyes brim with tears.

They follow Mr Samuel to the back door and leave the house.

'Heloise,' says Lister, 'as I was saying, you're pregnant.'

Mr Samuel comes back into the room as Heloise gives out her laughter.

Mr Samuel says, 'They've locked the doors of the car. Evidently they're going on a trip round the grounds.'

Mr McGuire goes to the window in the dark pantry office. 'They've gone round to the front of the house,' he says.

'Let them prowl,' says Lister. 'About your condition, Heloise. There's a solution to your problem.'

'It's no problem,' says Heloise.

'You marry the Baron,' says Lister, 'and become the Baroness.'

Pablo says, 'He's gone to meet his Maker. He shoots the wife and secretary when they talk too fast. Then he shoots himself, according to the script. He sorts out the mix-up the only way he knows.'

'Eleanor has found some new evidence,' Lister says. 'It was quite unforeseen, but one foresees the unforeseen. He in the attic is the Baron's younger brother. Heir to the title and, under the terms of the Trust, most of the fortune.'

'I thought he was related to her, not him,' says Hadrian.

'He's a nephew or something, isn't he?' Clovis says. 'If not, I have to amend the script.'

'A younger brother of the Baron.'

'He turns my milk,' says Heloise.

'Mine too,' says Lister. 'But he's the heir.'

'There's the young brother Rudolph in Brazil,' says Mr Samuel. 'He was always thought to be the heir. All that money.'

'The one in Brazil is younger than him in the attic,' Eleanor says. 'Him in the attic is next in line. He inherits. Sister Barton knew what she was doing when she sent for the Reverend tonight and offered to marry her patient out of pity.'

The Reverend has opened his eyes on hearing himself referred to. He has sat up, rather refreshed from his nap.

'My poor boy in the attic,' he says. 'Sister Barton is a fine woman. I think it should be done.'

'He in the attic has prior responsibilities,' says Lister. 'Does anyone know his Christian name?'

'I never heard it mentioned,' says Heloise.

'Sister Barton calls him Tony,' says the Reverend.

'His name,' says Lister, 'is Gustav Anthony Klopstock. It's on his birth certificate, his medical certificate exempting him from army service, and it's in their father's will.'

'The Registers?' says the Reverend.

'He's also mentioned in a social register for 1949. That's the latest we have in the house. It occurred to me he must have died, but I was wrong. I admit we were in error,' Lister says. 'But fortunately we left room for error, and having discovered it in time, here we are. There is a vast difference between events that arise from and those that merely follow after each other. Those that arise are preferable. And Clovis amends his script.'

'I wouldn't have married him for choice,' says Heloise. 'He doesn't cognate.'

'You don't have to cognate with him,' says Hadrian. 'You only need get your marriage-lines in black and white.'

'Reverend,' says Lister, 'do you recall that night last June when the Klopstocks were away and him in the attic got loose? Remember we called you in to catch him and calm him down?'

'Poor boy, I remember, of course,' says the Reverend. 'He didn't know what he was doing.'

'He's not officially certified,' says Eleanor. 'The Baron and Baroness wouldn't hear of it.'

'That's true,' Lister says. 'And I wish to draw the Reverend's attention to the result of that rampage last June.' Lister indicates Heloise who smiles at her stomach.

'Good gracious me!' says the Reverend. 'I wouldn't have thought he had it in him.'

'We must lose no time,' says Lister getting up. 'Prepare the drawing-room, Eleanor. It's past five o'clock. I'll go and give orders to Sister Barton.'

'I would need a few days,' says the Reverend firmly. 'You can't marry people like this.'

'It's a special case, Reverend. You can't refuse. In fact, you may not refuse. Look at poor Heloise, her condition.'

The central posy of violets is missing from the funeral wreath which lies under the shower in the scullery bathroom being gently sprinkled to keep it fresh. Heloise in her bedroom holds the posy in her hands. Pablo stands by admiringly. 'I've unpacked all my things again,' he says.

'What a business,' she says. 'Nobody needed to pack their things, after all. All those trunks and suitcases.'

Hadrian appears at the door of her room holding the white mink coat lately left in the cloak-room by Victor Passerat. 'Just right for the occasion,' she says, putting it on.

'Lister says it has to go back in the cloak-room immediately after the ceremony,' Hadrian says. 'The police will want to know what coat he was wearing. Lister is keen that the police should see this coat. It speaks volumes, Lister says.'

'It doesn't meet in the front,' Heloise says.

'You look nice,' Pablo says.

There is a knock at the door and Irene walks in.

'You really going to marry him?' she says.

'Sure,' says Heloise. 'Why not?'

'Then you'll need some music,' Irene says. 'How can you have a wedding without music?'

'Eleanor could play the grand piano,' says Hadrian.

'No,' says Heloise. 'I like Eleanor but she's got a lovely touch on the piano. I can't stand that lovely touch.'

'Mr Samuel plays the piano and also the guitar,' Pablo says. 'Mr Samuel energizes.'

'Bring down the gramophone,' says Heloise. 'That's better; because Mr Samuel will be taking the photographs and Mr McGuire has to do the sound-track. This thing's got to go on record. It's got to compass.'

'It's still stormy,' says Hadrian as a flash of lightning stands for a second in the square pane of the window. A clap of thunder follows it. 'There must be trees felled in the park,' he says.

'I shall arrange for them,' says Heloise, 'to be swept up some time tomorrow. Let's go down to the room. They're all waiting.'

Upstairs there is a scuffle and a howl.

'Isn't it usual for the bridegroom to arrive first?' says Irene.

'It's all right if he's late on account of his health,' says Pablo. 'Let's go.'

'Clara,' says the porter, 'your tea, dearest. It's nearly half-past five, and I'm early bringing it up. I've got the jitters, somehow. I've just got orders not to open the gate before eight and after that, let everyone in. "Absolutely everyone." Can you understand it? Why should everyone come at eight in the morning?'

'Oh, my dreams, Theo,' she says, sitting up in bed and reaching for her frilly bed-jacket. She puts it on and takes her tea from Theo's waiting hand.

'He said, "Let everyone in after eight o'clock, not before." This job's beyond me, Clara. We have to move on.'

'Oh, but I love this little house. It was always what I wanted. You know I think the Baroness got sentimental with one of the secretaries. I think she's going to run away with him.'

'Those two strange ones who came in the green car asking for Victor Passerat all the time,' Theo says. 'They came back up here a few minutes ago. They didn't get to see Victor Passerat. Now they're anxious to go home but I've got orders not to let them out. The gates don't open till eight, then everyone, absolutely everyone, can come and go as they please.'

'Where have they gone then, those two?'

'Back to the house to wait there.'

'Do you know, Theo, the one that sat beside the driver doesn't look like a lady. Very hard face. Like a man.'

'Don't dwell on it, Clara dearest.'

The drawing-room is being re-arranged for the wedding. Irene and Eleanor bustle and give orders to Pablo and Hadrian who are moving chairs and tables. The Reverend wanders with a perplexed air from one end of the room to the other, carefully piloting himself around the busy workers, weaving in and out between the minute tables and small sofas, and puzzling his brow absentmindedly at the tiny portraits and litter of small ornaments.

'I really think,' says the Reverend, pulling his press-cutting out of his pocket, 'that Baron Klopstock should take this pill.'

'Too far gone,' says Hadrian, standing back to see if the table he has placed beside another squares off neatly. 'He's past caring.'

Clovis comes in with an embroidered tablecloth which he lays carefully across the two oblong tables which Hadrian has placed end-to-end. 'It makes a very good altar, says Clovis. He snaps his fingers. 'A large candelabrum from the dining-room!' he shouts. Irene skips out of the room, while Lister with Heloise on his arm appears in the doorway of the ante-room at the far end.

The Reverend puts his press-cutting back in his pocket.

Eleanor says, 'We are to use the Book of Common Prayer appointed to be read in the Church of England.'

The Reverend says, 'I always marry according to the Evangelical Waldensian form, which is very free.'

'Heloise,' calls Eleanor, her voice rising on the last syllable, 'what religion are you?'

'None,' says Heloise. She lets go Lister's arm, comes in from the ante-room and relaxes into a comfortable chair.

'What religion were you brought up in?' says the Reverend.

'None,' says Heloise.

'Where were you born?'

'Lyons,' says Heloise, 'but that was by chance.'

'It should be Evangelical,' says the Reverend.

'In this house it is the Book of Common Prayer,' Eleanor says. 'Do you want her to have that child out of wedlock? We haven't all night to spend arguing, Reverend. The father has assented but he might change his mind.'

'Let me see the English book, then,' says the Reverend. 'I have it within my competence to make exceptions in a case like this. Perhaps I could simplify the English form. I don't read well in English, you know.'

Eleanor points to a flat, leather-bound book lying ready beside the small porcelain statuettes on a wall-table. 'That's it,' she says. 'It can't be simplified, it's impossible.'

Lister advances into the room, stopping to twist a bowl of flowers to better taste. He says, 'Eleanor, the bridegroom is C. of E., I think.'

'No, they're Catholics.'

'Oh well, he went to Winchester, an English school.'

'No, he never went to school. He was always unable.'

'He went for a week.'

'It isn't enough.'

'Eleanor,' says Lister, 'we can have any little irregularity put straight later.'

'That's right,' says Heloise. 'This coat's heavy.'

Irene comes in with a large branched candlestick in ornamental silver with long white candles set in its sockets. She places it on the covered table.

'Don't light the candles yet,' says Eleanor, raising her eyes to the ceiling, from above which comes the sound of a scuffle and a howl. 'Goodness knows what might happen. We don't want a fire.'

'He's had his injection,' Lister says.

'Well it hasn't taken yet,' says Heloise.

'Come back into the little room and stand with me,' Lister says to Heloise. 'The bride should enter last and enter last she will.'

The scuffle upstairs continues and is accompanied by a repeated banging.

'Is that the wind or is it him?' says Eleanor. 'Is it the shutters?'

'It could be either,' Pablo says listening expertly.

'I'd better go and help,' says robust Hadrian. He bounds out of the drawing-room and up the stairs.

Heloise has again joined Lister at the door between the ante-room and the drawing-room and from there he gives his final instructions. 'Remove the Sèvres vases – take them away, just in case. Irene, your skirt's too short, this is a ceremony.'

Heloise says, 'Irene likes to show her legs. Why not?'

'They're all she's got,' says Clovis.

'He's coming!' says Irene.

The wind now whistles round the house and the remote shutters bang as another latent storm wakes up. Footsteps descend heavily and the occasional howl that accompanies them becomes, as it approaches, more like a trumpet call.

Mr Samuel now enters with his camera. Mr McGuire follows with his tape-recorder which he places on a table in an angle of the room, unplugging a lamp to make way for the plug of his machine. He tests it out, then pulls up a chair and, folding his arms, waits.

As the footsteps and the trumpet-blast tumble their way down, Pablo puts a record on the gramophone with a pleased, but unsmiling expression. It is a new rendering of *Greensleeves*, played very fast even at the beginning, and plainly working up to something complex and speedy.

'Not so loud,' says the Reverend, but his words cannot be heard at the door of the ante-room, where Pablo has settled the gramophone by the side of Heloise and Lister. 'Play it more quietly,' Lister says.

Pablo turns it down.

'It seems unsuitable but one has to go along with them,' says the Reverend as Hadrian and Sister Barton edge into the drawing-room, supporting between them him from the attic. It is immediately noticeable that the patient's howls and trumpetings appear to be expressions of delight rather than pain, for he grins incessantly, his great eyes glittering with ecstatic gladness.

Lister, with Heloise on his arm, advances slowly to meet the bridegroom. 'What a noise he's making,' says Heloise.

'There must be at least eighty-two instruments in that band you've got for your wedding march,' Lister says, 'another can't be amiss.' An instant of quick lightning at the windows followed by a grumble of thunder reinforces his argument.

The zestful cretin's eyes fall first on Irene. He neighs jubilantly through his large teeth and shakes his long white wavy hair. He wears a jump-suit of dark red velvet fastened from crotch to collar-bone with a zip-fastener. This zipper is secured at the neck by a tiny padlock which very likely has been taken, for the purpose, from one of the Baroness Klopstock's Hermes handbags. Beside him, holding him fast with one arm round his shoulders and with the other hand gripping his arm, is a young nurse whose youthfulness does not help. Hadrian, his eyebrows tentatively raised, holds the other arm.

'My boy,' says the Reverend to him from the attic who now stands shaking off his keepers with his powerful shoulders.

The other servants stand back, and Hadrian joins them. Eleanor casts a glance behind her to the open door, and stands a little nearer to it.

'A vivacious husband,' says Lister. 'Miss Barton, try to hold him firm. It's an exciting moment in his life.'

'It's a scandal,' says young Sister Barton. 'It's me he wants to marry.'

At the moment he seems to prefer Irene, and, breaking loose, plunges upon her. Heloise says, 'He doesn't level, you can't really construe with him.'

He is lifted off Irene, who demands a cigarette, and he is then consigned, still wishfully carolling, to the strong arms of Hadrian and Pablo.

'Make it look like something,' says Mr Samuel, training his camera. Immediately they open their mouths in laughter to combine with his, and group themselves on either side of him so that their restraining arms are concealed, only Hadrian's arm of fellowship and Pablo's congratulatory hand in the bridegroom's being revealed. Mr McGuire's bobbins whirl sportively while the scene lasts.

'Just hold him there,' says Lister, 'for a minute.'

But now the captive has caught sight of the bride, tall, pink and plump, and indicates his welcome with a huge fanfare of delight, straining mightily towards her.

'Reverend,' says Miss Barton, 'this is not proper. He's had his injection and these girls are simply nullifying the effect. In his normal state he is very much attached to me.'

'This bit of group-therapy,' Lister tells her, 'is precisely what he needs. Poor man, confined up there all the time with you!'

'I am perplexed,' says the Reverend. 'I have to know which one he wants to marry.' He smiles at the prisoner and says, 'My boy, which of the ladies is your preference, if any?'

The bridegroom gives a cunning heave, triumphantly dragging Pablo and Hadrian in the direction of Heloise who is now taking a light for a cigarette from Irene's. He also spares a glance of beatitude for Eleanor, but continues to make for Heloise with determination.

Lister says, 'It's Heloise, obviously.' The storm beats on the windows and detonates in the park. The music comes to an end, causing him from the attic to crow and romp a little, and to touch the padlock of his zip lovingly.

'He wants to take his clothes off,' says Sister Barton. 'Take care. He's been known to do it.'

'Who is the father of your child?' says the Reverend desperately to Heloise.

'Well,' says Heloise, taking a chair, 'it isn't born yet. Four months and a bit to go. Pablo was busy helping the Baron every evening at the time and Hadrian was off-duty. Mr Samuel and Mr McGuire were in the Baron's team, too, following their respective professions. Then – '

'The Baron?' says the Reverend impatiently. 'Don't tell me he's never attempted to exercise *droit du seigneur*, because Baron Klopstock was well known in his youth.'

Lister says, 'A pornophile, merely. Pornophilia does not make for fatherhood, Reverend. At least, in my experience, it doesn't. Now, if the Baroness could have been the father in the course of nature she might have been, but the Baron, no.'

'Let me see,' says the Reverend, looking round the room. 'Who does that leave?'

'All the rest of them,' says Heloise. 'Let's have some music.'

'Someone from outside,' says the Reverend.

'Do you mean one of the guests at one of the banquets, Reverend?'

'No, one of their private affairs, perhaps.'

'Heloise was strictly on duty at the time,' says Lister. 'Very busy. The secretaries were fully occupied and there were no visiting cousins. You saw for yourself how it was the month of June. You were a constant visitor at large.'

'Then it rests between Clovis, the poor boy Klopstock here, and you, Lister,' says the Reverend, ticking them off again on his fingers while mentally going through the roll-call.

Lister whispers in the Reverend's ear.

'Oh,' says the Reverend. 'Well it isn't Clovis. That leaves you and the poor boy.'

'I am enamoured to the brim with Eleanor,' says Lister, 'and her prayer-book carry-on.'

'Lister,' says Eleanor.

'Eleanor,' he says.

'It's got to be him in the attic,' says Heloise. 'I'm waiting.'

'It could only be him or the Reverend,' Lister says.

'Let us begin,' says the Reverend. 'Bring him over – carefully, carefully. He must stand here with the girl.'

'The music,' says Heloise.

'Sister Barton,' says Pablo. 'If you don't come and help I can't go and put on the wedding record for Heloise.'

'It's atrocious,' says Sister Barton, weeping but not helping. 'To take him away from me now, after all I've done.'

The Reverend looks for a moment at Sister Barton then looks away as if finding her unsavoury. 'Have you got a Protestant Bible?' he says. 'If not, we'll do without.'

'The English Prayer Book,' says Eleanor, but she cannot be heard above the noise of the storm and the ecstasy of the man from the attic, whom Clovis is now assisting Hadrian to hold. Standing beside Heloise the patient is apparently dumbstruck and gazes at her with only his grin. *Greensleeves* starts up again.

'It's getting late,' says Lister.

'The Book of Common Prayer,' says Eleanor.

'It's within my competence as a pastor to perform a legal marriage in this country according to my own simple formula,' says the Reverend looking at his watch then at him from the attic, while pointing to Heloise. 'Gustav Anthony Klopstock, do you take this woman to be your wedded wife?' he says.

The bridegroom escapes, once more, to tumble upon Heloise.

'That means "I do",' says Pablo, helping with the others, to rescue the bride.

'Nobody can now say he wasn't in his right mind at the time of the marriage,' says Lister. 'He knows perfectly well what he's doing.'

'In my condition,' says Heloise.

When the couple are set in place again the Reverend says to Heloise, 'What is your father's name?'

'Klopstock,' says Heloise.

'Klopstock?'

A howl of delight is emitted by the Klopstock from the attic.

'Kindred and Affinity!' shrieks Eleanor above the boisterous instrumentals of the storm, the music and the groom.

'It is a coincidence,' Lister says, spreading his hands like a conductor of an orchestra pleading a *pianissimo*. 'Her father is a humble Klopstock, a riveter. No connection with the House of Klopstock whose residence this is, where galaxies of generals, ambassadors, and their bespangled consorts mingle with cardinals and exiled Arabians by night when the Baron and Baroness are not privately engaged.'

'Are you of age?' says the Reverend to Heloise.

'I'm twenty-two,' she says, swinging a little to the rock-music as it speeds up, and shaking the white mink coat.

'She's twenty-three!' says Sister Barton, still tearful.

'Well you're a major,' says the Reverend to Heloise. 'Heloise Klopstock,' he says, 'will you take this man to be your wedded husband?'

'I will,' says Heloise.

'They have no ring,' says the Reverend looking round irritably.

Lister produces a ring immediately.

'He'll only put it in his mouth and swallow it,' weeps Sister Barton.

'I shall place the ring on the bride's finger by proxy,' says Lister, doing so.

'I hereby pronounce you man and wife,' says the Reverend placing a hand on each shoulder of Heloise and her new husband who, now overjoyed, once more leaps out of reach, this time gambolling to the far end of the room. Numerous precious vases crash to the floor.

Mr McGuire hastens to protect his bobbins, while Mr Samuel says, clicking his camera, 'Marvellous! His laugh's very like a large-mouthed cry of elation such as any beauty queen might give at the moment of her election.'

'I would never resemble him to that,' says Heloise.

Her husband is sprightly and will not be caught. He rips the whole zip-fastener from the stuff of his suit and exultantly dances out of the garment. Then, capering lustily with carols and further damage to the furniture, he pulls the mink coat off his wife's back, drags her into a corner and falls on top of her.

Pablo rushes to intervene.

'Leave him be. He has every right,' says Lister.

'He has no right at a wedding,' says the Reverend. 'It's not the thing to do.'

Sister Barton sobs and the storm revels, while Heloise shoves with hard athleticism and finally escapes, fleeing to the safety of the sound and film-track area. 'Give me a comb,' she says.

Clovis is blowing out the candles.

Mr Samuel says, 'This will need a lot of editing.'

'In my condition,' says Heloise, 'and I've lost a shoe.'

The bridegroom is being held by Sister Barton, Hadrian and Pablo, and is being clothed with the embroidered table cloth by Eleanor.

'Bite his finger and keep him quiet,' says Clovis to Sister Barton.

'He was only doing his thing,' says Hadrian.

Lister says, 'Kings and queens of olden days used to consummate in public. They had four-poster beds with curtains. The court had to stand by to see the curtains shake when Mary Queen of Scots married the Dauphin of France, compared to whom our friend from the attic, here, is an Einstein. And so, my dear Heloise, nobody can now contest the validity of your nuptials on the grounds that they haven't been consummated.'

'They were not consummated,' say Heloise. 'Only almost.'

'To the eye of the candid camera,' says Lister, 'the marriage was consummated. Isn't that so, Mr Samuel?'

'Yes,' says Mr Samuel. But nobody is listening. Lister is offering a pen and two sheets of typewritten paper to the Reverend. 'The marriage certificate,' he says. 'Will you sign your witness, Reverend? I have already signed. In duplicate.'

The Reverend is looking round him as if wondering where he is.

'Sign?' he says. 'Oh yes, of course, I'll put my name. And the happy couple has to sign, too.' He beams at everyone, takes out his glasses, rests the piece of paper on Eleanor's flat prayer book and signs. 'The bridegroom,' he says, 'then the bride.'

'Bite his finger,' says Clovis to Sister Barton, 'or you're fired.'

Tearfully, she takes the little finger of the trumpeting patient in her mouth and bites. He starts to giggle and, although she lets go, does not stop. Lister places the pen in the giggler's hand and raising the paper and the hard book to a convenient level, moves the limp and helplessly amused hand over the space provided until the name is traced, Gustav A. Klopstock. 'The Anthony would have taken too long,' says Lister, very satisfied in his expression of face. 'You never know when his milder spells will stop. Now, Heloise.' Heloise takes the pen and writes her name above the typed address, in the space reserved for her. 'We register this tomorrow,' says Lister. 'It's a quarter to seven. Time has flown. Sister Barton, Pablo will assist you. Give him a nice warm drink and an injection.'

'I must go home to bed,' says the Reverend. 'Where did I leave my bike?' He looks around the very untidy drawing-room.

'In this storm,' Lister says, 'you can't ride back to Geneva, Reverend. We have a bed for you. We shall always have a bed for you, Reverend. Eleanor, show the Reverend to his room.'

'Nice of you, very kind under the circumstances,' says the Reverend. 'I want to show a press-cutting to Cecil Klopstock. Where is he?'

'The Baron is not to be disturbed.'

'Tell him I want to see him when he wakes up.'

V

'BEAR IN MIND,' SAYS LISTER, 'that when dealing with the rich, the journalists are mainly interested in backstairs chatter. The popular glossy magazines have replaced the servants' hall in modern society. Our position of privilege is unparalleled in history. The career of domestic service is the thing of the future. The private secretaries of the famous do well, too. Give me another cup of coffee, please, Eleanor. It's almost time to go up and change.'

They are seated round the large table where breakfast seems to be as rapidly begun as nearing its end. The storm has retreated from the near vicinity of the house, but continues to prowl on the lake and the mountain-sides. Every now and again there is a banging of fists, a shouted demand, on the back door. Nobody takes any notice.

'Are there any grapes in the house?' says Heloise.

'No, you had the last of them,' says Clovis.

'Well, you're wrong,' says Irene, 'because I brought her a huge big bunch from Geneva. They're in the pantry. I got them from that boyfriend who's a steward on the first class TWA.'

'Irene, what a treasure the Klopstocks have lost in you by their death!' says Lister.

Irene looks modestly at her crumby plate.

Clovis yawns and leans his elbow on the table and his head on his hands. 'I'm worn out,' he says. 'I'll be glad to get to bed.' He gets up, goes into the pantry and returns with a tray on which are set a plate of large green grapes, a bowl of water in which to dip them and a tiny pair of scissors with which to snip them off their twigs. He places them before Heloise. 'Long live the Baroness!' he says.

Heloise pats her stomach.

Mr Samuel then goes to open the back door. He can be heard saying, 'You'll have to wait. Victor Passerat's not available just yet.'

'We've lost the keys of the car!' says the woman's voice.

'Well, look for them.'

'The ground's all wet. We're soaked through. Can't we come in and telephone to a garage, or something?'

'Sorry, strangers aren't permitted.'

'What can we do? We can't get in the car, and we can't get out of the gate. The porter won't open it for us.'

'Take a stroll in the grounds,' advises Mr Samuel.

'It's wet. We'll get caught in another downpour. This is a terrible place.'

'You should always,' says Mr Samuel, 'avoid terrible places.'

Returning to the servants' dining-room he says, 'Amateurs. Where's my camera? It's just possible I could get a few shots of them to fit in an educational film I've got going. The young have to be taught about the average aberrant in the street.'

He takes his camera to the window and focuses.

Lister, dressed smartly for the day's work, stands at the open front door like a gloomy shopkeeper looking at the dark, rumbling sky as Theo comes up the drive on his bicycle. Theo makes a questioning sign, pointing round to the back of the house. 'No, come here,' says Lister.

Theo tremulously parks his bicycle against the dripping hedge and walks the rest of the way.

'I called for you, Theo, because there is something strange to report,' Lister says. 'Come right in.'

The others are coming downstairs, with sleeplessness in their movements and on their faces. The servants are dressed in their morning overalls. Behind them come Mr Samuel in a knee-length blue bath-robe and Mr McGuire in a black and white striped dressing-gown.

'What's going on?' says Mr Samuel.

Theo says, 'There's something peculiar been going on all night.'

'Do you like the job, Theo?' says Lister.

'Yes, Lister,' he says.

'Well, you can keep it. Only remember that nothing peculiar has been going on, as indeed it hasn't. I want only to inform you here and now that the light is on in the library as it was last night when we went to bed with orders not to disturb the Baron Klopstocks and their guest and, furthermore, this morning the door is locked from the inside and there is no response.'

'What's happened?' says Theo. 'You know, my Clara has had dreams, terrible dreams. Have you knocked hard enough?'

Lister goes to the library door, tries the handle, shakes it, then knocks loudly. 'Sir!' he says. 'Madam!'

'We'd better break it down,' says Theo, looking at the others one by one.

'I have orders not to disturb,' Lister says. 'We shall call the police.'

'Clara will be frightened,' says Theo.

'Tell her to confide in the police about her dreams, and get it off her chest,' says Lister. 'The more she says about her dreams when questioned, the better. As far as you two in the lodge are concerned we have been such stuff as dreams are made on all through the stormy night.'

'There's a couple been wandering the grounds all night,' says Theo. 'They came in the car and I wouldn't let them out, as you ordered. Now they've lost the keys of the car and they're taking shelter under a tree. They look a suspicious pair to me.'

'Forget them,' says Mr Samuel. 'They're only extras.'

'Better go back to Clara,' says Lister. 'It's nearly eight o'clock. See that the gates are opened.'

'All right, Lister,' says Theo is a hushed voice, looking towards the library. Then he departs quickly through the open door, mounts his bicycle and starts off up the drive. He gets drenched almost immediately for at that moment the storm descends with full concentration on the Klopstocks' country seat. Theo pedals vigorously, and rounding a bend he is forced to get off his bicycle and press forward on foot along the loud storm-darkened avenue, streaked every now and then as it is with a dart of lightning. On the way he passes a clump of trees under one of which, shrinking into the bark, are the couple of wandering friends from the car. Theo staggers onwards up the twisting drive and at the porch of his house lets fall the bicycle, bends through the torrent to the gates of the house, unlocks them and throws them open. Then he returns to the lodge and tumbles indoors.

Meanwhile the lightning, which strikes the clump of trees so that the two friends huddled there are killed instantly without pain, zig-zags across the lawns, illuminating the lily-pond and the sunken rose garden like a self-stricken flash-photographer, and like a zip-fastener ripped from its garment by a sexual maniac, it is flung slapdash across Lake Leman and back to skim the rooftops of the house, leaving intact, however, the well-insulated telephone wires which Lister, on the telephone to Geneva, has rather feared might break down.

Having alerted the police and quiveringly recommended an ambulance with attendant doctors and nurses, Lister now telephones to the discreet and well-appointed flat in Geneva which he prudently maintains, and extends a welcome to the four journalists who have been waiting up all night for the call, playing poker meanwhile, with the ash-trays piled high.

'Our four friends,' Lister then instructs the household, 'are to have first preference in anything you can say to them. They will, of course, have the scandal exclusives which Mr Samuel and Mr McGuire have prepared in the form of type-script, photographs and sound-recordings. The television, Associated Press and the local riff-raff are sure to question you wildly: answer likewise – say anything to them, just anything, but keep them happy. Isn't that right, Clovis?'

'Yes, the arrangements between our four special friends, ourselves, and our numbered accounts in the Swiss Trust Corporate can be left to Lister. We don't have any arrange-ments with the others. Keep them happy, that's all. For the television, throw your heads into your hands and sob, or display a sad disapproval of your late employers.'

'I want to go to bed,' says Heloise.

'I shall see that you are allowed to retire at the earliest possible moment, Heloise.'

'Listen to Lister,' says Eleanor.

Lister then books a telephone call to the residence of Count Rudolph Klopstock in Rio de Janeiro, and having done this, says to the others, 'There's a delay to Brazil and they're five hours back. We should get the Count somewhere between four and five a.m. Rio time, and allowing for human nature on the telephone exchange between here and there the news will get around pretty quickly.'

'The brother ought to know,' says Eleanor.

'Know what?' says Lister.

'About the brother,' says Eleanor.

'At the present moment,' says Lister, 'all we ourselves know is that the library door is locked with the Baron, the Baroness and their young friend unresponsive. We're justifiably apprehensive, that's all. Here comes the crime squad. Group yourselves apprehensively.'

He opens the front door to the sound of sirens in the storm. Two police cars pull up at the door followed by an ambulance. An inspector of police, a police detective, two plain-clothes men, three uniformed policemen and a police photographer troop in the open door. The ambulance crew alight and come in out of the rain.

'This is the door, Inspector,' says Lister, leading the way to the library.

The Inspector turns the handle, rattles it, bangs on the door and listens.

'Are you sure there's somebody inside?'

'We fear so. The light's still on as it was last night. The Baron gave orders they were not to be disturbed,' Lister says. 'I have already put through a call to the Baron's brother, as I felt it was right.'

'Open the door,' says the Inspector. Two hefty policemen break it down. The Inspector and his men crowd into the room. Lister follows while the rest of the household approaches the threshold. Mr Samuel's camera clicks. Mr McGuire has a small, light apparatus dangling from his wrist. The body of the Baroness is lying on the floor by the window in a large dark red stain. That of Victor Passerat lies curled against a bookcase which is well splashed with his blood. The Baron's body is slumped over a round table with a revolver not far from his fingers.

The women scream.

'Take the girls away,' says the Inspector to a plain-clothes man. 'Put them in the kitchen and make them calm down.'

Clovis leads the way to the servants' quarters while the Inspector says to Lister, 'Didn't you hear anything during the night? No shots? No shouting or screaming?'

The wind encircles the house and the shutters bang. From the attic comes a loud clatter. 'No, Inspector. It was a wild night,' says Lister.

Up the drive comes a caravan of cars.

The doctor has scrutinised the bodies, the police have taken their statements, they have examined and photographed the room. They have confiscated a letter written by the Baron, to the effect that he has just shot his wife and his secretary and is about to shoot himself, that this is the only solution and that he has no ill feelings against anyone. The Inspector has permitted Lister to read it but has refused it to the reporters who now swarm in the great hall and make a considerable hubbub.

The women have been released from the kitchen, having given their shaken and brief testimony, and again join the household group at the door of the library.

'I must have a last look,' says Eleanor. Heloise casts a doleful eye at a television camera which does not fail to register it. The noise from the reporters swells as, one by one, the covered bodies on their stretchers are borne out of the room. 'Here they come,' says Lister to his troop, 'Klopstock and barrel.'

The bodies are stowed away in the ambulance. The police seal off the main quarters of the house, pushing the reporters out into the subsiding storm, and requesting the servants to retire to their wing.

The doctor then suggests he takes away the ladies to be treated for shock, but they bravely resist. 'The porter's wife,' says the Inspector, 'could do with a bit of treatment. Better take her.'

'I should take them both, sir,' says Lister.

The reporters now crowd in the back door. 'Inspector,' says Lister, 'I shall deal with them briefly then turn them out. We're all rather shaken. If you want any further information we are here.'

'Very helpful,' says the Inspector. 'I'll leave a couple of my men to guard the house. Don't let anyone into the library or upstairs, any of you.'

Heloise says, 'They won't go upstairs, you can be sure of that. My Monet and my Goya are upstairs. One can't be too careful.'

'I beg your pardon?' says the Inspector.

'She is overwrought,' says Lister and says a word or two in the Inspector's ear.

'Yes, yes,' says the Inspector, eyeing Heloise.

Lister murmurs another few words, gesturing towards the ceiling.

'Oh yes,' says the Inspector, looking up. 'We know about him. Relative of the Baroness.'

'No, the Baron.'

'Really? – Oh, well. An unfortunate family.'

Lister adds a further piece of information in an undertone.

'Yes, well, if he's the father, you did the right thing,' says the Inspector, anxious to join his men in the police car which is now waiting at the back door. He shoves his way through the crowd, refusing comment, and drives off.

Very soon Lister's four friendly journalists go to their car with their brief-cases under their arms, and drive away.

'Now for the riff-raff,' Lister says to his clan. 'Eleanor and Clovis can take one bunch in the sitting-room. Heloise and I will hold our press conference in the pantry. Hadrian and Irene can sit round the kitchen table with Pablo, representing the young approach. Mr Samuel and Mr McGuire – you can go the rounds.'

They settle themselves accordingly. The cameras flash. Microphones are thrust forward to their mouths like hot-dogs being offered to hungry pilgrims.

The voices drown the hectic howl which descends from the breakfasting bridegroom.

Eleanor is saying, 'Like a runaway horse, not going anywhere and without a rider.'

Hadrian is saying, 'The flight of the homosexuals . . . ' to which his questioner, not having caught this comment through the noise, responds ' . . . the flight of the bumble-bee?' 'No,' says Hadrian.

Lister is saying, '. . . and at one time in my youth I was a professional claque. I applauded for some of the most famous singers in the world. It was quite well paid, but of course, hand-clapping is an art, it's a question of timing. . . . '

'Togetherness . . . ' says Irene.

Hadrian is saying, 'Death is that sort of thing that you can't sleep off. . . . '

Pablo's voice cuts in, ' . . . putting things in boxes. Squares, open cubes. It's a mentality. Framing them. . . . '

Eleanor says, 'Like children playing at weddings and funerals. I have piped and ye have not danced, I have mourned and ye have not wept.'

Lister, turning in his chair to a prober behind him, is saying, 'He didn't do his own cooking or press his own trousers. Why should he have consorted, excuse my language, with his own wife?'

Clovis says, ' . . . not on the typewriter – you wake the whole household, don't you? What I call midnight oil literature is only done by hand. It's an art. Yes, oh no, thanks, I intend to make other arrangements for publication.'

Irene is saying, 'No, he wanted it that way, I guess, until she did a Lady Chatterley on him . . . A Victorian novel, don't you know it? She was really quite typical at heart when it came to Victor.'

Lister is heard to recite, 'For the thing which I greatly feared is come upon me, and that which I was afraid of is come upon me. I was out in safety, neither had I rest, neither was I quiet.'

Eleanor is saying, 'No. No living relatives on her side.'

Pablo says, 'Ghosts and fantasies rising from sex-repression.'

Clovis says, 'Descendant of the Crusaders.'

' . . . somewhat like the war horse,' says Lister, 'in the Book of Job: He saith among the trumpets Ha! Ha! and he smelleth the battle afar off, the thunder of the captains and the shouting. . . . '

' . . . hardly ever seen,' Eleanor is saying. 'He wears a one-piece suit zipped and locked. The Swiss invented the zip-fastener. . . . '

'Well it's like this,' says Pablo, 'if you put friendship out to usury and draw the interest. . . . '

The Reverend has now come down for his breakfast and stands bewildered in the doorway of the servants' sitting-room where Eleanor and Clovis are holding their crowded conference. He has his press-cutting in his hand.

'Reverend!' says Eleanor, pushing over to him.

'There's a man on the landing outside my room. He made me come down the back stairs. Where's Cecil Klopstock? I want to show him this.'

Eleanor is swept away and replaced by five reporters. 'Reverend would you care to elaborate on your statement about the sex-drug . . . ? Did the Baron . . . ?'

Eleanor, herself surrounded once more, is saying, ' . . . frothing and churning inside like a washing machine in full programme.'

Lister, beside her, addresses another microphone, 'The glories,' he says, 'of our blood and state

> Are shadows, not substantial things;
> There is no armour against fate;
> Death lays his icy hand on kings:
>> Sceptre and crown
>> Must tumble down,
> And in the dust be equal made
> With the poor crooked scyth and spade.'

'Could you repeat that, sir?' says a voice. Clovis pushes his way through the mass of shoulders and reaches Lister. 'Phone call from Brazil,' he says. 'The butler won't fetch Count Klopstock to the phone. Absolutely refuses. He's locked in the study with some friends and he's on no account to be disturbed.'

'Leave word with the butler,' says Lister, 'that we have grave news and that we hope against hope to hear from the Count when morning dawns in Rio.'

Hadrian is saying, 'When my brother had the flower-stall at the Piazza del Popolo and Iolanda had a little pitch for the newspapers a few steps away . . . It was a windy corner.'

The Reverend, though trembling, is eating his breakfast in bed. The storm has passed and the sun begins to show itself on the wet bushes, the wide green lawns and the sodden rose-garden. The reporters with their microphones and cameras have trickled away. Lister is looking at the cigarette stubs on the floor. Clovis opens the kitchen window. A homely howl comes down from the attic.

A car approaches up the drive.

'No more,' says Lister. 'Send them away.'

'It's Prince Eugene,' says Eleanor. 'He's gone round the front.'

'Well, he'll be sent round the back,' says Lister, kicking a few cigarette stubs under the sideboard. 'Let us all go to bed.'

Footsteps can be heard squelching round the back of the house, and the top half of Prince Eugene's face appears at the open window.

'Have they all gone?' he says.

'It's our rest-hour, your Excellency.'

'I'm a Highness.'

Eleanor says, 'Was there something we can do for you, your Highness?'

'A word. Let me in.'

'Let his Highness in,' says Lister.

Prince Eugene enters timidly. He says, 'The neighbours have been parked out on the road all morning. They didn't have the courage to come. Admiral Meleager, the Baronne de Ventadour, Mrs Dix Silver, Emil de Vega, and all the rest. Anyway, I got here first. Can I have one word with you, Lister, my good man?'

'Come into the office,' says Lister, leading the way into the pantry office. Mr Samuel's camera flicks imperceptibly, just in case.

Prince Eugene takes the chair indicated by Lister. 'Any of you like to come over to my place? Have you thought it over? It's very comfortable. I can offer – '

'At the moment, sir,' says Lister, 'we want to go to sleep and we don't want to be disturbed.'

'Oh, quite,' says the Prince, rising. 'It's only that I wanted to get here before the others.'

'It's very understandable,' says Lister, rising, too. 'But in fact we've made our plans.'

'Miss Barton? – Would she consider a few light household duties? Surely the poor fellow can't go on living here?'

'Miss Barton will be needed. Heloise desires her to stay. Heloise was a parlour maid but she married the new Baron early this morning.'

'You don't say! They got married.'

Lister whispers in his ear.

'Oh, I understand. Quite drastic, though, isn't it?'

'They can marry or not marry, as they please, these days, sir,' says Lister. 'Times have changed. Take Irene, for instance.'

'Which one is Irene?'

'The very charming one. Quite the most attractive. A very good little cook, too.'

'I can offer her a very good wage.'

'These days,' says Lister, 'they want more.' He again murmurs a few words in the Prince's ear.

'I'm not the marrying type,' whispers the Prince shyly.

'It's the best I can offer, your Highness. She's happy enough with her evening off at the airport.'

'Well, I'd better be going,' says the Prince.

'Thank you for calling, sir.'

Lister leads the way to the back door, where Prince Eugene hesitates and says, 'Are you sure we can't make some alternative arrangement with Irene?'

'Yes,' says Lister. 'I have others in mind for her in this part of the world who would be grateful to have her seated at their table. She's a very capable young housekeeper. The Marquis of – '

'Very well, Lister. Arrange the details as soon as possible. Accept no other offers.'

The Prince tramples round once more to the front of the house, gets into his car and is seen to be driven off, sunk in the back seat, pondering.

The plain-clothes man in the hall is dozing on a chair, waiting for the relief man to come, as is also the plain-clothes man on the upstairs landing. The household is straggling up the back stairs to their beds. By noon they will be covered in the profound sleep of those who have kept faithful vigil all night, while outside the house the sunlight is laughing on the walls.

THE TAKEOVER

I

AT NEMI, THAT PREVIOUS SUMMER, there were three new houses of importance to the surrounding district. One of them was new in the strict sense; it had been built from the very foundations on cleared land where no other house had stood, and had been planned, plotted, discussed with an incomprehensible lawyer, and constructed, over a period of three years and two months ('and seven days, three hours and twenty minutes,' the present occupant would add. 'Three years, two months, seven days, three hours and twenty minutes from the moment of Maggie giving the go-ahead to the moment we moved in. I timed it. God, how I timed it!').

The other two houses were reconstructions of buildings already standing or half-standing; both had foundations of Roman antiquity, and of earlier origin if you should dig down far enough, it was said. Maggie Radcliffe had bought these two, and the land on which she had put up the third house.

One was intended eventually for her son, Michael; that was the farm-house. He was to live in it when he got married.

Maggie herself was never there that previous summer, was reputed to be there, was never seen, had been, had gone, was coming soon, had just departed for Lausanne, for London.

Hubert Mallindaine, in the new-built house, had news of Maggie; had seen, had just missed, Maggie; had had a long discussion with Maggie; was always equipped to discuss knowledgeably the ins and outs of Maggie's life. He had been for years Maggie's friend number one and her central information agent.

The third house had been a large villa in bad repair. It was now in good repair, sitting in handsome grounds, with a tennis court, a swimming-pool, the old lily-pond made wholesome and the lawns newly greened. Maggie could do everything. But it had taken years and years. The Italian sense of time and Maggie's lack of concentration due to her family troubles and involvements had held things up. But the villa, too, was ready that previous summer. In an access of financial morality, although it was quite unnecessary, Maggie had decided to let this house for a monthly rent to a rich businessman. She didn't need the money, but it put Maggie in a regular sort of position. Her present husband, Ralph Radcliffe, who also had money and never thought of anything else, had less justification to resent the whole idea when he could be reminded that Maggie was drawing a rent from one of the houses. This was the summer when it was said Maggie's marriage was going on the rocks.

Hubert Mallindaine's terrace had a view of the lake and the Alban hills folding beyond.

Hubert needed the best view: he had so encamped himself in his legend that Maggie had not questioned that he was entitled to the view. His secretaries from their bedrooms also had splendid views.

There were four secretaries that summer: Damian Runciwell, Kurt Hakens, Lauro Moretti, Ian Mackay. Only one, Damian, did the secretarial work.

'We can't stay here all summer, darling.'

'Darling, why not? I hate to travel.'

'Take off those earrings before you open the door to the butcher.'

'Darling, why?'

'Did you remember the garlic?'

'My dear Kurt-o, we do not need garlic today.'

'Ian, we do . . . The salad.'

'Dearie, we have a clove of garlic for the salad. More garlic we do not need today.'

'Oh, get out of my kitchen. Go on. You make me nervous.'

'My boredom,' said Hubert Mallindaine, the master of the house, 'makes you all look so tawdry.' He was addressing the others at the lunch table. 'Forgive me that I feel that way.'

'Feel what you like,' said one of them, 'but you shouldn't say it.'

'The mushrooms are soggy. They have been done in oil. Too much oil, too. They should have been done in butter and oil. Very little butter, very little oil.'

There was a heatwave so fierce you would have thought someone had turned it on somewhere by means of a tap, and had turned it too high, and then gone away for the summer.

Hubert lay on the sofa in his study and deplored Maggie's comparative lack of chivalry. It was siesta time and his room had been made dark. Hubert decided to talk to Maggie about air-conditioning. But this decision annoyed him. One should not find oneself in the position, he thought, of having to ask, having to wait for the opportunity to talk on practical matters with a woman of no routine. She might progress into the neighbourhood, looking gorgeous, at any moment, without advance notice. She had no sense of chivalry. A protectress of chivalry would not have left him dependent on her personal bounty for little things; Maggie should have made a settlement. Even the house, he thought, as he lay on the sofa at the onslaught of that previous summer, is not in one's own name

but in Maggie's. One has no claim to anything. Something
might happen to Maggie and one would have no claim. She
could be killed in an air crash. Hubert, staring at the ceiling,
pulled a hair from his beard, and the twinge of pain confirmed
and curiously consoled the thought. It was unlikely that anything would happen to Maggie. She was indestructible.

II

'MISS THIN,' HUBERT SAID, 'I wish you would not try to use your intelligence because you have so little of it. Just do as I say. Put them in date order.'

'I thought you would want to keep the personal separate from the professional,' said Pauline Thin belligerently. 'That would be the logical way.'

'There is no distinction between the two so far as I'm concerned,' Hubert said, looking, with a horror that had no connection whatsoever with Pauline Thin, at the great trunkfuls of old letters still to be gone through. Masses of old, old letters are very upsetting to contemplate, each one containing a world of past trivialities or passions forever pending. The surprise of words once overlooked and meanings newly realized, the record of debts unpaid or overpaid, of boredom unrequited or sweetness forever lost, came rising up to Hubert from the open boxes.

'Put them in chronological order,' Hubert said, 'a bundle for each year, then break each bundle up into months. That's all you have to do. Don't read them through and through, it's a waste of your working hours.'

'Mine not to reason why,' Pauline Thin answered, pulling towards her a pile of letters which she had set on the table.

'Yours *is* to reason why,' Hubert said. 'You can reason as much as you like if you know how to do it. You're free and

I'm free to reason about anything. Only keep it to yourself. Don't waste my time. Don't ask me for the reasons. Just put them in order of dates.'

Hubert walked to the door and went out to the shady verandah overlooking the lake. It was a warm day for March. Spring was ready. He thought maybe he had better try to get on well with the girl and start calling her Pauline. She already called him Hubert without the asking. His nerves were edgy since, at the beginning of the year, a sequence of financial misfortunes had begun to fall upon him, unexpectedly, shock after shock. Hubert thought of these setbacks as 'curious' and 'unexpected' although, he would presently be brought to reflect, they had not been actually unforeseeable and were linked by no stronger force of coincidence than Maggie's second divorce and a new marriage to an Italian nobleman, probably jealous, and to the deterioration of money in general, and the collapse of a shady company in Switzerland where Hubert had put some of his personal money in the hope of making a fortune. He didn't know quite what to do. But he had one resource. Its precise application was still forming in his mind and wandering lonely as a cloud, and meantime he was short of funds.

The very panorama of Nemi, the lake, the most lush vegetation on earth, the scene which had stirred the imagination of Sir James Frazer at the beginning of his massive testament to comparative religion, *The Golden Bough*, all this magical influence and scene which had never before failed in their effects, all the years he had known the place and in the months he had lived there, suddenly was too expensive. I can't afford the view, thought Hubert and turned back into the room.

The sight of Pauline stacking the papers gave him a slight euphoric turn. There, among the letters and documents of his life, he had that one secret resource and he had decided to exploit it. Maggie could never take Nemi away from him because, spiritually if not actually, the territory of Nemi was his.

Actually, of course, not even the house was his. Maggie was ... Maggie had been ... Maggie, Maggie ...

Pauline Thin was reading one of the letters. Sometimes when a letter was undated it was necessary for her to read it for a clue as to its appropriate place in the various piles of correspondence set out on the table. But Pauline was reading with a happy sort of interest and Hubert was not sure that he could afford Pauline Thin's happiness in her work, seeing she was theoretically paid by the hour. He was not sure, because on the one hand she was paid very little by the hour, and, further, she was greatly to be trusted and he relied on her now more than ever; he was not sure, on the other hand, if he could afford her at all, because, moreover, he owed her a lot of hours' pay, the debt increasing every hour in proportion as the likelihood decreased of his ever discharging it.

Hubert glanced back again at Pauline with her tiny face and her curly hair and felt the absence, now, of Ian, the boy from Inverness, and Damian, the Armenian boy with the curious surname of Runciwell who, as secretary, had been the best secretary, and he missed the other two with their petulance and their demands, their talents for cooking or interior design, their earrings and their neck-chains and their tight blue jeans and twin-apple behinds, fruit of the same tree. He felt their absence without specified regret; it was their kind he missed. Their departure was a fact which still paralysed him, belonging to a time so recent and yet so definitely last summer, in the past.

The morning news had announced the death of Noël Coward, calling it 'the passing of an era'. Everything since Maggie's sudden divorce and equally sudden Italian marriage last year had been to Hubert the passing of an era. Eras pass, thought Hubert. They pass every day. He felt dejected. He cheered up. Then he felt dejected again.

He glanced back at Miss Thin. She had finished reading the apparently absorbing letter and was bending with her back to him over the table stacking the piles of documents neatly. She was broad in the behind, too large. Where is the poetry of my life? Hubert thought. He retained an inkling that the poetry was still there and would return. Wordsworth defined poetry as 'emotion recollected in tranquillity'. Hubert took a tranquillizer, quite a mild one called Mitigil, and knew he would feel better in about ten minutes. To make sure, he took another. In the meantime a familiar white car turned into the drive and stopped before it reached the door. 'Oh God, it's him,' Hubert said and turning to Pauline Thin he called out, 'Miss Thin, this is a tiresome person. Please hang around and keep on bothering me with letters to sign. Remind me emphatically that I have a dinner date this evening. I'll give him one drink. This man's a pathological pest.'

The girl came out to see who had arrived. A medium-sized thin man in a clerical suit had got out of the car, had slammed the door and was walking towards them, smiling and waving.

'He's a Jesuit,' said Hubert, 'from Milwaukee.'

'I've seen him before,' Pauline said. 'He pesters everyone.'

'I know,' Hubert said, feeling friendly towards Miss Thin. He stepped forward a little way to meet the priest.

'Oh, Hubert, this is wonderful to find you in,' said the priest in a voice that twanged like a one-stringed guitar. 'I just drove from Rome as I wanted to talk to you.'

'How are you?' said Hubert politely. 'I'm afraid I'm going to be a bit pressed for time. If you'd have phoned me I could have made a date for you to come to dinner.'

'Oh, oh, are you going out . . . ?'

'About sevenish,' said Hubert putting on a weak smile. It was then sixish. 'I have to go and change soon' – Hubert indicated his old clothes – 'out of these things. Have you met Pauline Thin? – Pauline, this is Father Cuthbert Plaice.'

'Why, I think I know you, Pauline,' said the priest, shaking her hand and, it seemed, trying to locate her in his social register.

'I worked for Bobby Lester in Rome,' Pauline said.

'Why, of course! Yes. Well, now you're here?'

'Yes, I'm here.'

'Hubert, I've got a Jesuit friend down there in the car,' said the priest, 'that I want you to meet. I thought you would like to meet him, he's been studying the ancient ecological cults and in fact he's taken some tape recordings of modern nature-cultists which you have to hear. There are the conscious and the unconscious. It's fascinating. I thought we could have dinner together but anyway I'll just go call him and we can have a drink. I just wanted to tell you before you meet him, you see, that he's on your wave-length.' The priest made away towards the car stretching one arm behind him as if Hubert were straining away from him at the end of an invisible cord.

'Bloody pest,' said Hubert to Pauline. 'Why should I give them my drinks? He knows – I've told him – that I can't afford those lavish entertainments any more. And dinner – he wanted to stay with his friend for dinner. He marches in, and one's house isn't one's own. Priests can be very rough people, you know. Such a bore.'

'This one's an awful bore,' said Pauline. 'Bobby Lester couldn't stand him.'

Father Cuthbert was returning with a younger Jesuit of the same size to whom he was talking eagerly.

'Hubert,' he said, when he had reached the verandah, 'I want you to meet Father Gerard Harvey. Gerard has been doing studies of ecological paganism and I've told him all about you. Oh, this is Pauline Thin. She's working for Hubert. I knew Pauline before. She – '

'Come in and have a drink,' said Hubert.

'We can sit right here on the terrace. I want Gerard to see the view. What marvellous weather! That's the thing about Italy. You can sit outside in March, and – '

Hubert left them sitting on the terrace and went inside to fetch the drinks. Pauline followed him. 'Do you want me to stay with them?' she said.

'Yes, make a nuisance of yourself. Hang around looking silly so that they can't speak freely. Remember I'm supposed to get ready for dinner in about half an hour's time. These people need to be house-trained.'

Pauline went out on the terrace and sat down with the two men.

'Have you been in Italy long?' she said to the younger man.

'I've been here six months.'

She looked at her watch. 'Hubert has to go and change very soon,' she said. 'He's got a long drive ahead to arrive for eight. He has some letters to sign first.'

'Oh, where's he going?' said Father Cuthbert.

'You shouldn't ask,' she said.

'Well, now, that's not the way to talk,' said Cuthbert, looking very amazed.

'I guess she isn't a Catholic,' said Gerard soothingly.

'I'm a Catholic,' said Pauline. 'But that's got nothing to do with it. One doesn't tell people all one's business and all one's employer's business.'

Hubert appeared with a tray of drinks. The whisky bottle was one third full and the gin was slightly less. There was a box of ice and a bottle of mineral water.

'It's terrorism,' said Pauline.

104

'What's this?' Hubert said, setting down the tray.

'Priests,' said Pauline. 'They're terrorists. They hold you to ransom.'

The Jesuits looked at each other with delight. This was the sort of thing they felt at home with, priests being their favourite subject.

'Times have changed,' Hubert said to Pauline, 'since you were at school at the Sacred Heart, I'm afraid.'

'It isn't so long ago,' Pauline said, 'since I was at school. My last years, I went to Cheltenham.'

Father Gerard said, 'What goes on at Cheltenham?'

'Ladies' College,' said Hubert. 'If you look closely, it's written all over her face.'

'What do you have against us?' Father Cuthbert said, shifting about with excitement in his chair as if he were sexually as much as pastorally roused.

'It seems to me,' Hubert said, turning with gentle treachery towards Pauline, 'a bit inhospitable to carry on this conversation.' His Mitigil had started to work. He had put ice in the glasses. 'What will you drink?' he said to the guests.

'Whisky,' said both priests at once. Hubert looked sadly at his whisky bottle, lifted it and poured.

'Hubert,' said Pauline, 'that's all the whisky we have.'

'Yes,' said Hubert. 'I'm having gin. What about you, Miss Thin?'

'Plain tonic,' said Pauline.

The younger priest sipped his drink and looked out over the still lake in its deep crater and the thick wildwood of Nemi's fertile soil. 'Terrific ecology!' he said.

'You mean the view?' Pauline said.

Hubert sat in a chair with his back to the grand panorama and he sighed. 'I have to give it up,' he said. 'There's nothing for it. The house isn't mine and Maggie's changed so much since her new marriage. They're insisting on charging me rent. A high rent. I have to go.'

'Remember your dinner date,' Pauline said, 'and Hubert, would you sign some letters, please?'

'Dinner date . . . ?' said Hubert. Since Maggie's marriage following on her son Michael's marriage, and since the trouble with his money in Switzerland, he had been asked out less and less. He looked into his little drop of gin, while Father Cuthbert seized on the doubt about dinner. 'You're going to go out for dinner?'

'We've already told you so,' said Pauline.

'Oh, I didn't know if you meant it,' said the priest.

Hubert, remembering, said, 'Oh, yes, I am. I have to go and change very soon, I'm afraid. They eat early, these people.'

'What people?' said Father Cuthbert. 'Do I know them? Could we come along?'

His companion the ecologist began to show embarrassment. He said, 'No, no, Cuthbert. We can go back to Rome. Really, we mustn't intrude like this. Unexpectedly. We have to . . . ' He rose and looked nervously towards the car where it was parked halfway down the drive.

'Why don't you go and see Michael?' Hubert said, meaning Maggie's son, whose house was near by.

Father Cuthbert looked eager. 'Do you know if he's home?'

'I'm sure he is,' said Hubert 'They're both in Nemi just now. He got married himself recently. Marriage does seem to be a luxury set apart for the rich. I'm sure they'll be delighted to see you.'

While Hubert explained to the excited priest how to get there by car, his friend, Father Gerard, looked around him and across the lake. 'The environment,' he said. 'This is a wonderful environmental location.'

'It's your duty to visit Michael and Mary, really,' Pauline egged them on. 'They have sumptuous dinners. They had a shock when Maggie got divorced and married again, you know. It's been an upset for the Radcliffes. Her new husband's a pig.'

'Don't they see his father?'

'Oh, I dare say,' Hubert said. 'Radcliffe was Maggie's second husband, of course. The new one's the third. But it was so sudden. The family's all right financially of course. But I must say it's left me in a mess, personally speaking.'

When the priests had left, Hubert went with Pauline into the kitchen. He opened a tin of tuna fish while she made a potato salad. They then sat down to eat at the kitchen table, silently, reflectively.

It seemed as if Hubert had forgotten the priests. Pauline, as if anxious that he should not forget a subject that had served to bring them closer, assiduously said, 'Those priests . . . '

At first he didn't respond to the tiny needle. He merely said dreamily, 'It's not too much to wonder if they're not a bit too much,' and took in a mouthful of food.

'But so pressing, so insufferably pushy,' Pauline said, at which Hubert was roused into agreement, chummily communicating it: 'It's an extraordinary fact,' he said, 'that just at the precise moment when you're at your wits' end it's always the last people in the world you want to see who turn up, full of themselves, demanding total attention. It's always the exceptionally tiresome who barge in at the exceptionally difficult moment. Would you believe there was a time when a Jesuit was a gentleman, if you'll forgive the old-fashioned expression?'

Pauline passed him the potato salad. It had onion, too, in it, and mayonnaise. 'Forget them, Hubert,' she said, plainly intending him not to do so.

But Hubert smiled. 'Miss Thin,' he said as he took the salad bowl from her hand, 'I have inside me a laughter demon without which I would die.'

III

'DEMONS FREQUENTED THESE WOODS, protectors of the gods. Nymphs and dryads inhabited the place. Have you seen the remains of Diana's temple down there? It's terribly over-grown and the excavations are all filled in, but there's a great deal more to see than you might think.'

'No, I haven't seen it,' said Mary, curling her long legs as she sat, yoga-style, on a cushion on the pavement of the terrace. She was a young long-haired blonde girl from California, newly married to Michael Radcliffe. The priests were entertaining her enormously. She didn't want them to leave and pressed them to stay on for a late dinner. Michael had gone to Rome and wouldn't be back till nine. 'He said nine, which most probably will be ten,' she said.

'Pius the Second,' said Father Gerard, 'said that Nemi was the home of nymphs and dryads, when he passed through this area.'

'Really?'

An Italian manservant, young and dark-skinned in a white coat with shining buttons and elaborate epaulettes, brought in a tray of canapés and nuts which he placed on the terrace table beside the bottles. He looked with recognition at Father Cuthbert who, without looking at the manservant, took a handful of nuts, as also did Father Gerard. The ice clinked in the glasses, and they helped themselves to the drinks when their glasses were empty, refilling Mary's glass too. They were Americans together, abroad, with the unwatchful attitude of co-nationals who share some common experiences, however few.

'I majored in social science,' said Mary who had been to college in California.

'Did you come to Italy before?' said Father Gerard.

'No, never. I met Michael in Paris. Then we settled here. I love it.'

'How's your Italian?' said the other priest, beaming with idle pleasure – as who would not after two months' continuous residence in the priests' bleak house in Rome, anonymous and detached in its laws of life?

'Oh, my Italian's coming along. I took a crash course. I guess I'll get more fluent. How about yours?'

'Gerard's is pretty good,' said Father Cuthbert. 'He doesn't get enough practice. There are Italians at the Residence of course, but we only talk to the Americans. You know the way it gets. Or maybe the French – '

'Cuthbert speaks almost perfect Italian,' said Father Gerard. 'He's a great help when I'm talking to the locals around the country about their legends and beliefs.'

'Gerard,' said Father Cuthbert, 'is doing a study on pagan ecology.'

'Really? I thought the Italians were mostly all Catholics.'

'On the surface, yes, but underneath there's a large area of pagan remainder to be explored. And absorbed into Christianity. A very rich seam.'

'Well,' said the girl, 'I don't know if you've talked to Hubert Mallindaine about that . . . '

Hubert was a whole new subject, vibrating to be discussed. The priests began to speak in unison, questions and answers, then the girl broke in with laughing phrases and exclamation marks, until Father Cuthbert's voice, being the highest and most excitable, attained the first hearing. The manservant hovered at the terrace door, his eyes upon them, waiting to serve. Mary stretched her fine long suntanned legs and listened. 'We arrived this evening,' said Cuthbert, 'without letting him know in advance. Well, that's nothing new. As a matter of fact the last time I saw him, about six weeks ago, in Rome, he said, "Come to dinner any time. Sure, bring a friend, you're always welcome. There's no need to call me. I never go out. Just get into that car and come." That's what he said. Well. We arrived this evening – didn't we, Gerard?'

'We did,' said Gerard.

A person with a good ear might have questioned the accuracy of Cuthbert's report on the grounds that Hubert, not being American, was not likely to have used a phrase like, 'Sure, bring a friend . . . ' But it did seem that the priest had been in the habit of dropping in on Hubert from time to time, whether welcome or not. Clearly he regarded it as his right to do so, anywhere.

'I was embarrassed for Gerard,' Cuthbert was saying, 'especially as this was his first visit, you know. He had an awful secretary, a girl who used to work for another friend of mine in Rome. A terribly – '

Here Gerard broke in, and so did Mary. When they had finished exclaiming over Pauline, Cuthbert continued, 'I think she's got a problem. Then she kept telling Hubert he had to go out to dinner, which I'm sure wasn't true because of the way it was said, you know.' He finished his drink and the manservant came out of the shadows to replenish it. This time Cuthbert recognized the man's face but couldn't at first place it.

The servant lifted the glass with a well-paid and expert air and smiled.

'I know you, don't I?' said Cuthbert to the man.

'It's Lauro,' said Mary. 'He was one of Hubert's secretaries last summer.'

'Why, Lauro, I didn't recognize you in that uniform! Why Lauro!' The priest seemed confused, realizing the man had understood their conversation.

Lauro answered in easy, accented English. 'You surprised to see me here? I lost my job with Hubert and I went to a bar on the Via Veneto then I came back to Nemi to work for Mary and Michael.'

'Lauro's on first-name terms with us,' Mary said. 'The Embassy crowd are shocked. But we don't care.'

Lauro smiled and slipped back to his doorway.

'Lauro could tell you everything you want to know about Hubert,' Mary said. Lauro's shadowed form stooped to adjust a rose in a vase. Cuthbert looked carefully at Mary as if to see quite what she had meant by her words, but she had evidently meant far less than she might have done.

'Oh, I like Hubert. Don't misunderstand me,' said Cuthbert, and he looked towards Gerard who gave it as his opinion that Hubert had seemed very likeable.

'Well, I used to like him too,' said Mary. 'And I still do. But when Maggie and her husband number three got kind of mad at him we had to take her part; after all, she's Michael's mother. What can you do? There's been a bad feeling between the houses since Maggie got into this marriage. She wants Hubert to go. He says he won't and he can't pay rent. She's going to put him out. The furniture belongs to Maggie as well. But my, she's finding it difficult. The laws in this country . . . Hubert might get around them forever.'

They sat down to dinner soon after Mary's husband, Michael, arrived. They spoke of Hubert most of the time. Hubert was a subject sufficiently close to them to provide a day-to-day unfolding drama and yet it was sufficiently remote, by reason of their wealth, not to matter very much. Hubert himself, since the young couple had ceased to see him, had become someone else than the large-living and smart-spoken old friend they used to know when he was Maggie's favourite. Now that Maggie had turned against him he was, in their mythology, a parasite on society. 'He's not like the old Hubert at all,' Michael said. 'Something's changed him.'

'I dread one day maybe bumping into him in the village,' said Mary. 'I don't know what I'd say.'

First one Jesuit and then the other offered advice as to the coping with this eventuality. So dark, rather short but so somehow splendid, Lauro served the meal, assisted by a good-looking maid. The spring evening air from the terrace stood around them like another ubiquitous servant, tendering occasional wafts of a musky creeper's scent. The wine had been sent by Maggie's new husband from his own vineyards in the north.

'Hubert,' said Michael, 'of course considers he is a direct descendant of the goddess Diana of Nemi. He considers he's mystically and spiritually, if not actually, entitled to the place.'

'No kidding!' said Gerard.

'No kidding,' Mary said. 'That's what Hubert believes. It's a family tradition. All the Mallindaines have always believed it. Michael and I met an aunt of his in Paris. She was convinced of it. But I think her health had broken up.'

'She was old,' Michael said.

'Well,' said Gerard, 'I should look into this for my research.'

The other Jesuit said, 'I always thought, you know, the Diana mythology was just an interest of his. I didn't know it was in the family. We'll have to go see him again.'

One of the stories to be read from the ancient historians of Imperial Rome is that the Emperor Caligula enjoyed sex with the goddess Diana of Nemi. And indeed, two luxurious Roman ships, submerged for centuries in the lake and brought to land in recent times, have been attributed variously to the purpose of Imperial orgies on the lake of Nemi, and to service in the worship of Diana. These ships were brought to land in reconstructable condition only to be destroyed by some German soldiers during the Second World War; however, their remaining contents and fittings testified to the impression that something highly ritualistic took place on board, well into Christian times, although the worship of Diana at Nemi reaches back into the mythological childhood of the race. Hubert's ancestors . . .

But it is time, now, to take a closer look at Hubert on that spring evening, seeing that he had provided a full and wonderful stream of conversation for the party over there in the other house, where the frank spirits rose higher, Lauro glowed in the shadows and Mary, with her golden Californian colouring, her dark blue eyes and white teeth, was so far stimulated as to repeat for good measure a recent saying of Maggie's: 'The goddess Diana presents her compliments, and desires the company of her kinsman Mr Hubert Mallindaine at the Hunt Ball to be held at Nemi . . . '

Meanwhile, then, Hubert watched Pauline Thin wash up the plates. He carried their coffee through the sitting-room and out to the terrace. 'At my age,' Hubert said, 'I shouldn't drink coffee at night. But, Miss Thin, it doesn't always bear to think of what one should or shouldn't drink. There's a limit to every thing.'

'I can see that,' said Pauline, looking out over the marvellous lake.

'Miss Thin,' said Hubert, 'I have decided. I will not leave this house.' Hubert had shaved off his beard shortly after hearing of Maggie's divorce last year in the December of 1972. Then, a week after he heard, in the following January, that she had married the northern Marquis, he had shaved off his moustache. Not that he felt these actions were in any way connected with Maggie's. It does, however, obscurely seem that in these two shavings he was expressing some reaction to her divorce and marriage, or, more probably, preparing himself for something, maybe an ordeal, requiring a clean-cut appearance.

He looked younger, now. Pauline Thin, who had come to work for him this February, had never known him with his hairy maestro's face. She described him to her best friend in Italy, another English girl who was working in Rome, as 'dishy'.

Hubert was now forty-five. His generally good looks varied from day to day. Sometimes, when she went into Rome for shopping and stopped to lunch with her girlfriend, Pauline described him as 'a bit fagoty'. However that may be, Hubert undoubtedly had good looks, especially when anguished. By a system of panic-action whenever he started to be overweight, he had managed to keep his good line. The panic-system, which consisted of a total fast for a sufficient number of days, never more than twelve, to make him thoroughly skinny and underweight, allowed him then to put on weight comfortably with small indulgences in food and drink which otherwise he would never have enjoyed. Hubert had been told, much earlier in his life, that eventually this course would ruin his health but the event had never happened. Indeed, most of his active life was formed by panic-action and in the interludes he was content to dream or fret or for long periods simply enjoy sweet life. One such of these interludes was just coming to an end, which accounted for the especially good looks of his worried face. He was fairly dark-skinned with light blue eyes and sandy-grey hair. His features were separately nothing much, but his face and the way his head was set on his body were effective. Quite often, he was conscious of his physical assets, but more often he simply forgot them.

This house, with the best view of all Maggie's three houses in the neighbourhood, was furnished richly. After only a year's occupancy this new house still had newness penetrating its bones. Even the antiques, the many of them, were new. Maggie had brought back across the water from an apartment high in the air, on the east-sixties of Manhattan, large lifts of itinerant European furniture and pictures. The drawing-room furniture was Louis XIV; there had been six fine chairs, at present only five; one was away in a clever little workshop on the Via di Santa Maria dell'Anima in Rome, being sedulously copied. Hubert was short of money and, almost certain that Maggie would at least succeed in removing the furniture from the house, he was taking reasonable precautions for his future. The new chair was almost finished, and it only remained for the upholstery on the original to be tenderly removed and fitted on to the fake before Pauline should be ordered to go into Rome and fetch the chair. She had been told only that it was being mended. The original would remain in Rome for a while at Hubert's disposal. Like money in the bank, Hubert thought of switching and rearranging, perhaps, a few more items, and maybe, if there was time, another chair. Maggie had put on the drawing-room floor a seventeenth-century rug; Isfahan. Hubert brooded upon it: not at all possible to copy with excellence. He didn't use the drawing-room much these days; the heart had gone out of it.

Maggie's withdrawal from Hubert had taken place quite slowly. It was only to him that it seemed abrupt. To him it was the heedless by-product of a too-rich woman's whim or the effect of her new husband's influence, the new husband also being rich. But Hubert's memory was careless. As we have seen, as far back as the previous summer he was privately lamenting Maggie's lack of chivalry. His protectress had already started, even before that, to recede. She had let him occupy the new house, as one silently honouring a bad bargain; the house had been ordered to his taste more than three years before it was ready. But it was during those three years and more while the house was being made that she had gradually stopped confiding in him and even before that, perhaps, the disaffection and boredom of the relationship had set in for Maggie.

Hubert had been uneasy about his position, really, for many years more than he now admitted when he thought or spoke of Maggie. 'Like any other spoilt moneybags she used me when she needed me and then suddenly told me to go, to clear out of her house and her life. All my projects were based on her promises. We had an understanding . . . ' So he dramatized it in a nutshell, first to himself, then, later, to Pauline Thin.

Pauline assumed there had been a love affair till one night, when he was confiding in her for the sheer lack of anyone else to talk to about himself, he remarked, 'I never touched a woman. I love women but I never went near one. It would break the spell. There's a magic . . . women are magic. I can't live without women around me. Sex is far, far away out of the question in my mind where women are concerned.'

Which bewildered Pauline. Quickly rearranging her ideas, and in the spirit of the missionaries of old who held that conversion was only a matter of revealing the true doctrine, she ended with the conviction that he had not yet met a truly appetizing, faithful woman and decided more than ever to stick by Hubert in these reduced days of his.

I V

> 'Lo, Nemi! navell'd in the woody hills
> So far, that the uprooting wind which tears
> The oak from his foundation, and which spills
> The ocean o'er its boundary, and bears
> Its foam against the skies, reluctant spares
> The oval mirror of thy glassy lake;
> And calm as cherish'd hate, its surface wears
> A deep cold settled aspect nought can shake,
> All coil'd into itself and round, as sleeps the snake.'

'It's a perfect description,' said Nancy Cowan, the English tutor. 'Can you imagine what Byron meant by "calm as cherished hate"? – It's mysterious, isn't it? – Yet perfectly applicable. One can see that in the past, the historic long-ago, there was some evil hidden under the surface of the lake. Many evils, probably. Pagan customs were cruel. "Cherished hate" is a great evil, anyway.'

Her pupils pondered, perhaps being nice enough to feel they had missed the point. Letizia, a girl of eighteen, was not quite sure what the phrase meant. 'Hatred,' explained the tutor, 'which has been kept hidden, secret, never expressing itself behind its impassive face. That's why the poet wrote "calm as cherished hate".'

'It's very good,' said Pietro. He was twenty. Both Letizia and Pietro were cramming for entrance exams to American colleges.

The villa at Nemi where they sat in early summer with the English teacher had no view at all of the lake. One could only glimpse the castle tower from one of the windows. It was the third of Maggie Radcliffe's houses, the newly-restored one, recently let to the family. Letizia, a passionate Italian nationalist with an ardour for folklore and the voluntary helping of youthful drug-addicts, resented very much the fact that her father rented the house from an American. She was against the foreign ownership of Italian property, held that the youth of Italy was being corrupted by foreigners, especially in the line of drugs, and asserted herself, with her light skin and hair, large-boned athletic shapelessness, and religious unbelief, to be a representative of the new young Italy. The father, who was divorced from the mother, was extremely rich. She was in no accepting frame of mind to study for an American university entrance, and had already almost converted Miss Cowan, the tutor, to her view. Her brother Pietro, dark-eyed, long-lashed, with a pale oval face, wanted very much to be in a film and then to direct a film, and whenever he was free he spent his time among the courtiers of famous film directors, skimming the speed-routes by day and by night in his Porsche, his St Christopher medal dangling on his chest, speeding the length of the boot of Italy and back to be with some group of young men who clustered round the film director wherever the film should be in the making. Italy is a place much given to holding court. Pietro, when he was not at one or another court, was happier at home now than he had been in recent years because of the presence of Nancy Cowan.

She was thirty-six, well-informed, rather thin, long-nosed, tender-hearted towards anyone within her immediate radius at any one time. She had come in answer to an advertisement in *The Times*, bringing her Englishness, her pale summer dresses, her sense of fair play, and many other foreign things with

her. Letizia had been at first delighted to find that the English
tutor was so easy to walk all over in intellectual matters; it
was as if Miss Cowan had anything you like instead of views
of society or political stands. But at times she suspected that
Nancy Cowan really didn't feel it worth while to give her own
opinions; sometimes it almost seemed, in fact, as if Nancy was
making herself agreeable to either the brother or the sister
simply because they mattered very little to her. Letizia, when
this feeling struck her, would force her own views the more
strongly, and would sometimes speak her mind to the point
of insult. Pietro thought Nancy's malleability to be very fem-
inine, and with an intuitive artistic sense of economy, he set
out to get his father's money's worth out of her in his studies.
It seemed likely that their father was already sleeping with her.
It would have been possible to find out for sure, but Pietro felt
too young and sex-free to make the effort; it would have been
unhealthy, indelicate, but Pietro one night when they were taking their coffee after dinner in the garden, from the way Nancy
Cowan responded to the night-beauty, decided that his father
had wooed and won her there. She was also better-looking in
the moonlight, quite handsome as in a film; and then, again,
the manner towards Nancy of the big fat whiney parlour maid,
Clara, told Pietro something. He supposed it also told Letizia
something, but he didn't expect Letizia to acknowledge any
such unsevere facts about their father or their English tutor. It
was thoroughly in keeping, though, that Papa was getting all
full value out of Nancy Cowan, as was she from the job.

The brother and sister sat reading Byron with Nancy in the
shady garden a few yards from the house. It was six in the afternoon. To humour Letizia, Nancy had bent her English lessons
in the direction of local lore. A poor rescued drug-addict in the
wreckage of his twenties was cleaning out the swimming-pool
under the direction of a gardener and fat Clara. This simple

120

operation made a terrific background noise since Clara's only tone for all occasions was one of lament, and the gardener, in trying to make a simple instruction penetrate the saved youth's brain, treated him as if he were hard of hearing. The youth, who had been brought in by Letizia from Rome that morning, would be given a meal and an old pair of Pietro's trousers for his services before he was taken back to the welfare centre. A few such garden chores got done in this way; only garden chores, since Letizia did not bring these strange people into the house for fear of what they might see and be tempted either to take away or send their friends to procure. To her father, Letizia's protégés were more or less what in the old days were gypsies. To the eyes of Nancy Cowan they were young drug-addicts just like the London variety. Letizia referred to them as 'our new social phenomena' and this, oddly enough, was the title they liked best; they seemed to respond to Letizia, to her statistics and her sociological language which apparently gave them a status in life, and it was rarely that any one of them attempted to take undue advantage of her or ask her for money. Mostly they demonstrated an allergy to Pietro with his Bulgari steel watch, his Gucci shoes and belt, his expensive haircut, and with his Porsche being endlessly cleaned by the house's young lodge-keeper in overalls.

Big Clara lumbered up from the pool to the house, clutching her heart. She was not yet fifty but she looked much older and yet behaved like a child of twelve which evidently she still felt herself to be. 'A headache,' she said in her babyish whine. 'It's too hot. You need a professional to clean out the pool. He'll never understand the chlorine. I've got a headache. He has no capacity. You need a man, a real man. He'll never learn.'

Letizia sprang up from her seat beside Nancy Cowan, full of what it took to cope with Clara in their native tongue. Letizia's young skin glowed in the late afternoon, her pale

121

blue eyes had a fishy bulge. She swung around in her folklore skirt, her red platform clogs and smocked blouse, gesticulating with her healthy arms. As a specimen, Letizia at eighteen was rounded-off and complete; the finishing touches were already put, there was no room for further contention between character and contours, there was scope only, now, for wear and tear. She was much as she would be, she thought, much as she would think, and looked not much different from what she would look, at forty-eight.

The grumbling servant having been coped with, Letizia returned to her garden chair beside her brother and Nancy, with a grin full of healthy teeth.

Nancy Cowan held out her hand for the copy of Byron which Pietro had taken to look at.

'He must have come here in winter,' Pietro said, 'since he wrote about the wind tearing up the oak tree.'

Letizia leaned over Nancy Cowan to examine the lines. 'He says the wind spares the lake, which is true. Nemi is a very secluded spot. Was Byron at Nemi in winter, then?'

'Look, you'll have to get a Life of Byron . . . '

'I think Papa has a biography of Byron. Pietro, do you know?'

' . . . something you ought to know about, though. Byron's always – '

'He was a lame lord . . . ' Pietro had taken the book from Nancy and was reading aloud from the biographical foreword to the poems: ' . . . a spendthrift and a rake . . . '

'What is that – spendthrift . . . ?' Pietro reached for the dictionary. Nancy Cowan began explaining Byron while the air grew cooler, the light faded over the lawn and Letizia suddenly recollected a bit of Byron's history from her earlier schooldays.

Just then Letizia was called to the telephone and cursing in Italian went indoors to answer it.

Nancy caught Pietro looking closely at her, and turned her head to look back into his face.

'Would it embarrass you if I asked you a question?' he said.

'You've just asked me an embarrassing one,' she said to gain ground, and was never to know what Pietro's other embarrassing question might be, for Letizia returned by way of the kitchen door to say, 'Papa has asked our landlady to dinner. She phoned Papa at the office. Her name was Mrs Radcliffe but she got married again to an Italian. La Radcliffe wants to see us.'

'What's she like?' Nancy said.

'We've never seen her. She rents the house through an agent. She's a rich American, Madame Radcliffe, and now she's a Marchesa married to a nobleman from the north. I hate Papa for renting a house from an American in our own country. It should be round the other way. Why doesn't Papa buy a villa?'

'Italians own property in England,' said Nancy.

'That is different. They settled there for two, three generations. They was poor.' Letizia looked angry, unable to clarify her thoughts, if indeed her feelings existed in thought-form. She slightly lost her grip on correct English. 'There is many reasons,' she said. 'Here in Italy the foreigner takes everything.'

'Maybe you're right,' said Nancy. 'I really hadn't thought of it before.' She thought of it now, looking with purely formal anxiety into the distance.

'This was an old Italian villa, the foundations are ancient Roman,' said the girl calming down a little, 'then along came an American woman with the money. She restores the house. She's got other houses, all over Nemi, full of foreigners. We're the only Italians and we pay her rent. Papa pays a huge rent. We had to put in a downstairs sitting-room. Before there was no sitting-room downstairs. We had to make over one of the garages at Papa's expense. Papa likes the house so he pays and pays.'

The large maid came out with a tray of drinks and ice, wearing a baleful expression. Nancy smiled at her but this made Clara close her eyes as if in pain.

'You shouldn't criticize foreigners in Nancy's presence,' said Pietro. He was hoping to get a part in a foreign film just at that time and although it was unlikely that their English tutor had many friends among the thousands of foreigners in Italy, far less the Americans who were making the film, he felt there was nothing to lose by shutting his sister up a bit.

'But Papa pays her to help us with our English and we're talking English,' Letizia said. 'And tonight we have to talk English at dinner for our landlady.'

Their father's car could be heard coming up the drive, whereupon Nancy Cowan smiled.

A sixteenth-century refectory table with some antique chairs from Tuscany waited for the party in a green damask dining-room. Some special-looking green and gold china was arranged on shelves in four flood-lit alcoves. The candles were ready to be lit in the silver candlesticks, the table was set for six, which meant that the seats were twice as far apart as they need have been. Letizia looked sulkily over the table, said nothing one way or another to the waiting manservant, then left the room through folding doors which led to the drawing-room. The manservant slipped out of another door to report, apparently, no complaints.

In the drawing-room Letizia's father sat back on a sofa with his contented drink. Nancy Cowan sat by his side, tentatively and upright, near the edge of the seat. Letizia, coming in from the dining-room, said, 'We should have dined in the north room. The green dining-room is far too formal for six.'

The father, Dr Emilio Bernardini, elegantly thin with a pale skin and rather beautiful, very dark eyes behind a pair of scholarly spectacles, black-glossy hair and sharply defined eyebrows, had a look of the portraits of the Stuart monarchs. He was a business lawyer occupied between Rome, Milan and Zürich; in fact, a good part of his business was real estate, and the reason he had yet to sell his own family villa and had chosen to rent from Maggie Radcliffe the one in which he now sat was presumably known only to himself. Although it annoyed his daughter she was too well-fabricated within the business world of Italy to believe she could persuade the father to buy rather than rent. Whatever his reason, it was definitely in his own interest.

He replied in Italian, carelessly, that the dining-room was best for their landlady's visit. Pietro, in the meantime, was telling Nancy he admired her dress.

Nancy answered, in correct Italian, that it was a new one. She added, 'After my first long stay in Italy when I saw how Italians dressed, I felt I was underdressed in my London things, so I always get some clothes for the evening when I come to stay here.'

'Do you mean we're overdressed?' said the charming father of the family.

'In England, at this moment, for this occasion, we would be quite overdressed.'

The father contemplated his children and then herself with some happiness. 'I think we all look very elegant,' he said. 'I'm glad we overdo it. Not long ago we overdid it far more.'

A new young man was shown in, whom Letizia had hastily summoned to dinner to make a respectable number. He, at least, had not overdone it, but was wearing a dingy, grey cotton round-necked shirt and dark trousers, both very much too tight. He was small and plump, bulging with little rolls of flesh under the arms, above the belly, all over; it seemed he had never even started to care what he looked like; Letizia introduced him as Marino Vesperelli, adding, for her father's sake, that he was a Professor of Psychology. Dr Bernardini took him in good part, cast a hand to indicate a seat, rose to ask him what he would drink. At which Letizia took over, and the young man followed her to the wagon of bottles and ice at the far end of the room. Emilio Bernardini then murmured to Nancy, 'I hate to think of *him* breathing all over my daughter.'

'Maybe he's just a friend.'

'Where does she pick them up?'

'I expect this one works with her in her welfare work.'

'He needs a bit of welfare himself,' said the father.

However, as soon as the young psychologist had sat down with his drink Dr Bernardini tried to engage him in conversation as to his profession. The young man answered briefly and asked no return questions; plainly he felt that his odd-looking presence was sufficient social contribution to the evening; which, in its decided oddity, it rather was.

'There's a car arriving; it must be *her*,' said Pietro.

Maggie Radcliffe was so much in the long, long habit of making heads swim when she came into view that she still did so. She looked somewhere in her late forties but the precise age was irrelevant to the effect which was absolutely imperious in its demands for attention; and what was more, Maggie achieved it carelessly. She cared only, and closely, about what was going on around her. And so, as soon as she had given her hand to everyone in the room, she started to admire the Bernardinis' pictures whose authors she recognized, one by one. Still administering her entrance like drops of heart-medicine, she turned to the owner and reminded him how the Klimt over the mantelpiece had very nearly remained in the Austrian collection, thus establishing with him the higher market-place communion that exists between rich and rich.

Nancy Cowan stood waiting for the special guest to sit down. She pulled, through her dress, at the top of her panty-hose, setting herself to rights like a schoolgirl. She then moved her finger under her hair at the nape of her neck. Maggie sat down. The men sat down. Maggie, on being asked what she would drink, turned to the uncomely young psychologist and asked what he was drinking.

'Sherry on the rocks,' he said.

Maggie gave a soundless laugh, looking towards her host in merry collusion, and said she would have a vodka-tonic. She had overdressed very tastefully, with a mainly-white patterned dress brilliant against her shiny sun-tan. Her hair was silver-tipped, her eyes large and bright. She had a flood-lit look up to the teeth.

The air-conditioner was turned off before dinner seeing that the evening was cool. The windows of the dining-room were opened to the breeze of the Alban hills. They sat at the long refectory table, spaced out, murmuring pleasantly one to the other, waiting to be served. Emilio Bernardini at the top of the table had Maggie on his right, Nancy on his left. Letizia sat facing him with Pietro on her left and her boy-friend bundled in his chair on her right.

Wine, water, avocado, sauce. 'What do you think of your villa, Marchesa, now that we're in it?'

'You've made it charming, more delightful than I remembered having seen it before,' Maggie said.

'We made some alterations,' Letizia said. 'We had to get workmen. One of the garages is now a downstairs sitting-room. Otherwise, there wasn't – '

'I know,' said Maggie. 'My agent mentioned it.'

'The Marchesa must see it later,' said the father.

'Yes, I must,' said Maggie.

'If we're speaking English why do you say "Marchesa",' said Letizia, ' "Marchioness" is English.'

Pietro said, 'Because it sounds nicer.'

'Oh, yes, it does,' Maggie said and laid down her little spoon to drink some water. 'And "Signora" would be better. "Mrs" and "Miss" make you close your mouth for the ms but for "Signora" and "Signorina" you don't shut your mouth. "Mrs" and "Miss" form a sneer but "Signora" and "Signorina" are a hiss.'

Marino the psychologist leaned forward to catch Maggie's drift, puzzled. The others laughed while Letizia explained the point to Marino in rapid Italian undertones. He said, 'Why is a hiss better than a sneer?'

'It's better,' said the father as the glasses were filled with his good wine.

'Anyway,' said Maggie, 'Signora is perfectly all right for me as I'm now married to an Italian and Italy's a republic.'

'The Signora is of course the Marchesa di Tullio-Friole,' said Dr Bernardini with his cool good manners, at the same time drawing the line at any excess of a tiresome subject arising from Maggie's logic.

'Oh, Marchesa is so formal. It suits me only when I'm with my husband.'

'I was at school with his son, Pino,' said Dr Bernardini. 'I remember your husband very well. I stayed at the villa up in the Veneto, often. I've hunted there.'

'Then you must come again,' said Maggie. 'He's there now, seeing to the alterations to my bathroom.'

The candles flickered. Came the spinach soufflé, the crumbed veal and salad, the lemon ice and the fruit, while Maggie talked on about the two other houses she owned in the neighbourhood, her son's and Hubert Mallindaine's.

'Mr Mallindaine's is new,' said Letizia sharply, 'but your son's house is a sixteenth-century farm-house.'

Pietro said he had always admired the old farm-house. He seemed uneasy about his sister.

'It should be in Italian hands,' Letizia said. 'Our national patrimony.'

'It cost a fortune to put right,' Maggie said.

The father intercepted Letizia's foreseen reaction to say that he understood Maggie had restored the old house beautifully, and built the new house beautifully as well.

Pietro, it seemed, knew the young Radcliffes and had been to their house.

'Oh, those are the Americans you spoke of?' This was Letizia again, so much so that her boy-friend laughed.

'What's funny?' said Letizia, seeing that the others were laughing.

'Something,' said Maggie, 'about the way you said "Americans".'

'Letizia, don't be silly,' said the father.

Letizia said, 'Shall we have coffee outside, Papa?' Then, as she led the way through the French windows to the upper terrace, she said, 'I believe in Italy for the Italians.'

'Letizia!' said Emilio.

'You are so impolite,' said her brother.

'What about the English?' said Nancy. 'Are we unwanted here?'

'The English the same,' Letizia said as she waited for her guests to be seated.

The father was explaining to Maggie. 'It's only a toy gun she's playing with, or at least, a gun filled with blanks.'

Letizia said 'Oh!' protestingly.

Maggie said, 'Oh, I agree with her, really I do. I think the Americans soon won't be able to afford to stay in Italy. You know, since I married an Italian, I feel myself to be an Italian.'

The young psychologist said to the father, 'You talk of guns, Dr Bernardini. Playing with guns. That's interesting.'

'It's a sexual image,' Maggie said, and they all laughed except Letizia and her boy-friend.

Letizia sat down and the coffee was brought to the terrace table. Letizia started pouring while Nancy took round the cups. 'And the third house?' Letizia said.

'An Englishman,' Maggie said. 'As a matter of fact, Dr Bernardini, he's my problem. He's the problem I wanted to ask you about.'

'It's a beautiful house,' said the father. 'It must have a wonderful view.'

'It has the best view of all three houses,' Maggie said looking one by one at her rings. 'And what's more, the furniture is mine. Every piece. I've given him notice to quit.'

'But he belongs to Nemi,' said Letizia.

'Who belongs to Nemi?' said Pietro.

'The occupant. The Englishman. He has an ancestral claim.'

Emilio Bernardini called for the brandy and liqueurs.

'He has to quit,' Maggie said. 'My husband insists.' She turned to Emilio. 'You know,' she said, 'what Italians are like, of the old school. Very conservative. And really, I admire it.'

'In our country it's difficult to get rid of tenants,' Emilio said, not anxious to take the landlady's part against a tenant so near at hand. 'Very difficult indeed.'

'He pays no rent,' Maggie said. 'He has been a guest for a year and now his welcome is outworn.'

'I'm not sure we can help you,' Emilio said, as if reinforced by the rest of the company.

'I thought we might, perhaps, get up a neighbourhood petition,' said Maggie, prompt, too, with her 'we'. She added, 'My son and daughter-in-law, of course, will – '

'It would make a scandal,' Pietro said.

'But he himself is quite a scandalous person,' said Maggie. 'I'm sure you must have heard – '

'There is a secretary but no scandal. Miss Cowan knows her, don't you, Nancy?'

'Well, I wouldn't say I know her,' Nancy said. 'I believe I met her in Rome one time at the house of some English friends. She had a job in Rome.'

'Well,' said Maggie, 'before this secretary there were boys.'

'It's a Mediterranean custom and in Italy not a crime,' the host said. 'I sympathize with you, Marchesa, but a petition ... ' – he spread his hands – '. . . a petition to get a man out of his house because of boys . . . The scandal would fall on us, definitely, as Pietro says.'

'What does your lawyer say?' said the psychologist.

'Oh, he's working on it,' said Maggie, somewhat vaguely and without conveying much enthusiasm for her lawyer.

'But Mr Mallindaine has a claim to Nemi,' said Letizia. 'His ancestry goes back to ancient times. He can prove it.'

'You know him well?' Maggie said.

'No, I don't know him at all, but I heard – '

'Well, I,' said Maggie bending her head sorrowfully, 'know him well.' Since the subject of Hubert had been discussed, she seemed to have been unexpectedly put in the position of asking an unwelcome favour; her looks seemed to have lost their sensational quality.

In bed that night Emilio Bernardini said to Nancy, 'She's an animal.'

'She looked stunning when she came in.'

'Animals can look stupendous. I wonder what she really wanted to see me about. She rang me in the office this afternoon and said she'd like to see me. I asked her to dinner. I wonder if she just wanted to see what we'd done to her house.'

'I think she wanted you to help her to get the other tenant out.'

'He was probably her lover.'

'No. No, he wasn't. He likes boys.'

'He could take women too, I suppose.'

'No, they had a long relationship but there wasn't any sex in it,' Nancy said, lying beside him in the cool of the summer night, under the thin white sheet.

'I don't believe it. Who would believe it?'

Nancy cast aside her half of the sheet and stretched her body. Her underdeveloped skinniness and boniness was, if it was not regarded as a defect, her considerable speciality; so that without her clothes she was changed, in Emilio's view, from a nobody into a somebody. 'What are you thinking of?' she asked her lover.

'I'm admiring your non-figure,' said Emilio. 'You look so much as if you need a good dinner.'

'I had a good dinner,' she said. 'Maybe I don't look very lovable but I don't care.'

'How seldom one falls in love with the lovable!' he said. 'How seldom . . . Hardly ever.'

'How do you know when you're in love?' she said.

'The traffic in the city improves and the cost of living seems to be very low.'

V

'A TYPICAL BUSINESS-MAN, about forty-three, I should imagine rather conceited,' said Maggie, 'with a son who looks like a gigolo, a daughter, a kind of Girl Guide, I couldn't stand the girl; then there was a downtrodden English governess and the girl's boy-friend, awful little fellow from under some stone. The only good thing about them was their house, which isn't theirs, it's mine.'

'Oh, but I know Pietro and Michael likes him,' her daughter-in-law said.

'I admit the son was the best of the lot,' Maggie said, 'but it isn't saying much. Very bourgeois; of course they were terrified of lifting a finger to help me to get Hubert out.'

'I'll do everything I can to help you,' Mary said eagerly. She was terribly anxious to make a success of her marriage, as she would put it; her father was a success and her mother was a well-known success in advertising although she didn't by any means need the job; moreover, Mary's elder sister was busy making a success of her marriage. Mary had been successfully brought up, neither too much nor too little indulged. And so, still half under the general anaesthetic of her past years, Mary was not disposed to regard Maggie as critically as she would have done had Maggie not been her mother-in-law; it was part of making a success of her marriage. 'So long as I'm here on the spot, Maggie,' Mary said, 'I'll do my best.'

'I know I was foolish to let things get this way,' Maggie said. 'I realize that. It was just that when I was married to Ralph Radcliffe I got just so bored, I just took on a number of artists and intellectuals in a number of cities, and I just . . . Well, Hubert of course was really sort of someone, I really helped him to be what he was, but he's not all that a somebody. He's better known in Paris, of course, or rather was a few years back – after *Ce Soir Mon Frère*, that play, you know – '

'Oh yes! Did Hubert produce it?' Mary said.

'No, Hubert wrote it. Well, I took – '

'Was it a success?' Mary said.

'Well, in Paris it was. So I took Hubert on more and more. He was doing this play. And after a couple of years he was doing another. I helped him a lot with funds and so on, the rent. Sometimes he'd give me a bit of advice about pictures, when we went to the galleries, New York and Paris. Then, well, there was advice and counsel about so much furniture and rugs. He has taste and knowledge, but of course that's not everything. Then you know he kind of took over my life; even when I was away I felt dependent, I felt trapped, and I couldn't rely on Michael's father as a husband, not at all; no, Ralph Radcliffe couldn't have cared less. Of course Hubert's friendship with me was only platonic.'

'So what were you getting out of it?' Mary said.

'Exactly. In the end, that's what I asked. But who would believe it if there was a scandal? And you know these houses at Nemi, it was Hubert's idea to invest this way; he found two houses for me, and of course he wanted one for himself on that piece of land. I don't regret the houses, they're all good properties and appreciating in value, only I want out, out, out, where Hubert is concerned. When I remarried I told Berto about Hubert still occupying one of my houses, and all the best furniture in it. Berto said, "You're crazy, Maggie, crazy. He's a hanger-on. Just get him out. Tell him to go." But it's difficult, you know.'

'Hubert has the nerve!' said Mary. 'The nerve of him! I heard that he had a house full of queers last summer.'

'Yes, but I stopped the money. When I married Berto he said, "Stop sending money. Stop the money order at the bank." I didn't really know what to do. It's really hypnotic when you get in someone's clutches. Berto said, "Why are you hesitating? What are you afraid of? Just write and tell him you're stopping the money." Berto said he would write himself, if I wanted. I said, "Well, Berto, he knows you don't need the money and neither do I, and I don't give him very much." So –'

'That's not the point,' Mary said.

'Right. That's precisely what Berto said. It isn't the point. But now Hubert's being so stubborn, I don't want a scandal, especially as you and Michael live here and like it so much. It's a problem.'

'It's a very, very big problem,' said Mary, eager to be entirely with Maggie. 'It's a tremendous problem.'

'And there's that lesbian secretary living with him,' Maggie said.

'Is she lesbian?'

'I guess so. What else would she be?'

'I guess that's right,' said Mary.

'She couldn't be normal, living there with him.'

'Well, it could be platonic like when you were friends with him,' Mary said, 'but I guess it isn't.'

'A lesbian,' Maggie said, adding, as if to make her real point, 'a penniless lesbian.' With that much off her chest, Maggie now started to praise Hubert by little bits, placing Mary, who also had a few pleasant memories of Hubert, in a state of assenting duplicity.

'He has been careful of the furniture,' Maggie said. 'He appreciates fine furniture and understands it. In fact he helped me choose it. And now I hear he still sends the Louis XIV chairs to an antique expert in Rome to be checked regularly and put right if there's any little thing loose or frayed, you know, and maybe the wood treated. I heard only the other day. In some ways, Hubert was very thoughtful for me.'

'It's expensive, the maintenance of antiques,' Mary said. 'My father's – '

'Oh, I know. He can't be all that short of money, can he?'

Mary said, 'I'll find out what I can.'

'Not that it matters to me,' Maggie said. 'Only, I mean, he can't be all that badly off if he's looking after my furniture, can he?'

'No, he can't.'

'He didn't open the door to the official whom my lawyer sent with a notice to quit. Pretended he was out.'

'But he'd have to let you in,' Mary said. 'Why don't you go yourself and have it out with him? A confrontation is always the best.'

'Do you think so?'

'Well, maybe. I don't know. I mean, most of the time a confrontation is healthy when a relationship goes wrong.'

'There's nothing wrong with the relationship,' Maggie said. 'On my side, everything's the same. I just don't want to go on keeping him, that's all. No explanation necessary. I just don't want to go on.'

'I hear he changed the locks on all the doors.'

'Who told you that?' Maggie said.

'Pietro, the Bernardini son. He told us their tutor learned it from Hubert's secretary. They changed all the locks so your keys won't fit.'

'I wouldn't dream,' Maggie said wildly, 'of breaking into the house without his permission. What's he think I am? He's not all that bad.'

'Sure, he's got very good points. Very, very good points.'

'It would be nice,' Maggie said speaking softly now, 'to think he wasn't in need of actual food. I hope he has enough to eat.'

'He couldn't afford a secretary if he hasn't enough to eat,' Mary said in an equally low voice.

'Well, I don't know,' Maggie said, 'and it makes me thoughtful. There are some young secretaries foolish enough to work free for a man if they believe in him. And Hubert's secretary, the little time I saw her passing in that station-wagon of his, it was only once, for a second, well, I don't know . . . She may have ideas for the future.'

'But she's a lesbian!' Mary said.

'Who knows? Lesbians like to hook a man too, you know. Sex isn't everything. She might want a cover. And so might he.'

'Well, if he hasn't enough to eat he'll be starved out,' Mary said.

'Then there's the electricity, the gas and the telephone. They'll be cut off if the bills aren't paid,' Maggie said, and her voice had taken completely to a whisper, as if an utterance of such things could be unlucky.

'That will solve your problem, then,' Mary said. 'He'll have to leave.'

'Do you believe in the evil eye?' said Maggie still speaking very low.

'Well, no,' said Mary whispering back in concert, 'I believe I don't.' She bent closer to Maggie.

'It's possible,' Maggie breathed, 'that if there is such a thing, Hubert has the evil eye. His name, Mallindaine, is supposed to be derived from an old French form, "malline" which means of course malign, and "Diane" with the "i" and the "a" reversed. He told me once, and as he explained it, the family reversed those syllables as a kind of code, because of course the Church would have liquidated the whole family if their descent from a pagan goddess was known. And they always worshipped Diana. It was a stubborn family tradition, apparently.'

'It sounds very superstitious,' Mary said in her hush.

'I wouldn't think Hubert was malign, would you?' Maggie whispered.

'No, I wouldn't think that. I think he's a bum, that's all,' Mary said, shifting in her garden chair, while the treetops on the slope below their house rustled in a sudden warm gust of air and the dark lake showed through the branches, calm, sheltered by the steep banks.

'It makes me uneasy,' Maggie said. 'Could you keep a secret?' She moved her chair a little nearer to the daughter-in-law.

'Sure.'

'Even from Michael?'

'Well, if it wouldn't make any difference to our marriage . . . ' Mary said.

'I don't see how it could as it only concerns Hubert and me,' Maggie whispered.

'Oh, sure I can keep a secret,' the girl whispered back eagerly, as if the confidence might otherwise be withdrawn altogether.

'I want to send Hubert money from time to time. But he mustn't know it comes from me,' Maggie said. 'I also have to think of my marriage. Berto insists that I throw Hubert out. Well, I have to keep trying, and in a way I want to.'

'You don't have to tell Berto everything, do you?'

'He wants to know everything,' Maggie said. 'He's the old-fashioned Italian, it's part of the charm.'

'I can see that,' said the girl.

'How can I get this money to Hubert without him guessing?'

'Is it a lot of money?'

'Well, if I decide on a sum . . . enough for him to live on here at Nemi while I'm trying to get him out of the house.'

'I don't think I follow, really,' said Mary. 'But I see what you mean in a way.'

'It's a paradox,' Maggie said. 'But Hubert mustn't know how I feel.'

'He'd think you were frightened of him.'

They talked in hushes late into the afternoon.

'We're going a long way but we aren't getting anywhere,' Maggie said as the air grew cooler.

'I wish I could talk it over with Michael.'

'No! Michael would put a stop to it.'

'So he would, I guess. I'll try to think of a scheme.'

'You have to help me.'

'I'll help you, Maggie.'

They looked down on the incredible fertility beneath them. A head and small flash of face every now and again bobbed out of the trees as the country people came and went; one of these, approaching up a path through the dense woodland, presently emerged clearly as Lauro returning. He appeared and disappeared ever larger, seeming to spring from the trees a fuller person at every turn. A little to the north was a corner of Hubert's roof, and under the cliff below him at a point where the banks of the lake spread less steeply into a small plain lay the cultivated, furrowed and planted small fields of flowers and the dark green density of woodland that covered what Frazer in *The Golden Bough* described as 'the scene of the tragedy'.

The scene of the tragedy lay directly but far below Hubert's house, and meanwhile the stars contended with him. 'Hoping to inherit the earth as I do,' he said, 'I declare myself meek.'

This tragedy was only so in the classical and dramatic sense; its participants were in perfect collusion. In the historic sense it was a pathetic and greedy affair, The recurrent performance of the tragedy began before the dates of knowledge, in mythology, but repeating itself tenaciously well into known history.

The temple of the goddess Diana was, from remote antiquity, a famous pilgrim resort. To guard her sanctuary, Diana Nemorensis, Diana of the Wood, had a court of attendants ruled over by a powerful high priest. Legends and ancient chronicles have described this figure and it was upon him that J. G. Frazer's great curiosity was centred. Here is Frazer's celebrated account of the priesthood of Diana and its 'tragedy':

In the sacred grove there grew a certain tree round which at any time of the day, and probably far into the night, a grim figure might be seen to prowl. In his hand he carried a drawn sword, and he kept peering warily about him as if at every instant he expected to be set upon by an enemy. He was a priest and a murderer; and the man for whom he looked was sooner or later to murder him and hold the priesthood in his stead. Such was the rule of the sanctuary. A candidate for the priesthood could only succeed to office by slaying the priest, and having slain him, he retained office till he was himself slain by a stronger or craftier.

The post which he held by this precarious tenure carried with it the title of king; but surely no crowned head ever lay uneasier, or was visited by more evil dreams, than his. For year in year out, in summer and winter, in fair weather and in foul, he had to keep his lonely watch, and whenever he snatched a troubled slumber it was at the peril of his life. The least relaxation of his vigilance, the smallest abatement of his strength of limb or skill of fence, put him in jeopardy; grey hairs might seal his death-warrant . . . According to one story the worship of Diana at Nemi was instituted by Orestes, who, after killing Thoas, king of the Tauric Chersonese (the Crimea), fled with his sister to Italy, bringing with him the image of the Tauric Diana hidden in a faggot of sticks. After his death his bones were transported from Aricia to Rome and buried in front of the temple of Saturn, on the Capitoline slope, beside the temple of Concord. The bloody ritual which legend ascribed to the Tauric Diana is familiar to classical readers; it is said that every stranger who landed on the shore was sacrificed on her altar. But transported to Italy, the rite assumed a milder form. Within the sanctuary at Nemi grew a certain tree of which no branch might be broken. Only a runaway slave was allowed to break off, if he could, one of its boughs. Success in the attempt entitled him to fight the priest in single combat, and if he slew him he reigned in his stead with the title of King of the Wood (*Rex Nemorensis*). According to the public opinion of the ancients the fateful branch was that Golden Bough which, at the Sibyl's bidding, Aeneas plucked before he essayed the perilous journey to the world of the dead. The flight of the slave represented, it was said, the flight of Orestes; his combat with the priest was a reminiscence of the human sacrifices once offered to the Tauric Diana. This rule of succession by the sword was observed down to imperial times; for amongst his other freaks Caligula, thinking that the priest of Nemi had held office too long, hired a more stalwart ruffian to slay him; and a Greek traveller, who visited Italy in the age of the Antonines, remarks that down to his time the priesthood was still the prize of victory in a single combat.

Rigid and frigid as was the statue of Diana the huntress, still, after all, it became personified as a goddess of fertility. But how, Hubert would demand of his listeners, did the mad Emperor Caligula have sex with a statue? It was an orgy on a lake-ship: there must have been something more than a statue. Caligula took Diana aboard his ship under her guise as the full moon, according to Suetonius. Diana the goddess, Hubert explained, was adept at adding years to the life of a man – she had done so with her lover Hippolytus. She bore a child to the madly enamoured Emperor, added years to the infant's life so that he became instantly adult, and it was this young man, and not a Roman hireling, whom Caligula sent to supplant the reigning King of the Wood, the priest of Diana.

Hubert descended, then, from the Emperor, the goddess, and from her woodland priest; in reality this was nothing more than his synthesis of a persistent, yet far more vague, little story fostered by a couple of dotty aunts enamoured of the author-image of Sir James Frazer and misled by one of those quack genealogists who flourished in late Victorian times and around the turn of the century, and who still, when they take up the trade, never fail to flourish.

Modern Nemi, at the end of the last century, as more recently when Hubert Mallindaine settled there, appeared to Frazer to be curiously an image of Italy in the olden times; 'when the land was still sparsely peopled with tribes of savage hunters or wandering herdsmen'. Diana's temple had been feared by the Church. The long wall of high arched niches, once part of the temple-life, have perfectly survived antiquity, and these, at a later time, had been named 'the Devil's Grottoes'. Hubert, beating his way through the undergrowth along the rows of remaining cliff-chapels, would come upon the relics of traditional disrespect and of outcast life. There was a rubbish dump, incredibly rubbishy with the backs of yellow plastic chairs, petrol tins, muddy boots and cast-off rags piled up in those enormous Roman votive alcoves which soared above their desecration with stony dignity. And from this view the plateau was beautiful; it contained the rectangular site of the sanctuary itself, now filled up with earth and cultivated with a chrysanthemum crop.

Very few people now visited this spot as a temple. Hubert had seen reported in a recent article that it was 'still lost as far as the ordinary tourist is concerned'. 'No local folk,' complained the author of the article, 'seem to know where it is.' Which, of course, was instinctively the way with local people. Chrysanthemums enjoyed a commercial popularity in Italy on one day of the year, the Day of the Dead; otherwise they were considered unlucky.

The site of the rectangular sanctuary was marked unobtrusively by a withered tree in one corner. A rim of the temple wall still protruded a few inches from the ground on three of its sides. The reason the peasants had cultivated the soil once more over the late dig was that 'the money for the excavations had stopped', as one of them explained to Hubert.

One spring, when he was supervising the building of the house then destined by Maggie to be his, Hubert had walked down the cliff-path and talked to a man who was pruning a pear tree on the site of Diana's temple. The man was about forty-two. He remembered the excavations, he said, when he was a boy. Very beautiful. Red brick paving. A fireplace. Yes, said Hubert, that was for the vestal virgins; it was an everlasting flame. The man went on with his pruning. My ancestress, Diana, was worshipped here, Hubert said. The man continued his work, no doubt thinking Hubert's Italian was at fault.

Again, standing one winter day alone among the bare soughing branches of those thick woodlands, looking down at the furrowed rectangle where the goddess was worshipped long ago, he shouted aloud with great enthusiasm, 'It's mine! I am the King of Nemi! It is my divine right! I am Hubert Mallindaine the descendant of the Emperor of Rome and the Benevolent-Malign Diana of the Woods . . . ' And whether he was sincere or not; or whether, indeed, he was or was not connected so far back as the divinity-crazed Caligula – and if he was descended from any gods of mythology, purely on statistical grounds who is not? – at any rate, these words were what Hubert cried.

VI

MARY HAD NOT YET GOT USED to the Italian afternoon repose. Her hours were the Anglo-Saxon eight in the morning till midnight with a two-hour break for lunch. That Maggie went to bed between three and five in the afternoon she attributed to Maggie's middle-age. That nearly all Italians rested during that period of the day she attributed to Latin laziness. What her husband did with himself in Rome during these hours she had not begun to wonder; if she had done so she would have assumed that he regularly returned to his office after lunch, keeping American hours in lonely righteousness. In fact, Michael had a mistress in Rome in whose flat he spent the customary hours of repose; it was not unusual for Italian businessmen to spend the long free hours of lunch and after-lunch with their mistresses, but if Mary had suspected that Michael had acquired the habit, especially so early in their married life, she would have considered her marriage a failure beyond redemption.

Maggie was sleeping successfully that afternoon. Mary had, with some scruple, for she was a girl of many scruples, plied her mother-in-law with white wine. They had lunched together on the terrace, talking of next week. Then Maggie had given Mary the smart jewel-case of black calf-skin, slightly wider than a shoe-box, which, when opened, was dramatically and really very beautifully packed with gold coins of various sizes, dates and nationalities. 'There are no absolute collectors' items,' Maggie explained. Their two heads – Maggie's shimmering silver and Mary's long and fair – bent over the glittering and chinking hoard. 'But,' said Maggie, 'the collection as a whole is of course worth more than its weight in gold. Coins always are. My real collection is worth a great deal.' Mary's long fingers shifted the coins about. She lifted one, examined it, put it down and took up another, then another. 'Queen Victoria half-sovereign, King Edward sovereign, South African sovereign – whose head is that?' 'Kruger,' said Maggie. 'Kruger. Are these worth a lot of money, then?' 'Well,' Maggie said, 'it depends who you are, whether they are.'

The coins tinkled through Mary's hands, then hearing the coffee-cups being brought she shut the box, put it on her lap and looked over her shoulder. Lauro appeared, his eyes intent on the tray although he must have seen the black box on Mary's lap.

When he had left, Maggie said, 'Hubert mustn't have a clue who sent them.'

Mary said, 'I really don't see why he should have all these.'

'I have my own important collection,' Maggie said, 'and I can get more. Any time I want.'

'I know. But it's crazy . . .'

'Yes, it's crazy. But it's a way of getting rid of him in my own mind.'

'Oh, I do see that.'

'A cheque would tie him to me even more. I could never get rid of him.'

'No, I see that. He'd think he was in with you again. But gold is appreciating in value, isn't it?'

'Such a damn cheek,' Maggie said. 'I hate him.'

Later, in Maggie's room, they counted the coins and made a list. It was Mary's idea to make a list. She made lists of everything. A good part of her mornings was spent on list-making. She had lists for entertaining and for shopping. She listed her clothes, her expenditure and her correspondence. She kept lists of her books and music and furniture. She wrote them by hand, then typed them later in alphabetical or chronological order according as might be called for. Sometimes she made a card index when the subject was complex, such as the winter season's dinner parties, whom she had dined with and whom she had asked, what she had worn and when. Now she was making a list of the coins while Maggie took off her clothes, and got right into bed for her afternoon rest. Mary took her unfinished list and the coin-box quietly out of the room when Maggie fell asleep, and now she was in her own room sorting and writing seriously. She felt useful. Even though it was to be a secret from Michael, this help she was giving to Maggie was almost like helping Michael. Maggie, asleep in the next room, was much the same as if Michael were lying down there, having an afternoon sleep.

'Q. Vict.,' she wrote, '½ sov. 1842.'

She grasped quickly that there were no numismatic rarities; the value of the coins was largely commercial. At that, they added up to a considerable amount. They were mostly English half-sovereigns, early and late Victorian, bearing the Queen's young head and her older head. Mary found a sovereign of the reign of George IV and, realizing its extra value, wondered if Maggie had put it in by mistake. She put the coin aside, then, on the thought that Maggie might think her critical or stingy, put it back in the box and marked it on her list. The main idea was to please Maggie and show she understood her position. Maggie, after all, was being very delicate in her treatment of Hubert. Mary began to consider various means of conveying this treasure to him without betraying its origin. When she realized how impossible it would be for her to simply drive or walk over to the house herself and hand it over to him, she felt a waif-like longing to do so; she saw herself for a brief moment as an outcast from what appeared to her as a world of humour and sophistication which Hubert had brought with him during those few months she had known him, when he was still in Maggie's good favour. At the same time she disapproved of him as a proposition in Maggie's life. He really had no right to this golden fortune. Her mood swivelled and she imagined with satisfaction a dramatic little scene of handsome Hubert being thrown out of Maggie's house by the police.

Her list was complete. She closed the box and stood up. From the window she caught sight of a shining black head in the greenery below. She recognized Lauro and at the same time the idea came to her that, obviously, Lauro would be the person to carry this box to Hubert. She was convinced of his discretion and, after all, he had worked for Hubert once.

Mary went immediately to Maggie's room clutching the box. Maggie was still asleep. Her mouth was open and she slept noisily. The girl felt guilty, watching this uncomely sleep. Maggie, if wakened, would know she had been watched. Mary retreated, deciding to act on her own and rightly perceiving how gratified Maggie would be to wake up and find her plan accomplished; she would feel free in her heart and mind to turn Hubert out and give him hell and know that at least he wasn't starving. Mary was already on her way to meet Lauro, leaving the house by the back door. His white coat was hanging on the back of a kitchen chair. Mary swung down the hot winding path with her long brown legs and sandals and, seeing Lauro's black head once more below her, called to him, 'Lauro!'

He stopped and waited. She found him sitting down in the shade of the woods just off the path. 'Lauro,' she said,

'I've got something important to ask you. I want you to do something.'

She expected him to stand up immediately she approached but he let a moment pass before doing so. He was smiling as if he enjoyed the lonely scene, and as if the woods belonged to him. She felt strangely awkward as she had not been before when she had been alone with him in the house or in the car, or walking with him to the shops in the village street.

She spoke rapidly, as if giving some domestic instructions while her free mind, as it might be, was on something weightier. 'You have to keep a secret, Lauro,' she said. 'I have something here for Mr Mallindaine but he must not be told who sent it.'

'Okay,' said Lauro.

'I want you to take this box to Mr Mallindaine's house. He mustn't see you as he mustn't know where the box has come from. Find some way of leaving it where he's sure to find it. Do you know the lay-out of the house?'

'Sure, I know the house well. I lived there all last summer. What's in the box please, Mary?'

Mary opened it, trembling at what she was doing. 'They're old coins,' she was saying. 'I've made a list.' She displayed the rich tumble of gold with an expression which conveyed both her naïvety and the pleasure of showing off to the boy.

The sight of so much golden money in the rich, very rich, tall girl's hands inflamed him instantly with sexual desire. He grabbed the box and pulled her into the thick green glade. He pulled her down to the ground and with the box spilling beside them he would have raped her had she not quite yielded after the first gasp, and really, in the end, although she protested in fierce whispers, her eyes all over the green shrubbery lest someone should see, she put up no sort of struggle. 'That wasn't no good because you didn't relax,' Lauro said, his face, satyr-like, closing in on hers, his eyes gleaming with automatic hypnotism as he had seen it done on the films and television from his tiniest years, and acquired as a habit.

Mary, in a crisis of breath-shortage and an abundance of tears, pulled at her few clothes and managed to articulate, 'My husband will kill you.'

'He sooner screw me,' Lauro said.

'That, too, I'll tell him,' she said. 'I would hit you on the face if you were not a servant.'

He jumped up; flash and flutter went his eyes closing on her face, and tight went his hands on her bare arms, as if he were directing the film as well as playing the principal part. 'Next time, you relax,' Lauro said, smiling through his teeth. 'For the first time, no good.'

Mary closed her mouth tight and pushed back her hair with a gesture of everyday indifference. He turned and took up the jewel-box whose contents were half-spilled on the earth, and with her help scooped up the lurking gold. He laughed as if the coins were some sort of counters in a party-game, while Mary, still trembling and crying, stood up; she tugged at her clothes and smoothed her hair; she said, 'Give me that box.'

'I'll take it to Hubert,' he said, and started off in that direction.

Mary caught up with him. 'Are you sure you'll find the right place to leave it? It's not mine, it's Maggie's. Hubert mustn't know.'

He smiled, and turned to put his face close to hers again, smiling. 'Leave it to me, Mary,' he said. He clutched the box under his arms as if it were a man's business, and looked as if he had earned the takings within.

She turned and ran back to the house, not sure how far she was guilty, or what she must do next. She became uncertain whether Lauro could be trusted with those coins. She was perplexed about the relationship in which she stood with Lauro now, and above all she was anxious to take a shower.

Hubert was at that moment counting some coins which he had found in a curious way at six o'clock that afternoon.

Pauline had gone in to Rome in Hubert's station-wagon, taking with her, wrapped in lengths and strips of sackcloth, a second Louis XIV chair of Maggie's to be delivered to the address in Via di Santa Maria dell'Anima where the copies were made. Of these transactions Pauline knew nothing, thinking only that the chairs were being examined and repaired, and that the bill for this service would be sent to their mysterious all-pervasive owner, Maggie. Pauline had never seen Maggie; to Pauline she was a hovering name, an absent presence in Hubert's house and his life.

She delivered the chair, with its penitential sackcloth secured by a winding string round its beautiful legs and tied over its seat and back, ordering the man who carried it up the stairs to take care, great care. She left it with him while she went to find a legitimate parking place for the car. When she returned the man was with a younger man, tall, in blue jeans and a smart shirt; the chair had already been unshrouded and they were examining it with pride.

As Pauline approached the younger man disappeared into a back room from where he carried a chair identical in appearance to the one Pauline had brought. She had been instructed to fetch this back to the house; apparently it was the first of Maggie's best chairs to be sent for inspection and overhaul and, apparently, it was now in perfect order. In reality, it was a new and very clever fake; one of its legs was all that remained of Maggie's former chair. Most of these clever fakes contained at least one limb of the original, and in that way the dealer was entitled, or felt entitled, to proclaim it 'Louis XIV'. To Pauline, it did not matter very much what period the chair belonged to. She had her orders to collect it and she was anxious to get back to Hubert quickly. She asked the men to wrap the chair carefully, which they duly did, with new rags, and much wadding placed over the sparkling green silk of the seat. It was carried to the car.

'Tell Mr Mallindaine to pass by early next week,' said the smart young man in blue jeans.

'He isn't leaving Nemi much, at the moment,' Pauline said, thinking of Hubert, how he was afraid to leave the house in case Maggie should come and reclaim it in his absence.

But the man repeated his request.

Meantime Hubert, at Nemi, was counting the gold coins he had found at six o'clock. It was his usual tea time and he had gone into the kitchen to make it. As he had fetched down the teapot from the shelf he heard a strange rattling inside it. He took off the lid. He had found a quantity of gold money inside the pot.

He sat down at the kitchen table, looking inside the teapot. Then he looked round the kitchen to see what else, if anything, was amiss. Nothing seemed to be out of place. He wished for Pauline to return. He had emptied the gold coins on the table, and now was counting them.

There were, in fact, far fewer than the amount entrusted to Lauro who had kept the black box and more than half the gold. Indeed, his sense of prudence in carrying out Mary's orders was mixed with a feeling of decided benevolence that he had deposited any of these coins in Hubert's teapot. It had sunk into his mind that Mary had told him she had made a list of the coins. It had seemed to him both a fruitless thing to do and a suspicious thing, as touching on his honour.

By the time Hubert, at his customary hour for tea, was puzzling over and re-counting the coins, Lauro was back at the Radcliffes' house, and had changed into his smart houseman's coat. He filled the ice-buckets, arranged the drinks and the glasses, set the terrace furniture to rights, then, chatting with the cook in the pantry, he waited for the cocktail hour.

On her return to the house, after her careful shower and before going down to dinner, Mary had sat for a long while in her room, with her head in her hands, thinking God knows what. Then she skipped to her feet and changed into a long skirt and a blouse. She took up her list of coins, where it was lying on the writing table, and put it down again. She sat down at the table, and pulled out another piece of her list paper. At the top of the page she wrote 'Michael' and underneath it she wrote 'Lauro'. She settled for the thought that she could not have been faithful to Michael all her life, but she felt it was too soon because a year had not passed since her marriage. But then she considered how she had not herself planned the incident with Lauro. One way and another, she tidied up her mind, aligned the beauty preparations in their bottles on the dressing table, and put away the paper she had just written Lauro's name on with Michael's together with the coin-list, her guest-lists and her other lists, locking them up in her desk. Mary had then patted her face with a paper tissue, and had gone down, passing Michael, home from the office, on the stairs. Maggie was already sitting on the terrace waiting for her husband to arrive and her son to come down. Lauro came forward to hover till they were ready to say what they wanted to drink.

'Oh, Lauro,' Mary said very uppishly, 'did you remember that errand?'

'Yes, Mary,' he said in his usual friendly tone, 'how could I forget?'

Mary turned to Maggie and said in a decidedly natural voice, 'He's delivered the box. You see, Lauro knows the house so well, I sent it by him.'

'Oh!' said Maggie. 'But then Hubert will know where it came from and who sent it, and – '

'He didn't see me,' Lauro said. 'I got in through the bathroom window while he was sleeping upstairs. I put the box beside the teapot, so when he came to make his tea he'd be sure to find it.'

'That's brilliant. Lauro, you're brilliant,' Maggie said. 'Mary, darling, you're brilliant. I feel so much relieved now he's at least not likely to starve, because you know I have to get him out of the house. How I've been in the past to Hubert is no guide to how I shall be in the future.'

'Get the police and have him thrown out,' said Mary rather impatiently. 'Lauro, a Campari-soda, please.'

'Well, in our position we can't have a scandal. You know what the Italian papers are like, and all those Communists,' Maggie said.

'We do it discreet,' Lauro said.

'That's right, Lauro. A gin and tonic. Lauro's got the right ideas. Lauro, you're brilliant.'

Hubert, meanwhile, having counted the coins and made his tea, taking it outside on the handsome terrace, gazed out on the panoramic view and pondered. He then began an inspection of the house and decided that one of the ground-floor windows had been entered. There was a narrow pantry window and a narrow bathroom window. The bathroom window was open. It had not been forced. He decided to put bars on the ground-floor windows. He went on a tour of the whole house, opening drawers and cupboards. Nothing was disarranged, nothing missing; it seemed to Hubert that his burglar had been motivated by sheer benevolence towards him. It was a pity to have to bar the windows. Nothing could have been more clearly intended as a personal and rather touching present than those golden coins in his own teapot. For the first time for nearly a year, Hubert started to feel, singing within him, innocence and happiness.

He spread out the coins on the terrace table in the late bright sunlight: Queen Victoria still with a firm young profile and high curly bun, on the coin which was dated 1880 although she was born in 1819. St George and the Dragon, 1892, whose Queen Victoria on the reverse had now been minted with an incipient extra chin, a little coronet and a veil. Gulielmus IIII D: G: Britanniar: Rex F: D:, drooping jowls, a thick neck, a curly quiff on top of his head, 1837. Who, thought Hubert, adores me enough to send me all this glittering mint? And here's Nero wearing a laurel wreath tied with a pretty ribbon at the nape of his neck, or rather, it's Georgius IIII D: G: Britanniar: Rex F: D: 1833. And now, Sub. Hoc. Signo. Militamus – a Knights of Malta ten scudi, 1961. Another juicy young Victoria D: G: Britanniar: Reg: F: D: – darling Victoria, 1880, and that poor downtrodden dragon on the reverse. Render unto Caesar the things that are Caesar's and I wonder, thought Hubert, what utterly charming gentleman hath rendered these things unto me? It then occurred to Hubert that the actual bearer of the coins was hardly likely to be the sender. Hubert had instantly formed an image of largeness, if only of heart, for the sender; he was certainly rich, anyway, and would most likely have young men at his beck and call. Only a young man and slim could have got through the bathroom window so silently and softly. Then, it was someone who knew Hubert's habits and who knew the house. Someone rich. Who? He scooped up the many dozens of coins and took them into the kitchen, where he spread them out and looked at them again.

Pauline returned with the fake chair which they placed in the drawing-room and admired. 'He wants you to call in and see him. Better go soon,' Pauline said. 'I hope it isn't about the bill.'

'I hope not,' Hubert said. 'Maggie gets the bills for this servicing of her stuff. However, if you'll hold the fort I'll go and see him very soon. Always hold the fort. Let no one into the house. I'm thinking of getting bars put in these lower back windows as it seems to me someone might easily get in that way. Once they're in, they can take possession of the house and we're done for.'

It was in any case his intention to call on the furniture restorers and collect payment for the genuine parts of Louis XIV. It would be a considerable sum. Hubert looked at Pauline in a kind of dream, wondering how he could explain to her the good supply of drinks and food he intended to bring back from Rome with him. She had brought back a chicken and some meat and wine from Rome, the good girl; she had spent her own money and was about to prepare a special supper.

After a glass of wine he was moved to tell her about the gold coins.

'It's my opinion,' he said, 'that the spirit of my ancestors Caligula and Diana are responsible for this.' He gave Pauline two sovereigns.

She accepted them after a little hesitation. 'They could have been stolen,' she had said.

'Well, *we* didn't steal them. They were in my teapot, so they're plainly mine. My dear, they are our crock of gold and we have come to the end of the rainbow.'

'Someone must have got into the house.'

'Through the bathroom window,' Hubert said. 'So tomorrow we arrange to have the windows barred.'

'Then your ancestors won't be able to come again,' Pauline said, looking at her sovereigns.

'Those are not on account of wages,' said Hubert. 'Wages I'll pay later and in good measure. I don't like that touch of scepticism in your voice. Remember that my ancestor Diana is very much alive and she doesn't like being mocked. But of course if you're going to express doubts and behave like a French village atheist – '

'It could have been one of those boys who worked for you last summer,' Pauline said, looking at the pile of gold on the table and touching the coins tentatively from time to time.

'Not on your life,' said Hubert.

'It's someone who wants to help you,' Pauline said. 'A well-wisher. Why didn't they send you a cheque?'

Hubert found himself suddenly irritated by this speech. Her kindergarten teacher's tone, he thought. All this being penniless, he thought, has lowered my standards. I should have better company, witty, good minds around me. I find a pile of sovereigns in the teapot and all the silly bitch can say is, 'Someone wants to help you. Why didn't they send you a cheque?'

He took up the newspapers and weeklies she had brought in with her, and went off to his study to take a couple of tranquillizers and further hypnotize himself with the current American government scandals of which everyone's latent anarchism drank deep that summer.

Lauro left for Rome very early one morning with his list of shopping at the supermarket. His first stop, however, was at one of the little cave-like shops in the village, filled, as they were, with the richest of fruits, plants and cut flowers. It was perhaps unusual, but not noticeably so, that he locked the car when he left it outside the door on the village street. Lauro went in and waited his turn.

Figs, peaches, strawberries, all so local and proudly selected, there was not one inferior fruit to be seen. The flowers were mainly of the aster family, huge, medium-sized and smallish, in white, yellow, mauve and pink. Among them were some deeply-coloured small roses and a variety of ferns and leafy plants. The woman who was serving and she who had just been served looked at Lauro with the look of curiosity which comes over the faces of people to whom nothing much happens, and which, to people of more elaborate lives, looks likes hostility. The Radcliffes had their own orchards and rarely shopped here. However, the local people knew very well who Lauro was, and of his recent transference from Hubert's mysterious home to Mary Radcliffe's spectacularly rich one. Lauro, in his smart clothes, the transparent beige shirt and fine-striped pink trousers, was to be treated with a touch of deference. What would he desire? Grapes, peaches fresh this morning, fine tomatoes . . . ?

Lauro desired some plants, strong and lasting, with the roots, for transplanting.

What type of plants? What did the gardeners at the Radcliffes' advise?

'Oh, no,' Lauro said, rather impatiently, almost as if to suggest that not any roots, not any plants, would do, 'they're for my mother's grave. I'm going to visit her at the cemetery.'

The woman who had been served, although she had received her change, made no sign of leaving, but entered the discussion. Surely the Radcliffes had plenty of plants and to spare . . . ?

'For Mama,' said Lauro with a haughty masculine bark that sent the women scurrying, 'I prefer to pay.' And he bought four chrysanthemum plants not yet in flower and rattled his money while they were being carefully wrapped in newspaper and placed in an orange-coloured plastic shopping bag. He left, and was watched to his car. It was only when he was seen to unlock the empty car, there on the harmless street, that he looked behind him and saw the two women exchanging glances. Carefully, he spat on the pavement. Then he got into his car and drove away too fast. Suspicious old fat cows, what did it matter if they knew what he might be up to, and he knew that they knew that he knew, since, if he put his mind to it he could easily make as many accurate guesses about their doings as they about his. It was for this reason that he had not even bothered to take the precaution of buying his plants in Rome: in Rome they were twice the price, whereas in Nemi they were cheap and he didn't need to care what the people thought. So ended one of those telepathic encounters that go on all the time among compatriots who have foreigners in their midst.

Arriving in Rome, Lauro made first for the cemetery. He found his mother's grave, well-tended and neat, with its hovering marble angel and the little inset photograph. There was room here for his father; their five children would later buy their own burial-plots in the new cemetery, since this one would then be fully occupied. 'Cara Mama,' said Lauro. He had brought his packages in the bright orange plastic shopping bag from the car. He had unpacked the healthy plant-roots, the little strong trowel and another newspaper-wrapped package containing the black leather box with most of the coins that Mary had given over to him the afternoon before.

Some people passed, old people on the way to visit their dead. They gave Lauro a muted 'Buon giorno', inclining their heads towards him with approving piety. Lauro, on his knees, dutifully digging and tending his mother's flower-bed, looked up and returned the greeting with wistful repetition, one quiet 'Buon giorno' for each of the three figures who passed. He was a nice boy in their eyes, which made him feel nice as he dug. The figures, a fat woman in black, a thin man and another, less fat woman with difficult-walking feet, passed from his life. When he had dug enough and laid on the grass verge some of the flowers and plants he had dislodged in the process, he opened up the sheets of newspaper which contained the black leather box. He had almost thrown away the box, keeping only the coins to bury, but it was such a well-made, a well-bred box, such as Lauro sometimes saw in the shops and boutiques of Rome, and it was so connected, now, with the desirable coins and the casual and exclusive quality of Mary and Maggie in their inherited wealthiness, that he had decided to bury the box along with the coins, despite the nuisance. He opened the box, lifted the paper-tissues which he had stuffed inside to keep the coins from rattling, sifted a few of the beautiful golden disks through his brown fingers, quickly replaced the lot, put the black box in the orange plastic bag for safe preservation and, seeing that it was well-covered, he buried it deep. On top of this he replaced some of the short shrubs he had dug up.

He began also to plant the new chrysanthemum roots he had brought, working his way around the grave and, tidying up the border, tastefully arranged the colours; there were already a few nasturtiums, some asters in pink and purple shades and some dark green shoots the nature of which would not be revealed till the autumn. While he was at it he dug up, examined, and replaced two well-wrapped little parcels, one containing a huge sapphire ring and the other a pair of monogrammed cuff-links, these being objects he had picked up somewhere along the line from two earlier periods and encounters of his young life.

When the grave was ready, Lauro stood up and looked at the picture of his mother whom he remembered as deserving and energetic. Her huge voice had commanded until she died. She looked out unsmiling with her bold eyes and her short hair shining and fresh from the hairdresser's. The costly angel who spread his wings above her little oval picture looked frightened by comparison, and the downcast eyes of that pale, churchgoing, feathered adherent of the New-fangled Testament seemed shiftily afraid to meet those of the living Lauro.

Nobody except the family was permitted to touch the grave. Lauro had taken on this work exclusively to himself; the rest of the family, from whom, in any case, he had nothing to fear, were all too busy elsewhere to tend it. His father had married again and lived in Milan; his two sisters were married with children and lived in Turin. One brother was married in America, and the other, who lived with his father in Milan, was a student. Once a year at the beginning of November, on the Day of the Dead, those of the family and their spouses who were not in America or, as it might happen, confined in labour wards, came to visit Lauro's mother at the cemetery, bearing with them large bunches of long-petalled white and yellow chrysanthemums. These would be piled on the grave. The family would hover and weep, some lustily, some merely wetly. They would say how nicely Lauro kept it, how good he was, sparing them the expense of the cemetery-attendant's services. They kissed Mama's picture but did not touch the grave and asked no questions, not even of themselves. They felt Lauro was getting on quite well and admired his clothes. After the visit to the cemetery on the Day of the Dead the family would troop out with the other thousands of ancestor-visitors, get into their cars and proceed to a trattoria where they had booked a long table for a five-course family meal. Once a year.

Lauro looked round the cemetery, now, in early August, nearly deserted. Only one or two heads moved behind one or two tombstones. Lauro wrapped the leafy rubbish in a piece of his newspaper and the trowel in another. An attendant passed and wished him good morning. Lauro looked around with pleasure. What secrets lay buried in these small oblong territorial properties of the family dead!

VII

Dear Hubert,

    We are leaving for Sardinia next week – out of this frightful heat! I expect you too will have plans to go to the sea. After Sardinia I plan to return with Mary to the U.S. to spend some time on our own beautiful Atlantic beaches. Berto (my husband – he looks forward to the pleasure of meeting you one day!) plans to join me on the Emerald Coast for a few weeks and then goes on to Le Touquet to join his brother. They plan to look over some horses he plans to buy. I plan to join him in Rome, then Nemi for a week on October first after which our plans take us back to the Veneto.

    What I am writing about mainly is, if you can plan to vacate the house during the summer so that we can occupy it from October first, that would suit our plans. Will you let me know, please? Address your letter up till the end of August:

La Marchese Adalberto di Tullio-Friole,
Villa Stazzu,
Liscia di Vacca,
Costa Smeralda,
Sardegna.

After that my New York address (address me there Mrs Maggie Radcliffe as the apartment is still in my old name!)

till the end of September. Please leave the key with Mary's maid Agata, if you vacate in the month of August. Agata is coming in every day to feed the cat and dust. September, Lauro will be back so please leave the key with him if you have to vacate as late as the month of September. August would be preferable as this would enable me to plan for the decorators to come in from Rome in September so the house would be in shape for us.

A little bird told me you have been looking after my precious chairs! It was thoughtful of you and very, very simpatico. Bill me with the cost, of course. Maintenance is so very, very important.

One day when all the trivialities of life are settled I hope you will come and visit with me and Adalberto and tell us about your big project that you plan as I am sure you do. I hope it's shaping up!

Happy summer!

> As ever, love,
> Maggie.

Hubert took a large whisky and two Mitigils. He re-read the letter, paying less attention to what she actually said than to the tone and implication. A mass of ideas moved like nebulae in his mind. It was not until later in the day, after lunch, that he was able to isolate the germ: it was Maggie who, two days ago, had caused the gold coins to be placed in the teapot. The reason: plain guilt. But why buy him off in such an exotic manner?

And why, if she really wanted to make it easy for him to leave the house, had she sent so comparatively little? For, after all, small fortune though they amounted to, they were hardly the value and dimension of what one would call a settlement.

A settlement. In any case, for no money at all would he leave the house.

Again he read the letter. Over lunch he had read it out to Pauline Thin. 'Does she always go on like that about her plans?' Pauline said.

'Not in conversation so much as in her letters. She has an epistolary style which denotes an hysterical need for stability and order. In conversation she counts on her remarkable appearance to hypnotize the immediate environment into a kind of harmony. She learned about planning at college, I should think. It's a useful word in American education. She never understands the rules of anything, however, and her emphatic use of the word "plan" when she writes a letter is nothing but self-reassurance. Naturally, she will not stick to her plans. If she goes to Sardinia at all, she'll probably only stay one night. That's Maggie.'

Pauline said, 'If you look at things in her light, you wonder why she doesn't get her lawyer to press on with the eviction.'

'She doesn't want a scandal and it's difficult to evict.' Hubert, who was always impatient with others who failed to keep pace with his leaps of logic, conveyed impatience now.

Pauline found herself regretting the appearance of the gold coins; Hubert had been sweeter during their recent weeks of meagre living.

'Well, we should still go very carefully,' Pauline said. 'It may be a trick to lure us into carelessness. We mustn't leave the house unguarded in case they suddenly swoop and stage a takeover.'

Hubert considered this. 'You're a clever girl,' he said.

'And we should still be careful with the money. Are you going to sell the coins?'

'Tomorrow,' Hubert said, 'I shall go into Rome and sell a few. You'll have another present, too.'

'Oh, no,' Pauline said.

'Why not?' said Hubert. His mind was on the money he was going to collect for the chairs. He would have to leave early for Rome to give him time to collect the money comfortably and, in the event they didn't pay in cash, change the cheque before the banks closed. It was an exceptionally hot August. He didn't like Rome in the heat. 'I'll leave early in the morning,' Hubert said.

'Then I'll iron those shirts of yours,' she said, the wifely girl.

'Shirts? I've got plenty of shirts,' Hubert said absently, for his head had lifted to hear the sound of a car coming up the drive. A green Volkswagen that he did not recognize presently drew up at the door.

Pauline said, 'It's the Bernardini daughter.' She stood beside Hubert behind the glass doors of the terrace.

'Those people who live in one of Maggie's other houses?'

'Yes, she's the daughter, Letizia.'

Letizia had evidently brought a friend. She got out of the car in front of the house and went round to the other door. Presently, partly by persuasion and partly by force she brought out of the front seat before the eyes of Hubert and Pauline a tall lanky young man with a mop of reddish hair very like a giant chrysanthemum out of which peered a peaked and greyish face. He was trembling and wobbling, and obviously was in a bad way.

'That's Kurt Hakens,' Hubert said.

'Who?'

'One of my secretaries from last summer.' Hubert locked the terrace door. 'He looks drugged, and my laughter demon, which resides somewhere inside me, has ceased to laugh.' He stood back from the glass door of the terrace. 'Let them in,' he said. 'See what they want. Tell them I'm busy and can't be disturbed.'

The secretaries from last summer were not, in themselves, of any particular account to Hubert. There had been other secretaries and other summers in plenty. And other winters.

Once, at a New Year party, in those days when Maggie was discovering the wonders of Bohemian life through him, one of his secretaries deliberately burnt Maggie's hand, that right hand with which she had signed the cheques, and such grand and frequent cheques. 'Hold this,' had said the young man who, Hubert reflected as he recalled the scene, must now be thirty, maybe with a secretary of his own. 'Hold this,' he had said, out on the terrace of that other villa of those days. It was a firework. He put it in Maggie's hand then lit it; it was the live end of the firecracker that she held in her hand. It flared in her palm before she dropped it. She looked at the young man's smiling face and fuming eyes. 'He burnt my hand!' she screamed out to Hubert across the dark terrace. 'He did it purposely. I'm in agony.' She bent with pain. Hubert was dancing to the distant bells. He seemed to have lost his head to the New Year, and it was another secretary who took Maggie away to treat her hand with some type of cream. Helplessly, Maggie asked for her chauffeur. Another young man joined them. Both secretaries said the chauffeur was asleep in the servants' quarters. They wouldn't call the chauffeur. It was recounted thus later to Hubert first by Maggie and then by the two young men who had helped dress her burns.

'Where were you, Hubert?' Maggie had said. 'Why didn't you help me?'

'I didn't realize what had happened. I thought you were throwing a temperament,' Hubert replied. And he asked her, 'Why didn't you go into the kitchen yourself and demand your chauffeur if you wanted to go home?'

'I couldn't. I felt paralyzed. Something just prevented me.'

Maggie had slept in Hubert's bed. They had given her a strong pill. She slept till the party was over at five in the morning, then had got into the car with her bandaged hand, without having seen Hubert around anywhere. The rooms had been littered with used glasses and piled-up ash-trays. Hubert had gone to someone else's bed long before.

When he heard this story later, he saw it all swiftly from Maggie's point of view; he weighed up her nightmare-like experience of being unable to move of her own will to call her chauffeur, and her retiring to a deep sleep on his bed, and decided she was fairly hypnotized by him. For about five years after that, apparently indispensable to Maggie in practical affairs, he had been able to do what he liked with her until that time when gradually, at first unnoticed by him, she began to withdraw. In the meantime there had been secretaries, waves upon waves, season upon season of them. Last summer Kurt Hakens was a secretary, but that was when Maggie had already begun to retreat and was vaguely nowhere to be found. It was plain, now, that last summer she had actually been plotting. She was already getting rid of her ineffectual and purely nominal husband, preparing to marry the new one, and was emerging as a society woman, well-groomed, fully using her enormous wealth which had been lurking there in her favour all the time.

Pauline Thin was at the drawing-room door, apologetically. Hubert looked vexed but in reality he was relieved to see her, imprisoned as he had been, merely sitting it out on one of the still unfaked chairs, out of sight and earshot of his visitors. He had a paranoiac feeling that he was being discussed behind his back and, at the same time as he was very eager to know what was going on between the Bernardini girl, the very ill-looking Kurt Hakens and Pauline, he was afraid to know. Pauline came softly over to him, apologizing in low tones. She pointed to the floor and said, 'They're still down there. Letizia says couldn't you please come down a minute. It's very urgent.'

'What do they want?'

'She says Kurt used to be your secretary and he's an old friend of yours. He needs help.'

'I can't have him here,' Hubert said.

'I'm awfully sorry,' Pauline said.

'You mean you can't cope with them yourself?' Hubert said nastily, rising.

'Yes,' said Pauline humbly.

Hubert took his reading glasses from his pocket and followed her downstairs, looking very much as if he had been torn from his desk.

Letizia was on the terrace, drinking tea. Kurt was stretched out on the long canvas chair beside her, his eyes closed, his mouth quivering. 'How do you do?' Hubert said to the girl.

Letizia stood up, affably showing her teeth and fixing her clear eyes steadily on his face. 'I did not phone,' she said, 'because we haven't met. It was less complicated to come. My father is your neighbour, Emilio Bernardini. I am Letizia.'

Hubert said again, 'How do you do?'

They sat down, looking at the view which seemed always to ask to be looked at like a much-photographed actress. Kurt Hakens continued to lie with closed eyes and quivering lips.

In a while Hubert said, 'What's the matter with him?'

'He's taken an overdose of a drug. I occupy myself with these cases. Now I find me in a predicament because we leave tomorrow for our vacation. This man is a foreigner and he's a friend of yours – '

'Yes, in a way,' Hubert said. 'I gave him a job last summer. A few weeks, then he left. You shouldn't abandon your patients, you know.'

'Papa has made arrangements.'

'Is he getting treatment?'

'I don't know.'

'How does he live?'

'I don't know.'

'Then you want to leave him with me?'

'Yes.'

Pauline said, 'We'll have to call a doctor.'

'Do you know what would happen?' Letizia stood up, agitated. 'They would take him to the Neuro.' The 'Neuro' was the mental hospital in Rome where all cases of mental, nervous, psychopathic and psychotic sufferers who could not afford private clinics were indiscriminately housed in conditions, it was said, rather worse than the Rome prisons, which were reputedly infernal.

'What can I do with him? My dear girl, it's a year since I last saw him,' Hubert said, looking down at Kurt. 'He needs treatment and care. I have no money, my dear. Are the police looking for him? Nemi is in fact my ancestral home. It may be difficult for an Italian to realize, but it is so. My landlady is trying to put me out of the house. How can I take in this poor boy? – I can't do it.'

'Well, yes, as I say, we will do our best,' Hubert said.

Kurt had been helped, half-pushed, upstairs, crying, and without any resistance; he did not seem to know where he was but he knew his way instinctively to the bedroom he had occupied last summer. From time to time a small noise would come from his room to the three sitting downstairs on the terrace; he was faintly whining through his nose; he sounded like a young horse or a dog dreaming in its sleep. Hubert looked at the cheque Letizia had given him. He passed it to Pauline.

'I really don't like taking it,' he said.

'It's from our fund,' Letizia said. 'Papa gave me it for our funds, because I had Kurt on my hands and I didn't know what to do with him for the vacation. I would have had to

170

send him to a clinic, then they would ask him questions and maybe he would be in trouble.'

'It will go straight from your fund into ours,' Hubert said. 'I assure you we have a fund, too, for our unfortunates. Pauline, please put it in the fund.'

'All right,' Pauline said. 'Do you want a receipt, Letizia?'

'Oh, no!' She made a gesture of pushing away the offer with her open palms as if alarmed lest the exchange of any document should continue to bind her to the bought-off Kurt. She said, 'Papa was only too happy to help. We leave tomorrow on the boat for Greece and Turkey. Then we go to Ischia. Papa wants you to visit us when we come back.'

'If I'm still here,' Hubert said. 'Our padrona is trying to put us out.'

Pauline was upstairs trying to converse softly with Kurt and at the same time to persuade him to stay in bed. She sat near the door in a soft armchair, in a casual attitude, but ready to flee because Kurt, from time to time, demanded his clothes. Pauline had agreed with Hubert in family-type whispers to keep watch over him while Hubert continued his conversation with Letizia downstairs. Letizia had begun to interest him on the subject of Maggie and this, together with the good big cheque she had handed over, made up for the actual infliction of Kurt upon him; the actual problem of Kurt could be solved later.

The intermittent sound of Kurt's argumentative demands and Pauline's soothing replies seeped down to them. Letizia had accepted a sherry. Her face was lightly tanned, her eyes clear blue.

She paused in her account of the night that Maggie dined at her house, and Hubert, thinking she was troubled about Kurt, said, 'Oh, don't worry. We'll calm him down. I know a couple of Jesuits who'll give me advice. American Jesuits. They'll know how to cope with him.'

But Letizia was not, apparently, at all troubled by Kurt; he had become yesterday's problem. She had paused to consider whether, after all, it was wise of her to repeat how Maggie had tried to get her father's help to put Hubert put of the house. 'Yes, Jesuits, that's good,' she said.

'I suppose she wants your father to gang up with her,' Hubert said, coaxingly. The phrase 'gang up' was beyond her, and after it was explained she rattled on obligingly. 'Of course,' she said, 'we've no intention of making the gang with her. I mean, I have no intention and Papa will listen to me. At Casa Bernardini we're on your side. Papa has to think this way: if she can get one tenant out then we'll be the next.'

'This has the best view of all three houses,' Hubert said, wishing to establish a banal, greedy reason why Maggie should want to be rid of him.

'Oh, is that why she wants it? Well, Papa has spent a fortune in reconstruction so our house is now more worth than it was when we rented it.'

'Maggie,' pressed Hubert, 'covets the view.'

'She says you must go because her husband insists.'

'I dare say. He, too, appreciates the situation of the house. But I shan't go. I have an ancestral claim, you know, my dear.'

'I know! I know!' The girl jumped up and sat down again. 'Tell me more, please, about yourself, how you belong to Nemi and your –'

'Nemi . . . ' said Hubert, leaning back in the chair with his legs stretched out wide in front of him. 'Nemi is mine. It belongs to me, as a matter of fact. The offspring of Diana and Caligula became the high priest of Diana's sanctuary and I am his descendant.'

Kurt's voice could be heard in some sharp protest from above, joined with Pauline's impatient tones. It appeared, now, that Pauline had left the bedroom and was turning the key in the lock. Her footsteps could be heard coming down.

'I'm interested, so interested, Mr Mallindaine. Our English tutor and your English secretary have talked of your family tradition. I love so much the traditions. You shouldn't be sent away from your house.' She made her hands into fists and thumped one on top of another in a way most alarming to see in a young girl. 'My friends and I,' she shouted coarsely, 'will put the son of that American Marchesa out of his house. They will not send you away from your house. The farmhouse of the son is Italian property. The Curia had no right to sell it to her. The land where she built this house for you is Italian property. We want things Italian kept in the hands of the Italian people, we must remember our origins!'

Her oration finished, she breathed heavily with an overflow of indignation. Pauline had entered in the course of this speech and looked rather impatient of the rhetoric, in her English way. But Hubert, whatever he felt, looked impressed. He said, 'More Italian in origin than me you could not be . . . a direct descendant of a union between the Roman Emperor Caligula and the goddess Diana, here at Nemi. She must, of course, have been more than an idea; she was flesh, miraculous flesh, be sure of that. – Pauline, my dear, refill our glasses and help yourself. Letizia looks so like the very Diana of the Woods, she looks a true goddess of ancient Latium.' He shoved his glass towards Pauline who had sulkily fetched the sherry bottle. 'Diana, huntress, chaste and fair . . . ' Hubert said. 'It's true. She remained chaste at heart even after she became the great goddess of fertility of all Italy.'

'Do you have documents,' said practical Letizia, 'relating to the family?' Pauline was holding out the refilled glass of sherry; her hand wobbled and a few drops fell on Letizia's pink cotton skirt.

'Documents!' Hubert said, over and above the exchange of Pauline's squeal of apologies, Letizia's reassurances, and the sound of Kurt upstairs banging on his bedroom door. 'Documents! I have an avalanche of family letters and documents. We are working on them now. We're working against time. What do you think Pauline's here for?'

Pauline looked downcast, and indeed she felt so. Letizia, so very young and full of opinion, so very rich and so planted on her home ground, simply by her presence put Pauline in the position of an inferior. Upstairs, minding Kurt like the employee she was, while Letizia relaxed with Hubert on the terrace, Pauline had felt aggrieved. Letizia did not know quite how much au pair Pauline was; Pauline had been lending Hubert money to live on. She had paid his electricity bill. She had filled up the station-wagon with petrol to go back and forwards to Rome with those chairs.

Pauline sat silent, not being at all helpful to Hubert on the subject of the documents, because in the first place the documents she was putting in order had so far failed to prove, really, Hubert's ancestral claim, and secondly she did not feel in the mood to support him by so much as a misleading grunt. Hubert thought her obtuse. 'Pauline's been working on the documents,' he said. 'And I have sent for the important ones, which have been kept in England and in Malta. The Mallindaines lived for a long time in Malta.'

'It sounds most interesting,' said Letizia.

'It is most interesting,' said Hubert Mallindaine, and the words brought once more to mind his two aunts having passed the window on Lady Day. 'It sounds most interesting,' said the vicar who stood looking straight out from the bow-window with his hands in the pockets of his summer-grey clergyman's suit, rocking to and fro from his heels to his toes, while his mother sat sewing in the window-seat. The aunts had passed, without hats, which was strange for ladies in Hubert's childhood; their hair, moreover, was cut short, straight, grey and untidy. They were walking hand in hand, and his mother had finished explaining to the vicar that her sisters-in-law were convinced 'Mallindaine' was a corruption of 'maligne Diane'. 'Which is Old French,' his mother said. The aunts had not cared to turn their heads towards them as they passed the window. ' . . . on their way to Hampstead Heath; they do it every Lady Day,' his mother said, still intent on her embroidery. 'They light a bonfire and offer up prayers to the goddess Diana, and I expect there are other rites. They could be had up. Very eccentric. My poor husband could do nothing with them.'

'It sounds most interesting,' said the vicar.

'I dare say it is most interesting,' said his mother, 'but it's embarrassing for me, because of the boy.'

'Have they means?' said the vicar, gazing out on the sunny Hampstead pavement.

Hubert had a few letters referring to these aunts and their special eccentricity. He had come across the letters some years ago, in Paris, while sorting the first batch of his papers for his memoirs. From that moment he had cultivated the fact of these long-neglected aunts, one of whom had died in the meantime, allowing their fantasy to grow upon him. It may be that in those days he had felt a premonition, even before he had any outward sign, of Maggie's ultimate defection. Those were the years when he still had full control of Maggie's mind and it was he who convinced her to acquire the houses at Nemi 'where Diana, my ancestress, got laid by my ancestor the Roman Emperor'. It wasn't every woman whose escort and protector could make such claims. Submissively and carelessly Maggie had acquired two of the houses at Nemi and had the third built to Hubert's special stipulations; in the meantime she started an affair with a fine-looking young man who was a plain-clothes policeman and part-time actor, the very scourge of those other young men preferred by Hubert. She handed over the fretful details of the purchase of land and buildings at Nemi and had telephoned to Hubert from Rome in that special jargon used by people who at that time woke and took breakfast, as it might be, in Monte Carlo, flew to Venice for a special dinner, Milan next evening for the opera, Portugal for a game of golf and Gstaad for the week-end. 'J'ai compris – toute à Nemi – un avocat . . . called Dante de Lafoucauld, yes, really. – What do you mean, "my policeman lover", Hubert? – Il était gendarme, c'est vrai mais, mais . . . Well, darling, he's handsome. I have to sleep with someone, je dois – ma vie . . . Va bene, va bene, Hubert, ma cosa vuoi, tu? I tuoi ragazzi . . . I don't say a word about your boys, do I? Hubert, after all these years pensando che siamo sempre d'accordo . . . Look, I have to go . . . My maid has the luggage . . . ' Maggie always travelled with her maid and now, for a short while, until the affair of course ended, with her policeman.

Hubert's aunts, in the meantime, grew in the grace of his imagination. They sprouted ancestors before them, springing from nowhere into the ever more present past, until Hubert had a genealogy behind him. He started corresponding with the surviving aunt who in her poverty and dotage was greatly consoled by Hubert's complicity in her life-long belief. He had brought the aunt to meet Maggie in her flat in Paris. Maggie's son, Michael, was there, and Mary whom he was shortly to marry. 'Our forebear Diana,' said Hubert's aunt, 'sets us rather apart. That was why I never married, nor my sister. Hubert will always be a bachelor, too.'

He sat, now, on the terrace of the house at Nemi, secure in this lineage in which he could truly be said to have come to believe, seeing that his capacity for belief was in any case not much. He managed very well without sincerity and as little understood the lack of it as he missed his tonsils and his appendix which had been extracted long since.

He sat half-facing Letizia. 'Documents . . . Yes,' he said, 'the documents exist, of course. Pauline is sorting out the documents. I'm writing my memoirs, you know.'

Letizia turned her head to look uncomfortably inside the house where Kurt's noise was coming from.

'You know how to handle him?' she said.

'Of course. Don't worry,' said Hubert.

Pauline helped herself to sherry and sat down.

Hubert said, 'I was good to him before. He wasn't on drugs then.'

Kurt sounded as if he would break down his door. Pauline did not move. She was watching Letizia who was ready to leave, and was standing, now, a little way off, gazing up at Hubert with her young face. They walked off to the car, talking. The girl obviously was extremely relieved to get rid of Kurt, and was gratefully attributing to Hubert a kind of broad-shouldered glamour which Pauline just for that moment realized he did not possess. That Hubert, walking Letizia to her car, was assiduously playing up to this role made Pauline impotently furious. She could not hear what Hubert was saying as he smiled down at Letizia, held her hand, kissed her hand, laid his hand reassuringly on the girl's arm, and held open the door of her car for her. Letizia turned to wave to Pauline who, after a slight pause, waved back in the laziest way she could manage. Then Letizia was off, back to her sheltered privilege, her Papa and her holidays by the sea, while Hubert, really looking very handsome, strode back and up the steps to the verandah. Kurt was shouting and banging louder still. Hubert looked for help towards Pauline.

'What'll we do with him?' Hubert said.

'Get a doctor, I suppose,' Pauline said, not moving. 'It's your job. You've been paid to look after him.'

'Look, Pauline, we can't get a doctor. You know he'll be put straight into the loony-bin; my house will be searched; I'll be questioned by the police, you'll be questioned – '

'Oh, no I won't,' Pauline said. 'I'm leaving tonight. Going back to Rome tonight and tomorrow I'm going to the sea. If your bouncy admirer can get rid of her responsibilities and flip off to Greece tomorrow morning, why shouldn't I?'

'Pauline, it would be very dishonourable of you to let me down at this moment. Listen to him, up there!'

'How honest are you?' Pauline said, the words coming out in an unpremeditated access of insight. She had never questioned his honesty before.

Possibly suspecting that she already knew more about him than she actually did, he said, 'Dishonest I may be when pushed to it; it's a relative thing. But dishonourable, no.'

Pauline was by now very much upset, and this verbiage confused her. She said, 'We should go up and get him. Bring him down, and try to do something with him.'

'Come on, then,' said Hubert, loftily and pained. 'Let's see what we can do.'

The boy's panic subsided when they opened his door. He was laughing and crying as they brought him downstairs, Pauline holding him by the arm and Hubert following, exhorting him to keep calm, not to worry and to relax.

There was a canvas chair on the terrace that converted into a full-length couch. Hubert arranged this and they got Kurt stretched out on it crowing through his tears. His voice had the effect of ventriloquism, sounding sometimes from a point above and behind him, sometimes from the ground beside him. No words were distinguishable among these doom-like cries and sob-like spasms of laughter. He bayed like an animal. He fell back exhausted. Hubert fetched him a glass of mineral water and two of his Mitigil tranquillizers which the boy took with upturned mad eyes.

Pauline was trembling. 'Either you call a doctor or I do,' she said.

'He can't be seen by a doctor here in my house.'

In the end Hubert agreed to take him to Rome to see a doctor he knew who might even get Kurt into a private clinic. 'It will cost a fortune,' Hubert said roughly.

'Isn't Letizia's cheque enough for the clinic?' Pauline was eager to know how much.

'Barely,' Hubert said. 'We must hope for the best.'

It was nearly eleven that night when Hubert arrived in Rome with Kurt, who was somewhat stunned by a further dose of tranquillizers and trembling at the wrists and knees, in the front seat beside him. Hubert drew up at the foot of the Spanish Steps in the Piazza di Spagna, pressed a golden Victorian half-sovereign into Kurt's hand, told him it was exchangeable for a week's lodgings, and put the young man out on the pavement. Kurt made his way without looking back to a crowd of young vagrants and hippies who were sitting or reclining on the steps in the warm young night.

'That's that,' said Hubert when he returned. Pauline had waited up for him.

'A clinic?' she said.

'Yes, a clinic.'

'What clinic?'

'It's better you shouldn't know what clinic. If there are any questions, you know nothing. Just mind your own business, my dear.'

'It's Letizia Bernardini's problem. You should phone and let her know what's happened before she leaves for Greece.'

'Don't be disagreeable, Pauline. Let the girl go in peace.'

'She hates foreigners, actually. She's that type of Italian. She's only using you.'

'She appeared to be very charming. She's entitled to her bit of folk-schmaltz, it's fashionable among the young.'

'I don't need to be told by you what it feels like to be young.'

'But you can be taught by me, I see, what it feels like to be jealous.'

'How could I be jealous,' said Pauline, 'when you don't care for women, anyway? That's what you told me.'

'I do care for women. I don't have sex with them.'

Pauline started to cry. 'There was something passed between you and Letizia. I could see it. All that tenderness. I don't know what to believe.'

Hubert put his arm patiently around her shoulders, meting out an almost equal balance of tenderness. 'You can't leave me,' he said, 'because we're friends, and I need you.'

VIII

'NOW YOU PRIESTS,' HUBERT SAID, 'give me my money's worth. Ours is a friendship based on mutual advantage and so I expect some intellectual recompense for this materially superb dinner that we are about to receive.'

Father Cuthbert Plaice said coyly, 'Oh, Hubert!' Father Gerard gave a jocular smile to Pauline and lifted his fork.

'Pass the wine,' said Hubert. Pauline was wearing a long lavender-blue dress of floating chiffon; Hubert wore a deep purple patterned shirt of transparent cotton with expensive-looking blue jeans; the smart dining-room had been opened and the silver and fine glasses brought out; a cold buffet of elegant rarities was laid on the sideboard.

Cuthbert, having tasted his chilled salmon mousse, looked at Pauline across the candlelit table and said, 'Everything looks very sumptuous this evening.'

'He means opulent,' Hubert said, for no other reason than to be difficult.

'It's only a semblance of opulence,' said Pauline, warily; she was evidently thinking that their golden windfall must inevitably reach a point of exhaustion.

'But what is opulence,' said Hubert, 'but a semblance of opulence?'

'Well,' said Gerard, 'I would say there is a very, very great difference.'

'How ingenuous you are!' said Hubert.

'I don't understand,' said the young priest. 'How? – "ingenuous" . . . '

'If you imagine,' Hubert said, 'that appearance may belie the reality, then you are wrong. Appearances *are* reality.'

'Oh, come, Hubert,' said Father Cuthbert. 'Pauline has just said that you have here a semblance of opulence. "Semblance" was her word – wasn't it, Pauline?'

'Yes, it was,' said Pauline, 'and Hubert knows what I mean.'

'A vulgar concept,' Hubert said. 'Tonight we have opulence.'

'But it might not be everybody's idea of opulence,' ventured Gerard. 'I mean of course you're making reality out to be something very subjective, aren't you? People differ in their perceptions.'

'Reality is subjective,' said Hubert. 'In spite of what your religion claims, I say that even your religion is based on the individual perception of appearances only. Apart from these, there is no reality.'

'Try having a scientist agree with you,' said Cuthbert, making little excited movements in his chair.

'The more advanced scientists do agree with me; in fact they're almost mystics,' Hubert said. 'As am I.'

'Can you come to the sideboard?' said Pauline. 'Take your own plates and help yourselves.'

'It looks delicious,' said Gerard, following her to the sideboard. 'And you look very nice in that gown, Pauline.'

'It's new,' she said.

'Is Maggie back from her holidays?' Cuthbert meanwhile inquired softly of Hubert, as if treading a mined field.

But Hubert ignored the question, standing back and beckoning the guests towards the spread of cooked meats and the choiceworthy range of salads. When they were seated Hubert produced a different wine, recommending it with a grand and far-away voice.

It was mid-September and still the heat of summer hovered far into the nights of Rome and its surroundings. Tonight at Nemi there was a faint hill breeze, hardly enough to flicker the candles through the open doors of the dining-room balcony.

'Delicious,' said Cuthbert. 'Delicious wine.'

'Delicious,' said Gerard.

'And Maggie,' Cuthbert plodded on, ' . . . have you heard from her?'

'Not a word,' Pauline said, warming up to communicability which, with a little more wine, would presently become volubility. 'We had a letter from her before she left Nemi. She told us all her movements up to the end of this month. She should have been in America at the moment but I believe she didn't go. She's still in Italy. She wants us to get out of this house by the end of September, but – '

'Pauline!' said Hubert. 'Don't you think you might be boring these learned Fathers with this trivial gossip?'

'No, it isn't boring at all,' Cuthbert said.

'Isn't your chair comfortable, Cuthbert?' Hubert said.

'My chair? – Oh, yes, thank you kindly, it's quite comfortable, Hubert.'

'Cuthbert very often motionizes,' Gerard explained with well-wined pleasantness, 'while verbalizing, depending upon the emotive force of the topic in its relation to the scope and limitations inherent in the process of verbalization.'

'I see,' said Hubert, inclining himself very slightly in aristocratic acknowledgement of this exposition and with the same movement lifting his glass of deep red wine. He sipped and looked at a point above Pauline's head, as one who savours.

'Well, I wasn't being boring,' Pauline said. 'I was only saying that Maggie – and I've never seen her, mind you, I haven't met her at all – is simply impossibly spoilt. Too much money. She had a gentleman's agreement with Hubert and –'

'Maggie is not a gentleman,' Hubert said, 'and I find personalities a boring subject of conversation, Pauline, if you please.'

'What else is there to talk about?' Pauline said. 'Everyone reads the papers and we hear the news; I think it's boring to discuss what everyone's heard already. The point about Maggie is that she's holding this threat over our heads while she's sunning herself on some beach. We only have two weeks to go, and –'

'Pauline, enough!' Hubert said, loudly.

'Maybe we could be of help?' Cuthbert said. 'We found Mary, her daughter-in-law, a very charming, human person. Could I have a word with her? Gerard was in Ischia with them the beginning of August, you know. He –'

'Ischia – I thought they were going to Sardinia,' Pauline said.

'Maggie changed her plans,' said Gerard. 'I had an invitation from Mary to go study the surviving ecological legends of Ischia,' Father Gerard said. 'I stayed with them, it was very comfortable. And I must say that area is rich in legends of nature worship. Mary listed for me many cases of surviving nature-practices and superstitions in that area. They're devout Catholics, of course. I'm not saying anything against their faith; those peasants are great Catholics.'

'But they worship the tree-spirits and the water-spirits,' said Hubert.

'No, no, I wouldn't say worship. You've got it wrong. The Church continues to absorb many pagan nature-rituals because the Church is ecology-conscious.'

Pauline, who had been engaged in conversation with Cuthbert while the other priest was expounding all this to Hubert, suddenly broke in and, hurling the words across the table, said, 'Hubert – listen to this! Lauro, that Italian boy who was your secretary and works for the Radcliffes – well, he went to join them in Ischia and he's sleeping with Mary *and* Maggie. What d'you think of that?'

'Well, perhaps,' said Cuthbert, bouncing in his chair, 'I shouldn't have mentioned it. But, well, maybe – don't you think, Gerard? – it's something that Hubert and Pauline ought to know.'

Gerard, somewhat shaken, said hastily, 'Why, yes, in confidence, of course. As I told Cuthbert on my return from Ischia, this state of affairs arises from an impression, as it was indicated to me by primary coadjunctive factors, that formed in that location with the Radcliffes. But still, as I said, I found Mary very intelligent to be with and very, very helpful. I think, in her case, it's only a passing phase and that young Lauro should never have been allowed the freedom that he has. Mary was very helpful with her documentational listings.' When he had finished this speech he looked at Pauline reproachfully, as if by her outburst she had been a confessor who had burst out of the confessional proclaiming the outrage of a penitent's sins.

Pauline was not apparently concerned with his feelings. She was looking intently at Hubert. He looked back in aloof silence.

'Gerard,' said Father Cuthbert, 'is really very perceptive; since he told me about it, I thought about it and I decided this is something that you ought to know, Hubert, because both Lauro and Maggie have been friends of yours.'

'Personalities bore me,' said Hubert. 'I've spent too much of my life on perishable gossip. Cuthbert, let me change chairs with you; I can see that there's really something wrong with yours.' He got up and started moving his chair. Cuthbert looked bewildered.

'It's only a reflex of Cuthbert's,' said Father Gerard.

Hubert replaced his chair and before he sat down refilled their glasses. He said, 'Gossip and temporal trivialities. Whereas the intellectual principle endures. Cuthbert, be intellectual, for God's sake.'

Pauline took up her plate, holding it at arm's length from her new dress, and moved to the sideboard for a second helping.

'I thought you'd be interested, Hubert,' said Cuthbert, getting up to follow Pauline.

Pauline said, 'We've been hard at work all day. It's nice to relax at night.'

'Do you find it relaxing to think of Lauro busying himself with Maggie and Mary by turns?' Hubert said.

The priests giggled coyly.

Pauline said, 'I do.'

'Then you have a sexual problem, my dear,' Hubert said.

'Whose fault is that?' said Pauline.

'Maybe we'd better keep off personalities, as Hubert suggests,' Gerard said. 'There was a lot of that going on in Ischia, I'm afraid.'

'There always has been,' Hubert said. 'That's where your studies in pagan ecology should begin. Copulation has always been part of the worship and propitiation of nature.'

'Well, Christianity has given all that a very, very, new meaning,' said Cuthbert.

'To us,' said Hubert, 'who are descended from the ancient gods, your Christianity is simply a passing phase. To us, even the God of the Old Testament is a complete upstart and his Son was merely a popular divergence. Diana the huntress, the goddess of nature, and ultimately of fertility, lives on. If you poison her rivers and her trees she takes her revenge in a perfectly logical way. The God of the Christians and the Jews – where's the logic in him?'

'Hubert,' said Pauline, 'you know I'm a Catholic. I don't mind helping you but I won't have my religion insulted.'

Father Cuthbert said, 'Good, Pauline!'

'My dear, I knew you would take it personally,' Hubert said, 'and you look adorable tonight in your new dress. Go and get the sherbet ice out of the refrigerator and mind your frock.'

When the visitors had left, greatly cheered by the wine and liqueurs, the pleasant food, the physical prettiness of the evening and Hubert's exciting insults, Pauline went to change out of her new dress into a cotton nightdress in which she descended to join Hubert at the kitchen sink where he was stacking the dishes into the dish-washer. They started the machine buzzing, then Hubert poured whisky for both, and they sat at the kitchen table, sipping and sizing each other up for a silent while. Eventually Hubert said, 'Lauro and Maggie. Lauro and Mary. When will it be Lauro and Michael?'

'Just what I was wondering myself,' Pauline said. 'Only a few months ago I wouldn't have thought of it. But now since being here alone with you, Hubert, and sharing the trouble, we seem to think the same thoughts. I feel there's a real bond between us. An everlasting bond.'

'Everlasting!' said Hubert. 'A bond, my dear Miss Thin, is not very far from bondage. Don't frighten me, please.'

'Well, Hubert, you don't have to go back to calling me Miss Thin, suddenly, just at this moment. It's not very nice of you after all we've been through.'

'When I feel the bonds tightening, Miss Thin,' said Hubert, 'I break loose from them.'

'All right, I'll go away,' said Pauline.

'What have I done?' said Hubert. 'What have I done to deserve this?'

'Nothing,' said Pauline. 'That's the trouble. You've done nothing at all because you're a confirmed queer. Proximity to a man who does nothing gets on one's nerves after a time. I'm at the end of my tether and I'm leaving.'

'Before one speaks of sex I should have thought one considered the aspect of love,' Hubert said.

'I've got a boy-friend in Brussels working for the Common Market,' Pauline said. 'I can go to Brussels and consider the aspect of love with him.'

'Pauline, Pauline, how heartless you are! Love takes time,' Hubert said. 'And if you think you have a right to describe me as a queer when you don't know the first thing about my physical inclinations, then you've got a stupid and a common mind. If I were to impart to you the erotic details of what goes on in my mind they would excite you but *per se* would consequently cease to excite me.'

Pauline, successfully perplexed by this collage of clues, replied sulkily, 'Well, you once told me that you'd never slept with a woman; you said so yourself – '

'Which is not to say I can't.'

'Well, if you haven't, how do you know if you can?'

'Have you ever eaten blubber?'

'No,' said Pauline, ready to be very annoyed.

'Whale-blubber. I ate some once in a little fisherman's café in Normandy. It was on the menu so I thought I'd try it,' Hubert said. 'It tasted all right – fat and fishy – but I suppose there might be ways in which one could prepare it to make an absolutely delicious dish. However, you say you can't eat it – '

'I said I'd never eaten it. What's whale-blubber got to do with sex?'

'Practically everything, if you're an Eskimo. Survival first, sex second.' As he spoke Hubert, noticing a two-inch quantity of champagne at the bottom of the bottle, poured it into his own glass. He now drank it and waited for Pauline to snap back some reply to him, which she failed to do.

Hubert repeated dreamily, 'Blubber!'

'Do you mean to insult women by saying they're like blubber to sleep with?' Pauline said.

'I don't know what they're like to sleep with. But just because you haven't done a thing doesn't imply you can't.'

'Well, I've never eaten blubber and I'm damn sure I couldn't,' Pauline said. 'What has all this got to do with sex?'

'I thought we were talking about love,' Hubert said, persuasively. He considered it was time to go to bed but on the whole he decided another bottle of champagne between them would be a good investment and a good idea. It was appalling, he thought as he undid the cork, how much she wanted a lover and how much he needed a secretary-accomplice.

'What are you doing?' said Pauline, sitting winefully and sulkily in the corner of the big sofa.

'Opening another bottle of expensive champagne. With you in this mood, Miss Thin, I can't afford not to.'

'May I bring my lover in Brussels to stay with us for a while? He gets leave soon,' Pauline said.

'No,' he said, crossly. If she can try to be clever, he thought, I can be really clever. He filled their glasses, sank into his chair and raised his glass slightly to her before he sipped.

'You're using me,' she said.

'Of course. You'll be paid as soon as I have the money, Pauline.'

'I don't want to be paid.'

'You want to use me?' he said.

'No, I want to leave. Your behaviour . . . '

'You want,' said Hubert, 'to use me to satisfy your dreams. Which is wicked. I only want to use you as a secretary, which is perfectly reasonable behaviour. Are you in love with your lover in Brussels?'

'That's my business. Why do you keep talking about love?'

'My dear, it was you who started – '

'No, it was you.'

'Look,' said Hubert, 'one can't have sex with one's secretary. It doesn't work.'

'Now you're talking about sex,' she said.

'Well, it was you who started talking about sex, Miss Thin,' Hubert said, and refilled their glasses.

'We have to get new locks put on the doors tomorrow. The man's coming,' Pauline said, sleepily.

'Why are we getting new locks?'

'You told me to have them changed every month in case Maggie got hold of a key or something. Tomorrow's the sixteenth. I told the man to come tomorrow. Shall I put him off?'

'It's expensive, everything's expensive,' Hubert said, 'but no, my dear, don't put him off. You're very efficient.'

'Thank you,' she said. She put down her glass and started to walk carefully to the door, weaving only a little from her surplus intake of wine.

'Aren't you going to kiss me good night?' Hubert said when she reached the door. He made no motion to get up.

She looked back and felt the start of a drunken haze. She decided to use what lucidity remained to her to climb the stairs, clutching the banisters. 'No, of course not,' she said. 'What do you think I am? A piece of blubber?' She achieved an exit, leaving him to think over what she had said.

What he thought was that the worst was over for the time being. She had got out what was in her mind and might even regret having done so. However, the air was a little cleared and he could count on the *status quo* continuing until it was possible for him to develop a better and more stable *status quo*. Hubert finished the champagne, so musing, and enjoying the solitude of the night. He thought of Maggie in Ischia. She had not told him of her change of plans. He didn't know her house in Ischia. 'Maggie . . . ' mused Hubert, 'Maggie . . . ' At about three in the morning he had a sudden desire to telephone Maggie and wake her up, hear her voice. The Marchese would probably be snoring by her side in one of those huge matrimonial beds so prized by Italian families. Hubert felt he didn't care. He half rose from his chair to go into the study, get her number from the exchange and ring her up. Then he recalled with great sadness that the telephone of his house had long since been cut off.

IX

'NO REPLY FROM HUBERT,' Maggie said. 'I should have had the phone bill paid if only to keep in touch with him. But I didn't see why he should have the use of it free, calling San Francisco, Hong Kong, Cape Town, you name it. And that lesbian. I had the phone cut off. Anyway I sent him a telegram two days ago to ask if he's ready to vacate the house, and he hasn't replied.'

Her husband, Berto di Tullio-Friole, was intent on listening to a Beethoven symphony on the gramophone and frowned across the room at Maggie to keep her voice down; he made an irritable gesture with his hand to accompany the frown; he was not in the least disenthralled with Maggie; he only wanted very much to savour the mighty bang-crash and terror of sound which would soon be followed by the sweet 'never mind', so adorable to his ears, of the finale. He was a sentimental man. Maggie and Mary lowered their voices.

Berto closed his eyes till the record came to an end. Then he went to join the women at the other part of the long paved room with its windows opened to the sunlight of October and the sea beyond. Lauro appeared from nowhere and was ordered to fetch a whisky and soda for Berto. 'Si, Signor Marchese,' said Lauro. No first names with Berto, nor would Berto have tolerated his wife, her son and her daughter-in-law to be addressed by their first names by any servant in his presence. Lauro, understanding this perfectly, had not even tried. They were nearly ready for lunch, already missing the past summer's days with their morning rhythm of laze and swim, laze and swim, on and off their private rocky beach. This beach, a small promontory, was not entirely private by law, only the elevated rock was private. The pebbly shore where the waves lapped was like all other beaches in Italy, public property, a fact well-known to the blithe visitors who ostentatiously intruded whenever the whim seized them to bring their little boats ashore. It had happened that, one day during the summer, Maggie's swim had been disturbed by a girl in a rowing boat; she was washing her long hair over the side with a shampoo which bubbled Maggie's way. Maggie, aware of her impotence in territorial rights, shouted at the girl, 'You can't wash your hair in sea-water.' Whereupon the girl shouted back, 'It's a special sea-water shampoo.'

Maggie had been very upset and after a hard day's work on the telephone to the mainland had procured five private coastguards who still lounged along the rim of the shore below and on the rock and in front of Maggie's house, dressed up as 'intruders', thus to keep at a distance the real ones. 'The time is coming,' Maggie said severely, 'when we'll have to employ our own egg-throwers to throw eggs at us, and, my God, of course, miss their aim, when we go to the opera on a gala night.' She had sighed; a deep sigh, from the heart.

Meanwhile they sat in the room with the blinds lowered against both the fairly bright sunshine and those hired intruders, who Maggie thought were making a noise beyond the call of realism, while Berto waited for his drink and the two women continued their discussion of Hubert.

Berto, who was less rich than Maggie, but rich enough to understand the excessive and rather mysterious concerns of rich women of Maggie's generation, and did not object to them, listened with a touch of tolerance and another touch of jealousy. The war of 1973 in the Middle East was just coming to an end. Things would never be the same again, as Berto had been told by the owner of the only newspaper he read. Once when he had entertained at a shooting-party a journalist of considerable fame, descendant of a noble family from Verona, who had ordered the delivery of three newspapers of conflicting politics, Berto had been highly indignant; his roof had been insulated and his hearth befouled; how could anyone read a Communist or a slightly left-wing newspaper, how could any friend of his read anything but the established paper of the right wing with its news reported fairly and its list of important deaths? The mild and middle-aged gentleman of Verona had tried very hard to point out that his profession required him to read all slants of opinion, but had not succeeded in conveying this to Berto who was convinced that all the needs of objectivity were supplied by the one and only newspaper permitted within his walls and whose owner he had known all his life. The journalist gave in and cancelled his wild order, being a man of agreeable temperament, and a desire to shoot some animals being one of the purposes of his visit.

'By law,' Maggie was saying to Mary, 'when you turn someone out of a furnished house in Italy, you send a certain number of warnings, then the authorities send a van for the stuff. By law they have to leave behind the bed, the washing machine and the contents of the files. I would love to take everything away and leave him with the bed, the washing machine and his ridiculous papers and let him share them with Miss Thin.'

'What about the man himself?' Mary said. 'How do you get rid of the person?'

'It's a different process and it's difficult because first of all the neighbours gang up to protect the guy, and then you have the Press and the photographers and the police. But before it comes to all that you have to – '

'Maggie dear!' Berto said. 'Maggie, my love, you'll just have to forget it, you know. Leave him alone; starve him out. He'll leave of his own accord one day, you'll see.'

'Now, Berto, you know you advised me to turn him out!' Maggie said.

'Yes,' said Mary. 'Berto – you did say to turn him out.'

'But,' said Berto slowly, exasperated by their lack of his local logic which he fully thought to be the universal logic, 'if the lawyer has told you the law, and it's going to make a scandal, then you can't succeed. You have to face the fact that the man has tricked you and has stolen your property. And you have to put that man right out of your mind because you can't put him out of your house and make a scandal for the Communists to make capital of in the papers.'

'Italy is a strange place,' Maggie said.

'It's the same everywhere,' Berto said. 'Times are changing rapidly and things will never be the same again.'

'I hate Hubert Mallindaine!' Maggie cried out. 'I loathe Hubert Mallindaine!' And as she exploded further about her feelings against Hubert, her husband was overcome by a tremendous jealousy; Maggie's emotions against Hubert were stronger by far than any she displayed towards himself; and Berto, suspecting in his jealous anxiety that she did not love him with the intensity that she hated Hubert, was too agitated to care whether she expressed love or hate; he cared only lest Maggie felt something for Hubert and nothing for him.

'Hubert,' Maggie said, 'is a man that I despise, loathe and hate, and absolutely detest.'

'He is very contemptible,' Mary said.

'The servants will hear you, Maggie,' Berto said aimlessly, while staring at her as one appalled at his own fate. Lauro, representing the servants, appeared to inquire if he should serve more drinks. Berto had cancelled his trip to Le Touquet to buy horses. He had thought well before doing so; he had thought well, all the time knowing that he would decide to cancel the trip. Maggie had watched this process of decision with the eye of one watching a horse race, knowing full well which horse ought to win, and seeing it win.

'I'm thinking of getting married,' Lauro said.

'Really? To anyone in particular?' said Maggie.

Lauro looked put out. 'She's a fine girl from a very fine family. She did a year at the University of Pisa studying sociology, and she's only twenty.'

'And what does she do now, then?'

'She works in a boutique in Rome. Her mother also works in a boutique. Her father is dead; I don't know where he is.'

'What do you mean . . . ?'

'I don't know anything of the father. Maybe there isn't a father. The mother's family has land at Nemi, two fields.'

'Well, Lauro,' said Maggie, 'you're a lucky man. Is she beautiful?'

'Oh, yes,' said Lauro as if it went without saying.

'Well, why don't you bring her here to see us?' Maggie said.

'The Marchese wouldn't mix,' Lauro said with a laugh.

The Marchese had gone out and Lauro was sitting on the arm of one of the blue cotton-covered armchairs in the long paved room. He had opened the blinds to let in the mild sunlight of the late October afternoon. Berto was upstairs asleep. Mary and Michael had also disappeared upstairs where their voices sounded faintly in a continuous everyday tone. The rest of the staff had dispersed, some to the cottages behind the villa where their quarters were, others to hang around with their local friends at the bars which stretched along the quayside and where the incoming ferries brought ever-new talkative life from Naples, and the outgoing ferries carried away those multilingual visitors who had done their day, or stayed their weeks, on the islands of Ischia. Lauro perched at his ease, in a fresh shirt and blue jeans, sipping from a glass of cloudy grapefruit juice and talking to Maggie. She sat back in her immaculate bright-coloured house-pyjamas, against the blue cotton covers of her chair, and smiled through her bright eyes and even as it seemed through the deep bronze of her skin.

Maggie was wondering whether Lauro had decided to talk of the girl he wanted to marry from the sheer naturalness of his kind, or whether he wanted to assert his male pride and put her in her place in some way, since he made love to her often in Berto's absence and when Berto returned was so very much the old-fashioned servant; or did he, thought Maggie, smiling still, want a sum of money on the excuse that he needed it for his wedding and in the knowledge that, so far, she had always been generous to him with money? Maggie pondered on these alternatives as Lauro spoke in his casual manner about his girl and the boutique where she worked, and how she was unaware that he was employed as a domestic. 'I am Mary's secretary,' Lauro advised Maggie, who murmured gaily, 'Quite right, Lauro.' Meantime Maggie's mind ran on the alternatives of Lauro's motives, mistakenly assuming that they were in fact alternatives and that Lauro was capable of analyzing his own motives, or bothered to do so, since it had never been in the least necessary for him to find one reason only for doing any one thing.

Then Lauro said, 'I hope that Mary will not take it to heart.'

'Oh,' said Maggie, 'she won't object to calling you her secretary. She'll play along. What's the difference?'

'I mean that I hope my marriage will not upset Mary.'

Maggie was about to ask, 'Why should it?' But, thinking quickly, she refrained. She gave a little laugh instead and said, 'There's no question of upsetting Mary.' And she was gratified to see that Lauro was put out. He's trying to upset me, she thought.

'You know about Mary and me?' Lauro said.

'I know you're a very active boy,' said Maggie, laughing softly again and gazing openly in his face.

'Well, you Americans . . . ' Lauro said, gazing back.

'What about us?'

'Strange women,' he said, and in Italian repeated, 'donne strane.'

'Look, Lauro, I'll give you a wedding present, a handsome one. Mary, too, will give you a present; from her and Michael. Isn't that what you're talking about?'

'No, it isn't what I'm talking about,' said Lauro. He was furious and began to shout, 'You think you can buy everything, don't you? I was a secretary to Hubert Mallindaine and now I'm only the butler.'

'Well, I wouldn't say "butler",' Maggie said. 'A butler is a very special type of professional with a very special training. You wouldn't fit in as a butler, really. I always thought of you as our friend who looked after us, as – '

'As a servant,' Lauro shouted. 'I have to wear that white coat, those black pants.'

'Well, Lauro, that's the custom and we pay you well. You do better with us than you ever did with Hubert, and besides you were only his houseman, really, among other things. The word "secretary" – ' She stopped and motioned towards the staircase where footsteps descended.

Lauro stood up and Berto appeared in the bend of the staircase. 'What's going on?' he said to Maggie. 'Who's shouting?'

'Lauro wants to be known as our secretary from now on,' Maggie said. 'I don't see why he shouldn't be a secretary. He's going to get married.'

'Secretary? What do you mean? I don't understand,' Berto said.

Lauro stood in a state of confusion. He was exasperated by Maggie's coolness and quickness of mind and by the fact that he had put himself in the wrong by raising his voice. Maggie, smiling in her chair, was fully conscious that even if the younger man burst out at this moment with the wildest truths about his relations with Maggie and, possibly, Mary, he would be disbelieved on principle; and in fact he would be in deep trouble.

Lauro stood looking at Berto's angry face. 'I finish being a servant,' is what he said.

'All right, all right,' said Berto. 'You can go. Take your things and go. Come back tomorrow morning and I'll give you your wages and your severance pay and your holiday pay and all your other damned communistic rights for domestics, but don't stand there abusing the Marchesa. You don't raise your voice in my house, understand.'

The thought flitted into Maggie's mind that Berto was behaving out of character, but then the thought flitted away in the heat of things.

'Now, you listen a minute,' screamed Lauro, ready for a long hysteria-match such as he had been involved in several times before in his life, not only with Hubert but with the owner of a nightclub, with another Marchese, with a policeman known familiarly as Contessa, with his late mother and very many others. In torrential Italian he listed the indignities he had been subjected to in the service of the Radcliffes and threatened to denounce to the Ministry of Inland Revenue the family's faulty tax returns, this being a safe guess; he said he would sue for being overworked and having to keep late hours with the result that he now suffered a nervous crisis. Tears came to his eyes as he bawled his accusations, convincing himself by his own voice, more and more, how humiliated he had been and how Berto had even done the unspeakable by addressing him with the familiar 'tu' instead of the third person 'lei' required by the law.

'Go!' screamed Berto and gave him the 'tu' again: 'Vai!'

Maggie now stood up majestically, spreading her golden arms in a peace-appeal. From upstairs Mary called down, 'Maggie!'

Maggie went to the foot of the staircase, leaving the two men glaring at each other, and called up, 'It's all right, Mary.'

Michael looked over the banisters. 'What's wrong?'

'Stay there, both of you,' Maggie said. 'Nothing's wrong.' Then she returned to the combatants. 'I haven't understood a word of all this Italian,' she said, 'but it sounds awful. Berto, I have to speak with you privately. Lauro's only a young man and they're all like that these days.'

Lauro spat on the floor between them and left the scene, mounting the main staircase to his room where he banged the door hard. Against the further banging of Lauro's cupboard door and his suitcases, Maggie settled once again in her chair with her hand to her head.

'I'm sorry, Maggie,' said Berto gently and quite surprisingly.

'Oh, these things happen.'

'Can I get you a drink?'

'Yes. Anything.'

He brought her a whisky and soda and she could hear the clink of ice in the glass as he brought it over. His hand was trembling.

Upstairs, Michael could now be heard in urgent conversation with Lauro, possibly trying to calm him down.

Berto brought over his own drink and perched where Lauro had lately perched. The ice in his glass pelted against the sides. He was agitated. 'I'm sorry,' he said.

'Well, Berto, it's sweet of you to feel sorry for me, but really he wasn't so bad before you appeared.'

'I'm sorry.'

'I don't want him to leave,' Maggie said. 'At least not yet. He might start saying things and cause a scandal.'

'Did he say anything about me? What did he say about me?'

'Nothing,' Maggie said, smiling again, 'except what he said to your face, and that was enough.'

'Oh, I just wondered if the little swine had said anything about me, as you say he might go around talking – '

'I mean Mary. He might talk about Mary.'

'What can he say about Mary?'

'I don't know. Between ourselves, Berto, I don't know if Mary hasn't been foolish with Lauro. He seemed to hint something like that.'

'Mary!' he said.

'Yes, Mary.'

'I can't believe that. These boys are capable of saying anything. They're dangerous. What did he want? Money?'

'I guess so. But you know he's proud and he went a long way round to ask for it.'

'He went the wrong way round.'

'I guess so.'

'He has to leave this house,' Berto said, rather factually and with a melancholy tone which invited contradiction.

'Maybe it will blow over,' Maggie said. 'I don't mind calling him our secretary. I don't see that it makes any difference what he's called. He says he's going to get married and the girl thinks he's a secretary.'

'I don't believe there's a girl.'

'No? Why not?'

'There are things you don't understand, Maggie. You know, at least, that he was Mallindaine's boy.'

'I dare say he goes with boys and girls regardless.'

'Amazing,' said Berto, obviously not much amazed.

'You should talk to him like a father, Berto.'

'Me?' he said. 'Look, I don't want any more to do with him. He's a whore. Coming into my house and raising his voice to my wife . . . Are you sure of what he said about Mary?'

'Well, he hinted. I don't remember the actual words.'

'He's a liar. I'm sorry.'

Maggie, suddenly unable to resist the impression that Berto had said 'I'm sorry' rather often, threw out a small bait. 'If we let him go, what could he say against *you*, Berto?'

'Anything,' he said. 'Anything. But it wouldn't be true, naturally.'

'Then we'll throw him out,' she said. 'Servants are a boring subject. So that's settled. Michael can drive him to the ferry.'

'He'll make a scandal of it,' Berto said. 'I think, in fact. he'll calm down.' He looked up to the ceiling. 'Michael seems to be dealing with him.' Berto was agitated, speaking softly and loudly by turns. Loudly now, he said, 'And he'd better apologize.'

Maggie said, 'I'm going to have a shower.' She put down her glass and got up, looking back at her empty chair. Berto stood up politely beside her, hovering and anxious to please. What a lot one can learn, she thought, just by sitting still for one hour in a chair. She recalled the long gaze of anger that had passed between Lauro and her husband a short while ago. It had been a knowing anger. She said to herself that she had not seen Berto lose his temper with the other servants or with any of his

202

business employees whatever their stupidity, or however much they lost theirs; Berto habitually subdued them by placing a thousand miles of ice between himself and them. On the other hand, she had seen him involved in brief shouting and glaring exchanges, like that with Lauro, when discussing a horse with his brother or politics with an acquaintance.

'Michael seems to have done the trick,' Maggie said, smiling as she went to the stairs. There was silence above. 'I'm sorry, Maggie,' said Berto as she left him.

Lauro came along the passage from the farther end, where his room was, and confronted her before she could reach her room. She put a finger to her lips. Michael threw open the door of his room, meanwhile. 'Mother,' he said, 'you upset Lauro.'

Mary appeared behind him. 'We have to call Lauro our secretary, Maggie,' she said. 'It's only fair.'

'I quite agree,' Maggie said. 'After all, Lauro is our secretary in a very real sense. A secretary is one who keeps secrets. What is the Italian for "secretary" anyway?'

Nobody answered her. She went into her room, glancing swiftly at Michael. God knows, she thought, what next to expect; anything might have been going on under my nose, anything. She took off her clothes and went to turn on her shower. But of course, she thought, it hasn't been under my nose. It's been somewhere I wasn't. Lauro with Mary. Lauro with Berto, of all people; Berto. Michael . . . God knows.

Berto, she mused to herself as she took her shower, is in love with me all the same. Mary and Michael I suppose love each other. Who loves Lauro? Who cares? And he knows he isn't loved in this little family; that's what the row was really about, I guess. She soaped her breasts and pummelled them between her fingers luxuriously. Lauro, she thought, knows a lot, and a man like that is useful to know.

By the evening their holiday guests, the Bernardinis, had returned with their English tutor from a three-day progress to various friends along the Amalfi coast. By the time Berto returned from the chemist's with medicine for Lauro's migraine, the visitors were sitting out on the terrace overlooking the sea. Berto handed the bottle of tablets to one of the maids and told her to take it to Lauro in his room: two with a glass of water; then he rubbed his hands, cheered up and kissed Letizia Bernardini and Nancy Cowan, once on each cheek, both girls. Then he went and fetched a shawl for Maggie.

At dinner they spoke of Hubert, and of Nemi to where they were all planning shortly to return. It was not in their minds at the time that this last quarter of the year they had entered, that of 1973, was in fact the beginning of something new in their world; a change in the meaning of property and money. They all understood these were changing in value, and they talked from time to time of recession and inflation, of losses on the stock-market, failures in business, bargains in real-estate; they habitually bandied the phrases of the newspaper economists and unquestioningly used the newspaper writers' figures of speech. They talked of hedges against inflation, as if mathematics could contain actual air and some row of hawthorn could stop an army of numbers from marching over it. They spoke of the mood of the stock-market, the health of the economy as if these were living creatures with moods and blood. And thus they personalized and demonologized the abstractions of their lives, believing them to be fundamentally real, indeed changeless. But it did not occur to one of those spirited and in various ways intelligent people round Berto's table that a complete mutation of our means of nourishment had already come into being where the concept of money and property were concerned, a complete mutation not merely to be defined as a collapse of the capitalist system, or a global recession, but such

a sea-change in the nature of reality as could not have been en-
visaged by Karl Marx or Sigmund Freud. Such a mutation that
what were assets were to be liabilities and no armed guards
could be found and fed sufficient to guard those armed guards
who failed to protect the properties they guarded, whether
hoarded in banks or built on confined territories, whether they
were priceless works of art, or merely hieroglyphics registered
in the computers. Innocent of all this future they sat round the
table and, since all were attached to Nemi, talked of Hubert.
Maggie had him very much on her mind and the wormwood
of her attention focused on him as the battle in the Middle East
hiccuped to a pause in the warm late October of 1973.

Letizia Bernardini, with her youth dedicated to an ideal
plan of territorial nationalism, had she been able to envisage
at that moment the reality to come would have considered it,
wrongly, to be a life not worth living. At any rate, at Berto's
table in Ischia that evening, Letizia conversationally em-
barked once more on the leaky ship of Hubert.

'There's a certain magic about him,' Letizia said, causing
Maggie to glare at her and her father to smile. 'There's something of the high priest about him,' Letizia went on. 'I want
to see more of him when we return to Nemi.'

Nancy Cowan said, 'I think he's pure fake.'

'What!' said Letizia.

'Why?' said Maggie at the same time as her husband said
'Fake what?'

One way and another, Nancy's quiet little words produced
an uproar of argument, all about Hubert, so that they hardly noticed the good food they were eating or heard the very
professional robbery of Maggie's summer jewels going on
upstairs in the meantime. Here are the details of the burglary:

Maggie's summer collection of jewellery was worth a
vast fortune, even although it was far less valuable than her

winter jewels, and considerably less again than the jewellery she kept in the bank summer and winter, except for the rarest and most important occasions. Her jewellery was difficult to insure against theft in any way that meant business; the insurance companies' requirements for so large a risk were not only so expensive as to defeat the purpose of insurance, but inconvenient as well. The companies insisted on the jewellery being housed in all types of safes and secured by innumerable safeguards, and even then were becoming more and more unwilling to insure jewellery of Maggie's sort. Generally, she avoided hotels and when she did stay in one she took very little jewellery, which she lodged in the hotel safe when she was not wearing it. Maggie's main problem was to prevent jewel-robberies at home. Burglar-alarms had become less and less effective as the burglars themselves became more and more adept at inventing, patenting, selling and subsequently exploiting them.

Two summers ago, Maggie had thought up a scheme to outwit the burglars, provoked as she had been at that time by a passing thief's discovery that she kept some of her jewels in a hot-water bottle. Her new scheme was to have a tiny kitchen built on an upper landing of every house she owned and frequented. This kitchen, complete with stove, refrigerator and sink, was ostensibly for the use of house-guests who wanted to be independent and who might take it into their heads to cook bacon and eggs in the middle of the night, or mix a drink. These upper kitchens were never used but were always elaborately stocked with food and drinks. They were always approached by a little step about four inches in height. This step was in reality a drawer, and in this drawer went Maggie's jewellery, unlocked and unnoticed.

Maggie had not been robbed for two years until this evening at Ischia during dinner. Lauro was sleeping off his migraine, heavily dosed with the pain-relieving drugs that Berto had brought from the chemist. The other servants were occupied downstairs with the serving. A boat drew up quietly and unremarked on the rocks below Maggie's villa from where a lift ascended to the top of the house. One man was left in the boat on the look-out. Two others, young in their T-shirts and blue jeans, went up in the lift with fixed and sad expressions on their faces. They got out precisely at the landing where the little upper kitchen stood. The dinner proceeded downstairs and Lauro slept heavily in his room.

They left the lift door open, went straight to the kitchen door and within a few seconds had opened the drawer in the step. They emptied it and stuffed most of it bulgily under their shirts. All the rest, enclosed in their leather cases, they held in their hands and tucked under their arms as they sadly and expertly descended to the waiting boat. This operation was the fruit of six weeks' research into Maggie's habits, casual questioning at local bars of builders connected with the latest construction of Maggie's upper kitchens, of boatmen connected with the villa, of unwitting servants who chattered about how ridiculous it was that the Marchesa had kitchens built at the top of her houses, always unused, and of simple deduction from a builder's boy's remark that she had quite unnecessarily called in a different builder from Milan to construct the step up to the kitchen. Summer jewellery though it was, the haul was high in the chronicles of summer robberies that year.

It was just towards the end of the dinner, with feelings and exchanges still vibrating across the table on the subject of Hubert, and Nancy Cowan quietly insisting that he was a fake, and Letizia rowdily defending him, with a murmur of scorn and an exclamation of despair here and there from Maggie, that the sound of an outboard-motor rapidly leaving the site of their landing-stage caused one of the servants to run out on the terrace and look over the cliff at the departing boat below. Suspicious of what he had seen he called out to one of the maids and ran to the lift. He pressed the button. Nothing happened. It was stuck down at sea-rock level, with the doors open.

It was when the maid returned to the terrace outside the dining-room window and started calling down vainly to Maggie's house-guards that the diners at the table were aware that something had happened.

'What's going on?' said Maggie, waving her arm towards the beautiful night outside the open French windows.

The maid and the manservant both appeared together in the dining-room, worried. 'There's a boat seems to have just left here, Marchesa. It left with great speed and we can't find the house-guards. Those boys are terrible. I always say they're negligent. They must have gone to a bar, Signora Marchesa.'

'Go down and find them,' said Maggie.

'And the lift doors have been left open,' said the girl. 'The lift's stuck downstairs.'

'Then go down the steps,' said Berto, rising, bothered by the fuss. The man and the girl made off across the terrace to the winding steps that led down the cliff to Maggie's rock-beach. Berto stood looking after them.

The boat had already disappeared across the bay, heading probably for another island or some remote inlet of the Neapolitan shore. Maggie said to the others at the table, 'Don't get up. Letizia, Nancy, go and get the fruit, please, will you? These servants are hysterical.' The cook had joined Berto on the terrace and was shouting inquiries to the maid and the manservant who had now reached the rock-beach. They were presently joined by those two of the five house-guards who were supposed to be on duty; they were amazed that their absence should have caused such a stir. Berto called roughly down to them to ask where they had been while the cook sent down vilifications of a rich and strange Italian variety.

Nancy and Letizia brought fruit and cheese to the table, but Maggie was standing now, and Emilio Bernardini with her, his pale smooth oval face gleaming beside her brown and splendid one. She looked from the terrace to him, then to the terrace again, and then back to Emilio, into his brown eyes behind his judicious spectacles. 'Do you know,' she said, 'I'm going upstairs to check my jewellery.' Emilio looked anxious but he smiled and said, 'Oh, I hardly think . . . '

Maggie was still upstairs when another visitor arrived, by car at the front door. He rang several times before Emilio let him in. A short man with very black dyed-looking hair and a taut, very cosmetically-surgeoned face. He seemed understandably surprised that no servants had appeared at the door to take his luggage and he greeted Emilio, who was obviously an old friend, with an absent-eyed geniality.

'Maggie's upstairs; she'll be down soon. The servants have made some mystery about an unknown boat that took off from the landing-stage in a hurry. Berto's down at the shore, investigating. Leave everything in the hall. Come in. Have you had dinner?'

The man said he had already eaten in Naples. Nancy and Letizia had left the table and were on their way down the sea-steps to join Berto and the servants. Emilio took his friend into the drawing-room where his son Pietro sat, sulkily uninterested in the fuss and ostentatiously unmoving. Emilio helplessly pressed a bell. As if in answer to it, Maggie appeared with her arms waving and her lips moving silently up and down in an effort of dumbstruck wild speech. Her arms waved and her dress glittered. On her arms and round her neck she wore the jewellery she had put on for dinner: bracelets and long necklaces of seashells which she had taken the whim to have set by a jeweller in conjunction with rubies and diamonds. These jewels. which were now all the summer jewellery she had left, made a sound like little dolls' teacups being washed up in some toy kitchen as her arms waved and her mouth gasped. She sat down on a sofa as Emilio came to help her. His friend had also stood up, quite bewildered by the whole business. Pietro sat still with a supercilious air.

'What happened, Maggie?' said Emilio, sitting down beside her.

Maggie pointed at the stranger, and this time her voice came through. 'Who is that?' she said, her pointing arm outstretched with its expensive shells.

'Maggie, what's happened? You've had a shock.'

'Who is he?' Maggie said. 'Call the police. Arrest him.'

'Maggie, don't you remember, you asked him to stay. He was expected, Maggie. What's wrong with you, my dear? This is my friend Coco de Renault.'

Berto returned followed by Letizia and Nancy. 'Nothing down there,' he reported. 'Someone took the lift down to the water and left the doors open. Must have been one of the servants, though of course they deny it.'

'Arrest him!' Maggie said, still pointing to Coco de Renault, who said, 'What the – '

'He's stolen my jewellery!' Maggie said.

At this moment Coco de Renault took charge. 'This lady,' he said gently, 'has had a shock.'

'I think so,' said Berto, while Emilio said, 'What's happened, Maggie?'

'My jewellery has gone,' Maggie said. 'It was upstairs in the kitchen step and it's gone. Call the police and arrest this man.'

210

But Coco de Renault was already pouring out a brandy and soda for Maggie. He came and stood over her like a doctor and said in a firm, almost harsh, voice, 'Drink this.' Maggie took the glass and drank. Monsieur de Renault then ordered the two girls to help Maggie stretch out on the sofa; on the strength of Maggie's words, 'My jewellery . . . the up-stairs kitchen . . . ' and assuming his hostess was unbalanced by nature and in a mixed-up mood, he ordered Berto to go up to Maggie's room and investigate, and he ordered Emilio into the kitchen to investigate. He then ordered Pietro to have his luggage taken to his room and unpacked. Maggie lay on the sofa, moaning. Looking cross, Berto none the less went upstairs and Emilio with alacrity went into the kitchen where the servants were complaining and arguing loudly amongst themselves. Pietro did not move from his chair but stretched out his hand and tinkled a little china bell which was to hand. 'The servants are spoilt in this house,' Pietro remarked.

Monsieur de Renault stood in the middle of the room watching his orders being executed. His head was poised like the conductor of an orchestra. Lauro then appeared in the doorway, bare-chested and bare-foot, wearing only his day-time jeans. 'Who are you?' said Coco de Renault.

'I'm the Marchesa's personal secretary,' said Lauro.

'Then go and put on some respectable clothes,' barked the stranger-in-charge. Lauro fled.

At this moment, Berto's voice preceded his footsteps down the staircase. 'There's been a robbery! Maggie's jewels have been taken from their hiding-place. Call the police, call the – '

'Call the police,' Coco de Renault said to Pietro. 'Quickly, your mother's jewellery – '

'She isn't my mother,' Pietro said.

'Then who are you?' said de Renault as if he owned the place, and his question was so imperative that it seemed to

211

include Berto himself who had now appeared in a state of agitation. Pietro said, 'I'm Bernardini's son,' and Berto said, 'I'm Tullio-Friole, the Marchesa's husband.' Pietro dialled the emergency number.

'How do you do?' said Coco de Renault to Berto. 'I'm Emilio's friend – '

'Oh, yes, Maggie was expecting you. I'm sorry about all this . . .'

Emilio returned from the kitchen and said, 'There's nothing missing from there. The servants are – '

'Please come immediately,' Pietro said into the telephone. 'Casa Tullio-Friole, the Marchese. There's been a robbery.'

Lauro appeared again, still half-dressed, and this time ready to express his summoned-up indignation. Maggie feebly pointed at Coco de Renault. 'He stole my jewellery . . .' she murmured.

'Maggie,' said Emilio patiently, 'this is Monsieur Coco de Renault, my friend from the Argentine whom you invited here. Your jewellery has been stolen by someone, probably common thieves who have got away by boat. Monsieur de Renault has just arrived in this distressing situation, but I'm naturally very embarrassed – '

'Maggie, Monsieur de Renault is our guest,' Berto said, while Nancy pressed a table napkin folded round ice from the drinks-trolley on to Maggie's forehead, and Letizia held her hand.

'I really am not embarrassed,' said de Renault. 'I understand shock. It's hardly conceivable that anyone would seriously take me for a jewel thief.'

The servants were questioned by the two policemen who presently arrived. Coco de Renault's documents were looked over as were Nancy Cowan's. The police took the numbers of the passports. They looked with a certain scorn at the drawer in the upstairs kitchen step. They expressed their doubts that the thieves would ever be found: 'The jewels will likely be broken up by now somewhere in the *quartieri* of Naples.' They inquired if the jewellery had been insured. Then they inquired why not. And on learning that its value was beyond the range of the insurance companies, exchanged glances. They assured Berto they would do their best, and Berto assured them, quietly, that there would of course be a reward if the jewellery should be found. The elder of the policemen exchanged some wry Italian colloquialisms with Berto: the stuff would never be found, and they knew it. Lauro, however, was taken away to the police station, in a fuming rage, to be questioned, much against Maggie's protestations but very much with Coco de Renault's approval.

'You can't trust *anybody*,' said de Renault when the police car had gone. And there was in fact this much in what he said, that he himself, within the next year, was to trick Maggie into handing over to him the bulk of her fortune, such a bulk as to make the more entirely absurd her concern about Hubert's occupancy of the house, or the little earnings of Lauro, or the theft, that evening, of her summer jewellery.

None the less, later that evening Maggie had so far recovered as to sit clanking her remaining bracelets on her arm as she reached for her drink, and asked Coco de Renault's advice as to how Hubert should be removed from the house at Nemi. Lauro returned from the police station by this time, soothed by the fact that Berto had followed the police car and had gone right into the office of the Commissioner himself to vouch for him, and had telephoned to the Prefect at Naples, and had altogether given Lauro such a good name as to be almost equal to promotion from private to general in the army. Lauro sat, now, in his jeans and the light cotton sweater he had put on to go to the police. He sat arrogantly, as arrogant as young Pietro.

'TRUTH,' SAID HUBERT, 'is not literally true. The literal truth is a common little concept, born of the materialistic mind.' He raised his right arm gracefully from the lectern before him, and with it the sleeve of his green and silver liturgical vestment. The raised arm seemed to signal an expectancy; the congregation obediently drew its breath; Hubert's eye rested on Pauline Thin in the third row, and he proceeded as if uttering a prophecy directed to all the world, but aimed especially at her.

'Brothers and sisters of Apollo and Diana,' Hubert went on, with his eyes focused defiantly on Pauline, 'we hear on all sides about the evil effects of inflation and the disastrous state of the economy. Gross materialism, I say. The concepts of property and material possession are the direct causes of such concepts as perjury, lying, deception and fraud. In the world of symbol and the worlds of magic, of allegory and mysticism, deceit has no meaning, lies do not exist, fraud is impossible. These concepts are impossible because the materialist standards of conduct from which they arise are non-existent. Ponder well on these words. Hail to the sacred Diana! Hail to Apollo!'

'Hail!' responded the assembly. 'All hail to Diana and Apollo!'

In the second row, the Jesuit Fathers Cuthbert and Gerard whispered together excitedly.

A little over a year had passed since the Middle East war of 1973, and Hubert was fairly flourishing on the ensuing crisis. He had founded a church. It cultivated the worship of Diana according to its final phases when Christianity began to overcast her image with Mary the Mother of God. It was the late Diana and the early Mary that Hubert now preached, and since the oil trauma had inaugurated the Dark Ages II he had acquired a following of a rich variety and ever more full of numbers.

It was the autumn of 1974 and Maggie had not succeeded in turning Hubert out of her villa, partly because she had been distracted throughout that year by little thumps of suspicion within her mind at roughly six-week intervals concerning the manipulation of her fortune, with all its ramifications from Switzerland to the Dutch Antilles and the Bahamas, from the distilleries of Canada through New York to the chain-storedom of California, and from the military bases of Greenland's icy mountains to the hotel business of India's coral strand. Brilliant Monsieur de Renault was now the overlord of Maggie's network. Mysterious and intangible, money of Maggie's sort was able to take lightning trips round the world without ever packing its bags or booking its seat on a plane. Indeed, money of any sort is, in reality, unspendable and unwasteable; it can only pass hands wisely or unwisely, or else by means of violence, and, colourless, odourless and tasteless, it is a token for the exchange of colours, smells and savours, for food and shelter and clothing and for representations of beauty, however beauty may be defined by the person who buys it. Only in appearances does money multiply itself; in reality it multiplies the human race, so that even money lavished on funerals is not wasted, neither directly nor indirectly, since it nourishes the undertaker's children's children as the body fertilizes the earth.

Anyway, back to Maggie's fortune: Coco de Renault had reorganized her financial network throughout the past year; he had made something of a masterpiece of it. Like so many others in that year he began using the new crisis terminology introduced by the current famous American Secretary of State; Coco de Renault's favourite word was 'global'. He produced an appealing global plan for Maggie's fortune, so intricate that it might have been devised primordially by the angels as a mathematical blueprint to guide God in the creation of the world. It was quite unfathomable, but Maggie, whose rich contemporaries were beginning to look at each other with wild alarm, at first felt a great satisfaction at having acted in time. She felt that brilliant Monsieur de Renault from the Argentine was a sort of perfected bomb-shelter. But as the months of 1974 passed from those of spring and summer into the autumn, she had experienced these intervals of anxiety, sudden little shocks. On one occasion she realized that her administration headquarters, which previously occupied an entire floor of offices in a New York block, with three full-time lawyers, twelve accountants and a noisy number of filing clerks and secretaries who fell silent on the few occasions that Maggie made a visitation thereupon, was now all disbanded. Pensions and parting gifts had been bestowed on the staff. The lately administering lawyers had lawsuits pending against Maggie for breach of contract, but Coco de Renault was dealing with such trivial nuisances out of court. Coco explained to Maggie, the first time she had one of her little shocks on realizing her estate had no business headquarters any more, that a headquarters was the very thing she had to avoid. He was her headquarters and she must realize he was dealing with her affairs globally. Maggie calmed down. Another time, she failed to find him on any of his telephone numbers on the globe. She went frantic, rattling the receiver for long hours over a period of three days and a half, in the course of which a strike of the international telephone service took place in the Veneto, from where she was calling. Vainly dialling the Minister of Posts and Telegraphs in Rome, Maggie looked out of the window of Berto's Palladian villa and saw her husband talking to the groom as if the world were not coming to an end. It came to her that if she were to die there would be an enormous lachrymose funeral with the Italian nobility speeding up to the Veneto to attend it and lay her in Berto's family tomb; then two days later Berto would be out in the garden as usual talking to the groom, while her son Michael would be busy on the question of her fortune. Maggie drove off to Venice and booked into an hotel from where she tried to telephone to Coco. The strike on the international exchange still prevailed. She looked out of the window and saw a placard which said 'The Postal Strike of the Veneto Must Be Confronted Globally'. She remained frantic after the strike was over, and still in the hotel room tried one number after another in search of Coco and her power of attorney. She tried San Diego, California, Port au Prince, Hong Kong, London, Zürich, Geneva and St Thomas in the Virgin Islands. Then she tried Madras. She had been in Venice two days when Berto called her to ask what she was doing. Had she been to the del Macchis' masked ball? How was Peggy? She said she was trying to find Coco de Renault. He replied that he thought there had been a call from de Renault if he wasn't mistaken. Maggie returned to the villa and located Coco within a few more agonizing days. The fear passed once more. 'I've been at Nemi, at Emilio Bernardini's,' he said, and laughed at the news that she had looked for him everywhere.

These distractions took her mind off Hubert but every now and again she was brought back to her frustration over his stubborn occupancy of the house. At the beginning of the summer of 1974 unknown to Berto she had handed the whole story of Hubert, in her own revised version, to an obscure lawyer in Rome, with instructions to get Hubert out of the house and to do it without a scandal. The lawyer promptly agreed to do it, and not only did he point out that the new Italian laws made it difficult to turn anyone out of any habitation whatsoever, but he exaggerated the difficulties. Maggie duly paid the man the large deposit he demanded to match the exceptional difficulties of the job he had undertaken. As it happened, this lawyer, having sentimental sympathies towards the political left wing, although no longer the extreme leftist he had been in his poor student days, loathed what he conceived Maggie to stand for at the same time as he was put into an ambivalent state of excitement by her glowing and wealthy presence. The one time she presented herself with her case in his absolutely ordinary office became an obsessive memory; as the months passed and the unseen presence of Maggie lingered here and there, with her voice on the phone to remind him on the one hand of his undertaking and, on the other, of her vital self and her money, his office and his life seemed in his eyes to be even more sad and ordinary. So that he was more short-tempered now, with his wife and with his secretary, than before. The secretary, indeed, left and he had to make do with another, inferior one; meantime Maggie was living her life all unaware of the effect she had produced on the lawyer. As to getting Hubert out of the house, the lawyer had written him a letter in a somewhat vague manner. Hubert had sent it back scrawled at the bottom with the message, 'Mr Hubert Mallindaine is at a loss to understand this missive and, assuming that it is misdirected, returns it to the sender.'

'You see,' explained the lawyer on the telephone to Maggie, 'he knows well the Italian laws. If you take out a court order even, this makes two years before you can disencumber him.

He will make the newspaper scandal that your husband fears and he might win the case if he proves that the house was built by his instructions for his own use. The laws are now on the side of the tenant, always. And if he loses the case everyone will assume he has been your *amante* and you are tired of him.'

'Don't you know,' Maggie said, 'there's a big recession on? We can't afford to give away houses and there is valuable furniture inside. My Louis XIV furniture . . .'

'You have said he had them restored?'

'I believe he's looking after my things. Yes. There's a Gauguin painting, too. I want it.'

'If he is spending money to care for the property he could argue that the property was his, else why should he spend the money?'

'Are you my lawyer or his?' Maggie said.

'Marchesa, I see the case objectively and I will try. I have my heart's sympathy with your side. Everyone knows what our laws are like in the world of today. I have landlords and proprietors at my office lamenting every day that they cannot remove their tenants and they cannot raise the rents – '

'But he's paying no rent, and it's fully furnished, my house.'

'That is all the more argument for him. Marchesa, you permitted him to stay too long. Now is probably too late, in effect. In effect, I will try and I can only promise to continue to try. If you are not satisfied with my efforts, Marchesa – '

'Oh, please carry on. Please do. I quite understand the difficulties,' Maggie said. 'But I have many problems just at this terrible moment in the economical situation of the world and I do wish to have the house to be near my son.'

'The law says that if you already have a habitation, Marchesa, you cannot evict a tenant on the grounds that you need the house. Only if you are homeless – '

'I know. I know. Go ahead, please; I have complete faith in you – '

'If you would care to lunch with me on your visit to Rome, I could better explain my plan of next procedure, or you could call in again at my office – '

'No, it won't be necessary – '

'It would be a pleasure. Or could I come to visit you at the Veneto? It is a country I well know – '

'What do you mean, "country"? It's still in Italy.'

'That is our manner of speaking. In Italy are many countries. I would be happy to visit – '

'Just at the moment I can't make plans,' Maggie said. 'Please go on trying and keep in touch with me.'

The lawyer wrote again to Hubert, a strong firm letter, cunningly phrased with many citations of law, number this and section that, including the commas. It was the sort of letter that would send the civil courts of Italy into a frenzy of sympathy for the tenant, at the same time as it left the lawyer professionally irreproachable. To this bureaucratic communication Hubert replied from the local bar at Nemi, by telephone.

'Look,' he said to the lawyer, 'this house is mine. The lady gave it to me. I've nowhere else to go. Why don't you just take me to court?'

'What number are you calling from?' said the wary lawyer, anxious about a possible telephone tap.

'The bar,' said Hubert, 'here at Nemi. Can't you hear the noise? I can't afford a telephone at my house. The Marchesa had it cut off.'

'Tell me the number and I'll call you back,' said the lawyer. He checked the number that Hubert gave him, and rang back to the bar.

'Now,' said the lawyer, 'it's like this. I have to do my duty, and I have sent you a letter. You have nothing to worry about.'

'I have plenty of things to worry about,' Hubert said, 'but the house isn't one of them. Why do you send me these absurd letters?'

'I am at the Marchesa's command,' the lawyer said. 'You want my advice? You write me a reply that you are not well and enclose a medical certificate. When you are recovered you will see your lawyer.'

'I'm in the best of health,' Hubert said. 'No doctor would give me a certificate, and anyway, I don't know any doctor in Italy.'

'Write me the letter,' said the lawyer, 'and I will arrange for the certificate.'

'This is unusually kind of you,' Hubert said. 'Why don't you come here and have a chat? I should be delighted to show you my house and my wooded grounds. And then, after all, I don't know how far involved you are with Maggie. I'd like to be reassured.'

The lawyer, who was fat, laughed with the full fruition of the fat. 'Sunday,' he said, 'I could make a little escape and getaway. After lunch, Sunday. Good?'

'Good,' said Hubert.

By the autumn, all the Louis XIV chairs had been replaced by very beautiful fakes, the Gauguin had been replaced by a copy for which Hubert had paid a very high price, but not, of course, a price of such an altitude as that fetched by the Gauguin, now safely smuggled into Switzerland. He had also replaced a Constable with a fair enough copy, the original of which, in any case, had been kept in a dark corner so that the many fine points of difference between this and the fake were obscured by the gloom. A Sickert painting still awaited treatment because the price of a good copy was by now reaching excessively blackmail proportions and Hubert was investigating another organization which provided a discreet art-copyist and export service. He had similar plans for an inoffensive Corot in the lavatory, with its little red blot in the right foreground, and also an umbrageous Turner which, although it was small, overpowered the wall of the upstairs landing, but this, one of the experts in clandestinity had informed Hubert, was already a fake; an expensive fake, but not marketable enough to have copied.

In this way, Hubert was very comfortably off by the time the collapse of money as a concept occurred. 'I refuse,' he said, 'to eke out my existence or change my philosophy of life according to the cost of oil per barrel – '

All the same, he took care to continue changing the locks on the doors of the house frequently. He did not flaunt his newly-acquired money. The telephone remained cut off, the garden was weeded to the minimum and the paint on the outside doors and windows was left to peel and flake with poverty.

The expert self-faker usually succeeds by means of a manifest self-confidence which is itself by no means a faked confidence. On the contrary, it is one of the few authentic elements in a character which is successfully fraudulent. To such an extent is this confidence exercised that it frequently over-rides with an orgulous scorn any small blatant contradictory facts which might lead a simple mind to feel a reasonable perplexity and a sharp mind to feel definite suspicion.

Pauline Thin's mind was not particularly sharp. But in her second year as Hubert's companion and secretary she had acquired enough experience of him, of his documents and his daily sayings, that she couldn't fail to realize that something was amiss between Hubert's claims and the facts. It was just when, with the aid of his new ally, Maggie's plump lawyer, Hubert had founded his religious organization that Pauline had discovered among Hubert's papers clear evidence that his aunts, infatuated by Sir James Frazer and his *Golden Bough*, had been in correspondence with the quack genealogist; they had instructed him in the plainest terms to establish their descent from the goddess Diana.

Hubert had looked Pauline straight in the eyes and with some arrogance informed her that she was misreading his aunts' intention, that she was terribly ignorant on some matters, but that he entertained many fond feelings for her, none the less.

Impressed by his cool confidence Pauline read the letters again, and was again dumbfounded. And once more, Hubert, actually looking over the batch of letters that Pauline had placed in his very hands, said only that she was a nice little fool, threw them aside, and went off about some other business.

It was the next day, at the meeting of the Brothers and Sisters of Diana and Apollo, that Hubert was preaching his sermon on the nature of truth. He had turned the dining-room, which led off the entrance hall beyond the terrace, into a chapel. The new world which was arising out of the ashes of the old, avid for immaterialism, had begun to sprout forth its responsive worshippers.

'Truth,' Hubert repeated as he wound up his sermon, his eyes bending severely on Pauline, 'is not literally true. Truth is never the whole truth. Nothing but the truth is always a lie. The world is ours; it is in metaphorical terms our capital. I remember how my aunts, devotees as they were of Diana and Apollo, used always to say, "Never, never, touch the capital. Live on the interest, not on the capital." The world is ours to conserve, and ours are the fruits thereof to consume. We should never consume the capital, ever. If we do, we are left with the barren and literal truth. Let us give praise to Diana, goddess of the moon, goddess of the tides, the Earth-mother of fertility, and to Apollo, the sun and the ripener, her brother. Hail to Diana! Hail to Apollo!'

'Hail!' said the majority of his congregation, while Father Cuthbert Plaice whispered to his fellow-Jesuit Gerard, 'There's a lot of truth in what he says.'

'I like the bit about the earth being our capital,' replied Gerard, ever ecologically minded, 'but he mixes it up with a lot of shit, doesn't he?'

'Oh, well,' said Cuthbert, 'it's like manure and even if it's shit it gets people thinking about religion, doesn't it?'

'Yes, I suppose it's an experience, isn't it?'

Hubert, splendid as a bishop *in pontificalibus*, folded in his vestments of green and silver, proceeded up the aisle giving his benediction to right and left before disappearing into the downstairs bathroom which had now been transformed into a vestry.

'Miss Thin,' said Hubert as Pauline came in behind him, 'remind me to apply for an unlisted, repeat unlisted, telephone number.'

XI

'THE TROUBLE WITH BERTO,' Maggie said quietly to Mary, 'is that his *tempo* is all wrong. He starts off *adagio, adagio*. Second phase, well, you might call it *allegro ma non troppo* and pretty nervy. Third movement, a little passage *con brio*. Then comes a kind of righteous and dutiful *larghetto*, sometimes accompanied by a bit of high-pitched *recitativo*, and he goes on, *lento*, you know, *andante, andante* until suddenly without warning three grunts and it's all over. What kind of an art of love is that?'

'Rhythm is very, very important,' said Mary reflectively, 'in every field of endeavour. What is the *recitativo* bit?'

'I don't understand dialect Italian,' Maggie said. 'Ordinary Italian is difficult enough, but this is some sort of dialect that Berto uses on these particular occasions. Afterwards he talks about horses, how a horse may go off his feed from too much exercise or too little or how sometimes horses get lumps on their skin from over-exercise or under-exercise, I forget which. Anyway, he frequently talks about horses afterwards. What kind of an art of love is that?'

'I could tell you a lot about Michael,' Mary said, 'but as he's your son it makes an obstacle.'

'I hardly think of him as my son any more,' Maggie said. 'Michael can be very inconsiderate. I think of him more as his father's son and if he's anything like Ralph Radcliffe then you have a problem there. Ralph was a problem but very, very attractive. Berto is no problem at all, but it's boring to go to bed with him, especially when you're my age. In your case you have your whole lifetime in front of you.'

'Not all of it,' Mary said. 'I feel I'm wasting my best years sometimes, and I know Michael's got a girl in Rome, too. But I want to make a success of my marriage, I really do.'

'You can always take time off,' said Maggie, 'while Michael's in Rome with the girl.'

'Well, I wouldn't like to.'

'You must think I'm pretty dumb,' said Maggie, 'if you think I don't know that you take time off with Lauro.'

Mary said, 'Oh, no! This is terrible. You mustn't say such a thing.'

'Keep calm,' said Maggie. 'Nobody else knows anything about you and Lauro.'

The girl started to cry. 'I wanted my marriage to be a success.'

'Go on wanting it, is my advice,' said Maggie, while Mary dried her tears on a paper tissue from the box beside her and drank a large gulp of her vodka and soda, spilling some of it on her body.

They were in bathing suits on the concealed sun-terrace of Berto's Palladian villa in the Veneto in the spring sunshine of 1975. They lay side by side on the dark blue mattresses soaking up the sunny vitamins of May in the hours between noon and lunch at two. Maggie reached out for her body lotion and smeared it over her legs, her breasts and shoulders, then, playfully, she smeared the remainder on her hands over Mary's belly, so that the girl became less nervy; she lay back somewhat becalmed and murmured solemnly, 'Lauro doesn't mean anything to me.'

'He satisfies the appetite,' said Maggie, 'but not the passions, I agree.'

A bright smile came suddenly to her face as Lauro himself appeared on the terrace, carrying a mute transistor radio and a bottle of Vermouth. 'Why, Lauro!' she said, 'I thought you were taking the morning off.'

'I shouldn't have come to this house at all. I repent it. The staff is terrible. They are vulgar domestics. They hate me. I came to help you out. I should have stayed at Nemi where I work for Mary and Michael. I am not obliged to follow the family.'

'Oh, Lauro, you can go back to Nemi any time you like,' Mary said.

He removed his white coat, put the bottle on the drinks trolley and stretched on a mattress beside them, and then got some pop music on his radio.

'God, Berto will see you, Lauro!' said Maggie. 'And I'll get the blame for fraternizing.'

Lauro threw the radio to the other end of the terrace where it stopped playing; he jumped up in a neurotic fit, spitting Italian obscenities, put on his white coat, and left.

'Well, I've finished with him as a person,' Mary said. 'He really means to get married to that girl in Nemi.'

'You'd better keep him on as a houseman,' Maggie said. 'Trained servants are hard to get. And he is well trained, you know.'

So much could be recounted about the winter past, so many sudden alarms as to the whereabouts of Coco de Renault and so many frantic messages sent by telex to non-existent offices far away; always, Coco turned up with an explanation and enough ready money to put Maggie back in a stable frame of mind.

He had on one occasion gently and consolingly hinted that she was the victim of the menopause, and this act of stupidity on his part nearly finished his relationship with Maggie, so violently did she react. Berto had to intervene and explain away Coco's mistake. He told Maggie that Coco was probably in love with her. 'This is a way in which a man in love tries to provoke a woman,' he told Maggie. 'When there is no hope for him, he provokes.' And to Coco, privately, he said, 'If what you think is true, as it probably is, then the last thing you should suggest is the truth, since the truth is the original irritant.' Coco meekly humoured Maggie and presently told her that her financial affairs were blooming only a little less than her lovely self.

There had been so many bad scenes that past winter with Lauro, and a cruise with Mary and Michael for Christmas in the Caribbean, followed by a week together in New York where Berto joined them. Berto now expressed strong doubts about Coco's integrity and escorted them home. Maggie defended Coco expansively; Coco was nagging her to have her portrait painted by a young artist friend of his.

And all along, Maggie had reverted to her passion for evicting Hubert from the house at Nemi. So much could be recounted. 'Eras pass,' said Hubert, in the new comfort of his life, 'they pass.' He had just read in the newspaper of 15 February that year that Julian Huxley and P. G. Wodehouse were dead: 'The passing of an era . . .' the newspapers had commented.

But this day in May 1975, in the sun of the north Italian spring, chose itself from among those others to be that sort of day when complications ripen, since inevitably there is always one particular day when discoveries come to being, when incidents put out shoots and start to bring into force from the winter's potentialities the first green blades of a crisis. Maggie and Mary stretched out on the sun-terrace before lunch while downstairs the probabilities foregathered to form what are the most probable events of all, which is to say, the improbable ones.

Meantime, Maggie said to Mary, 'We should go off to Nemi soon. I have to get Hubert out of the house. The Church authorities should be on my side. He's committing a great sacrilege in my house with that cult of his. He's got to be exposed, because of course he's sheer fake.'

'I'd like to go to one of the meetings,' Mary said. 'If only I could do so in disguise. You know, Letizia Bernardini says the services are terribly elating, really like magic.'

'Could we both go in disguise?' Maggie said.

'He'd be sure to find out. He's very, very discerning,' Mary said.

'I could kill that man, I really could,' said Maggie. 'It isn't so much the property, it's the idea of being done down that makes me furious with him.'

'Yes, and he wasn't even your lover,' said Mary, egging her on as usual, since the theme of Hubert had become one of Mary's favourite serialized entertainments.

'He wouldn't know what to do with a woman,' Maggie said. Twelve guests for dinner tonight; with Michael, Mary, herself and Berto that made sixteen. There were dinner parties practically every night. New friends, old friends visiting Italy from America, old and new friends of Berto's. Maggie sat for Coco's young artist; then it was Mary's turn. 'He's got you both out of focus,' Berto had said. In a world of jumping sequences, the problem of Hubert was a point of continuity, although Maggie herself had no idea how gratefully she clung to it.

Berto's Palladian villa was a famous one. It had been photographed from the beginning of photography and, before that, etched, sketched, painted, minutely described inside and out, poetically laboured upon, visited by scholars and drooled over by the world's architects. The Villa Tullio was indeed a beauty; the Villas Foscari, Emo, Sarego, D'Este, Barbaro, Capra, with their elegant and economical delights still in comparison with the smaller Villa Tullio, seemed to some tastes to be more in the nature of architectural projects and propositions. The Villa Tullio was somehow magically complete and at rest. It was a farm-house built for the agricultural industry of the original Tullios, for the charm of its position beside a reclaimed waterway and the civilized comfort of Berto's prosperous ancestors. Now, the plans of this house, every angle, every detail of its structure, being known throughout the world, photographs of the interior and exterior, and the original plan of the lay-out from every side having been published for centuries in studious manuals and picture books, it was hardly worth the while or the price for a gang of expert thieves to send their men to case the lay-out. However, they did.

It was ten minutes past twelve when two smart-looking men drove up to the marvellous front door in a white touring car. On to the upper balcony came Berto from the library where he had been glooming behind the French windows. Out he came into the shadows cast by the sweetness and light of that harmonious pediment. He did not recognize the people. They were too early for lunch, and therefore probably were not friends of Maggie's. Most likely, then, they were visitors come to inquire if they could see the house. Berto's arrangements for sightseers were very haphazard. He kept no porter at the lodge. While he was away his old butler was accustomed to use his sixth sense as to whom he admitted into the house and whom he sent away. There were no regular visiting days as had been established in the grand and more famous buildings of Palladio. Mostly, the visitors who wanted to see over the villa wrote in advance, or were written for by their universities or, as it might be, some friend of Berto's family. It was well known that Berto had changed nothing of the structure; only, over the years, in the interior, had new drainage systems been installed and bathrooms fitted in.

Berto was proud of his Palladian jewel, and his heart bent towards the two arrivals with such a desire that they should be educated tourists wanting to see the house that he invested them at first sight with various nice qualities. They mounted the fine steps, a tall, white-haired man and an equally tall youth, presentably dressed in fresh shirts and pale trousers; they approached the house with the right visitors' modesty and lost themselves under the balcony where Berto hovered and awaited their ring of the door-bell.

After a few seconds, during which Berto imagined them to be admiring the portico, that harmonious little temple, and the well-calculated panorama therefrom, the bell rang. Berto withdrew from the porch into the library and heard below the shuffle of Guillaume going to open the door. Guillaume was the old butler, who had been brought as a small boy from Marseilles sixty-two years ago by Berto's father and who, having had no surname that he knew of, was long since equipped with one: Marsigliese; he fairly ran the villa, and Berto who had grown up under his eye rarely questioned his judgement. Berto enjoyed with Guillaume a kind of reciprocal telepathy by which Berto understood precisely which of his friends Guillaume meant when he said that the French had telephoned, or the Germans had called, or that the Romans might be arriving, although, in fact, Berto had a good number of friends who might fit each definition. Guillaume Marsigliese likewise knew exactly which Americans were expected to dinner when Berto said he had invited 'the Americans'; no doubt there was a slightly different inflection of their voices for each designation, but no friend discussed between them in that way was ever confused with another. 'The Americans' also covered Mary and Michael, and, before her marriage to Berto, Maggie.

Now Guillaume had started to climb the beautiful sweeping staircase and Berto, to save him the fatigue, came out of the library door to meet him, leaning over the well of the circling banister.

Guillaume looked up. 'People,' he announced, without further elaboration – '*Gente*', by which he conveyed that the visitors were, as Berto plainly expected, people who wanted to see over the house. And the fact that he had invited them to wait inside and given them some hope that Berto would receive them demonstrated that he considered the newcomers not, so far, unworthy, without committing himself further to the road of positive approval.

'A few moments,' Berto said, giving himself time to put away the papers he had been studying and the visitors time, no doubt, to admire the care that had gone into the maintenance of the villa inside and out, starting with the hall and its superb outlook.

'Go down and tell them to wait.' His commands to the servants always struck Maggie and Mary as being on the abrupt and haughty side: they felt embarrassed and guilty when Berto gave orders to his old butler especially. But to Guillaume's ears Berto's tone was perfectly normal; the old man judged only what his master said, whether it was sensible or not sensible. Guillaume's life had been considerably upset by the fraternization that went on between Lauro and the Americans. Now, he turned and shuffled to the hallway, deeming Berto's orders to be sensible.

Berto descended in his own time and, courteously shaking hands with each of the men, inquired their names. At the same time he took in the well-silvered hair and the interesting light blue and white fine stripes of his trousers, the jacket of which he held over his arm. The younger man, who wore well-tailored fawn trousers of some uncrushable and impeccable material, was holding a shiny slim catalogue of an artistic nature. They gave their names, apologized for the intrusion, and asked if they might see over the exquisite villa. They bore no resemblance whatsoever to Caliban the beast, with intent to rape and destroy Prospero's daughter who, some have it, represents the precious Muse of Shakespeare. 'Come along,' said Berto. 'With pleasure, come along.' The younger man left his catalogue on the hall table, while Guillaume came forward to take the older man's jacket from his arm.

Meanwhile Maggie, on the sun-terrace, turned over her splendid body, winter-tanned from the Caribbean, and lay on her belly; she continued smoothing her arms with sun-tan oil. 'I want my house at Nemi and my furniture and my pictures,' she said. 'It's a simple thing to ask. That man makes me have bloody thoughts; they drip with blood.'

'Do you think he's practising some kind of magic?' Mary said.

'We ought to go to the police. But Berto's so conservative,' Maggie said. 'Berto would prefer magic to a scandal.'

Lauro appeared once more, and sulkily ambled over to where he had thrown the transistor radio. He picked up the battered object, tried it, shook it, opened it and readjusted the batteries, but apparently it was dead from violence. He threw it back on the terrace floor and went to pour himself a drink.

'Where is my husband?' Maggie said, nervously.

'Showing visitors over the house.'

'What visitors?'

'I don't know. They just came and asked to see the house. Guillaume let them in. Two men, well-dressed.'

'Berto will get us all killed one day,' Maggie said. 'They are all well-dressed. They could be armed. We could all be tied up and shot through the head while they loot the place.'

Mary dipped into her bag for her powder-compact and lipstick. She combed her long hair.

'Your husband is too much a gentleman,' Lauro told Maggie, 'and old Guillaume is too much an old bastard in all the senses of the word. He never knew his parents. He was off the streets. No family.'

'What recommendations do they have?' Maggie said. 'Who sent them?'

'I don't know. Perhaps nobody. They are art historians.'

'They are all art historians,' Maggie said. 'You read about them every day in the papers. And look what happened to me the summer before last at Ischia.'

'Those were boys from Naples,' Lauro said. 'These men here are Americans.'

'I wouldn't be surprised if Berto doesn't ask them to stay to lunch,' said Maggie.

Mary closed her powder-compact. 'There are only six of us for lunch today. Two more won't make any difference.'

'They could tie us all up, shoot us, take everything,' Maggie said.

'I got a gun,' Lauro said. 'Don't worry. I go now and get my gun.'

'Oh, we don't want any shooting!' said Mary. 'Please don't start carrying revolvers in the house. It makes me jumpy.'

'Lauro's wonderful,' said Maggie, standing up like a brown statue in her gleaming white two-piece bathing suit. She swung her orange striped towel wrap from the back of a chair and put it on, haughtily. Mary got up too, lean and long. 'I'm going down to the pool for a swim,' she said as she too wrapped herself up neatly in a bathrobe.

234

'I'm going to my room,' Maggie said. 'One thing they can't do is see over my bedroom. I just won't have it, even if it is one of the most interesting sections of the upper floor.'

'I bring you a drink at the pool, Mary,' Lauro said.

'Lauro, you're sweet.'

They descended from the sun-terrace together, listening for voices but hearing none.

'In fact,' Mary said, 'I think I heard them outside. Berto must be showing them the grounds.'

'Well, if you're keen to see them try to get rid of them before lunch,' said Maggie. 'I don't want them to stay.' She swung into the little lift that descended to her room.

'Maggie,' said Berto, 'these gentlemen are staying to lunch.'

Two middle-aged women, Berto's cousins who were expected to lunch, had already arrived and Maggie saw the two unfamiliar men chatting easily with them in the hall. The younger man was saying 'Byzantium was a state of mind . . .'

Maggie came over regally to be introduced, on her way passing the console table where the young man had left his catalogue. Mary stood with her back to it and when she saw Maggie she murmured, 'The damn pool water wasn't heated – the gardener forgot – '

'How are you? Come on in,' said Maggie to her husband's cousins, and then she held out her hand to welcome the new visitors who stood with Berto. The little group at the console table parted and Maggie's eye caught the picture on the cover of the catalogue just as she had her hand in the elder art historian's. She let her hand drop and her smiling mouth formed a gasp. 'What's this?' she said, grabbing the catalogue.

It bore on its lovely cover, in tasteful print, the name Neuilles-Pfortzheimer, a Swiss auction house famous among collectors of paintings and fine arts. Under this was a reproduction of an Impressionist painting. 'What's this?' Maggie shrieked, and the circle of friends around her stood back a little as if in holy dread. 'What's *what*?' said Berto looking over her shoulder.

'My Gauguin!' Maggie said. 'It was in my house at Nemi. What is it doing in this catalogue? Is it up for sale?'

The younger of the visiting art historians said, 'Why, that was sold last week. We were there. You must be mistaken, ma'am.'

'How can I be mistaken?' Maggie screamed. 'Don't I know my own Gauguin? There's the garden seat and the shed.'

Everyone spoke at once with ideas pouring forth: ring the police; no, never the police, you don't want *them* to know what you've got; get your lawyer; ring the gallery, yes, call Neuilles-Pfortzheimer, I know the director well; I know Alex Pfortzheimer; call your home at Nemi, who is the caretaker? . . . 'Art thieves!' Maggie screamed, pointing at the two visitors who looked decidedly uncomfortable, having come predominantly to find the best means of entry to the little Chinese sitting-room with its rare collection of jade, to plan a future jewel-robbery at least, and certainly they were alert also to where Maggie's room, with its wall-safe, was situated, since it was known she had taken her large ruby pendant, part of the diaspora of the Hungarian crown jewels, out of the bank to wear to one or two of the season's balls, even though she ostentatiously insisted, as was the fashion, that it was a fake. The visitors had also noted, with an eye to its whereabouts, Berto's sublime Veronese about which they had already heard, at the top of the staircase. They were innocent, however, of Maggie's Gauguin and the more she cried out against them, there in the graceful hall among the astonished friends, the more it seemed how demonstrably wronged the strangers were; the only discomfort in the affair, for them, was the risk involved should the police be called in, for they were already in some embarrassment in France.

Berto looked at them and said, quietly, 'I *am* sorry. I do apologize. My wife is distraught,' at the same time as he put his arm round Maggie as if to protect her from the menaces of a malignant spirit.

Mary joined the group and, shortly, Michael too, seeming, as he more and more frequently did, that he had too much on his mind to take notice of a domestic emergency. He eyed his watch. Mary was looking rather enviously at Berto's gesture of concern for Maggie, for in fact he looked very handsome at those moments of spontaneous charm belonging as it did to his own type and generation; it did not occur to Mary how silly Michael would have looked, how affected, bending his eyes upon herself as Berto bent his, so frankly with love, over Maggie. She only admired handsome Berto and envied Maggie who, pouring out her accusations, did not, in Mary's view, really deserve so fine a solicitude. If Mary had suspected the theft of any of her property she would have gone about it silently and with a well-justifiable slyness. Maggie, in the meantime, shrieked on, and Berto murmured over her as if she greatly mattered in the first place, the guests in his house next, and the Gauguin not at all.

Lunch was delayed forty minutes, but the hubbub had been whisked away little by little by Berto's tactics, and the guests had been waved into the green sitting-room, had been served drinks and their several troubled souls variously feather-dusted, while Maggie, refusing her room, lay on a sofa and allowed herself also to be somewhat becalmed. Berto was considerably aided in his efforts by the two cousins, women of authority and many wiles, who had pulled themselves together quickly for the purpose of family solidarity and the pressing need to avoid the threat of a lawsuit against themselves for defamation of character. Quite soon the embarrassed art historians were given new courage, full explanations, and were begged to stay; the elder remained slightly nervous, but both magnanimously overlooked Maggie's accusations which, from her sofa, she blurted out from time to time, ever more feebly, for thirty-odd minutes. A short space, and they went into lunch.

Berto had refused to do anything whatsoever about the Gauguin mystery before lunch. 'Later, later, it must wait,' he said. 'If the picture is stolen . . . well, first we have to make a plan of inquiry, and first we sit down and have a drink before lunch. Maggie, my dear . . . Love, be tranquil. We have a drink, all. Only the worst can happen. Only the worst . . . It is not so very terrible . . . The worst is always happening to many people everywhere. And only the worst can happen, Maggie, my dear.'

Now they sat in the perfect dining-room overlooking the artificial lake. Berto looked attentively towards his cousin Marisa; she was the newsbearer, grand as a Roman statue and anxious to get these pettifogging hysterics of Maggie's over and done with so that she could impart news of the world that mattered to the assembled company, whether they understood what she was talking about or not; for Marisa's world concerned the heavily populated cousinship of their family, and only she could know which of their Colonna cousins was in love with which Lancelotti, and how much the dowry would be; only Marisa could know who was expected to inherit when the ancient Torlonia should die, probably within the next few days; she alone knew that the Baring nephews had been staying in Paris with the Milanese Pignatellis in an endeavour to find a settlement about the companies in Switzerland; all this Marisa only was able to know since only she had the mornings on the telephone with a family information service from all parts. Very often, when the family themselves failed to telephone or were not to be found at home, she would get the required information from an old housekeeper. All these facts she was waiting to impart to Berto and her other cousin, the thin religious widow Viola, at lunch, for she had a strong sense of what was right for lunch, what to eat, what to wear, what to say; she expected fully that these family concerns would enthral every listener; if not, what were the strangers doing at Berto's table? She was as confident of the fascination of her subject to everyone as were the ancient dramatists who held their audiences with incessant variations on the activities of the gods and heroes of legend. And indeed, such was her confidence that she did manage to hold the attention of the outsider, for however unintelligible the substance of her talk she brought a sense of glamorous realism to the Italian mythology of the old families.

Maggie had brought her glass of strong rye whisky to the table, trembling still, but settling somewhat under the influence of Berto's solicitude and induced into an effort of self-control by a determination not to be overborne by the tourist-attraction, Marisa. Maggie now sat gleaming in her shaken beauty at the top of the oval table. On her right was the elder of the intruders who had been pressed to stay for lunch, and who went by the name of Malcolm Stuyvesant. Next to him, Mary, with Berto on her other hand, and next to Berto at the other end of the table his other cousin, the black-dressed pale little Princess Viola Borgognona, very thin of neck among her strings of seed-pearls; Viola was agog to hear Marisa's new serial in the family saga, for it always gave her an excuse to be morally scandalized and to recall the family scandals, misalliances and intrigues of the past.

She, like Berto, was aware that this inter-family talk had little relevance to the world of foreign visitors or of newcomers to the family, but she felt that it should be common knowledge even if it wasn't and, anyway, it was plain that people were not bored by it. Marisa had already started talking. 'Dino is sure to get married again when the year is up. He goes every morning to the cemetery, and then rides with Clementine, but of course the parents think he's too old. What can one say?' She turned appealingly to her neighbours, Michael on her left and then, on her right, to the younger of the two intruders, George Falk by name. 'What can one say?' she asked first one and then the other.

Berto, however, was still concerned for Maggie, and now started on a course that was distinctively his own and which he reserved for occasions when the atmosphere required to be soothed. It consisted of the introduction of certain words into the conversation which formed a magic circle of sweet suggestiveness, and, such was his instinct and skill, that he managed to do this without definitely changing the subject. 'When I was young,' Berto now said, 'I was very much in love with a Spanish girl who had been married to a man much older than herself; he was killed in the war. But although I was very much in love I didn't marry her because I felt that she would always desire an older man, and I, of course, was not much older.'

'Well, in the case of Dino,' Marisa went on, 'let me tell you that he does ride with her every morning after visiting poor Lidia's tomb.'

'It is so fragrant and cool in that cemetery,' Berto said. 'You know, it's quite romantic. I went once to visit our German aunts who are buried in that little cemetery, tucked away in the Vatican, and I heard the nightingale, suddenly, as if paradise were there among the treetops. I also would have liked, afterwards, to have gone riding with a beautiful lady and kiss her.'

So he went on with his groupings of 'I was in love' and his 'fragrants', his 'heaven' and his 'beautiful lady' and all the pleasant numbers of romantic poetry – trite in themselves but accumulatively evocative of a better life than the actual and present one; so he went on, and presently he could see Maggie's wrists relaxing on the table and her shoulders responding as a cat which has been upset responds to the soft stroking hand.

He could see that the danger was past that she should again open her mouth and let forth accusations like the dead pouring out of their tombs, crazed, on All Souls' Night. If she had been a cat she would by now have started against her better judgement to purr, and if an analytical critic had been taking a careful note of all that was said, Berto's magic technique would have been a feast more special than the very good lunch they were eating. Mary looked at Michael who alone among the company was brooding over whatever it was he had on his mind, and then she looked at Berto and once more thought how attractive he was in spite of his age; she hadn't noticed before how good-looking was Berto, what marvellous eyes he had.

'And before they went to Baden they were getting that new pool in the garden,' Marisa was saying. 'They had to dig much deeper, and do you know they found a marble head of the first century? Dino says they are now digging deeper to find the rest of it.'

'The Belle Arti will stop everything,' said Cousin Viola. 'They'll take it for the nation and someone will steal it and smuggle it abroad.'

'Well, they had to leave for Baden,' said Marisa. 'But I'm sure, I'm sure, that they haven't breathed a word to the Belle

Arti.' Again she appealed to her neighbours. 'The Belle Arti,' she said to Michael on her left and to the young criminal who went by the name of George Falk on her right, 'is our cultural protection agency, but they stop work on anything the moment you report a find. In Italy you only have to dig a few metres and you have a find. If one reported every find to the Belle Arti nobody would get a house built or a swimming pool.'

'Can they trust the servants?' said Cousin Viola.

'It happened once to me,' Berto said, 'that I was helping Guillaume to put up a rabbit hutch as he was sure the rabbits we bought to eat were poisonous and he wanted to breed our own rabbits. We were digging a trench out there behind the orchard and I felt my spade touch on a stone, but not a stone. It felt not like the stones of the garden. So I put aside the spade and went down on my knees. Guillaume was amazed and he said, "But what are you doing, Marchese!" I scratched at the earth with my hands and I saw a colour, blue, then another, red. It was a moment I could never forget, such a moment of all my dreams – you remember, Viola, the Byzantine vase. It was in fragments, of course.'

'It's in the museum in Verona,' said Viola, calmly eating.

'Oh, yes, it went to the museum.'

'You could have kept it,' Marisa said.

'How could I have kept it? But the moment of discovery, it's a moment that no one can take away from me, not even the Communists. I went back that night to look at the pieces in the moonlight. We left them where we found them, afraid to break them, and Guillaume constructed a little wire fence around them. I looked up at the clouds passing over the moon thinking of Guillaume's tenderness as he made the fence. It was *una cosa molto bella, molto bella* – '

'You have many fine things in this house,' said the younger criminal.

'Exquisite,' said Mr Stuyvesant, the older one, for whom under another name Interpol were looking to help them with their
inquiries. 'It must have been wonderful to grow up with them.'

'I was not here very much as a child,' Berto said. 'I was
a great deal in Switzerland, and then at school. But when I
was a very young man just before the outbreak of the war I
remember we had a masked ball here. It was considered a
small house for a masked ball, but it was a summer night, you
can imagine for young people in those days how exciting . . .'

The troubadour host turned inquiringly to Lauro who
stood quietly by his chair waiting for him to finish speaking.
Lauro had appeared unexpectedly, for he did not serve at
table here in Berto's villa, clashing so much as he did with
Guillaume and the cook. Berto looked up at the brown face
with a little questioning smile. Lauro spoke in rapid Italian,
very excited and happy and Berto listened with his eyes on
Maggie till Lauro had finished, and had turned and left the
dining-room.

'The masked ball,' said Marisa across the table to her cousin Viola, 'was where Mimi de Bourbon met Aunt Clothilde.
She had just broken off from the Thurn und Taxis – '

'Maggie!' said Berto, 'do you know what Lauro has just
told me? *Your* Gauguin is perfectly safe at Nemi; it's there in
your house and hasn't been moved.'

'Oh, darling!' said Maggie, who was by now sweetly mel-
lowed by the fragrant distillations of Berto's talk.

Viola, more mesmerized by her cousin Marisa than by her
cousin Berto, set her pale head at a saintly angle, and said,
'Aunt Clothilde is still President of the Orphans of St Joachim.
She does good work. She has not changed since the old days.'

'Well, she should have,' said Marisa, 'but that's a different
topic. I remember – ' Meanwhile, Berto recounted how Lauro
had telephoned to his girl-friend at Nemi, and she had gone

on a pretext to Hubert's house, and there had seen the leafy Gauguin in its usual place.

'How did she know,' said Mary, 'where to look for that picture?'

'Apparently Lauro's fiancée goes to Mallindaine's dreadful meetings regularly. Moon-worshippers. You can imagine – '

Maggie turned to Mr Stuyvesant. '*Your* Gauguin must be a fake,' she said, happily.

'It isn't my Gauguin,' said the art-thief. 'It belonged to Neuilles-Pfortzheimer's client, and it has been sold as an authentic. One should inform them.'

'Could it possibly be,' said George Falk, the younger crook, 'that the Gauguin at your home is a fake?'

'It is authentic,' said Maggie, and rose to lead her guests into the garden-room for coffee.

Michael woke from his self-absorbed dream and said, 'Mallindaine could have had a copy made. He could have sold the original.'

'Oh, come,' said Berto, as he stood aside to let his guests move out of the dining-room.

'We should get the experts,' Michael said, 'and, anyway, get the picture out of Hubert Mallindaine's hands.'

'That I do agree,' said Maggie.

Berto was about to catch Maggie's arm, to waylay her before she left, and whisper in her ear that she really might, now that she knew her picture was safe, and her initial shock had blown over, apologize to Mr Stuyvesant and Mr Falk. He was about to say she really should, when he was himself waylaid by Guillaume, Maggie in the meantime sailing ahead. Guillaume, alone with Berto in the dining-room, now confided his change of mind about the two visitors of whom he had earlier approved. 'I think they're up to no good,' said Guillaume.

'But why, Guillaume? What makes you say so?'

Guillaume seemed uncertain what precisely to reply. 'The senior visitor spilled *ragoût* on his trousers,' he ventured somewhat wildly. 'It's embarrassing him – a great red stain, and he's trying to cover it up. Right in the front.'

Berto, stifling all reasonable thoughts, and only recalling that it is the easiest thing in the world to splash on one's clothes some of that tomato sauce swimming in which Italian cooks love to present their pasta, was immediately troubled. Plainly, Guillaume had merely only offered an outward symbol for an inward insight, and it was the insight that Berto trusted.

'See if you can do anything for his trousers,' Berto said. 'Offer him some talcum powder. *Ragoût* is always a messy dish. I don't see what it has remotely to do with trusting the unfortunate man, anyway. An accident can happen to the best of us. No reflection whatsoever on his character.'

In the garden-room Berto found Mr Stuyvesant sitting in a crouched position, leaning well forward, with his legs crossed, holding his coffee. But one could still see, on the pale thin-striped trousers that Berto had so much admired, numerous red blotches and smears. He was glad he had not asked Maggie to apologize to these men. It struck him, now, that it was strange how neither of them had seemed to expect an apology, even after news had arrived that Maggie's picture was still in her house. They had not been offended, only embarrassed, by Maggie's outburst. That could be a sign of guilt. One had to be careful who one let into one's house. He looked out of the French windows to where the young Mr Falk was walking on the lawn between Maggie and Cousin Viola, and he looked again at Mr Stuyvesant crouched over his coffee. Guillaume had come in to hover. 'Why don't you go with Guillaume to the pantry,' said Berto, 'and let him do something to your trousers?'

Mr Stuyvesant looked helplessly at his splashed suit and gave a short laugh. 'Not the pantry,' Guillaume said. 'If the gentleman will go to the guest cloakroom I will bring some materials to clean.'

Ah, yes, yes, thought Berto. Guillaume is thinking of the silver depository. Not the pantry, not the pantry. Stuyvesant rose to follow Guillaume while Berto, Knight of the Round Table, courteously remarked, 'Beastly stuff, *ragoût*.'

He hung around the window watching his guests and his wife wandering around the garden in the May sunlight. Lauro and Michael stood under the lovely portico which gave off to the back of the house. Lauro was talking quietly but urgently, Michael listening sullenly. Lauro glanced towards the French window, caught Berto's eye where he stood watching, grinned, and resumed his talk. Berto watched Lauro with tolerant resignation; he had little doubt that Lauro was raising a moderate sum of money every so often from Michael; not much, but a moderate amount, just to keep quiet about the mistress in Rome. Berto looked at Lauro's shining head with its expensive hair-cut. It was difficult to think of him keeping a secret or doing anything free of charge. 'Once a whore,' Berto mused to himself, 'always a whore. That's my philosophy.'

Guillaume's efforts to clean the trousers were not a great success. Mr Stuyvesant asked for his coat, saying he would hold it over the stain to hide it. So his coat was brought, and holding it draped over his arm he collected his friend and said good-bye to the party very quickly. Berto, with Guillaume hovering behind, watched them leave from the front door. They revved up and left with unusual speed. 'Guillaume,' said Berto. 'I think you're right about those people. They drove off as if it was a getaway from a bank robbery.'

Guillaume muttered to himself in his French-Italian. Berto went to telephone to Alex Pfortzheimer.

XII

Dear Marchesa Tullio-Friole,

Having written in capacity your legal advocate to Mr Hubert Mallindaine at Nemi with regarding the opera of art painted by Paul Gauguin in view of your righteous inquiry in light of the sale of said painting in Switzerland, and having myself accompanied our expert to examine said painting at Nemi by Mr Hubert Mallindaine's request I have to report as it is suspected by the distinguished House Neuilles-Pfortzheimer that this picture at Nemi is a copy of original.

From which arises the complication which I myself have foreseen but not wishing to disturb without necessity have not mentioned to you since this moment. That is, the above-written Mr Mallindaine is hoping to claim of you the cost of original which he is declaring to be part of agreement settled upon him at your handing over to him in the year of 1968 the land and promise of house which he undertook for three years plus housebuilding to his requirements personally in accordance his needs; and the above-written Mallindaine was given contents in the year 1972, July 1, which makes, combined, the remuneration to his services of ten years adviser in your affairs. Always according to Mr Mallindaine's advice, the opera of Paul Gauguin was said at your moment of gift to be original which he has been accepting as such. This is the situation which naturally I hold off with every means from making a confrontation at the present time, as Mr Mallindaine has not yet employed legal offices in the case.

It is my hope you will approve my actions which I should explain you if you should be disposed to be my guest for lunch at the good restaurant that I most admire where we can discuss in tranquillity on the day of your choice.

Very soon hoping to have your telephonic communication my dear Marchesa,

Yours cordially,
Massimo de Vita.

Massimo de Vita, the obscure lawyer whom Maggie had engaged to evict Hubert from his house, sat in one of the copies of Maggie's Louis XIV chairs and looked out at the lake below, while Hubert read through this letter which the lawyer proposed to post from Rome next morning. As he gazed at the still green lake he thought of Maggie, and pictured her, perhaps bursting into his office, Queen of Sheba, making the secretary even more indignant than she constitutionally was, and demanding, with the rings flashing on her fingers, that Hubert be denounced to the police; whereupon, so the lawyer day-dreamed while Hubert studied the letter, one could have a beautiful time calming her down.

'Excellent,' said Hubert. 'The sentiments are accurate and the English is wrong just right. You must understand that with a woman like the Marchesa everything must be done in style. If your style wavers she takes immediate advantage of it and walks all over you. No doubt she believes the Gauguin is genuine. Certainly, she had it smuggled into the country along with many others, in the first place, so she can hardly make a public fuss. I myself have never doubted its authenticity or naturally I would never have accepted it in part settlement.'

'Style, style,' said Massimo de Vita grasping at the idea as if it were a crust, and he starving for it, as indeed he was. He was a brutally ugly man, which in itself could not be counted a disadvantage if he had not made it so by a continual unconscious betrayal of his thoughts which were low-pitched all the time and really quite base. He thought, in fact, that he exercised a quality which he called style, but was in reality an aggressive cynicism. Style, in the sense that he believed himself to possess it, needs a certain basic humility; and without it there can never be any distinction of manner or of anything whatsoever. 'Style,' he repeated, smiling at Hubert who, on occasion, did have a certain style.

'Send her this letter,' Hubert said, handing it back.

Some people could be heard coming up the stairs and presently Pauline entered the drawing-room with a lanky young man. Massimo de Vita got up and greeted her warmly while Hubert sat on in an expressionless way.

Pauline introduced the young man to the lawyer as Walter. He was her boy-friend from the Common Market Headquarters at Brussels, taking his vacation in Italy now that May was passing into June, and was staying in the house as Hubert's guest. He had yellow hair and a moustache of a darker yellow. Hubert tolerated him even though, as he said to Pauline, 'Walter is too occidental for my taste.' At first she thought he had said 'accidental', and was puzzled. He had repeated 'occidental', whereupon she was still puzzled but rather less so.

Walter now plonked himself, tired from his walk, on the sofa, while Pauline busied herself with the letter which the lawyer offered her for a second opinion.

'The English is all wrong. I'll put it right,' she said when she had read it through.

'You will leave the English alone,' Hubert said. 'It express-es Massimo's personality, and besides, if there's any real un-pleasantness one can always fall back on the plea that there was some linguistic misunderstanding.'

'What misunderstanding could there be?' Pauline said. 'We thought all along the Gauguin was genuine. We could have counted on it for our bread and butter. Now it turns out to be a fake. I think that woman knew all along it was a fake.'

'I wouldn't be surprised,' Hubert said.

'And we spent all that money on getting it cleaned,' Pauline said.

'You had it cleaned?' the lawyer said.

'Yes, I took it into Rome myself. I was terrified of a hold-up and being robbed or kidnapped on the way. I needn't have been,' Pauline said.

'You needn't say anything to anyone about the cleaning,' Hubert said. 'It would make people laugh. Spending good money on cleaning a fake. It could damage the work of the Brothers and Sisters of Diana and Apollo. The Movement comes first.'

'If the picture went to be cleaned,' said the lawyer, 'this should not be mentioned. The Marchesa must not believe you have money to burn.'

'It's a really lovely picture,' Pauline said. 'It's real to me, anyway.'

Walter said, 'That's all that matters,' and he looked at Hubert with an expression a little more sour than befits a guest.

Bulging Clara, the Bernardinis' chronically victimized maid, stopped in the main street of Nemi, and put down her plastic shopping bags, bulging like herself as they were. Agata, the pretty housemaid from the Radcliffes' house, stopped too.

She had approached from the end of the narrow street where
the grey castle stood bulkily with its tall and ancient tower,
looking like a crazed and bulging woman wearing an absurd
top hat, ready to dive off over the cliff into the lake far away
below her. Agata was decidedly swollen round the hips and
belly, pregnant as a well-founded good hope.

'Well,' said Clara. 'Well, Agata, any news?'

Agata stood into the wall to let the men who were un-
loading fruit cases from a truck go about their business. She
looked back up the haphazard street of fertile Nemi which,
by some long-ago access of euphoria or wishful thinking,
when Italy was still a kingdom, had been named, doubtless
to the peal of bells and the high notes of trumpets, the Corso
Vittorio Emmanuele. She already had her paper-tissue handkerchief to her eyes. Agata then named the private parts of
numerous animals, including humans, and ended the litany
by declaring that, to sum it up, the man was a ne'er-do-well.

'And all his dead!' responded Clara, meaning precisely
that all the dead relations of the man in question should by
rights endure damnation alike with him.

They stood talking in the sunny main street of Nemi
while life bustled by them, the machines in the smithy went
on grinding, the electrician skimmed by in his bright Opel,
the fruit van backed up and then manoeuvred forward,
backed up again and then was off while the fruit shop as-
sistants noisily discussed where the fruit should go in the
banked-up crates outside the tiny shop. Clara, with her sly
eyes moving occasionally towards the fruit shop, to see how
the prices were set on the newly-graded qualities, listened to
the young wronged Agata; she listened with her sly ears and
puffed out her breath with sympathetic paranoia. Across the
street outside the recreation centre stood a carabiniere in his
brown uniform, the town clerk in his pressed suit and clean

collar and tie, looking on at an exchange of banter between a schoolboy and a white-frocked friar. The two women were greeted occasionally by busy shoppers who passed and swept a glance, along with their smiles, at Agata's hard-done-by belly of shame, while the whole of eternal life carried on regardless, invisible and implacable, this being what no skinny craving cat with its gleaming eyes by night had ever pounced upon, no tender mole of the earth in the hills above had ever discovered down there under the damp soil, no lucky spider had caught, nor the white flocks of little clouds could reveal when they separated continually, eternal life untraceable and persistent, that not even the excavators, long-dead, who had dug up the fields of Diana's sanctuary had found; they had taken away the statues and the effigies, the votive offerings to the goddess of fertility, terracotta replicas of private parts and public parts, but eternal life had never been shipped off with the loot; and even the lizard on the cliff-rocks in its jerky fits had never been startled by the shadow or motion of that eternal life which remained, past all accounting, while Clara and Agata chattered on, tremendously blocking everyone's path although no one cared in the slightest that they did so.

'Could it be anyone else's?' Clara said.

'No, it could only be Lauro's,' said Agata. 'He wants me to put it on Mr Michael but Mr Michael wasn't there at the time. It couldn't have been Mr Michael, but Mr Michael offered to pay for an abortion and Lauro says the offer is a proof of responsibility, and he's getting married to his fiancée right soon; anything to save himself the responsibility. I said, "Lauro, there will be a blood test and I can prove the paternity," but Lauro said, "Well, Michael's group O and I'm group O, so you can just go to *that country* and prove paternity." It was terrible to hear him swearing at me like that after all those times I was good to him when he needed it.'

Clara looked judicious about this. 'You shouldn't have been good to him.' And she added, 'I'm never good to them,' as if she had plenty of opportunities. Then she observed the obvious: 'If Mr Michael wants to pay for an abortion he must have a reason.'

'I never went with him,' said Agata. 'But I know about his woman in Rome. I know all about that. He even brought her to the house once.'

'What did the Signora Mary say?'

'She was away. Anyway, he wants to help me, and maybe he wants me to keep quiet, too. Maybe he just wanted to help me, to be kind; I don't know. Anyway, I wouldn't have had an abortion, not even – '

'They never do anything just to be kind. Imagine it, just figure to yourself!' Clara said.

'Well, maybe Michael will give me something to help.'

'He'll have to. He'll have to,' Clara said. 'He has no option. The master of the house . . . Work it out for yourself and take my advice. Be advised by me.'

Lauro sat in the sitting-room of the new bungalow high on the terraced cliffs among the woods and caves of Nemi, one of a new group of small houses that looked as if they belonged to tidy Snow White. His relations-to-be sat around him, a good-looking, long-legged set, modern and, with the exception of his fiancée, slender. His future mother-in-law had a fine tanned face and streaked short hair, a woman who could pass, at sight, for any of the Radcliffes' friends. The same was not quite true of his fiancée with her long dark hair and slightly over-ripe figure dressed in a shirt and blue jeans; Lauro considered that he could slim her down after they were married. The two uncles, however, brothers on the mother's side, were also good-looking; one, in his late thirties, with lightish hair, well-tinted and cared for and of a length to cover his ears; and the other, about fifty years old, grey-haired, bespectacled and professorial of appearance. The latter's wife was a fashionably skinny woman with a close-cropped silvered hair-style. They all looked as if they worked in the fashion business or the film industry or else ran a nightclub, and went to the hairdresser a great deal for tints and cuts and for manicures. Lauro, gloomily perceptive, was proud enough of his new family's appearance, now that it had come to the point where he was goaded into actual marriage by the demands of the wretched servant-girl, Agata. It would have been unthinkable for him to marry Agata, a man of considerable pride like Lauro who had been accepted into the familiar confidences and the beds of the Radcliffes and the Tullio-Frioles, not to mention the distinguished and equally care-free company of the past. It was the lack of that very heart-easy quality in his new family, fine-looking as they were, that depressed Lauro. He flicked ash from his cigarette into a clean ceramic ash-tray, and as he did so his impending mother-in-law, good woman that she was, rose and took the ash-tray and shook the frail ash out of the window, so that Lauro was left with a clean ash-tray again to finish his cigarette with. It was like eating from a plate where they gave you a clean one half-way through the dish. To the tips of her red varnished finger-nails, the mother-in-law was spick-and-span. It made Lauro unhappy although he could not precisely say why, since Maggie, too, and Mary and all the others were always neat and well-groomed enough. It bothered him too that his fiancée, Elisabetta by name, called herself Betty. It troubled him deeply that these people were talking about the wedding-feast in the best trattoria in Nemi with grade one French champagne, seven courses, and at least two hundred people, counting all cousins and friends on both sides, at the expense of the bride's family, no matter how much per head, money no object on such an occasion and seven courses; seven, eight courses, light courses, Betty's sleek, smart aunt was saying, just as if she was a fat country woman, seven courses so that you start with the antipasto, maybe ham and melon; then the soup, a cold consommé very chic for summer; and for pasta you want two, three kinds, say a fine cannelloni of game or spinach and cream cheese inside and a lovely ravioli with tomato sauce and a good fettucine al burro with parmigiano over it, a choice; then you have to have the fish, scampi dipped in a batter; and then a salad, tomatoes and endives with condiments; you have to have the cold meat next, like for instance veal sliced thin and chicken breasts, or pheasant and for the next course something original, maybe a shish kebab which is to say beef on skewers surrounded by small carrots, green beans and rice; and then a green salad of lettuce and basil, very fresh, and so to a cream cake, for example St Honoré, and then the fruit, fresh fruit or macedonia, you could give them a choice, which could be served with petits-fours and some nuts on the table, too; then of course the cheese and coffee; the chocolates you pass round with the liqueur, sambuca, Cointreau, cognac, and the bride cuts the cake which goes round; Betty's eldest relation should toast the *sposi* in champagne as the champagne glasses are always kept full throughout the meal, and the *sposo* replies to toast the relatives of the bride and Betty's eldest uncle toasts the relatives of the groom; and you give cigars; the waiters should come from Rome so they would know what to do and serve with white gloves. The bride should give away flowers from her bouquet, then you must remember . . .

Lauro looked at his young bride-to-be with panic on his face but she failed to notice. He panicked all the more that she was listening, enthralled, to her aunt, after all the two years' association with Lauro, and then becoming engaged to him and all the times he had described the sort of life he led, with Michael and Mary, with Maggie and Berto, and their friends in Sardinia, at Ischia, in the Veneto, at Mary's house at Nemi, with its well-served meals of which nobody ate very much so that it was all sent back to the kitchen for the servants to guzzle and drink, and the funny, quite outrageous, chatter and gossip with always little bits of laughter but never a real rowdy laugh. In the world Lauro knew, there was silence in between the talk, and afterwards music and space, and nobody talked of the food at all; they took the good food for granted and if the men discussed wines or the women certain dishes, it was all like a subject that you study in a university like art history or wildlife. For two years Lauro had distilled all this into Betty's ear, but now, it seemed, to no avail, for she was chattering away about the wedding-feast, as loudly and eagerly and rapidly as everyone else, breaking into the half-finished sentences of the others as indeed they were all doing. It was a big food-babble, rising louder and louder and dinning around Lauro's ears, he being only half able to isolate the source of his unhappiness since certainly the family looked very good and up-to-date and prosperous and distinguished. Lauro wanted to run, but he thought of Agata in the Radcliffes' kitchen with one hand on her hip and the other pointing at him, and her screaming accusations and all those tears threatening the vengeance of her father and her brothers. He had nowhere to run to; once he was married to Betty it would be too late and Agata would become a muttering bundle of impotent umbrage, violated for life.

The food affair died down and now they were discussing the money and the marriage portion and the financial arrangements for the couple and their house. Betty should keep her job in the boutique in Rome and she had her car.

Betty's mother was about to open a new boutique in Rome, at which point Lauro could give up his job as secretary to the Radcliffes and get the money due to him for liquidation of the contract with a good bit besides; those people had plenty of money.

There came a moment when they let Betty's eldest uncle speak. It was a moment of gravity. Betty's mother filled the liqueur glasses with a sweet syrupy drink and handed them round accompanied each by a lace-edged napkin with a little lacey circlet to rest the glass on. The uncle spoke.

'Betty,' he said, 'is entitled to her share of the land. We have a bit of land.' And he pulled the black, smart brief-case that rested on the arm of the sofa beside him on to his knee, opened it, and extracted a folder. From this he brought a much-folded large document and a map which he spread out on the marble-topped dining-table.

Lauro began to take some notice, and the thought of Agata and his fury against her subsided, together with the memory of her accusations and the slightly older memory of the occasion when, just at the magic moment he had wanted to withdraw, the calculating bitch had told him she was on the pill, it was all right. These rankling images, as at the cinema, changed into that of the actual scene before him, Betty's uncle and her land.

Betty's family comprised her mother's side; the father was unknown and said to be dead. The grandparents, too, were dead and there remained only the uncles, co-proprietors of the fields represented in the big map open on the table.

Lauro bent over it with his arm affectionately round plump Betty's shoulder. He played with her hair and touched her neck as he looked, for he was excited by the surprising idea that she had so much land of her own. They traced a line. Betty's portion was about ten acres, on a plateau among the cliffs of Nemi. 'But it can't be there,' Lauro said.

The uncle's finger traced the boundaries. 'Of course it's there,' he said, and patiently he took out of his brief-case the title deeds, tracing their history for five generations right into young Betty's hands.

'This is good land,' said the younger uncle. 'Better a few *ettari* of good land than a hundred kilometres of waste.'

'But some of that land has been sold. There's a house there. The Marchesa bought it and a Mr Mallindaine, an eccentric Englishman, lives there. I used to work for him.'

Betty's mother started to laugh and so did the uncle. 'She bought it, yes, but not from us,' said Betty's well-groomed mother. 'Some lawyer came along and sold it to her. He said he represented the Church and it was Church property. She got false deeds. We didn't protest, naturally, when she put up the house. It's just as well to bide one's time.'

'It isn't hers,' Betty said, 'and the house is illegal. It's *abusivo*. We can make them take it down.'

'Any time we like. If we like. We can denounce them.'

'Send the police along to that house,' said Betty's skinny aunt.

'Why should we? Better let them pay us than pay a fine to the State,' the elder uncle said. 'We can sue. But she won't take it to court; she'll pay.'

'Once you leave the job, Lauro,' Betty's mother said, 'you can give the Marchesa a piece of news: she's got an illegal house and is trespassing on your land.'

Betty's mother took Lauro's ash-tray, almost empty as it was, into the kitchen and brought it back clean.

'The title deeds of the land,' said Hubert, 'were transferred to Maggie on 8 February 1968, a date I can never forget; and at the end of April this house was started on cleared land where no house previously had stood. The house took three years and two months to construct.'

'The building permit?' said Massimo de Vita. 'Was that a fake, too, or didn't you have one?'

'Maggie had a building permit, of course,' Hubert said. 'I don't know what she's done with it. She probably has it in her company offices for safe keeping.'

'A pity she didn't come to me sooner,' said Massimo. He was growing a beard, as yet not long enough to cover the extra chins which would not go away. He looked excited and hastily dressed, as one who had been, as in fact he had, working long hours for several days. In that time he had established beyond doubt that the lawyer who had arranged for Maggie to buy the property at Nemi was not to be found and his name nowhere on the legal records of Italy. He had further discovered that Lauro's impudent claim that the land on which Hubert's house was built belonged to his fiancée was not impudent at all, it was true. The whole of the transaction had been a fake, including the documents, and the land presumed to have been Church property belonged to Lauro's prospective bride at this moment.

'She should have had me for her lawyer in those days,' said Massimo. 'Now I have to write her a letter and see how I can get her out of this mess.'

'She gave me this house,' Hubert said sulkily. 'It is mine. I supervised the building of it for three years and two months; it was agony; getting things done in Italy is agony; then I moved in and a few months later Maggie cut off the funds she had promised in order to maintain it. I can sue.'

'It's up to me,' said the lawyer, 'to say whether you can sue or not. Meantime, let us look at the facts. You occupy this house – no?'

'Yes,' said Hubert, meekly.

The library door opened and Pauline Thin put her head round it. 'Coffee?' she said chirpily.

'Get out!' barked Hubert. Pauline withdrew.

'But you had no building permit.'

'There was indeed a building permit,' Hubert said. 'I re-member obtaining photo-copies from the lawyer to satisfy the building contractors. Everything was regular.'

'Well, it wasn't regular,' said Massimo, 'and the lawyer least of all. Dante de Lafoucauld, what a name for an Italian lawyer . . . You should have known . . . You should have – '

'What's the matter?' said an aggressive male voice from the door. It belonged to a skinny sun-bronzed chest, shoul-ders and pair of arms topped by a yellow-haired head: Walter, with his deep yellow moustache, having been called in from his sunbath and, bored by Nemi and resentful of Hubert, being now only too keen to take up a quarrel on Pauline's behalf. Some other voices, male and female, questioned and commented behind him; Pauline had brought some of the local young people to the house for the day. She did this many, many days now, gradually building up something like a commune under the protective wings of the Brotherhood of Diana and Apollo; so far, Hubert had felt it wise to refrain from expressing all the alarm that he felt, even although these young people had seemed to take over the house, left a mess behind them all over the place and never did any work.

Hubert shouted at Walter, 'Get out! I'm discussing serious business with my lawyer.' He rose and lumbered over to the door, gave the young man a hefty push, slammed the door shut and locked it. A clamour of protest arose from the other side of the door, subsiding after a few minutes as the footsteps of the lithe and sandalled young set flip-flopped down the staircase into the overgrown garden where these people were wont to lie and watch the intertwining of the weeds and get their bodies ever browner by the good offices of Apollo.

'Now,' said Hubert when he had simmered down a bit, 'one problem at a time, if you please. *Una cosa alla volta.*'

'Precisely,' said the lawyer, on the defensive. 'It's hardly my fault that – '

'Down to business,' said Hubert. 'Presumably, when Lauro gets married, he will start putting me out of the house.'

'I don't know about that,' said Massimo.

'Or they will want some money. A lot of money,' Hubert said, 'to keep their mouths shut.'

'There could be several legal opinions,' said Massimo. 'The law is very contradictory. Certainly they will want some money. Certainly. But can they claim it? The house does not exist.'

'I mean this house,' Hubert said.

'It does not exist. How can it exist? It is not on the records. In Italy if a house is not on the records, it has been constructed illegally and we call it *abusivo*. An *abusivo* construction does not exist in legal terms. The family who own the land can make the Marchesa pull it down.'

'But will they?'

'It depends on their frame of mind and if they can come to terms. It depends also on whether the land they own is only the top soil. In Italy, sometimes the sub-soil belongs to somebody else; it could belong to the Church or the State. At any rate the family can make trouble for the Marchesa.'

'She will have to pay,' Hubert said. 'Maggie will have to pay them off.'

'Even then,' said the lawyer, 'the police or the town council might discover that it is *abusivo* and cause the house to be destroyed, but it is unlikely they will know that the house is *abusivo* unless the family reports it.'

'Well, it's my house. Maggie gave it to me.'

'She had no right to do so. It doesn't exist.'

'She will have to make reparation if the house is pulled down,' Hubert said.

'Oh, certainly she would have to do that if she gave it to you. The legal transfer of the house to your name fortunately did not take place. Technically the house is still hers. Although of course I believe you, it is obvious that verbally she gave you the house. But now it is certain, anyway, that she can't put you out. There are many tenants in *abusivo* houses who cannot be put out and who need not pay rent, either. Because the house does not exist.'

'And the contents of the house?' Hubert said.

'It would be difficult,' said Massimo, moving his plump hands in the air as he spoke, 'to say anything about the contents of a house that does not exist. How can a non-existent house contain contents? How can it have a tenant? You don't exist when you inhabit a house that is *abusivo*.'

'Under Italian law?' said Hubert.

'It could be argued,' the lawyer said. 'It could be argued for a very long time and the longer you stay in a house the more difficult it is to get you out.'

'Italian law,' said Hubert, 'is very exciting. Positively mystical. I approve strongly of Italian law.'

Massimo laughed merrily and looked at his watch, very flat, very gold with its golden band encircling his plump wrist. He said something about lunch-time, but Hubert was musing on a private dream of his own from which he presently emerged to say, 'This house seems to me to be perfectly safe as the headquarters of the Brother-Sisterhood of Diana and Apollo. We can ignore Maggie's protests about the use the house is being put to; that's my opinion.'

'And mine,' said Maggie's lawyer. 'I tear up the letter now which the Marchesa sent me to that effect. I never received it.'

He took a letter from his brief-case and tore it in small pieces.

'It doesn't exist,' Hubert observed.

'I never received it,' said Massimo. 'She did not register it and so it is easy never to receive a letter with the postal situation in our country being what it is.'

The door opened and Pauline stood on the threshold of the library. 'Why have you unplugged the telephone?' she said. 'Someone is wanting to use it.'

'I don't want to be disturbed,' Hubert said. 'Miss Thin, are you my secretary or are you not?'

'I'm hungry. We're all hungry,' she said, 'and the lunch is ready and the cook is getting angry.'

'How much pleasanter it was,' said Hubert to the lawyer, 'before we had our good fortune.' He rose with the lawyer and swept past Pauline, declaring that the blessings deriving from his ancestor the goddess Diana were mixed ones indeed.

As he descended the stairs Massimo loitered to grasp Pauline and press her against the wall of the landing; then he kissed her heavily whether she liked it or not.

XIII

'HAVE YOU READ THE PAPERS?' Berto said, his eyes reposing on an abyss of horror.

Maggie was in Switzerland intently but vainly hunting Coco de Renault through the woods and thickets of the Zürich banks, of the Genevan financial advisory companies, the investment counselling services of Berne, and through the wildwoods of Zug where the computers whirred and winked unsleepingly in their walls, where the office furniture was cream leather in the tall buildings, and the dummy directors of elaborately-titled corporations entered the glass front-doors set into the marbled façades, walked up the staircases lined with the cedars of Lebanon, to take their places at their large desks at ten in the morning, after a massage and a swim in the pool.

Mary and Michael had gone to the Greek islands on a yacht to get away from it all, to get to know each other again and for a number of other purposes described in similar phrases which Mary had written down on a list. They were gone and the house at Nemi was closed up, the pretty maid having left their service with her aunt who, in view of the girl's condition, had carried the suitcases, refusing all help from Michael and Mary, but serving them with polite but pregnant assurances that justice would be done on the girl's behalf and Michael would be hearing from their lawyer. Mary had stood

beside Michael in a very positive way, cool and blonde, rich
and loyal. She had said the right thing: 'My husband is innocent.' Then she had said the wrong thing: 'We're not afraid
of your Communist lawyer.' This had brought a duet of re-
torts from the niece and aunt, to the effect that Mary would
pay for those words, the politics of their lawyer were not her
business; she had committed an outrage against the Republic
of Italy by speaking disrespectfully of their lawyer and his
politics; she was a whore who slept with everybody including
Lauro and she had also been seen in bed with her mother-in-
law. Mary had stood on, her arm in Michael's, cold-lipped,
till the women got into the car and drove off.

Lauro, too, was away. He was on his honeymoon, having first spent a morning with Maggie, at Michael's house,
breaking gently to her the news that none of her three houses
at Nemi was really hers and that Hubert's in particular was
built on the dowry of Lauro's bride. Maggie had assumed at
first that Lauro was weaving a fantasy in some obscure desire
to rouse her passions and end up with a love-making scene.
She had been indulgent about his stories, assuring him sweetly
that she held the title-deeds of all her properties everywhere,
or at least Coco de Renault did; Maggie took her cheque book
out of its charming little drawer and wrote out a very large
cheque to Lauro for a wedding present, which he received
graciously and lovingly. When they got up from the sofa,
pulling their clothes straight, however, Lauro again came
round to his incredible story. 'Really, Maggie, that lawyer
was a crook. He can't be found in Italy. He's sold you land
and houses that didn't belong to him. He chose a couple of
abandoned houses and a piece of vacant land and falsified the
papers, that's all.'

'The real owners would have come forward by now,'
Maggie said.

'In the case of this house of Michael's,' Lauro said, 'it belongs to a large family, twelve, fourteen, cousins, all of them in America. That crook was clever. But when one of those cousins comes home for a visit you'll have trouble. In the case of the Bernardini house, it once belonged to a cousin of my fiancée who died, but his son is the heir; he has a job in England, a very important job in a chemical factory. He won't like to see someone occupying his house if he returns to look for it in Italy.'

'The Bernardini house was a total ruin,' Maggie said, 'a complete wreck, and I spent a fortune on the reconstruction; I put in the tennis court and the pool; I put in the lily-pond and I laid the lawns; then the Bernardinis started all over again making big changes. The same with this house here; Michael had it before he was married; we flew one of the best architects in Los Angeles over here to restore this house; it was a wreck when I bought it.'

'You didn't buy it, Maggie,' said Lauro, quietly. 'You only thought you did. Take Hubert's house which you put on Betty's land, for instance, well, it just doesn't exist officially.'

He comforted Maggie greatly that morning as she telephoned one after the other office in Rome to try and trace that lawyer Dante de Lafoucauld whom it now appeared nobody had ever heard of, and whom Maggie herself had met only twice, in Rome, in the Grand Hotel in the winter of 1968. Nobody had heard of him at all. Maggie rang the office of Massimo de Vita, who was out. She left her name with an answering service, and then went into hysterics, blaming Massimo for everything and saying how awfully suspicious it was that he didn't have a secretary any more, only an answering service attached to his phone. 'Only crook lawyers have answering services,' Maggie moaned, while Lauro poured her out a brandy and said, 'Maggie, Maggie, drink this, Maggie

266

dear. I love you, Maggie. You didn't have Massimo de Vita for a lawyer in 1968, did you? You only went to de Vita for the first time a year ago, didn't you? How can he be to blame?'

'They're all in it together,' Maggie screamed. 'Why hasn't he got a proper office with a secretary? It was the seediest office I ever saw. Now he hasn't even got a secretary. I hate to deal with answering services.' The telephone rang just then, from Massimo de Vita in response to her message on the answering service. He was just about to write to her, he said.

'I have to talk to you,' said Maggie. 'Have you ever heard of an Italian lawyer called Dante de Lafoucauld?'

'Yes,' he said. 'I heard that name last week. He isn't any sort of Italian lawyer. I don't know who he is. He's a crook. Apparently, you see, Marchesa, you were badly advised, and this man, whoever he is, forged some documents for some houses which don't belong to you – '

'You know him?' Maggie said. 'Then you know the man?'

'I never heard of him till a week ago, when I was looking into the matter of the eviction of Mr Mallindaine. Then it all – '

'He had a beard,' wailed Maggie. 'He had a dark beard.'

'So have I,' said Massimo. 'Marchesa, since last we met, I have grown a beard. I will do what I can for you in this affair, although you realize, Marchesa, that when the houses are not yours – '

'Crooks, all of you!' Maggie yelled, whereupon her voice was immediately overlaid by that of Lauro who had taken the telephone from her hand. 'Doctor de Vita,' said Lauro, 'you must excuse the Marchesa. She's very upset. I will be in touch with you and arrange a meeting.'

The lawyer said a few words in Italian for Lauro's ears only, partly legal in substance, partly sexual.

'*Si, si, Dottore,*' said Lauro, and hanging up the receiver continued his work of calming Maggie down. He was somewhat successful until she got it into her head to ring Coco de Renault. The lines were engaged for every number she tried where Coco might be: Nemi–Paris, Nemi–Geneva, Nemi–Zürich. 'It's lunch time; it's one o'clock,' said Lauro. 'Everyone will be out. I'll fix you some lunch, Maggie. Leave the telephone and I'll tell you all you need to do in the case of Betty's land. It's simple and, after all, you can afford it.'

Maggie rang Berto and gave him the story, which he didn't believe. He replied quietly, thinking her to be temporarily deranged, and said he would join her shortly at Nemi. He sounded reluctant to do so; he said he was occupied with problems to do with the safety from robbers of his house in the Veneto.

'We can't stay here. There are no servants,' Maggie said. 'Lauro's getting married on Saturday and Agata's left. I have all these houses and nowhere to stay.'

'We can stay in Rome. Or we could stay with the Bernardinis,' said Berto. Maggie hung up and rang the Bernardinis. Emilio would not be home till six. The young people were out. Maggie collapsed into tears and presently let Lauro bring her a delicate lunch-tray.

That stormy morning over, Maggie set off the next day with Berto's car and driver for Rome where she had a full-scale massage treatment, then onwards, glowing and resolute, for Switzerland in pursuit of Coco de Renault. She was anxious to see him in any case about the lack of funds. Something was happening to her monthly cheques which were not arriving at the Rome bank as usual, so that she had been unable to pay her bodyguard. She said nothing to Berto. The bodyguard had left. That was embarrassing enough. And now it was imperative to get from Coco the title-deeds of her houses and so prove them hers.

Berto was staying with the Bernardinis meanwhile and had wearily realized the truth about the houses at Nemi. 'If I had met Maggie earlier,' Berto told Emilio, 'she would never have done anything so foolish. There's nothing for it but for Maggie to pay reparations or else surrender the properties; she can manage that all right. I wish she would try to see things in proportion.'

'It would be hard on us,' said Emilio Bernardini, 'to have to leave here after all the work we've put into the house.'

'I dare say something can be arranged,' Berto said.

'I dare say,' said Emilio, smiling to reassure his friend.

'Do you trust Coco de Renault?' said Berto, gazing across the trees towards the tower of the castle and the rows of little houses built into the cliff below it, huddled in half-circular terraces round the castle like the keys of an antiquated typewriter. He looked away from the view and into Emilio's face, suddenly realizing that the man was not quite his usual cool self.

'I did trust him, of course,' said Emilio. 'When I introduced him to Maggie of course I trusted him. He handled some affairs of mine, very badly as it has turned out. I can't say, honestly, that I trust de Renault now. It's very embarrassing, and I wish I'd never brought him together with you and Maggie. But I had no idea she would hand over so vast a part of her fortune to him to manage. In fact, I think she put everything in his hands, which was a foolish, an unheard of, thing to do. I would never have expected her to hand over *everything*.'

'Has she done that?' said Berto.

'I think so, yes.'

'And you have doubts about de Renault?'

'I do, yes. I have had quite a shock in my own case. There is something shady about him, and I'm very sorry, very embarrassed.'

'Poor Maggie,' Berto said mildly, 'I hope she won't get any more shocks. I think only of Maggie herself, you know. A wonderful woman, a wonderful woman. She doesn't need money to make her a wonderful woman. It's only that she's used to it.' Berto added after a while, 'It's hardly your fault, Emilio. I should myself have taken more interest in Maggie's affairs. Perhaps I could have persuaded her not to put her trust in de Renault. For my part, how could I hold you responsible? After all, I've known you since you were a schoolboy.'

Emilio said, 'Thank you, but, you know very well, you can't trust every man who was at school with your son. These days, whom can you trust?'

'One's friends,' said Berto. 'You know, Emilio, you're too sad by nature. Why are you so sad?' And this question, the asking of which would have seemed quite absurd in another society, was really quite normal at Nemi, on the outskirts of Rome in the middle of June 1975, for Berto and Emilio.

'Why are you so sad by nature?'

'Life is sad.'

It was the next morning, reading the newspaper, that Berto said to Emilio, 'Have you read the papers?' This was an unnecessary question since the news, on that morning and the next, was a national event: the regional elections throughout Italy had confirmed a popular swerve to the political left. It could fairly be said that Italy had turned half-Communist overnight. Both halves were fairly stunned by the results.

Berto, keening at the wake in those days, detained Emilio from going about his morning's business, with prophecies and lamentations. The Communists became 'They', the Italian 'Loro'. Berto said, '*Loro, loro, loro* . . . They, they . . .'

'It's the will of the people,' Emilio said, but he spoke into heedless morning air, and Berto continued, 'Look how they write in the newspaper; they say one has the sensation that something is finished for always. And whatever they mean by that, it's the truth. Something is finished. Loro, loro . . . They, they . . . They will come and take away everything from you. They took away everything from us in Dalmatia. They will take, will carry away . . . Loro . . . ti prenderanno, ti porteranno via tutto . . . They will come and take . . . Everything you possess . . .' The gardener's son, passing by and catching these words, wondered how that could be, his possession being a motor-scooter. 'They will kill . . . ti liquideranno . . .' said Berto. 'They will take over, and they will – '

Emilio, who, although not himself a Communist adherent, had none the less voted Communist in these elections to express his exasperation with Italy's government-in-residence, did not have the heart to say so to the older man. After all, he had been at school with Berto's son, and Emilio would not shatter Berto's kindly affection. Emilio kept his dark, young secret and merely observed, sadly, 'After the capitalists have finished with us I doubt if there will be anything left for the Communists to take over. De Renault, for example – '

'Better her money should go to a swindler than to the Communists,' Berto said.

XIV

WITH THE ELECTIONS AND THE strawberry festival in the air, and Maggie, so far as Hubert had ascertained, on a trip to Switzerland, and with Lauro away on his honeymoon, Hubert felt it wise to call a rally of his followers and prepare for battle with any such apocalyptic events and trials as are bound to befall the leaders of light and enlightened movements, anywhere, in any age.

Maggie, he hoped, had gone to Switzerland to arrange for the surreptitious payment of his claim for the fake Gauguin, and maybe to raise funds to meet the demands of Lauro's bride and the eventual claims of the other owners of the properties she had thought were hers; she would do this, he reckoned wrongly, without breathing a word to her pig of a husband. He was wrong not only in this reckoning, but also in the assumption that Maggie had received her lawyer's letter about his demand to be compensated for the fake Gauguin. The letter had indeed been sent to her by registered post, but the mails from Rome were fairly disordered, and the letter had not in fact reached Maggie at the Veneto before she had left the villa. Guillaume had signed for it and put it aside, on the tray in the hall, where it innocently awaited the most peculiar circumstances of her return. Hubert did not know this, and in fact he had got into a habit of false assumptions by the imperceptible encroachment of his new cult; so ardently had he been preaching the efficacy of prayer that he now, without thinking, silently invoked the name of Diana for every desire that passed through his head, wildly believing that her will not only existed but would certainly come to pass. Thus, like ministers of any other religion, he was estranged from reality in proportion as he mistook the nature of prayer, offering up his words of praise, of gratitude, penitence, intercession and urgent petition in the satisfaction that his god would reply in kind, hear, smile, and wave a wand. So that, merely because he had known in the past that the unforeseen stroke of luck can happen, and that events which are nothing short of a miracle can take place, Hubert had come secretly to take it with a super-stitious literalness that the miraculous may happen in front of your eyes; speak the word, Diana, and my wish will be fulfilled. Whereas, in reality, no farmer prays for rain unless the rain is long overdue; and if a miracle of good fortune occurs it is always at the moment of grace unthought-of and when everybody is looking the other way. However, Hubert, largely through his isolation at Nemi and from not having seen Maggie in person for a number of years, believed that Diana of the Woods could somehow enter Maggie's mind, twist a kind of screw there, and force her to do something she would not otherwise have done.

Moreover, he had not allowed for a change in Maggie, a hardening. In the carefree past she had been more or less a docile pushover where money was concerned, and Hubert miscalculated the effect upon her of being married to steady-minded Berto, of having had her suspicions aroused to the point of almost-justified paranoia by various threats to her moneyed peace, and, most of all, by the new economic crisis which Hubert had mentally absorbed in those months from what he read and heard, but which had not closely touched him.

Maggie would come back from Switzerland, he felt sure, and make a settlement for the Gauguin. Indeed, he could hardly think of Maggie without the word settlement coming to his mind.

Lauro and his buxom horror-beauty of a wife would also return and, should it please the gods, Lauro might even join the Fellowship of Diana and Apollo, in the same way that the three other boys had returned to him, those secretaries of the first, beautiful summer at Nemi, when the house was newly built, in 1972, that year of joy and of outrage, when Hubert was free to leave his doors unlocked, could come and go as he pleased, but when Maggie began to desert him, searching as he did after strange gods and getting married to Tullio-Friole. As it happened, the return of the secretaries was a mixed blessing, but Hubert thanked Diana for them all the same.

In the meantime he thought it well to declare a special congress of his flock. Pauline Thin, who in kindly moments Hubert called 'Our Mercury', sent messages by telephone and by grapevine word of mouth to numerous fellow-worshippers who lived within easy travelling distance of Nemi; she also sent out a number of telegrams, cautiously-worded in each case, in order to get together a preliminary meeting of kindred souls, the elect Friends of Diana and Apollo, and so prepare for an even grander gathering which Hubert projected for the following autumn and which he spoke of variously as an 'international synod', a 'world congress' and a 'global convergence'. Hubert was aware that the ecclesiastical authorities as well as the carabinieri already viewed his house with suspicion and that his activities were regarded with a certain amount of local disfavour. 'They can't pin anything on me,' Hubert said, 'not drugs nor orgies nor fraud. We are an honest religious cult. All the same, we have to be careful.' Mostly he feared Lauro and the Radcliffe family, feeling sure they would, if they could, use any eventual excuse to bring trouble on his Fellowship, which was covering expenses by now, very nicely. What Hubert had in mind for his final project was to try and syphon off, in the interests of his ancestors Diana and her twin brother Apollo, some of the great crowds that had converged on Rome as pilgrims for the Holy Year, amongst whom were vast numbers of new adherents to the Charismatic Renewal movement of the Roman Catholic Church. News had also come to Hubert of other Christian movements which described themselves as charismatic, from all parts of Europe and America; a Church of England movement, for instance, and another called the Children of God. Studying their ecstatic forms of worship and their brotherly claims it seemed to him quite plain that the leaders of these multitudes were encroaching on his territory. He felt a burning urge to bring to the notice of these revivalist enthusiasts who proliferated in Italy during the Holy Year that they were nothing but schismatics from the true and original pagan cult of Diana. It infuriated him to think of the crowds of charismatics in St Peter's Square, thumbing their guitars, swinging and singing their frightful hymns while waiting for the Pope to come out on the balcony. Not far from Nemi was the Pope's summer residence in Castelgandolfo. Next month, he fumed, they will crowd into Castelgandolfo, and they should be here with me.

Pauline, meanwhile, was having the time of her life. Men pressed her against the wall and kissed her whether she liked it or not. She found herself at the centre of Hubert's young following, surrounded by attentive people and to spare. She was determined to keep her privileged position of having been in with Hubert from the start, holding on to it partly by a habit she had of reminding Hubert by little hints, privately from time to time, that some of those records she had been obliged to put in order over the past three years still puzzled her. Pauline's allusions to the records inevitably subdued any attempt by Hubert to get rid of her, as he could now afford to do. He, meanwhile, on these occasions, finding himself stuck with her in this uneasy relationship, got himself quickly out of his troubled state of mind by telling himself he was fond of Pauline, very, very fond. When he told himself this for a few minutes continuously, he believed it, and did not appear in the least aware of having capitulated to a piece of blackmail, except that on such occasions he called her Miss Thin for the rest of the day. Perhaps it was his age; at all events he associated his pagan cult with his own very survival and was ready at least to endure Pauline for it; he was prepared to love her as far as he could and to let her fill the house and garden with anyone whomsoever, so long as they didn't bring in forbidden drugs, use up the hot water in the house, and provided they subscribed to the Fellowship. On these conditions he was content with the arrangements that Pauline made and especially with her rule that nobody could approach him except through her; that suited him very well.

Pauline herself had put a number of young people to work for the cult. She had roped in Letizia Bernardini as press officer and Pietro Bernardini as public relations officer. There was an older man, Pino Tullio-Friole, Berto's son, who also made regular pilgrimages to the home of Hubert, descendant of Diana, bringing contributions of money and precious objects and some of his wealthy friends who liked to attend the religious services and afterwards sleep with whoever was available. Pino, who was in his early forties, despised Maggie and resented her marriage to his father.

Hubert brooded especially over one of the many press cuttings Letizia had produced for him. It was dated 18 May, and was taken from the English-speaking paper of Italy, *The Daily American*. 'Cardinals, bishops meet, dance in Rome,' was the headline. It said:

Rome, 17 May (AP) – Bishops, archbishops and cardinals, struggling to keep their hats in place, sang and danced in ecstasy, embracing one another and raising their arms to heaven.

The Most Rev. Joseph McKinney, auxiliary bishop of Grand Rapids, Mich., joined hands with the Most Rev. James Hayes, archbishop of Halifax, who in turn linked arms with Leo, Cardinal Suenens of Belgium.

The unlikely chorus yesterday opened the Ninth International conference on charismatic Renewal in the Roman Catholic Church.

The conference theme of 'renewal and reconciliation' – the theme of Holy Year – underlines the movement's search for wholehearted approval in the official Church.

A crowd of about 8,000, most of them Americans, gathered at the catacombs of St Callixtus, burial place of the early Christian martyrs, for the opening ceremony. A young band led the congress in song, and delegates from Quebec to Bombay testified to the growth of the movement in all continents.

Cardinal Suenens, archbishop of Malines, urged participants to use the four-day reunion 'to renew your faith, to renew your hope in the future, to love each other like you never did before'.

The Charismatic Movement, a predominantly lay movement claiming more than half a million followers, emerged in main line Protestant churches in the early 1960s and in Roman Catholicism in 1967, among students and professors at Duquesne University in Pittsburg.

It is characterized by fervent prayer meetings, gifts of the spirit such as 'speaking in tongues' and efforts to breathe new life into personal religion.

In a recent report, American Catholic bishops credited the movement with 'many positive signs . . . a new sense of spiritual values, a heightened consciousness of the action

of the Holy Spirit, the praise of God and a deepening personal commitment to God.'

But they warned of dangers inherent in the revival –
divergence from the official Church, fundamentalism, ex-
aggeration of the importance of the gifts of prophecy and
speaking in tongues.

'Tongues is not the important thing; the important
thing is the change in your life,' said Bob Cavnar, a retired
U.S. Air Force colonel who came here for the meeting
from Dallas, Tex.

Cavnar, introduced to the movement by his son Jim,
was one of 70 congress elite renowned for speaking in
tongues and selected to receive messages to the conference
from the Holy Spirit.

Hubert kept many such cuttings, read and re-read them,
with a sense of having been cheated of his birthright. He had
sent Pauline at the beginning of June to one of these meetings and afterwards had locked himself with Pauline into the
drawing-room, or rather, locked out the rest of the drifting
acolytes and lovers who at present made up his household,
to hear her story.

'It started off,' said Pauline, 'with a mass.'

'In church?'

'No, no. It was an altar set up in this flat in the Via Giulia.
I don't know whose flat it was. Well, they had a mass, there
was a Catholic priest with his vestments, and the congregation, about thirty people.'

'What sort of people? Rich, poor, how did they strike you?
All English-speaking? What language was the mass?'

'It was in English, but there were lots of Italians and
French, all sorts. All sorts of people and some nuns. Quite a
lot of nuns in their habits; and later I found some were nuns

and priests in ordinary clothes. They seemed all ages, really, but only one or two really old, and they were nuns.'

'It is from ordinary people that the great revenues come,' said Hubert. 'They are filching the inheritance of the great Diana of Nemi, the mother of nature from time immemorial.'

'I did talk about Diana, don't worry,' Pauline said. 'A number of people were very interested. And do you know who was there? – Those Jesuits, Cuthbert Plaice and his friend Gerard Harvey the nature-study man, were there. Father Gerard, in fact, was urging some of the young men to come to one of our meetings and telling everyone how wonderful Nemi was, how the environment comes right up to the back door and so on. Father Cuthbert was asking me a lot about your personal origins, Hubert, and I told him well, it was a long story. Then – '

'Miss Thin,' said Hubert, 'I want the whole picture of this charismatic meeting and you can tell me afterwards what the Jesuits said. At the same time, my dear, I must say it was most commendable of you to get your word in about the true Fellowship. You're wonderful, Miss Thin, you really are. Tell me about the mass.'

'Well, the mass only preceded the meeting. It was an ordinary mass except for the swinging hymns, and the fact that the Kiss of Peace was real kisses, everyone kissed everyone. That sort of thing. The nuns seemed to like it and there was lots of embracing and singing.'

'We should have nuns in the Fellowship,' Hubert said. 'Diana always had her vestal virgins. We should have vestal virgins watching a flame on the altar day and night.'

'Well, they would have to be part-time,' Pauline said. 'Who is going to come and watch a flame all day?'

'When we have a greater following,' Hubert said, 'all these things will fall into place. Did the Jesuits participate in this orgy?'

'Well, I wouldn't say it was an orgy. The Jesuits were there as observers, anyway. The prayer meeting that followed the mass was more exciting, when they spoke with tongues and made emotional comments on the scriptures. They made a sound like an Eastern language, Hebrew, or Persian maybe, or Greek. I don't know what; but that's speaking with tongues. Then they prophesy. There was a woman there, about thirty-five, she prophesied a lot, and would you believe it, she was a doctor. She proclaimed a passage from the Gospels and closed her eyes and threw up her hands. Everyone said "Amen". Then we sang and clapped hands in syncopation, and sort of danced – '

'What passage from the Gospels?' said Hubert.

'Oh, I don't know. Something about St Paul in his travels.'

'That is not the Gospels. It is probably the Acts of the Apostles. What was the text?'

'Oh, I don't remember. Something about the Lord. It was all so noisy, and everybody was excited, you know. It wasn't so important what the words were, I think.'

'It never is,' Hubert said. 'And what were the Jesuits doing?'

'Well, they didn't join in but they seemed to be enjoying it all. Their eyes were all over the place. Cuthbert Plaice saw me. He said "Hi, Pauline, how do you like it?" I said I liked it tremendously, and I really did as a matter of fact, but the feeling wore off afterwards, you know.'

'We must step up our services in the Fellowship,' Hubert said, 'that's clear.'

It was a hazy hot afternoon towards the end of June. Beyond the ranges of the Alban hills you had to imagine the sea, for indeed it was there, far away, merging invisibly into the heat-blurred sky-line.

Pauline had been busy over the past ten days, putting such a massive amount of energy into the task she had undertaken that in fact she felt she would never again in the course of her life find it in her to repeat the effort, even although Hubert kept reminding her that this was only a preliminary little gathering to the one planned for the autumn.

At the end of ten days Pauline had arranged a fairly big gathering of Hubert's faithful to be held in the large overgrown garden behind the house stretching to the dark, moist woods. She had announced the event as a 'secret meeting', totally avoiding any written messages. Pauline had spent many hours on the telephone and had travelled around in Hubert's car to notify the Friends of Diana and to exhort attendance. The object of this meeting was to form a nucleus around which the future cells of the Fellowship were to collect.

Pauline had not been able to get much done with the garden, but she had cleared enough to put up an altar and a flowery canopy, and to prepare a covered marquee for the fruit juice and sandwiches.

'What will we do if it rains?' she had asked Hubert snappily on one of those frantic ten days of preparation.

'It will not rain,' thundered Hubert.

On the last day she had been to Rome to get her hair cut and set, and also to buy the remarkable outfit which she now, as the expected throng began to accumulate, triumphantly wore. Too late, Hubert had seen her and exclaimed, 'You can't wear that!' This was a khaki cotton trouser-suit with metal-gold buttons on the coat and its four pockets; Pauline had tucked the trouser-legs into a pair of high canvas boots, so that the whole dress looked like a safari suit. The hunting effect was increased by a pale straw cocked hat which perched on her short curled hair.

'What do you mean?' Pauline said when Hubert, already waiting in his leafy bower, bedecked in his silver-green priestly vestments, had exclaimed 'You can't wear that!'

'It's entirely out of keeping, and irreverent. You look like the commandant of a concentration camp or something out of a London brothel.'

'It signifies the hunt,' Pauline said. 'Diana is a huntress, isn't she?'

'She is always portrayed wearing a tunic,' Hubert said, 'and a quiver full of arrows.' It was a hot day, and his vestments were heavy, which made him feel sicker than ever.

'Well, I can't wear a tunic,' said Pauline, 'I haven't the figure.'

'The figure!' shouted Hubert from under his greenery and his robes. 'The figure . . . ' he shouted across the garden. 'If you think your figure fits into that outfit, with your haunches like a buffalo's – '

Pauline started to cry, pulling from her satchel-bag a large red handkerchief with white spots which it would seem was designed, even the handkerchief, to enrage Hubert. Pauline's skinny boy-friend Walter came out of the house, and stopped in some astonishment at the scene. He had not seen Hubert before in his robes nor Pauline in her new outfit, although he had seen her cry at various times.

Hubert, who had taken some care to pose himself under the bower, was unwilling to disarrange the effect. He stood motionless with his arm raised to receive in benediction the people whom he could already hear arriving at the front of the house. Motionless as he was, he screamed in his heat and fury, 'That woman has no sense of stage management. Tell her to go and remove those objectionable clothes. She's supposed to be the chief of Diana's vestals and she looks like Puss-in-Boots at the pantomime. Don't forget I've had experience with the theatre, I've had a lot of success, and when I ran my play in Paris, *Ce Soir Mon Frère*, I took responsibility for all the costumes.'

Walter, unable to make sense of the quarrel, said to Pauline, 'What's the matter with him?'

'I have to wear something to symbolize my authority in the Fellowship,' Pauline wailed from behind her red handkerchief. 'Otherwise I'll just be taken for one of the rest. I know what I'm doing and I've worked myself to death for ten days. The running about, the phoning, the fruit juice, the hairdresser, the sandwiches, and choosing my suit and getting it altered, and making the list and typing the order of business for the meeting.'

'Why don't you take off the boots and the hat?' said Walter against the background of more explosive sounds from Hubert at the other end of the garden. 'You'll be too hot in all that stuff. It looks fine, but – '

'Here they come,' said Pauline, as a group of people walked up the side-path, chattering, to reach the back of the house. 'I'm on duty.' She strode to the little gate that divided the pathway from the garden, threw it open and began to receive.

Some had come from enthusiasm, some from curiosity, and a few peasants and trade-workers of the district who had already been initiated into the cult had come because they liked the international and egalitarian atmosphere.

Pauline had put out benches in front of the throne under the leafy bower where Hubert stood. She scrutinized each person, greeting them with an aloof, red-eyed smile, as she waved them to their seats.

'Why, Pauline,' said Father Cuthbert, 'you look very sporty.' Pauline waved him on, while Walter, beside her, in his blue jeans and open-necked shirt, smiled nervously. The priest passed on, accompanied by his fellow-Jesuit Gerard Harvey.

One local woman whispered to another, 'Those Jesuits always come, both of them.'

'The Jesuits always go two together, never alone,' said her friend.

'Like carabinieri,' said the other, 'because one can read and the other can write,' and her laughter crackled in the air like a fire in the grass until Pauline's frown quenched it.

By four o'clock they were all assembled and the gate was locked. Pauline had confiscated a motion-picture camera from Letizia Bernardini who had brought her brother Pietro to take a film of the proceedings. Letizia looked sour but did not challenge the booted leader. Berto's son Pino was also of the party, he having been especially attracted to this meeting because of Maggie's feud with Hubert.

Not long ago, Letizia's friend, the psychiatrist Marino Vesperelli, whom she had brought to dinner to meet Maggie that night at her father's house two years before, had discovered in the big general mental hospital in Rome a Swedish patient who had no relations who bothered with him, no friends, but who was apparently cured of the drug addiction which had landed him in that place two summers ago. In conversation with the patient Marino learned that he had been at Nemi with Hubert, working, he said, as a secretarial aide; and in this way, with Letizia's help, Kurt had been safely restored to Hubert who was horrified but impotent to protest; besides, Pauline had taken the boy's part. Kurt was now an acolyte in the Fellowship. He got up late and went out often in a little *cinque cento* car that Letizia had lent him: Hubert prowled around Kurt's room and searched his pockets while he lay asleep, hoping to find traces of narcotic drugs or a hypodermic needle, and so an excuse for getting rid of him. However, Kurt was so far blameless, only somewhat lazy, and here he was as part of the household to help with the meeting in the wild-grown leafy garden.

Pauline's energies had brought back two other lost sheep, named Damian Runciwell and Ian Mackay, only a little changed in appearance and very happy to come and spend another summer with Hubert as in the idyllic past of 1972 when they had all lazed and lain around together, wearing fantastic jewellery and cooking fantastic food. Pauline had often heard Hubert talk nostalgically of those days before she had come to work for him, and before Maggie's marriage had spoiled everything. Like a good sheep-dog Pauline had rounded up three of those four secretaries, and brought them happily before Hubert. Hubert had much to bear in these days of his new prosperity. 'I would have brought you Lauro, too, if I could have done,' Pauline assured him.

'I'm sure you would,' Hubert had said.

'Well, all I want to do is to make you happy, Hubert,' said Pauline.

'It's the thought that matters, Miss Thin,' Hubert said. 'Diana be praised.'

'Oh, aren't you glad to see these old friends? You know how you always talk about that summer before I came to help you out. Now you can relive it all over again. Except, of course, for Lauro. I'm sorry about Lauro. Only, you know, he's absolutely over there on the Radcliffe side and making a fortune. And getting married, too.'

Hubert would have thrown Pauline out that very evening, the three young men with her, had it not been that she knew too much, she knew too much. And here they were among the crowd of selected followers in the garden.

Hubert smiled on them all benevolently when they were seated. About thirty people, he thought. Pauline Thin must be out of her mind, he thought, to call a secret meeting of thirty-odd people. What sort of secret is that?

He decided to change his plan somewhat, and to refrain from discussing anything that might be deemed illicit by the Italian or ecclesiastical authorities, such as the raising of funds and the missionary work necessary to internationalize the Fellowship. A service of worship and a testimony of faith might equally serve this purpose, together with a deliberate accent on the charismatic features of the old, old religion of nature.

'I am the direct descendant of the goddess Diana,' he announced, 'Diana of Nemi, Diana of the Woods and so, indirectly, of her brother the god Apollo.'

Sitting apart from the congregation the two Jesuit observers gave out charismatic smiles in all directions and made way for a late arrival whom Pauline had sent to sit with them. Another observer, Hubert thought. How many observers do you have at a secret meeting? He glared at Pauline who looked angrily back, with fury on her face under her ridiculous hat. Evidently she was still dwelling on Hubert's insults. As well she might, Hubert thought with desperate resentment of the woman as he looked at her, ordering people around, placing them here, guiding them there, with those boots on her awful legs. Hubert, under the leafy trellis, breathed deeply. He noticed that Pauline now held a black-bound book in the hand that indicated the seats; Hubert thought it looked like his Bible but then he put the thought aside, not seeing what she could possibly want to do with it. As she also held the confiscated camera at this moment, Hubert assumed she had also, probably quite needlessly, taken charge of someone's book: bossy little nobody.

Walter, the weak fool, was beside her, holding a list and ticking off names. Who were all these people? Pauline had told Hubert from time to time of new people who could be trusted. But he had no idea they amounted to so many. Two American art historians, very cultured, very rich, Pauline had said. A girl from Rome, 'my best friend there', Pauline had said. Then she had said on one occasion, 'a girl-friend of my friend and she happens to be Michael Radcliffe's mistress'.

Hubert had felt satisfaction at this. Yes, but how did they add up to so many? Hubert did not know most of these people who sat before him.

From the house stepped another robed figure. He was dressed in a toga-like garment which bunched and bundled about his tubby body. It was the lawyer Massimo de Vita; he had come to stand by Hubert's throne and give a simultaneous translation for the benefit of the Italians present. 'Friends,' said Hubert, holding out his arms in benediction, while Massimo announced, '*Amici*'.

'Friends,' Hubert said. 'Brothers and Sisters of Nature. As I have said, I am the descendant of Diana and Apollo, the gods of the old religion that goes back beyond the dawn of history, into the far and timeless regions of mythology where centuries and aeons do not count.'

Massimo de Vita kept even pace behind Hubert, who spoke slowly, somehow without his usual energetic conviction; he was still ruffled by Pauline Thin; she had put him off his stroke. 'Diana,' he went on, 'Goddess of Wildlife, is older than man. She fought on the field of Troy and was humiliated by her jealous step-mother who, as it is written in Homer, took the quiver of arrows from Diana's shoulders and whacked her with it. But such was the charisma of Diana, the virgin goddess, protectress of nature, that she took no revenge, but rather decided to come to Italy, change her name, and dwell amongst us at Nemi. You must know that her name in Greece was Artemis and not far away from the hill upon which we are gathered here in this garden is Monte Artemisio; and down below us lies the sanctuary of Diana, my ancestress, ravished and pillaged . . . ' And with worthy self-effacement Massimo de Vita recited, 'Diana, *la mia antenata, rapita e saccheggiata . . .* '

Meanwhile the sudden voice of a woman cried out the determined statement, 'I'm going to testify.' Hubert, startled, looked towards the voice, while the toga'd advocate, also surprised, instantly pulled himself together, and, believing this to be part of the show, since the voice was Pauline's, continued his dutiful translation ' . . . *adesso vengo testimoniare* . . . '

'What is this interruption?' said Hubert, as everyone turned to look at Pauline.

'*Cos'è questo disturbo*?' translated Massimo into his loudspeaker, although his eyes looked desperately about him for some guidance. He got none whatsoever. He looked towards Pauline, seeing her for the first time that day in her strange sporty outfit and immediately presumed that this interruption was a prearranged affair: a sort of dialogue, all part of that sense of theatre Hubert had so often said was necessary for the success of the Fellowship.

'Miss Thin,' Hubert bellowed into his amplifier, 'do you realize you are in Church in every important sense?'

Massimo continued translating.

Pauline bounded up to the leafy bower and stood beside Hubert, grabbing the loudspeaker. 'I have a right to testify and prophesy,' she proclaimed, 'and I want to testify from the New Testament.'

Father Cuthbert jumped up and down in his seat while his companion, Gerard, smiled eagerly. The rest of the congregation stirred and asked of each other what was it all about, and then fell silent as Pauline's voice boomed out, 'The First Epistle to Timothy, Chapter 1, verses 3 and 4:

As I besought thee to abide still at Ephesus, when I went into Macedonia, that thou mightest charge some that they teach no other doctrine,

Neither give heed to fables and endless genealogies, which minister questions, rather than godly edifying which is in faith . . . '

The congregation remained silent, waiting for further enlightenment which it was clear Pauline, adjusting the loudspeaker, was preparing to give. Only Cuthbert Plaice moved to whisper something with gleaming eyes into his fellow-Jesuit's ear. Hubert, immediately sensing sabotage, attempted first to possess himself of the microphone. But Pauline hung on to it. Hubert therefore, in terror of what she might say next, all in one gesture made as if he were adjusting the instrument for her better to speak and then stretched his left arm at right angles to his body so that it rested across her shoulders in a protective attitude. Thus he made it appear that Pauline's interruption was part of the service, and even his first exclamation – 'What is this interruption?' – might have been part of a dramatic litany. Pauline looked amazed, and turned to Hubert as if to ask if he really meant it.

Massimo, meanwhile, was still catching up with the Italian translation of Pauline's text, which he found difficult.

'Proceed,' said Hubert, grandly.

Two young men in the congregation who had been drawn to the meeting by the rumour that Maggie, whom they both knew slightly, was to be present, sat near the front. One was a former chauffeur of Maggie's and the other was that portrait-painter who had been recommended by Coco de Renault, and for whom she and Mary had somewhat disastrously and very expensively sat. Before setting out for Nemi they had pepped themselves up with trial injections of a new amphetamine drug. The scene before them gave the two young men to believe that the new drug was a very great advance on any previous drug they had sampled, and, as Massimo's garbled version wobbled over his loudspeaker, the two young men began to clap their hands in rhythm.

Pauline pulled herself together to proceed with her testimony under the surprise of Hubert's bidding. With Hubert's arm fondly resting on her shoulders she changed her tone of fury to one of breathless timidity. 'I only wanted to point out,' she told the congregation, 'that the words of the Apostle Paul refer to Diana of Ephesus, where there was a cult of Diana, and that's what inspired me. If you remember in the Acts, and I could find the place, I think – ' She started to look through the Bible in her hand, while the loud rhythmic clapping increased, others of the congregation being encouraged to join in. As she floundered, Father Gerard, perceiving her difficulty, charismatically rose and called out, 'Chapter 19.'

'The Acts, Chapter 19,' said Pauline, turning to the place, while Hubert stood loathing her, imprisoned with his arm in its draped and silvery-green sleeve resting consolingly on her shoulder. 'Read,' he commanded his jailer; whereupon the Jesuits exchanged joy-laden glances. 'He's being very broad-minded, isn't he?' whispered Cuthbert Plaice. The hand-clapping increased and some of the congregation began to sway. Pauline visibly cheered up and now read aloud to this rhythm, with her finger on the place,

'For a certain man named Demetrius, a silversmith, which made silver shrines for Diana, brought no small gain unto the craftsmen;

Whom he called together with the workmen of like occupation, and said, Sirs, ye know that by this craft we have our wealth . . . '

'*Piano, piano,*' pleaded Massimo. 'Read slowly, Miss, I can't keep up.' Pauline began to change her rhythm, stumbling along until she was reading in a kind of syncopated time to the loud hand-clapping, allowing two beats of theirs to one of hers. 'Courage!' bawled Hubert grimly. 'Read to the end.'

' . . . Moreover ye see and hear, that not alone at Ephesus, but almost throughout all Asia, this Paul hath persuaded and turned away much people, saying that they be no gods, which are made with hands:

So that not only this our craft is in danger to be set at nought; but also that the temple of the great goddess Diana should be despised, and her magnificence should be destroyed, whom all Asia and the world worshippeth.

And when they heard these sayings, they were full of wrath, and cried out, saying, Great is Diana of the Ephesians.'

'Enough, enough,' said Hubert, drawing the microphone away from her. Massimo had by no means caught up, but he skipped a good part, few people present being any the wiser, and ended up, '*Basta, basta! Evviva la Diana d'Efeso.*'

Hubert turned to Pauline, who was now thoroughly bewildered by his actions, and embraced her on both cheeks, with the ritualistic gesture of the kiss of peace. He then made a sweeping indication that she was dismissed, and, to the ever-louder clapping of the crowd she descended amongst them. They were making other noises too, now, and standing on the benches.

'And I say unto you,' crooned Hubert into the microphone, 'that Diana of Ephesus was brought to Nemi to become the great earth mother. Great is Diana of Nemi!'

'Diana of Nemi!' yelled someone in the crowd, which inspired Pauline's boy-friend Walter to strike up his guitar. Soon everyone was chanting, 'Diana of Nemi! Diana of Nemi!' The seats were empty, the congregation in raptures all over the place, dancing, clapping, shouting. Hubert gazed on the scene with benevolent satisfaction, relieved that nobody seemed to have taken in the true meaning of the passage. He smiled indulgently, there under the leaves. Then he sat down on his throne, gathering his robes about him, smiling even upon Pauline who was dancing and singing ecstatically with the others and looking such an absolute mess, believing herself once more in Hubert's favour and not caring in the least that he had turned her treachery to his own account.

'I want to testify!'

Hubert turned from his musing, annoyed to find a thin girl standing before the microphone at his side. He recognized Nancy Cowan, the former English tutor to Letizia and Pietro Bernardini who was now simply part of their household, waiting for Bernardini to marry her in the course of time. Hubert rose, uncertain what to do, since the people who were jumping about the garden had come to a standstill at the sound of her voice, and Walter, the damned fool, stopped strumming his guitar.

'I want to say,' said Nancy, 'that the biblical passage you have heard is a condemnation of the pagan goddess Diana. It implies that the cult of Diana was only a silversmith's lobby and pure commercialism. Christianity was supposed to put an end to all that, but it hasn't. It – '

'Well said,' Hubert boomed into the microphone. He had taken over, edging her out of place, and he now put a hand on her shoulder as he continued. 'Our Sister Nancy tells us that Diana of Ephesus was betrayed. Christianity was betrayed, and now we have the great mother of nature again, Diana of the Woods, Diana of Nemi. Great is Diana of Nemi!'

Massimo, who had joined the crowd, returned to his place in time to translate a portion of this speech, but meanwhile something was going wrong with the ritualistic side under Hubert's leafy bower, for, as he had spoken, Nancy had thrown his hand off her shoulder and was now tugging and tearing violently at his robes.

The clapping recommenced, everyone crowding round to see the new event taking place before Hubert's throne. It looked like a fight, and the bemused congregation turned into an audience. Walter, assuming that this affair, too, was part of a previous plan, strummed up once more. 'Great is Diana of Nemi! Long live Diana of Nemi!' Nancy was fairly strong, but Hubert now had her by the hair. His sleeve was half torn off. Presently Letizia excitedly came to help Nancy in whatever role it was she was playing; she was probably drawn to the girl's assistance by the fact that she felt in conflict about Hubert, disliking him personally but fascinated by his nature cult. The sound of hand-clapping mounted again, all round the fighters; Letizia was fairly carried away, so that, in passing, having drawn blood from Hubert's cheeks with her nails she frenziedly tore off her own blouse under which she wore nothing. She fought on, topless, while Nancy concentrated on tearing the green and shining robes piece by piece from Hubert's back.

The noise in the garden was louder than ever. The two priests stood some way from that throne and scene of battle, exhorting frantically. Cuthbert came a little too close and received a casual swipe from Hubert which sent him to the ground. Soon the clothes were torn from the Jesuits, and in fact everyone in the garden was involved in the riot within a very short time.

Mr Stuyvesant and his young friend George Falk did a tour of the house, meantime, to see if there was anything worthwhile. They puzzled for a long time over the good fake Gauguin, then passed on, touching nothing and apparently just breathing as they walked. They noted several valuable objects and the lack of any burglar alarm, unaware as they were that the house would very shortly be emptied of its contents even before they had time to inform their friends what the contents were.

In their self-contained way, they walked back through the ecstatically distressed crowd in the garden, got into their car and drove off.

The party in the garden did not end abruptly, but piece by piece, stagger by stagger. Marino Vesperelli, the psychiatrist who had steadily wooed Letizia for the past three years, lay naked and very fat under a mulberry tree, repeating fragmentary phrases with his eyes staring at the twinkly-blue of the sky between the leaves. 'Exhausted. Group therapy,' he said. 'Letizia. The group.' She, meanwhile, lay on her back across him, gazing up likewise at the branches wherefrom was hanging, for some reason, the twisted and bashed-in skeleton of Walter's guitar. Letizia looked down at her breasts and turned over to comfort her plump suitor.

Pauline wandered in the overgrown and now overwrought garden, looking vainly for her hat while Walter waited for her in the road, his car already packed with some of their possessions. Hubert had in fact thrown her out. He gave her twenty minutes in which to leave, refusing absolutely her offer to bathe a wound on his hand. 'I'll kill you,' Hubert said.

'I thought you were charismatic,' said Pauline. 'At the reading of my testimony from the Bible you showed charisma.'

'Look at my head, Miss Thin,' said Hubert.

'I didn't do it,' Pauline shrieked.

'To all intents and purposes,' Hubert said, 'you did.'

Massimo de Vita came to Pauline's room shortly afterwards and told her she was in trouble, she must pack and go. 'Italian prisons are not very nice. You brought drugs to this house. You created the orgy. People have been hurt and disturbed greatly. Soon it will be all over the countryside and the carabinieri will inquire.' She packed a few things, but not all, unwilling to make such a clean break. To give Hubert a last chance she returned to look for her hat in the garden, as she explained to the waiting Walter. Under Hubert's window Pauline called up, 'Hubert!'

His bloody head appeared. 'I'll wish you good afternoon,' he said. This was followed by one of the heavy metal taps that had been wrenched from every bathroom and washbasin in the house. It hit her on the head and blood spurted down her face. She ran, then, out to Walter and the car, and set off with him towards Paris.

The young portrait-painter had lost a tooth but he felt that the trip which his new amphetamine-based drug had induced was well worth it; and he said as much to his friend, Maggie's former chauffeur, as they sat indoors, squeezed together on the draining-board of the kitchen sink with their feet dabbling in the basin which was filled with cold water.

'It's all over,' Hubert moaned. 'My hopes . . . my . . . I'll kill that woman Pauline Thin if I see her again. I shall have to leave Nemi, but I'll see Miss Thin shall die.'

He was lying on his bed with Massimo hovering over him. His cheeks and hands were scarred and swollen with scratches from the fight, but the most visible wound, a cut on his forehead stretching from the eyebrow to his fairly receded hairline, had come about from his precipitate flight into the house, when he simply banged his head on the lintel of the door.

Massimo, who had early taken refuge from the riot in the garden, was trembling but unharmed. He wrung out a towel in a basin of water beside Hubert's bed, and applied it to the wounded head. He said, 'What do we say when come the journalists? If arrive the police . . . ?'

'I will kill her. She has to die,' Hubert said. 'I shall make her die wherever she is, because I will it. I will send emissaries to kill her.'

The door opened then, and Hubert's three restored secretaries appeared. Kurt Hakens, his red hair now short-cut, with his arms looking like legs and his legs all uncontrolled. Ian Mackay, squat and tough, looking far more like a swarthy Sicilian than a Scotsman, and Damian Runciwell, the big-boned Armenian who had once been the best of the secretaries as secretary. This Damian looked at Massimo and said, 'Get out.'

There was something in the secretaries' attitude that made Massimo place the bowl of water on the floor, drop the damp towel into it and stand up, ready to go.

'Boys, boys!' said Hubert. 'This is no time to be rude. Go and kill Pauline Thin. She must be hovering around somewhere. She'll never leave.'

'Out,' said Damian to Massimo, who went.

'Boys, I've been wounded severely,' said Hubert. 'Look at my head.'

'We've come to kill you,' said Ian, producing an ugly, long and old-fashioned revolver from his trousers pocket.

'Put that silly toy away and bathe my head,' Hubert said. 'Do you want me to have to go to hospital? As it is, I wouldn't be surprised if the carabinieri arrived at any moment.'

Kurt had taken out a revolver, too. His was shiny and modern-looking. 'For God's sake, what are you doing? It might go off,' Hubert said.

Damian now turned nervously to the others and said something that Hubert couldn't hear. He jerked his head towards the door, perhaps indicating that they should leave, or perhaps referring in some way to Massimo, who had been the last to depart.

Ian, with his revolver pointed at Hubert said, 'Who was he?'

'Who? Massimo de Vita? He's my lawyer,' Hubert said, sitting up in some alarm, with his hand to his wounded head.

Damian walked to the door, opened it and stood half in and half out of the bedroom. He said to the other two men, 'Come here a second.' They followed, Ian still keeping a watch on Hubert, and started arguing in whispers which presently began to sound like the spits and hisses of recrimination.

Hubert screamed, 'What the hell's going on?' and started to get out of bed. Whereupon the three surrounded him and pressed him back. Damian was crying all over his broad face.

'Hubert,' he said, 'can you give us a drink? It's all too unnerving, my dearie. It's all too much.'

Ian put his revolver back into his trousers pocket where it bulged unbecomingly. Kurt rather coyly went over to the bed and placed his smart little gun upon it.

'Have you boys been taking drugs?' said Hubert.

'My word of honour,' said Kurt. 'I'm cured. My psychiatrist will tell you.'

'Drugs,' said Ian. 'All he can think of is drugs when there's a threat on his life. He doesn't think that certain people might have a certain reason to pay us to kill him.'

'We never meant to do it, Hubert,' said Damian, weeping still. 'Not really.'

'Bathe my wound,' said Hubert, 'and tell me who sent you to scare me.'

Damian started washing Hubert's wound at the point that Massimo had left off. 'We need a drink,' said Ian.

'Well, go and fetch a drink. Fetch some disinfectant and a dressing of some sort,' Hubert said. 'I don't want to get stitches in my head. I shall bear the scar of Pauline Thin all my life. When you've had a drink you can go and find her, shoot her, and hide her body in the woods.'

'Hubert, the Marchesa de Tullio-Friole sent us to kill you. Really she did,' said Damian.

'Maggie? She offered you money?'

They were silent then, and obviously embarrassed. Hubert said, 'Then you'd have done so if you hadn't bungled it, if you hadn't come in when my friend Massimo was here?'

'No, Hubert, it was all a pretence. We would have hid you and shared the money with you.'

'Would you go to court and swear that Maggie bribed you to murder me?' Hubert said.

'No,' said Ian.

'No,' said Damian, 'I wouldn't like to go into the horrible criminal atmosphere of a law court, Hubert.'

'No, I wouldn't go near the police ever again,' said Kurt.

'I might force you to testify,' said Hubert. Ian's hand went to his bulgy pocket. 'But I won't,' said Hubert. 'Descendant as I am of the great Diana of Nemi, I have been struck by disaster after disaster all in one afternoon. Such is the fate of the gods. Have you ever read Homer? Has any one of you read Homer? Worse things than this occurred to the gods and their descendants in those days, and so it isn't surprising if they happen to me in times like these. In fact, it proves my rights and titles. *Rex Nemorensis*, the King of Nemi, king of the woods, favoured son of Diana the mother of nature.'

Ian came back with a bottle of brandy, four glasses, a bottle of kitchen alcohol and a wad of cotton wool. 'It's all I could find,' he said. 'This house is not at all as well equipped as it was in the old days when we were running it.'

'Tell me,' said Hubert, 'did you really come here to kill me?'

'Of course not,' said Damian, crying again. 'Don't remind me,' he said.

'Ian, I want that revolver, please. Give it to me.'

Ian handed it over. Hubert examined it well. Then he examined the gun that Kurt had placed on his bed. 'Who gave you these?' he said.

'Maggie. She got them out of her husband's armoury. Mary was with her,' Ian said.

'Yes, Mary was there,' said Kurt.

'How much did she offer you?'

'She didn't specify. She said she'd pay a fortune but month by month in instalments, in case we talked. She said Mary was her witness as an alibi that she was somewhere else with Mary that day, so if we got into trouble it was useless to try to incriminate them. She meant it, Hubert.'

'You tell me you had nothing in advance? She paid you nothing?'

'Not a dollar, not one little dime,' said Ian, very quickly and definitely, and the other two murmured agreement.

'Then you are imbeciles,' Hubert said. 'I know that woman. She once said to me, "Faggots are things that you put on the fire." Very amusing. She thinks you're expendable. I will never know for sure whether you three boys meant it, either.' He locked the two guns and, placing them under the sheet beside him, lay back. 'Give me some brandy,' he said. 'I don't think you would have had the nerve to go through with it, anyway. Maggie has always been utterly foolish. She never consults the experts.'

Early next morning, Massimo returned to the house ostentatiously with a removal van, waving a file of documents that might have contained anything. To establish himself well as an outsider he stopped at the post office to ask the way to Hubert's house, volubly explaining that he had come on behalf of his client, the Marchesa Tullio-Friole to order the house to be vacated.

One by one the contents were stacked into the van and taken away to a safe place. Hubert was left with a bed, a stove, his everyday clothes, the television, the refrigerator, four kitchen chairs and four deck chairs. His tattered green robes as well as the good ones went with the van. His documents, so neatly arranged by Pauline in their boxes, went too. The pictures, fake and real, were stacked carefully and so was the furniture, expertly packed in the movers' cartons. Off went all these goods, under the tutelage of Massimo de Vita, and Hubert sat in the kitchen with his boys. 'It's like that previous summer before Maggie got married,' he said. 'Darlings, find something to cook.'

After lunch Hubert telephoned to Massimo de Vita 'Just to check,' he said, 'that the goods are in a safe place.'

'They are safe, don't worry,' said Massimo.

'When will they be leaving the country?'

'Be careful on the telephone,' said Massimo softly and then, in a louder voice, he said, 'With valuable stuff you have to be careful of thieves listening in, you know. Your possessions, Mr Mallindaine, will be leaving Italy within a few days. I have an export permit and all the documents. As a foreigner, you are easier to export than many other clients.'

XV

MAGGIE WAS BEING DRIVEN by car from Geneva to Lausanne when she remembered the hired assassins she had sent to Hubert. Seen in the light of the greater outrage perpetrated upon her by Coco de Renault, the arrangements she had made with these frightful people now seemed foolish. She hoped they had been too weak or had lacked the opportunity to carry out her orders. She had made no advance payments, only a gold watch apiece, each one slightly different to show good taste; and Mary would have to stand by her if there were any accusations. When she reached Lausanne Maggie put a call through to Mary from her hotel.

'Mary,' said Maggie, lying on the bed wrapped in towels, for the call had come through while she was in her bath, 'I've drawn the ace of spades in the game of life.'

'Excuse me?' said Mary.

'I say I've met with disaster.'

'Oh, have you had an accident?'

'Coco de Renault has completely disappeared with all my money.'

'That's impossible,' Mary said.

'I have to find him,' said Maggie, 'and I have to get back home. My cheques here are bouncing and my bank managers are not in the office when I want to see them; they are all otherwise occupied to a theatrical degree. I've never felt so humiliated in my life. Tell Berto to send me some money.'

'All right, Maggie. But there must be something wrong.'

'Don't tell Berto about Coco's disappearance. I don't want to give him a shock. He'd be furious.'

'Berto's in trouble,' said Mary. 'He had a burglary.'

'But I thought he warned the police about those two men who came to case the joint.'

'I know. Two detectives went along, and they said the burglar alarm was O.K., then the next day, it was only on Tuesday, Guillaume let in a couple of carabinieri, only they weren't carabinieri, they were people dressed up like carabinieri. They tied up the servants and they took the Veronese and all the silver, and they also took that portrait, school of Titian. Berto says they will hold the paintings for ransom as they're no use on the market, but Berto won't pay ransom. He says his hairs have gone grey overnight, but he already had grey hair. I like Berto so much, Maggie.'

'What about my jewellery?' Maggie said.

'They took that too, Maggie.'

'Guillaume!' shrieked Maggie. 'I don't trust that Guillaume. He must have been in with it. It was an inside job. Guillaume has to go. I'll tell Berto. It's either Guillaume or me. Berto must choose.'

'Maggie, the police questioned all the servants and the police believe the servants. Guillaume got hurt in the struggle, too. Didn't you read the papers? It happened Tuesday and it was all in the papers yesterday. Berto says – '

'My jewellery,' Maggie said, 'is the important thing to me at this moment, and Guillaume has it.'

'Maggie, there's an echo on the line; it's an awfully bad line.'

'It wasn't in the papers here,' Maggie said.

'It was in the Italian newspapers. Maybe it isn't a big enough robbery to make the international headlines,' said Mary. 'There have been an awful lot of robberies.'

'A Veronese is an international robbery,' Maggie shouted frantically.

'Well, some art thieves took a Rembrandt from Vienna the same day. Did you read about that?'

'No, I didn't. The press is hushing it all up,' said Maggie.

'I guess there are too many to report,' Mary said.

'Look,' said Maggie, 'I'm coming home. Tell Berto to get me some money here by tomorrow morning. I have to get out my best jewellery from the bank and sell it, and Berto has to sell some of his land. We're paupers. Guillaume has to go to jail and I have to get the contents of my house from Hubert. I hope nothing has happened to him, Mary; it was silly of us to – '

'Not on the phone,' Mary said. 'I told Michael what we'd done. He was so furious. He said not to mention it on the phone. Anyway those boys are staying over there in that house with Hubert and all the furniture's been taken away by your lawyer. They had an orgy, couple of weeks ago, but I wasn't there, myself. Everyone else was.'

'Which lawyer took my stuff?' Maggie said.

'Massimo something. The one in Rome.'

'He's a crook,' said Maggie. 'He's a Communist and he's working for Hubert. I gave Hubert's boys each a gold watch and all they can do is have an orgy. Did the police break it up? Why didn't you call the police?'

'I wasn't there. Nobody denounced them to the police. Everyone was afraid and they got away. The police went round last week to have a look but all they found was Hubert and the boys in the empty house.'

'Berto will never believe it,' Maggie said, 'and I'm going to fight every inch of – '

'Berto doesn't know a thing,' Mary said. 'We can't hurt Berto. He's too nice.'

'And what about me?' Maggie said. 'Doesn't anyone have any feelings for me?'

'Oh, yes, we do, Maggie,' Mary said. 'Oh, yes, we do. We love you and we care for you a lot.'

The first thing Maggie did when she put down the telephone was to order as many Italian newspapers as possible. Maggie was still, so far as was known, one of the hotel's wealthiest clients, but the best the night porter could do at that hour, well after midnight, was to send to the station for the early morning edition of *Il Tempo* which he delivered to Maggie at about one-thirty. She was still awake, putting her disasters in order of priority. There was no word of the robbery at Berto's villa; it had evidently become old news. But the headline in the Roman crime section caused her to put another call through to Mary.

'Oh, can't you sleep, Maggie?' said Mary anxiously. 'Michael said I shouldn't have told you all those things, I should have waited. Berto is going to call his bank in Geneva tomorrow morning. He tried to call you but he couldn't get through. It's terribly difficult from the villa. Can't you sleep? Berto says I shouldn't have told you about your jewellery because he should have liked to be with you when you heard.'

'Well, I want to know about your jewellery,' Maggie said. 'You said you were putting it in an out-of-the-way bank for safety.'

'Oh, goodness, yes. It's all in a bank, I don't know, Michael's trying to get to sleep. It's on the Via Appia.'

'Banco di Santo Spirito?' said Maggie.

'Yes, that's it. If you need money that bad, Maggie, I can get you a loan without pawning my jewellery. You just talk to Michael when you come home; I can talk to Daddy, and – '

'Number 836 Via Appia?' said Maggie.

'Well, I don't know. I guess there's only one Santo Spirito on the Via Appia.'

'Get up and look,' Maggie said. 'I must know the exact bank and the exact number of the exact street. There has been a robbery at the Santo Spirito. It says here in this morning's *Tempo*, Wednesday, 16 July, that there was a robbery over the week-end and they found on Monday that the gang ransacked the strong-boxes. Get up and see if that's your bank.'

'Oh, no! Oh, no!' Mary said. 'It can't be. I haven't heard anything. Maybe they tried to get me. We just got back this morning from the villa . . . ' Maggie then heard her say, 'Michael, wake up, my jewellery's been robbed. What is the address of my bank?'

It was indeed Mary's bank which the belated report referred to. Mary also informed Maggie that she hadn't insured this jewellery, believing it to be safe in its vault. Her voice was strange; she spoke with awe as if she was in church. 'What an experience for you!' Maggie said. 'You poor child, what an ordeal to have to wait till the bank opens in the morning before you can find out whether your box was one of the unlucky ones or not.' She spoke with genuine concern, thinking mainly of a special diamond brooch and an emerald ring of great value that she herself had given to Mary. But Michael came on the telephone, unreasonable with anxiety and short-tempered. 'What sort of a woman,' he said, 'would ring us up in the middle of the night, twice, with the very worst news? You could have let us sleep till the morning. Now Mary's crying. She wants me to call the bank manager. How can I call him in the middle of the night, what good will it do? I don't know him. Mary isn't a bit materialistic, that's what you don't realize, Mother. There's an economic crisis and you've got to face it. It's what – '

'We're ruined!' Maggie shrieked back. 'We've all become paupers overnight, and the first thing that happens when a family is ruined is always a quarrel unless they are very rare people, very exceptional. And I'm just so sorry to see that you are very, very ordinary, and also common from the Radcliffe side. The whole family quarrelled over their trusts and their wills, and what's more, it was only an hour ago that Mary told me you all cared for me and loved me. It isn't my fault if Mary's lost her jewellery. Maybe she hasn't. I hope not. I'm going to speak to Berto.' Maggie hung up at this point, looked at herself in the glass and was amazed to find herself still glowing and handsome. She took a bath, telephoned for a bottle of champagne, asked to be wakened at eight, and went to bed where she slowly sipped three glasses before she went to sleep.

It made Lauro very happy indeed to be summoned from his honeymoon cruise by Maggie, although he was putting on a great air to the effect that she had done something outrageous in putting through a call to the captain of the *Panorama di Nozze*, that cruise ship with twenty-one newly-wedded couples on board on which he and Betty had been spending their honeymoon. Lauro had already, in times past, visited the Greek islands with Maggie's entourage, he had seen the labyrinthine home of the Minotaur and he had been to the Acropolis. The tone of the honeymoon company appalled him. Twenty-one pairs of newlyweds; every morning a round of sniggery remarks; dancing until three in the morning with uproarious jokes about exchanging partners and which is the way to *your* cabin? The awful brides whispering together over cocktails, and Betty no better than the rest.

He sat with Betty now in the comfortable lobby of the hotel in Lausanne, while Maggie, reassuringly radiant, heard

out his outraged complaints with an obligingly penitent expression that meant only that she had more important things
on her mind than to waste words in defending herself.

'You're so right, Lauro,' she said. 'I should have realized . . .
I should have been more thoughtful . . . Your honeymoon. It
happens once in a lifetime, doesn't it?' She turned to plump,
bridal Betty who had clearly been to the hairdresser and
had dressed very carefully for this meeting. 'I do apologize,'
Maggie said, 'if I may call you Betty?'

Betty drooped her lids and shrugged, as if not prepared to
show any lack of support for her husband's complaint. 'We
nearly didn't come,' she said. 'But then the captain made out
it was so urgent, and the transport being all arranged, Lauro
thought maybe you were ill and so we came ashore that day.'

'Lauro could easily have come alone,' said Maggie, 'and
left you to finish the cruise.'

'What a suggestion,' said Lauro. 'How could I leave my
wife alone on a honeymoon cruise, Maggie, are you crazy?'

'Well, now that you're here, Lauro, may I have a word
with you?' Maggie said.

'Go ahead,' said Lauro, refilling all three glasses with the
champagne that Maggie had ordered for the party.

'Well, it's business, Lauro. Betty must, of course, get used
to business practice, and as you are my confidant and secretary I must speak to you alone. If Betty will give us half an
hour. I'm sure there's some shopping she wants to do. The
boutiques of Lausanne are charming; she can get some ideas
for her boutique in Rome, don't you think?'

Betty said, 'Just what I was thinking myself,' and put down
her glass with a sharp tinkle.

Lauro considered the matter importantly, with his lips
pouted together. Then he said, 'Yes, I think Maggie is in the
right. Come back in half an hour, Betty, all right?'

'Fine,' she said brightly, 'lovely.'

They watched her as she passed through the lane of little tables to the vestibule, and out of the swing doors, in her cream and brown linen suit.

'Are you happy?' said Maggie to Lauro.

'Of course,' said Lauro. 'Betty is a wonderful wife. She's beautiful and also intelligent. We Italians, you know, like women to be women, and to be shapely.'

'I often think Italian girls are very mature in their appearance,' Maggie said, 'a little over-full, but it's a matter of taste.'

'I won't hear a word against Italian girls,' said Lauro, 'and especially my wife.'

'You're perfectly right,' Maggie said in hasty conciliation. 'I only meant that maybe the trouble is that they have their Confirmation too early. In the Anglo-Saxon countries they aren't confirmed till they're fourteen.' She waved the subject vaguely aside. 'It's a matter of national custom, that's all. I'm sure I'm not bigoted. Well, Lauro, I've got something really serious to discuss with you. It's serious and it's private, and I can't thank you enough for breaking off your mass-honeymoon for me, Lauro.'

'It was a very lovely and very expensive, exclusive honeymoon cruise,' said Lauro. 'Today we were to go on donkey-back into the mountains.'

'All on donkeys together, twenty-one *sposi*!' marvelled Maggie.

Lauro looked sour.

'But Lauro, I'm in trouble, darling,' Maggie said. 'I really am.'

Lauro cheered up. 'What's your problem?' he said.

'I see in the newspapers,' said Maggie, 'that a lot of people are getting kidnapped. In Italy it's becoming a national sport. Every day there's someone new. Where are all the millions going to?'

'It's a criminal affair,' Lauro said, 'mainly run by the Mafia but there are independent gangs, maybe political. I don't know. Why don't you keep your bodyguard? What happened to your gorilla?'

'I can't afford a bodyguard. I'm broke,' said Maggie.

Lauro laughed. 'If that were true why would you be afraid of being kidnapped?'

'When it's known that Coco de Renault has disappeared completely with all my holdings, all my real estate, all my trusts, all my capital, I won't have to fear being kidnapped.'

'What are you talking about, Maggie?' Lauro said. 'You ask about kidnaps, then you tell me this story of de Renault. I think you try to make out you're poor because you're afraid. But no one will believe you, Maggie. You have to take care. It's not nice to be kidnapped. Sometimes the victim never comes home. Remember how they cut off young Getty's ear. They keep you in a dungeon for weeks.'

'Coco has disappeared. I've tried to trace him. I've had private detectives and my lawyers trying to trace him. They say he's somewhere in the Argentine; that's all the news I can get. I'm not sure if they're right or wrong. Maybe the investigators can't be bothered any more. In the meantime the detectives have to be paid, lawyers' fees have to be paid.'

'And the police?'

'Which police? He belongs to no country. Then if I make a scandal, the tax people will start nosing into my affairs, that's all. I want to kidnap Coco, that's what I want to do. I want to extort my money out of him. At least I might get a part of it, something. I want to kidnap Coco de Renault.'

Lauro said, 'It's a criminal offence, kidnapping.'

'Oh, I know,' Maggie said. 'I know. Why shouldn't I be a criminal? Everyone else is.'

'Maggie, your husband – '

'He'll never know,' said Maggie.

Lauro sat back in a worldly way with an unworldly expression. 'You're a wonderful woman, Maggie. What's in it for me?'

'Ten per cent,' said Maggie.

'Twenty,' said Lauro.

'Including the expenses and the pay-offs, though,' Maggie said.

'No, no,' said Lauro. 'There's a big risk for those poor people who do the actual work. They risk a life's imprisonment if they don't get shot by the police. Then they have to find the people to do the first part, take the prisoner; then they have to find the good hiding places; they have to find the family and make the telephone calls, and they have to feed the man.'

'All right, thirty per cent inclusive,' Maggie said.

'Who is the family?'

'An American wife, rather ancient-looking, living here in Lausanne. I've seen her at a distance, poor dreary soul. The investigators say she swears she hasn't seen him for five months, but they don't believe her; neither do I.'

'You think he'll visit her one day?'

'I don't know. I think he's probably changed his appearance by plastic surgery. The reason I think so is that he's done it twice before.'

'He'll never come back to Switzerland,' Lauro said. 'If he's now a millionaire in the Argentine, why should he want to see an old wife?'

'There's a daughter at college in America,' said Maggie. 'She'll be home with her mother this summer. I think he might want to see the daughter.'

'You would have to demand a very large ransom,' said Lauro, 'to make it worth your while.'

'I'll demand a large ransom,' Maggie said. 'After all, it's my money, isn't it?'

'My contacts don't run to the Mafia,' Lauro said. 'I'm not in touch with the underworld at all.'

'Oh, come,' said Maggie, 'don't exaggerate, Lauro.'

'I know very few,' Lauro said.

'If I sell my big ruby pendant,' said Maggie, 'I can offer to those very few friends of yours a good sum in advance. My ruby is one of the few things that haven't yet been stolen. I've had some jewellery stolen from the villa and I think Mary has probably lost hers in that job at the Banco di Santo Spirito the other day.' She was crying now.

'I don't know what to believe,' said Lauro, 'but somehow I believe you, or you wouldn't have torn me away from my bride and my honeymoon.' He, too, had tears in his eyes at the thought of his lost paradise as it now existed in his head, if not in fact.

'Betty will be back soon. Can you get rid of her for the afternoon? She can use my car,' Maggie said.

'I suppose so,' Lauro said. 'I get rid of her and I take you up to bed. Isn't that your idea?'

'It's usually your idea,' said Maggie, 'isn't it?'

'I suppose so,' Lauro said.

Dusk had fallen when Maggie arrived two days later at the Villa Tullio. Berto was not expecting her; he had heard no word from her and had been unable to find her at any of the Swiss hotels she usually stayed at. Berto was worried; he could not quite understand why she had needed money. He made arrangements for the money to reach her, but afterwards, when he had tried to reach her by telephone at Lausanne, she had just left the hotel.

Mary also had tried to reach her, overjoyed that her safety-box, being one of those set high in the wall of the bank-vault, had escaped the gang's frenzied operation. Mary had telephoned to Berto in the Veneto. 'I'm worried about Maggie. Where is she?'

'I don't know,' Berto said. 'She's left Lausanne, and I can't find her anywhere else. I'm worried, too. Have you seen this morning's paper? Another kidnapping.'

'Oh, Berto, darling, don't worry,' Mary said. 'Would you like me to come and keep you company?'

'No, my dear, don't think of it.'

The chauffeur who drove Maggie home to the Villa Tullio that night was thoroughly puzzled. The Marchesa had dressed herself up so peculiarly. She had gone to a flea-market in a small town on the way home, all on an impulse while he waited in the car-park. This chauffeur had long been in Berto's service and had very few original thoughts about Maggie. He respected her considerably because she was Berto's wife and hence the Marchesa, and he felt it natural that she should have illogical impulses. He had taken her all over Switzerland on a mystifying route, not consequentially, not economically planned; first the Zürich area, then the Geneva area, then Zug, then Lausanne. To him, it was all a great *non sequitur* but Maggie was always careful to see that he had good rooms and ate well and was comfortable, as a lady should. It had not caused him to quibble in his thoughts when Lauro and his bride turned up at Lausanne, that Lauro at Maggie's request had then sent him on a trip around the valleys and up the mountains on a sight-seeing tour with Betty for the whole afternoon, from twelve-thirty to six-thirty. The chauffeur had lunched at pretty little Caux, high up on a mountain path, Betty sitting at one table, he at another, despite the girl's invitation to sit at the table with her. Betty had marvelled at the little chalets, and the chauffeur had agreed with a totally unscientific will to please. 'My husband, my poor husband,' Betty had said, 'is busy with that Marchesa all the afternoon and he's on his honeymoon.' The chauffeur merely said that such was life. 'Her houses at Nemi are built on my land,' said Betty. 'They're *abusivo*; she has to pull down those houses or else pay us. That's what they have to discuss, and believe me – '

As she spoke the chauffeur pulled up at a cottage-weave shop and asked Betty if she would like to look round it. Betty spent some time there, buying embroidered placemats and a shawl, then re-entered the car, into the back seat, daintily, with the door held open for her by Berto's chauffeur.

The next day Maggie had gone to Geneva and dropped Betty at the airport to catch a plane for Rome. Then, with Lauro, she had gone to a newly constructed block of flats where there was no concierge but a press-button phone at the entrance. Lauro pressed a button but there was no answer. The big glass-fronted doors were locked. Maggie got back into the car and waited. Lauro walked up and down the little pathway with its tidy new plants on either side; he pressed the button again from time to time; he looked up at the windows; he looked at his watch.

Maggie, who seldom explained anything, had evidently felt it necessary to explain to the chauffeur that they were waiting for a dressmaker, very brilliant and not yet famous, whom she simply had to see. They had an appointment, she explained.

It was too bad, said the chauffeur, to keep the Marchesa waiting. They waited twenty more minutes before a Peugeot drew up. Three youngish men got out, very quickly, and made for the entrance where Lauro was waiting. The chauffeur had not been able to see their faces for they kept them quite averted from him. One of the men, saying something to Lauro, indicated vulgarly with his thumb the car where Maggie sat with the chauffeur and said something in French, which the chauffeur didn't understand, but which sounded disapproving. Maybe the man had not wanted to be seen. At any rate one of the men had opened the door with a key, and Lauro was answering back, looking at his watch. Maggie then got out of the car with her charming smile and followed the four men into the building. That took up the rest of the morning. Maggie emerged without Lauro, and they were off, back to the Veneto, stopping for meals on the way, and then, unaccountably, at a little market-town where Maggie had spent an hour while the chauffeur waited in the car-park.

He had waited, which is to say he had taken an occasional walk around. From what he saw and what he heard, Maggie had no rendezvous with anyone this time. A rendezvous, although its purpose might escape Berto's good chauffeur, might at least have been explicable. What was thoroughly inconsistent was that Maggie had stood there at a stall, innocently buying a heap of dreadful clothes; and they were plainly intended for herself for she held up these rags against her body to get a rough idea if they would fit. A worn-out long skirt of black cotton, a pair of soiled tennis shoes which she actually tried on there in the street, a once-pink head scarf, a cotton blouse, not second-hand but cheap, piped with white, and terrible. The chauffeur wandered back to the car and waited. Maggie appeared before long, with her sunniness intact, and her light-hearted walk, holding in her arms the bundle of these frightful garments, not even wrapped in a piece of paper.

The chauffeur took them from her and placed them carefully in the boot. All he said was, 'The Marchesa should leave her handbag with me when she goes shopping. There are bad people about.' Whereupon Maggie searched in her handbag, quite alarmed; but everything was all right. They drove on.

Towards dusk next day Maggie wanted to stop in Venice for a rest and a drink. She left the chauffeur at the quay and, hiring a water-taxi, directed it to a smart bar. Later she returned in a water-taxi and kept it waiting while she demanded of the chauffeur the old clothes from the back of the car. Wrapping them, for very shame, in a tartan car-rug, the chauffeur handed them over. Maggie redirected the taxi to the bar.

She returned looking so like a tramp that the chauffeur failed to recognize her at first. 'Marchesa!' he then exclaimed.

'I changed in the ladies' room,' Maggie had said. 'Did I give you a fright? I want to play a joke on my husband.'

Onward to the villa. It was dark as they approached. 'The back entrance,' Maggie ordered. 'I have the key.'

The chauffeur, still puzzled, drove round the villa to the firmly locked and heavy back gate in the wall which led into the paddock, the orchard, the kitchen garden, and finally to the great back door.

'Let me accompany the Marchesa,' he said, fetching out his big electric torch. He had in mind those masked balls he had heard of, and felt a little guilty and low-class, lacking that sense of humour of the sophisticated. He decided to try to enter the spirit of the thing.

Maggie attacked the big gate with her key while the chauffeur's torch shone on it. With the first touch, a furious din broke loose. Barking of dogs, the screams of women, male voices roaring out the worst possible obscenities, and above all the words, 'Ladri! Ladri! polizia!' – Thieves, police . . . Maggie screamed, but bells were ringing now, searchlights beamed from the rooftop of the villa and Berto's dalmatian, Pavoncino, came streaking towards the gate, barking only less loudly than the barking in the air.

The pandemonium continued while the chauffeur pulled Maggie back into the car, bundling her into the front seat beside him. He drove off at full speed round to the front of the house and got out to ring the bell.

Here, Pavoncino awaited them, barking. But soon, having recognized Maggie, he was wagging his tail. Maggie sat on and waited. A police car drew up, then another.

In the midst of the turmoil Berto appeared with Guillaume, both armed with guns.

The police had taken Maggie into custody and were holding the chauffeur with his hands behind his back.

'Berto, it's me,' Maggie called out.

'Where are you, Maggie? I can't see you,' Berto called. 'Are you all right?'

'No, I'm not,' Maggie said.

The police could not understand English and had already bundled her, in her rags, into a police car, around which the dog pranced joyfully, barking loudly.

The noises in the air ceased abruptly. Guillaume slowly opened the front gate, still with his gun poised. Then, perceiving the dog's demonstrations of welcome, cautiously approached the police car where Maggie sat meekly, handcuffed to two burly carabinieri.

At first he didn't recognize her, and could hardly believe her voice when she called 'Berto!'

'That's my wife,' Berto said. 'Maggie, what are you doing? You've set off my new burglar alarm and all the loudspeakers and the electronic communication with the police station. What's wrong?'

Maggie was released in due course of time, and brandy administered to the chauffeur. The policemen were invited inside and apologized to, refusing, however, to drink while on duty; they seemed happy enough to have a nice glance round the drawing-room.

'I dressed up as a pauper,' Maggie explained in the best Italian she could manage. 'Because I am a pauper. I'm ruined. I just wanted everyone to know.'

316

Berto, placing to one side for the moment his bewilderment, translated this with considerable modifications. He explained, in fact, that the Marchesa had only meant it as a joke; she had not known of the burglar alarm.

Many more apologies from Berto. Sincere and profound apologies. The police went away and Berto stood looking at his bedraggled wife, still handsome and gleaming through it all as she was.

XVI

Dear Hubert,

On my return from a business trip to Switzerland I found a letter from my lawyer, Avvocato Massimo de Vita, in which he tells me you are claiming that I gave you my Gauguin, and that moreover my Gauguin is a fake.

As it happens, I did not give you my Gauguin and my Gauguin is not a fake.

I plan, in fact, to sell my Gauguin. In these days of tight money one has to plan one's budget, and Berto plans to take my Gauguin to London to sell it. I plan also to dispose of my Louis XIV furniture. I heard an absurd rumour that my furniture and pictures had already been taken away from the house, but naturally you would have informed me had they been stolen. There are so many rumors! However, I plan the move for Wednesday. As you know I'm not so very keen on Louis XIV and I don't need it anyway really. I don't use it, do I? We are planning to collect it next week Wednesday August 27. It is such a long time since we met. We are planning to pay you a visit, Hubert, to discuss your future plans, as we are selling the villa to Lauro as it appears the land on which it is built belongs to Lauro's beautiful new bride. Isn't it fortunate that Lauro has been our friend all these years? Would you believe it, but he even cut short his honeymoon to come

318

and discuss my plans with me! What good fortune that the land does not belong to a stranger! In the meantime of course I am taking action against Mr de Lafoucauld who arranged for the purchase of my properties at Nemi as it seems he was most untrustworthy. That is not his real name, of course, but Berto has talked to the police, they have found him in Milan and certainly he will go to prison. Berto has said he no longer cares if his name gets into the papers in connection with a criminal action as we are the innocent party, always have been and always will be.

I hope you can find some other spot in Nemi to continue your plans for your new religion. It sounds very exciting and I would have loved to have been there, too, but I was in Switzerland and besides, Berto is so conventional, he would hate it if I got mixed up with drugs, orgies, etc. etc. Isn't it good that Lauro is willing to make a little arrangement with me for the house, as it is really an illegal house although I didn't know it at the time, of course. I plan to move in as soon as possible. Berto, of course, was angry about the orgy but he would naturally prefer you to go quietly. I mean, we don't want to complain to the authorities as that would be unpleasant. It has been good of you to keep my pictures and my furniture in good condition. I have tried to get in touch with Massimo de Vita to tell him personally what my plans are, but his office telephone number doesn't answer. A few weeks ago I read in the papers that the Lake of Nemi is 'biologically dead' which means it is polluted, but they are building a new sewage system for that clinic, so it doesn't all go into the lake. I am sure your ancestors would turn in their graves and I do feel for you, after those beautiful ships of antiquity sailed so proudly on its tranquil surface. Of course, Nemi is beautiful and Mary will be sorry to leave, but their house is also illegal and I don't know if they can make arrangements with the owners of the land, and in any case Michael says we shouldn't have to pay twice for a house. It is a worry for the Bernardinis also, especially as his wedding to Nancy is to take place soon. She is a very fine young woman and will be a very good housekeeper for him I am quite sure.

If you see Avvocato Massimo de Vita please tell him he has got it all wrong about my Gauguin. I really feel that lawyers these days are very slipshod in their work. Hardly any of them care about their clients any more. I plan to go to another lawyer.

Don't forget Wednesday, 27, the van will be coming, naturally with an armed escort as one can't be too careful these days.

Arrivederci and all my love,

Maggie

P.S. It is terrible the times we are living in. I just read in the *Herald Tribune* about a dear friend of mine, a financier from the Argentine, Coco de Renault, being kidnaped. Apparently they are asking a fantastic ransom and the poor wife and daughter in Switzerland are absolutely frantic. I put through a call to them immediately but they didn't want to talk so as to keep the line free for the kidnapers to negotiate. The family say they haven't seen Coco for months and they don't know where he is, which is terrible, but the newspapers say he has to send them a power of attorney to release all his money for the kidnapers, and it's possible the banks will not accept his word in which case he could be killed. It is terrible to read about these events and even more frightening when it is someone you know and it reaches your own door. Personally, I think the wife has already got all his money tucked away somewhere in Switzerland, though the talk of powers of attorney is her way of trying to drive a bargain. They usually put their money in the wife's name or in a numbered account so I hope my friend will be released unharmed, but how dreadful to pay it all to criminals!

Hubert read the letter slowly to Pauline Thin who had returned the day after Hubert's three former secretaries had left.

Since the furniture had been taken away there had been quarrels every day amongst them all; the boys simply didn't have the stamina to sit it out for a month all sleeping on camp-beds and eating in the kitchen. A month was all Hubert had asked of them, just for the sake of appearances.

Maggie's furniture and her pictures had already been sold in London. Even those pictures which had been copies, and the set of Louis XIV furniture which had been reconstructed, with an original leg here, an arm there, had fetched quite a fat sum, while those original paintings and articles of furniture which remained had fetched a fortune. After Massimo's half-share had been deducted there still remained a fortune for Hubert, that fortune which he had felt all along that Maggie should have settled on him. It was now only a matter of keeping up an appearance of poverty for a month or maybe a little longer, so there should be no question that he had made off with Maggie's property. Massimo had left for some unknown destination; he had said California, which meant, certainly, elsewhere; evidently he was used to departing speedily for elsewhere from time to time. Hubert's half-share of the sale was safely in that nursery-garden of planted money, Switzerland.

'Miss Thin,' said Hubert when Pauline arrived at the house the day after the departure of his three discontented friends, 'if you have come to collect your remaining goods and chattels you have come in vain. The bailiffs have been. They have taken everything, including your knickers. All they have left me are the bare necessities and I, descendant of the gods, am a pauper. What is more, Miss Thin, you have much to account for.'

Pauline said, 'So have you. Five months' pay for a start.'

'Don't be vulgar,' he said. All the same, he opened the kitchen cupboard and took a bundle of notes out of a tin. He counted out her pay. 'Women,' he said, 'are incredibly materialistic.'

She sat down on a kitchen chair and checked the money. 'Your boy-friends have gone,' she said. 'I dare say they left for idealistic, not materialistic, reasons. That's why they left you all alone here, without any comfortable furniture. Where did you get this money from, Hubert?'

'It's no business of yours and you're no longer my secretary. You wrecked my Fellowship and you wrecked my reputation. I have had an anonymous letter from someone in the village comparing me to some false Catholic prelate who set himself up at Nemi with his gang of acolytes two years ago in a villa, with all his holy pictures and his crucifixes and his apostolic papers in order. He claimed to have a commission from the Holy See to purchase vast stocks of merchandise, and when the police finally surrounded the villa he committed suicide. I have all the details here. The author of the letter enclosed the press cutting.'

He had passed it over to Pauline. 'See what the bloody fool killed himself with,' he said, 'a glass of *vino al tropicida*! It sounds like some speciality in a restaurant, but it's rat-poison in wine. A very low-class suicide, and I wouldn't care to know the author of this anonymous letter who suggests I do the same.'

'The hand-writing's pretty awful,' said Pauline.

'So is the spelling. Some village woman. What does it matter?'

'Oh, Hubert! You would never think of suicide, would you?' Pauline said. 'I don't want this money, really. Take it back. Here it is.'

'Suicide is not remotely in my mind,' Hubert said. 'But I'll put my money back in the tin for safe-keeping. I hope you've learnt your lesson, Miss Thin.'

'I'll go shopping and I'll cook for you,' Pauline said.

'I had another letter,' Hubert had said, and he then had proceeded to read aloud to her Maggie's letter.

'That woman is dangerous,' Pauline said. 'Where's her furniture at the moment?'

'How do I know? Her lawyer took it away.'

'And your manuscripts, Hubert, where are your documents?'

'In Rome,' Hubert said. 'Transferred to Rome, as was the cult of Diana which, for political and very democratic reasons, spread to Rome in the fourth century B.C.'

'I saw Father Cuthbert in Rome,' Pauline said.

'I dare say you spoke about me. What else would you have to talk about, my dear?'

'Well, Hubert, I think he's got a good idea that you should take up the Charismatic Movement in the Church and run the prayer meetings. You do the murmuring rite so well and Cuthbert said it wouldn't be in conflict with Diana as the preserver of nature, not at all.'

'It is a long time,' Hubert said, 'since Homer sang the wonders of Artemis who came to be Diana. He called her the Lady of Wildlife. There's much to be said for charisma and wildlife.'

'They're the new idea,' Pauline said, meekly. 'You have to make a living somehow, Hubert. You can't stay here with these kitchen chairs.'

'One way and another, Miss Thin,' Hubert said, 'I haven't done so badly.'

'We leave tonight at midnight,' Hubert informed Pauline. It was Tuesday, 26 August, thirteen days after the Feast of Diana and one day before the date fixed by Maggie for the removal of her furniture which wasn't there. That morning, when Pauline returned from her trip to the village to buy provisions, he had taken the newspapers out of her hand, as usual, waiting for her to serve the coffee. 'We leave at midnight,' he said.

Over coffee he handed her a newspaper, folded back to reveal a picture of a decapitated statue. 'This is a sign,' said Hubert. Two statues flanking a fountain in Palermo had been mutilated by vandals; the newspaper had printed the one which had suffered most. The headline read, 'Diana Decapitated', and the picture showed a sturdy and headless nude Diana with her hound and her stag. 'It's a definite sign,' Hubert said, 'for us, don't you think so, Miss Thin?'

'One good thing,' said Hubert, 'about having nothing left to protect is that I can go for a walk.'

He left before sunset, while Pauline set about putting their few household possessions in the back of the station-wagon ready for their transfer to Rome. Bobby Lester, her previous employer so long ago, and a friend of Father Cuthbert, had lent them his flat overlooking the Piazza del Popolo. She placed the tin box with Hubert's money on the kitchen table to keep an eye on it and sat down beside it dutifully and happily doing nothing but reading small paragraphs in the newspaper and listening to the transistor radio. She wore a black cotton blouse and a red skirt that made her hips seem wider than ever; they spilt over the kitchen chair in a proprietary way, and she knew she was indispensable to Hubert's future.

Hubert, meantime, had decided to take his last look at beautiful Nemi, where from every point appeared a different view, every view a picture postcard except that it was real. Down the old Roman road he went, past the old town-council building and into the village. All during July and August Nemi had been crowded with holidaymakers; even a few foreign tourists and some of the pilgrim crowds of Holy Year, lately coveted by Hubert, had brimmed over from near-by Castelgandolfo where the Pope held court in his summer residence. But now, as the road grew darker, there were few newcomers to be seen; most of them had returned to the lodgings which had been provided with great efficiency by the neighbouring convents. After dark, a few local people grouped around the bars and various courting couples leaned over the wall beside the castle, looking at the moon.

Outside the church a mosaic plaque had been put up to commemorate the Pope's visit to Nemi in 1969. Hubert paused on his way to look at it and saw by the road lamp how it bore on the left the crest of Nemi, blue, white, yellow, rich red and gold, surrounded by the motto *Diane Nemus*: the Woods of Diana; on the right was a gleaming emblem of a local Christian order of monks, and above them the Montini papal coat of arms, that of Paul VI, crossed by the gold and silver keys of St Peter. Hubert's walks in Nemi had been few. 'Nemi is mine,' he murmured, 'but I must move on to Rome.' In fact, he felt carefree and rather glad to be leaving, seeing that he was now in funds and how his future prospects, in collaboration with the Jesuits, seemed full of hope and drama, the two things Hubert valued most in life, all things being equal on the material side.

Down he went to the garden walk on the steep cliffs by the lake, across the bridge, towards Diana's temple. The moon was almost three-quarters full and on the wane. 'Always cut wood when the moon is on the wane,' an old countryman had told him during his first years at Nemi when he had gone out to gather firewood. He smiled at the moon, with no one to see him, and felt very deeply that he was descended from Diana the moon goddess.

The spot where Diana's temple had been located was not accessible to the public, and even the local people never went to the thickly overgrown alcoves that remained of her cult. But Hubert knew the way to that area which had been named, in more historic times, the Devil's Grottoes. Not only were the relics of antiquity to be found there, but also numerous caves leading deep into the heart of the cliff under the castle, where vagrants, in the days of lesser prosperity, could take refuge. These caves were now abandoned and overgrown, some of them totally concealed by dense greenery. He plodded through the thick undergrowth, over uneven ground, stopping to hack off a stout branch to help him to beat his path. 'Always cut wood when the moon is on the wane.' The branch broke easily from the low tree.

Suddenly Hubert saw a shape approaching, an old woman, it seemed, probably a gypsy, picking her way towards him. She lit her steps with the aid of a flashlamp. Behind her, but much further into the dark thickness of the wooded cliff, he thought he heard an exchange of voices, but then, stopping still, he heard nothing. The crone, dressed drably with a scarf round her head, came closer and was about to pass him with the usual 'Buona sera' of the countryside. 'Maggie!' said Hubert. She stopped and shone the torch on him, and started to laugh.

They sat together looking at the lake and the bashed-in circle of the moon for only a little space. Maggie, of course, had taken up almost from where she had left off, and, without any explanation for her appearance or her presence in that deserted spot, said first that she was fine thank you, how was he? 'Fine,' said Hubert.

So they found a place to sit and Maggie said, 'You would never believe it, Hubert, but my daughter-in-law, Mary, has fallen desperately in love with Berto and he's awfully embarrassed because he loves me exclusively, as you can imagine. He's trying to pass her off to a journalist friend of his, rather elderly, as he feels that Mary really wants an older man, a sort of father figure. It's rather pathetic, but it's all Michael's fault; although he's my own son I know he's neglected Mary and is altogether inadequate, between you and me.'

'It will sort itself out,' Hubert said. 'You look wonderful, Maggie, in spite of all these clothes and things.'

'Hubert, you're always so charming! My clothes are a symbol of my new poverty, of course. And then, dressed like this, one hopes to avoid being kidnapped. It's such a danger, these days. One is in peril.'

'Oh, I know. You told me in your letter about poor Coco de Renault. Any news of him?'

'Well, I wouldn't say *poor* Coco. But maybe he's going to be poor after he pays the ransom. What about you, Hubert? Are you prospering?'

'Mildly,' said Hubert.

'Of course,' said Maggie, 'I happen to know that you've sold all my furniture and pictures. My letter was just to satisfy Berto, and be above-board, you know. Where is Massimo de Vita?'

'Honestly I don't know, Maggie. There isn't a thing you can do about it.'

'I know,' she said, cheerfully.

'I'm sorry to hear that Renault made off with all your fortune,' Hubert said.

327

'I'm getting it back. In fact it has already been arranged,' Maggie said. 'Less thirty per cent.'

'That would be the kidnappers' share,' Hubert said.

'That's right,' said Maggie.

'Where have they got him?' Hubert said. 'The papers seem to have dropped the story, so I suppose he isn't in Italy.'

'Well, some say California and some say Brazil,' Maggie said. 'But in fact he's right here in a cave in this cliff, well guarded. I've just been to visit. Hubert, I simply had to go and gloat.'

'I can well understand that,' said Hubert. 'Is he to be released soon?'

'Some time tonight or early tomorrow morning. The wife delayed a lot and that made Coco very angry. But in the end she had to make over everything to me in Switzerland, all of it. I wouldn't settle for less.'

'Can he be trusted not to report you?' Hubert said.

'Well, naturally, he couldn't indict me. He's too indictable himself. There are times when one can trust a crook.'

'There's something in that,' Hubert said.

She said good night very sweetly and, lifting her dingy skirts, picked her way along the leafy path, hardly needing her flashlamp, so bright was the moon, three-quarters full, illuminating the lush lakeside and, in the fields beyond, the kindly fruits of the earth.

THE ONLY PROBLEM

PART I

I

HE WAS DRIVING ALONG THE ROAD in France from St Dié to Nancy in the district of Meurthe; it was straight and almost white, through thick woods of fir and birch. He came to the grass track on the right that he was looking for. It wasn't what he had expected. Nothing ever is, he thought. Not that Edward Jansen could now recall exactly what he had expected; he tried, but the image he had formed faded before the reality like a dream on waking. He pulled off at the track, forked left and stopped. He would have found it interesting to remember exactly how he had imagined the little house before he saw it, but that, too, had gone.

He sat in the car and looked for a while at an old green garden fence and a closed gate, leading to a piece of overgrown garden. There was no longer a visible path to the stone house, which was something like a lodgekeeper's cottage with loose tiles and dark, neglected windows. Two shacks of crumbling wood stood apart from the house. A wider path, on Edward's side of the gate, presumably led to the château where he had no present interest. But he noticed that the cartracks on the path were overgrown, very infrequently used, and yet the grass that spread over that path was greener than on the ground before him, inside the gate. If his wife had been there he would have pointed this out to her as a feature of Harvey Gotham, the man he had come to see; for he had a theory, too unsubstantiated to be formulated in public, but which he could share with Ruth, that people have an effect on the natural greenery around them regardless of whether they lay hands on it or not; some people, he would remark, induce fertility in their environment and some the desert, simply by psychic force. Ruth would agree with him at least in this case, for she didn't seem to like Harvey, try as she might. It had already got to the point that everything Harvey did and said, if it was only good night, to her mind made him worse and worse. It was true there are ways and ways of saying good night. Yet Edward wondered if there wasn't something of demonology in those confidences he shared with Ruth about Harvey; Ruth didn't know him as well as Edward did. They had certainly built up a case against Harvey between themselves which they wouldn't have aired openly. It was for this reason that Edward had thought it fair that he should come alone, although at first he expected Ruth to come with him. She had said she couldn't face it. Perhaps, Edward had thought, I might be more fair to Harvey.

And yet, here he was, sitting in the car before his house, noting how the grass everywhere else was greener than that immediately surrounding the cottage. Edward got out and slammed the door with a bang, hoping to provoke the dark front door of the house or at least one of the windows into action. He went to the gate. It was closed with a rusty wire loop which he loosened. He creaked open the gate and walked up the path to the door and knocked. It was ten past three, and Harvey was expecting him; it had all been arranged. But he knocked and there was silence. This, too, was typical. He walked round the back of the house, looking for a car or a motor-cycle, which he supposed Harvey had. He found there a wide path, a sort of drive which led away from the back door, through the woods; this path had been hidden from the main road. There was no motor-cycle, but a newish small Renault, light brown, under a rush-covered shelter. Harvey, then, was probably at home. The back door was his front door, so Edward banged on that. Harvey opened it immediately and stood with that look of his, to the effect that he had done his utmost.

'You haven't cut your hair,' he said.

Edward had the answer ready, heated-up from the pre-cooking, so many times had he told Harvey much the same thing. 'It's my hair, not your hair. It's my beard, not your beard.' Edward stepped into the house as he said this, so that Harvey had to make way for him.

Harvey was predictable only up to a point. 'What are you trying to prove, Edward,' he said, 'wearing that poncho at your age?' In the living room he pushed some chairs out of the way. 'And your hair hanging down your back,' he said.

Edward's hair was in fact shoulder-length. 'I'm growing it for a part in a film,' he said, then wished he hadn't given any excuse at all since anyway it was his hair, not Harvey's hair. Red hair.

'You've got a part?'

'Yes.'

'What are you doing here, then? Why aren't you rehearsing?'

'Rehearsals start on Monday.'

'Where?'

'Elstree.'

'Elstree.' Harvey said it as if there was a third party listening – as if to draw the attention of this third party to that definite word, Elstree, and whatever connotations it might breed.

Edward wished himself back in time by twenty minutes, driving along the country road from St Dié to Nancy, feeling the spring weather. The spring weather, the cherry trees in flower, and all the budding green on the road from St Dié had supported him, while here inside Harvey's room there was no outward support. He almost said, 'What am I doing here?' but refrained because that would be mere rhetoric. He had come about his sister-in-law Effie, Harvey's wife.

'Your wire was too long,' said Harvey. 'You could have saved five words.'

'I can see you're busy,' said Edward.

Effie was very far from Edward's heart of hearts, but Ruth worried about her. Long ago he'd had an affair with beautiful Effie, but that was a thing of the past. He had come here for Ruth's sake. He reminded himself carefully that he would do almost anything for Ruth.

'What's the act?' said Harvey. 'You are somehow not yourself, Edward.'

It seemed to Edward that Harvey always suspected him of putting on an act.

'Maybe I can speak for actors in general; that, I don't know,' Edward said. 'But I suppose that the nature of my profession is mirrored in my own experience; at least, for certain, I can speak for myself. That, I can most certainly do. In fact I know when I'm playing a part and when I'm not. It isn't every actor who knows the difference. The majority act better off stage than on.'

Edward went into the little sitting room that Harvey had put together, the minimum of stuff to keep him going while he did the job he had set himself. Indeed, the shabby, green plush chairs with the stuffing coming out of them and the quite small work-table with the papers and writing materials piled on it (he wrote by hand) seemed out of all proportion to the project. Harvey was only studying a subject, preparing an essay, a thesis. Why all this spectacular neglect of material things?

God knows, thought Edward, from where he has collected his furniture. There was a kitchen visible beyond the room, with a loaf of bread and a coffee mug on the table. It looked like a nineteenth-century narrative painting. Edward supposed there were habitable rooms upstairs. He sat down when Harvey told him to. From where he sat he could see through a window a washing-line with baby clothes on it. There was no sign of a baby in the house, so Edward presumed this washing had nothing to do with Harvey; maybe it belonged to a daily help who brought along her child's clothes to wash.

Harvey said, 'I'm awfully busy.'

'I've come about Effie,' Edward said.

Harvey took a long time to respond. This, thought Edward, is a habit of his when he wants an effect of weightiness.

Then, 'Oh, Effie,' said Harvey, looking suddenly relieved; he actually began to smile as if to say he had feared to be confronted with some problem that really counted.

Harvey had written Effie off that time on the Italian *autostrada* about a year ago, when they were driving from Bologna to Florence – Ruth, Edward, Effie, Harvey and Nathan, a young student-friend of Ruth's. They stopped for a refill of petrol; Effie and Ruth went off to the Ladies', then they came back to the car where it was still waiting in line. It was a cool, late afternoon in April, rather cloudy, not one of those hot Italian days where you feel you must have a cold drink or an ice every time you stop. It was sheer consumerism that made Harvey – or maybe it was Nathan – suggest that they should go and get something from the snack-bar; this was a big catering monopoly with huge windows in which were arranged straw baskets and pottery from Hong Kong and fantastically shaped bottles of Italian liqueurs. It was, 'What shall we have from the bar?' – 'A sandwich, a coffee?' – 'No, I don't want any more of those lousy sandwiches.' Effie went off to see what there was to buy, and came back with some chocolate. – 'Yes, that's what I'd like.' – She had two large bars. The tank was now full. Edward paid the man at the pump. Effie got in the front with him. They were all in the car and Edward drove off. Effie started dividing the chocolate and handing it round. Nathan, Ruth and Harvey at the back, all took a piece. Edward took a piece and Effie started eating her piece.

With her mouth full of chocolate she turned and said to Harvey at the back, 'It's good, isn't it? I stole it. Have another piece.'

'You what?' said Harvey. Ruth said something, too, to the same effect. Edward said he didn't believe it.

Effie said, 'Why shouldn't we help ourselves? These multi-nationals and monopolies are capitalising on us, and two-thirds of the world is suffering.'

She tore open the second slab, crammed more chocolate angrily into her mouth, and, with her mouth gluttonously full of stolen chocolate, went on raving about how two-thirds of the world was starving.

'You make it worse for them and worse for all of us if you steal,' Edward said.

'That's right,' said Ruth, 'it really does make it worse for everyone. Besides, it's dishonest.'

'Well, I don't know,' Nathan said.

But Harvey didn't wait to hear more. 'Pull in at the side,' he said. They were going at a hundred kilometres an hour, but he had his hand on the back door on the dangerous side of the road. Edward pulled in. He forgot, now, how it was that they reasoned Harvey out of leaving the car there on the *autostrada*; however, he sat in silence while Effie ate her chocolate inveighing, meanwhile, against the capitalist system. None of the others would accept any more of the chocolate.

Just before the next exit Harvey said, 'Pull in here, I want to pee.' They waited for him while he went to the men's lavatory. Edward was suspicious all along that he wouldn't come back and when the minutes went by he got out of the car to have a look, and was just in time to see Harvey get up into a truck beside the driver; away he went.

They lost the truck at some point along the road, after they reached Florence. Harvey's disappearance ruined Effie's holiday. She was furious, and went on against him so much that Ruth made that always infuriating point: 'If he's so bad, why are you angry with him for leaving you?' The rest of them were upset and uneasy for a day or two but after that they let it go. After all, they were on holiday. Edward refused to discuss the subject for the next two weeks; they were travelling along the Tuscan coast stopping here and there. It would have been a glorious trip but for Effie's fury and unhappiness.

Up to the time Edward went to see Harvey in France on her behalf, she still hadn't seen any more of him. They had no children and he had simply left her life, with all his possessions and the electricity bills and other clutter of married living on her hands. All over a bit of chocolate. And yet, no.

Ruth thought, and Edward agreed with her, that a lot must have led up to that final parting of Harvey from Effie.

Edward deeply envied Harvey, he didn't know exactly what for. Or rather, perhaps he had better not probe deeply enough into the possibility that if Ruth wasn't Ruth and, if they weren't always so much in agreement, he would have liked to walk off, just like that. When Harvey talked of his marriage it was always as if he were thinking of something else, and he never talked about it unless someone else did first. And then, it was as if the other person had mentioned something quite irrelevant to his life, provoking from him a puzzled look, then a frown, an effort of concentration, it seemed, then an impatient dismissal of the apparently alien subject. It seemed, it seemed, Edward thought; because one can only judge by appearances. How could Edward know Harvey wasn't putting on an act, as he so often implied that Edward did? To some extent we all put on acts.

Harvey began to be more sociable, for he had somehow dismissed the subject of Effie. He must have known Edward would bring up Effie later, that in fact all he had come for was to talk about her. Well, perhaps not all. Edward was an old friend. Harvey poured him a drink, and, for the moment Edward gave up trying to get on to the subject of Effie.

'Tell me,' said Harvey, 'about the new film. What's it called? What sort of part are you playing?'

'It's called *The Love-Hate Relationship*. That's only provisional as a title. I don't think it'll sell as a film on that title. But it's based on a novel called *The Love-Hate Relationship*. And that's what the film is about. There's a married couple and another man, a brother, in the middle. I'm playing the other man, the brother.' (Was Harvey listening? He was looking round into the other room.)

'If there's anything I can't stand it's a love-hate relationship,' Harvey said, turning back to Edward at last. 'The element of love in such a relation simply isn't worthy of the name. It boils down to hatred pure and simple in the end. Love comprises among other things a desire for the well-being and spiritual freedom of the one who is loved. There's an objective quality about love. Love-hate is obsessive, it is possessive. It can be evil in effect.'

'Oh well,' Edward said, 'love-hate is a frequent human problem. It's a very important problem, you can't deny it.'

'It's part of the greater problem,' said Harvey after a while. Edward knew what Harvey was coming round to and was pleased, now that he was sitting here with his drink and his old friend. It was the problem of suffering as it is dealt with in the biblical *Book of Job*. It was for this, in the first place, that Harvey had come to study here in the French countryside away from the environment of his family business and his friends.

Harvey was a rich man; he was in his mid-thirties. He had started writing a monograph about the *Book of Job* and the problem it deals with. For he could not face that a benevolent Creator, one whose charming and delicious light descended and spread over the world, and being powerful everywhere, could condone the unspeakable sufferings of the world; that God did permit all suffering and was therefore, by logic of his omnipotence, the actual author of it, he was at a loss how to square with the existence of God, given the premise that God is good.

'It is the only problem,' Harvey had always said. Now, Harvey believed in God, and this was what tormented him. 'It's the only problem, in fact, worth discussing.'

It was just under a year after Harvey had disappeared that Effie traced him to St Dié. She hadn't been to see him herself, but she had written several times through his lawyer asking him what was the matter. She described to him the process by which she had tracked him down; when she read Edward the letter before she posted it he felt she could have left that part out, for she had traced him quite simply, but by trickery, of which Harvey would not see the charm; furthermore, her revelation of the trick compromised an innocent, if foolish, person, and this fact would not be lost on Harvey. His moral sense was always intensified where Effie was concerned.

'Don't tell him, Effie,' Edward said, 'how you got his address. He'll think you unprincipled.'

'He thinks that already,' she said.

'Well, this might be the finishing touch. There's no need to tell.'

'I don't want him back.'

'You only want his money,' Edward said.

'Oh, God, Edward, if you only knew what he was like to live with.'

Edward could guess. But he said, 'What people are like to live with . . . It isn't a good test to generalise on.'

'He's rich,' said Effie. 'He's spoilt.' Effie had a lover, Ernie Howe, an electronics expert. Effie was very good-looking and it was hardly to be expected that she would resist, year after year, the opportunities for love affairs that came her way all the time; she was really beautiful. Ernie Howe was a nice-looking man, too, but he lacked the sort of money Harvey had and Effie was used to. Ernie had his job, and quite a good one; Edward supposed that Effie, who herself had a job with an advertising firm, might have been content with the simpler life with him, if she was in love with Ernie. It was only that now she was expecting a baby she felt she might persuade Harvey to divorce her with a large settlement. Edward didn't see why this should not be.

Harvey had never replied to any of Effie's letters. She continued to write, care of his lawyer. She told him of her love-affair and mentioned a divorce.

Finally she managed to find his actual whereabouts in St Dié, in a quite unpremeditated way. She had in fact visited the lawyer to try to persuade him to reveal the address. He answered that he could only forward a letter. Effie went home and wrote a letter, calling with it at the lawyer's office the next day to save the extra time it would have taken in the post. She gave it to the receptionist and asked that it be forwarded. There were two or three letters on the girl's desk, in a neat pile, already stamped. Acting on a brainwave Effie said, casually, 'If you like, as I'm passing the post box, I'll pop them all in.'

'Oh, thanks,' said the foolish girl, 'I have to go beyond the bus stop to post letters.' So she hastily filled in Harvey's address and handed the letters to Effie with a smile. And although Edward said to Effie, 'You shouldn't tell Harvey how you got his address. It'll put him right off. Counter-productive. And rather unfair on the poor girl at the lawyer's office,' she went ahead and wrote to Harvey direct, telling him of her little trick. 'He'll realise all the more how urgent it is,' she said.

But still Harvey didn't reply.

That was how Edward came to be on this errand to Harvey on her behalf. Incidentally, Edward also hoped for a loan. He was short of money till he got paid under his contract with the film people.

Edward used to confide in Harvey, and he in Edward, during their student life together. Harvey had never, to Edward's knowledge, broken any of these confidences in the sense of revealing them to other people; but he had a way of play-ing them back to Edward at inopportune moments; it was disconcerting, it made Edward uncomfortable, especially as Harvey chose to remind him of things he had said which he would rather have forgotten. Harvey seemed especially to choose the negative remarks he made all those years ago, ten, twelve, years ago, such as when he had said something unfa-vourable about Ruth, something that sounded witty, perhaps, at the time, but which he probably didn't mean. Scarcely ever did Harvey remind him of the praise he devoted in sincere abundance to others, Ruth included. So many sweet things seemed to have spilled out of his ears as soon as they entered them; so many of the sour and the sharp, the unripe and frivolously carping observations he made, Harvey had saved up in his memory-bank at compound interest; it seemed to Edward that he capitalised on these past confidences at a time when they were likely to have the most deflating effect on him; he called this a breach of confidence in a very special sense. Harvey would deny this, of course; he would claim that he had a clear memory, that his reminders were salutary, that Edward was inclined to fool himself, and that the uncomfortable truths of the past were always happier in their outcome than convenient illusions.

And undoubtedly Harvey was often right. That he had a cold side was no doubt a personal matter. In Edward's view it wasn't incompatible with Harvey's extremely good mind and his occasional flashes of generosity. And indeed his moral judgement. Perhaps a bit too much moral judgement.

Edward always spoke a lot about himself and Harvey as they were in their young days, even to people who didn't know them. But few people listen carefully to the reminiscences of someone who has achieved nothing much in life; the end-product of a personal record has somehow to justify the telling. What did come across to Edward's friends was that he had Harvey more or less on his mind. Edward wished something to happen in his own life to make him forget Harvey, get his influence out of his system. Only some big change in my life could do that, Edward thought. Divorce from Ruth, which was unthinkable (then how did I come to think it?). Or great success as an actor; something I haven't got.

Eventually Edward said, as he sat in Harvey's cottage in France, 'I've come about Effie, mainly. Ruth's anxious about her, very anxious. I've come here for Ruth's sake.'

'I recall,' Harvey said, 'how you told me once, when you first married Ruth, "Ruth is a curate's wife and always will be."'

344

Edward was disconcerted. 'Oh, I was only putting on an act. You know how it was in those days.'

In those days Edward had been a curate, doing so well with church theatricals that he was in demand from other parishes up and down the country. It wasn't so very long before he realised he was an actor, not a curate, not a vicar in bud. Only his sermons interested him and that was because he had his own little stage up there in the pulpit, and an audience. The congregation loved his voice and his delivery. When he resigned, what they said mostly in their letters was 'You were always so genuine in your sermons,' and 'One knew you felt every word.' Well, in fact Edward was and did. But in fact he was more involved in the delivery of his sermons than in the substance. He said good-bye to the fund-raising performances of *The Admirable Crichton* and *The Silver Box*, not to mention *A Midsummer Night's Dream* on the one chilly midsummer night when he was a curate.

He had played parts in repertory theatre, then that principal part (in *The Curate's Egg*) on the West End, and was well launched in his film career, spasmodic and limited though it was, by the time he sat talking to Harvey on Effie's behalf, largely for Ruth's sake. To himself, Edward now described his acting career as 'limited' in the sense that too often he had been cast as a clergyman, an unfrocked priest or a welfare worker. But, at present, in the film provisionally entitled *The Love-Hate Relationship*, he had been cast in a different role, to his great pleasure; he was playing a sardonic scholar, a philosopher. Thinking himself into the part had made him feel extraordinarily equal to his discussion with Harvey; and he returned, with the confidence of the part, to the subject of Effie.

'She wants a divorce,' he said, and waited the inevitable few seconds for Harvey's reply.

'Nothing to stop her.'

'She wants to get married, she's expecting a baby by Ernie Howe. And you know very well she's written to you about it.'

'What she wrote to me about was money. She wants money to get married with. I'm a busy man with things to do. Money; not enough money, but a lot. That's what Effie boils down to.'

'Oh, not entirely. I should have thought you wanted her to be happy. After all, you left her. You left Effie abruptly.'

Harvey waited a while. Time was not of an essence, here. 'Well, she soon found consolation. But she can get a divorce quite easily. Ernie Howe has a job.'

Edward said, 'I don't know if you realise how hateful you can be, Harvey. If it wasn't for your money you wouldn't speak like that.' For it struck him that, since Harvey had recently come into a vast share of a Canadian uncle's fortune, he ought not to carry on as if he were the moderately well-off Harvey of old. This treatment of Effie was brutal.

'I don't know what you mean,' said Harvey, in his time. 'I really don't care what you mean, what you say. I'll give you a letter to Stewart Cowper, my lawyer in London, with suitable instructions.' Harvey got up and reached on a bookshelf for a block of writing paper and one envelope. He said, 'I'll write it now. Then you can go away.'

He wrote without much reflection, almost as if he had come to an earlier decision about the paying off of Effie, and by how much, and had just been waiting for the moment Edward arrived to make a settlement. He addressed the envelope, put in the folded letter, then sealed it down. He handed it to Edward. 'You can take it straight to him yourself. Quicker than posting it.'

Edward was astonished that Harvey had sealed the letter since he was to be the bearer. Bloody indelicate. He wondered why Harvey was trying to diminish him.

'Harvey,' he said, 'are you putting on an act? Are you playing the part of a man who's a swine merely because he can afford to be?'

Harvey took a lot of thought. Then, 'Yes,' he said.

'Well, it doesn't suit you. One meets that sort of character amongst the older generation of the motion picture and theatre world. I remember hearing a producer say to a script writer, "It's the man who writes the cheque who has the final say in the script. And I'm the man who writes the cheque." One still hears that sort of thing. He had yellow eye-balls.'

Harvey sat with folded arms staring at his loaded worktable.

'I suppose you're playing this part to relieve your feelings?' Edward said.

'I imagine you are relieving yours, Edward.'

'I suppose you're fairly disgusted with things,' Edward said. 'With Effie and so on. I know you left her that day in disgust when she was eating her stolen chocolate and talking about the sufferings of the hungry. All that. But Effie has some good points, you know. Some very good points.'

'If you want a loan why don't you ask for it?' Harvey said, staring at his papers as if nostalgic for their lonely company.

Anxiety, suffering, were recorded in his face; that was certain. Edward wasn't sure that this was not self-induced. Harvey had once said, 'There can be only one answer to the question of why people suffer, irrespective of whether they are innocent or guilty; to the question of why suffering has no relation to the moral quality of the individual, of the tribe or of the nation, one way or another. If you believe that there is a Creator, a God, and that he is good, the only logical answer to the problem of suffering is that the individual soul has made a pact with God before he is born, that he will suffer during his lifetime. We are born forgetful of this pact, of course; but we have made it. Sufferers would, in this hypothesis, be pre-conscious volunteers. The same might apply to tribes or nations, especially in the past.'

Edward had been very impressed by this, by then the latest, idea of Harvey's. (How many ideas about *Job* they had formulated in the past!) But he had said he still couldn't see the need for suffering.

'Oh, development involves suffering,' Harvey had said.

'I wonder if I made that agreement with God before I was born,' said Edward at that time, 'for I've suffered.'

'We have all suffered,' said Harvey, 'but I'm talking about the great multitudes who are starving to death every year, for instance. The glaze-eyed infants.'

'Could your theory be borne out by science?'

'I think possibly there might be a genetic interpretation of it. But I'm talking theologically.'

When, now, Edward looked at his friend's face and saw stress on it, rich and authoritative as Harvey was, swine as he could be, he envied him for the detachment with which he was able to set himself to working on the problem through the *Book of Job*. It was possible for a man like Harvey to be detached and involved at the same time. As an actor, Edward envied him. He also envied the ease with which he could write to his lawyer about his divorce from Effie without a thought for the money involved. As for Edward's loan, Harvey had already written a cheque without a word, knowing, of course, that Edward would pay it back in time. And then, although Harvey wasn't consistently generous, and had ignored Effie's letters, Edward remembered how only a few months ago he had arranged bail through his ever-ready lawyer for Effie and Ruth's student, Nathan, when they were arrested during a demonstration, and been had up for riot and affray. Effie didn't need the bail money, for her lover came to the rescue

THE ONLY PROBLEM

first, but Nathan did. They were both bound over to keep the peace. Harvey's money was so casual. Edward envied him that, and felt guilty, glimpsing again, for that sharp unthinkable instant, the possibility that he might like to part from Ruth as abruptly and as easily. Edward closed the subject in his mind quickly, very quickly. It had been established that Ruth and Edward always thought alike. Edward didn't want to dwell on that thought, either.

As a theological student Edward had spent many an hour lying with Harvey Gotham on the grass in the great green university square if the weather was fine in the early summer, while the croquet mallets clicked on another part of the green, and the croquet players' voices made slight exclamations, and together he and Harvey discussed the *Book of Job*, which they believed was not only as important, as amazing, a poem as it was generally considered to be, but also the pivotal book of the Bible.

Edward had always maintained that the link – or should he say fetter? – that first bound him to Harvey was their deep old love of marvellous Job, their studies, their analyses, their theories. Harvey used to lie on his back on the grass, one leg stretched out, the other bent at the knee, while Edward sat by his side sunning his face and contemplating the old castle, while he listened with another part of his mind to Harvey's talk. 'It is the only problem. The problem of suffering is the only problem. It all boils down to that.'

'Did you know,' Edward remembered saying, 'that when Job was finally restored to prosperity and family abundance, one of his daughters was called Box of Eye-Paint? Can we really imagine our tormented hero enjoying his actual reward?'

'No,' said Harvey. 'He continued to suffer.'

'Not according to the Bible.'

'Still, I'm convinced he suffered on. Perhaps more.'

'It seems odd, doesn't it,' Edward had said, 'after he sat on a dung-heap and suffered from skin-sores and put up with his friends' gloating, and lost his family and his cattle, that he should have to go on suffering.'

'It became a habit,' Harvey said, 'for he not only argued the problem of suffering, he suffered the problem of argument. And that is incurable.'

'But he wanted to argue with God.'

'Yes, but God as a character comes out badly, very badly. Thunder and bluster and I'm Me, who are you? Putting on an act. Behold now Leviathan. Behold now Behemoth. Ha, ha among the trumpets. Where wast thou when I laid the foundations of the earth? And Job, insincerely and wrongly, says, "I am vile." And God says, All right, that being understood, I give you back double your goods, you can have fourteen thousand sheep and six thousand camels and a thousand yoke of oxen, and a thousand she-asses. And seven sons and three daughters. The third daughter was Kerenhappuch – that was Eye-Paint.'

Towards evening, on the day when Edward visited Harvey at his place near St Dié, Harvey went out and brought in the baby clothes. He didn't fold them; he just dumped them on a chair in the little scullery at the back of the kitchen. He seemed to forget that he was impatient for Edward to leave. He brought out some wine, some glasses, cheese and bread. In fact, Edward could see that Harvey didn't want him to leave, lest he should feel lonely afterwards. Edward had been feeling rather guilty at interrupting what was probably a fairly contented solitude. Now, it was not that he regretted imposing his presence, but that by doing so he must impose the absence to follow. For Harvey more and more seemed to want him to remain. Edward said something about catching a night ferry. He thought, Surely Harvey's involved with the mother of the baby whose clothes he's just brought in off the line. They must be the clothes of an infant not more than a year old. Where are the mother and child?

There was no sign of any mother or child apart from the clothes Harvey had dumped on a chair. Edward was envious, too. He was envious of Harvey's woman and his child. He wanted, at that moment, to be free like Harvey and to have a girl somewhere, but not visible, with a baby.

Harvey said, 'It's fairly lonely here.' By which Edward knew for certain that Harvey was suddenly very lonely indeed at the thought of his leaving. The mother and child were probably away for the night.

'Stay the night,' said Harvey. 'There's plenty of room.'

Edward wanted to know where Harvey had been and what he'd been doing since he disappeared on the *autostrada*. But they did not talk of that. Harvey told him that Effie was writing a thesis on child-labourers in the Western democracies, basing much of it on Kingsley's *The Water Babies*. She hadn't told Edward this. Harvey seemed pleased that he had a bit more news of her than Edward had. But then they had a laugh over Effie and her zeal in the sociological industry.

Harvey made up a bed for him in a sort of cupboard-room upstairs. It was nearly four in the morning when he pulled the extra rough covers over a mattress and piled two cushions for a pillow. From the doorway into Harvey's bedroom Edward could see that the bed was narrow, the furniture quite spare in a cheap new way. He said, 'Where's the baby?'

'What baby?' Harvey said.

'The baby whose washing was out on the line.'

'Oh that,' said Harvey; 'that's only my safeguard. I put baby clothes out on the line every day and bring them in at night. I change the clothes every other day, naturally.'

Edward wondered if Harvey had really gone mad.

'Well, I don't understand,' Edward said, turning away as if it didn't matter.

'You see,' said Harvey, 'the police don't break in and shoot if there's likely to be a baby inside. Otherwise they might just break in and shoot.'

'Go to hell,' Edward said.

'Well, if I told you the truth you wouldn't understand.'

'Thanks,' he said.

'You wouldn't believe,' said Harvey.

'All right, I don't want to know.'

'When I settled here I strung up the clothes-line. I have a sure system of keeping away the well-meaning women who always come round a lone man, wanting to cook and launder and mend socks and do the shopping; they love a bachelor; even in cities – no trouble at all getting domestic help for a single man. In my wanderings since I left Effie I've always found that a line of baby clothes, varying from day to day, keeps these solicitous women away; they imagine without thinking more of it, that there's already a woman around.'

But Edward knew him too well; it was surely one of those demonstrative acts by which Harvey attempted to communicate with a world whose intelligence he felt was away behind his own. Harvey was always in a state of exasperation, and, it was true, always ten thoughts ahead of everybody around him. Always likely to be outrageous. The baby clothes probably belonged to his girl.

Edward left three hours later before Harvey was up. He still felt envious of Harvey for his invisible and probably non-existent girl and her baby.

II

NATHAN FOX WAS SITTING UP with Ruth when Edward got back to London. It was a Sunday, a Pimlico Sunday with vacant parking spaces and lights in some of the windows.

Nathan had graduated in English literature, at the university where Ruth was now teaching, over a year before. He couldn't get a job. Ruth looked after him most of the time. Edward always said he himself would do almost anything for Ruth; they saw eye to eye. So Nathan was quite welcome. But just that night on his return from France, very tired, and needing to get to bed for an early rise the next morning – he was due at the studio at seven – just that night Edward wished Nathan Fox wasn't there. Edward was not at all sure how they would manage without Nathan. Nathan wasn't ashamed of calling himself an intellectual, which, for people like themselves, made life so much easier; not that he was, in fact, an intellectual, really; he was only educated. But they could talk to Nathan about anything; and at the same time he made himself useful in the house. Indeed, he was a very fair cook. To a working couple like Ruth and Edward he was an invaluable friend.

It was just that night, and on a few previous occasions, Edward wished he wasn't there. Edward wanted to talk to Ruth, to get to bed early. Nathan sat there in his tight jeans and his T-shirt with 'Poetry Is Emotion Recollected In Tranquillity' printed on it. He was a good-looking boy, tall,

353

with an oval face, very smooth and rather silvery-green in colour – really olive. His eyebrows were smooth, black and arched, his hair heavy and sleek, quite black. But he wasn't vain at all. He got up in the morning, took a shower, shaved and dressed, all in less than seven minutes. It seemed to Edward that the alarm in their room had only just gone off when he could smell the coffee brewing in the kitchen, and hear Nathan already setting the places for breakfast. Ruth, too, wondered how he managed it. His morning smile was delightful; he had a mouth like a Michelangelo angel and teeth so good, clear, strong and shapely it seemed to Edward, secretly, that they were the sexiest thing about him.

The only problem with Nathan was how to explain what he saw in them. They paid him and fed him as well as they could, but it was supposed to be only a fill-in job. They were together as on a North Sea oil platform. It wasn't that Nathan wouldn't leave them, it now seemed he couldn't. Edward thought, He is hankering after Effie, and we are the nearest he can get to her. Edward often wondered whether Effie would really marry Ernie Howe when she got her divorce from Harvey.

When Edward got back from France they had supper; he told Nathan and Ruth what had happened at Harvey's cottage, almost from start to finish. Ruth wanted actually to see with her eyes the sealed letter to the lawyer; so that Edward got up from the table and fished it out of his duffel bag.

She turned it over and over in her hand; she examined it closely; she almost smelt it. She said, 'How rude to seal down a letter you were to carry by hand.'

'Why?' said Nathan.

'Because one doesn't,' Ruth piped primly, 'seal letters that other people are to carry.'

'What about the postman?'

'Oh, I mean one's friends.'

'Well, open it,' said Nathan.

Edward had been rather hoping he would suggest this, and he knew Ruth had the same idea in mind. If they'd been alone, neither of them would have suggested it out loud, although it would certainly have occurred to them, so eager were they to know what Harvey had settled on Effie in this letter to his solicitors. They would have left the letter and their secret desires unopened. They were still somewhat of the curate and his wife, Ruth and himself.

But Nathan seemed to serve them like a gentleman who takes a high hand in matters of form, or an unselfconscious angel. In a way, that is what he was there for, if he had to be there. He often said things out of his inexperience and cheerful ignorance that they themselves wanted to say but did not dare.

'Open it?' said Ruth.

'Oh, we can't do that,' said Edward.

'You can steam it open,' suggested Nathan, as if they didn't know. 'You only need a kettle.'

'Really?' said Ruth.

Nathan proceeded, very know-all: 'It won't be noticed. You can seal it up again. My mother steamed open my aunt's letters. Only wanted to know what was in them, that's all. Then later my aunt would tell a lot of lies about what was in the letters, but my mother knew the truth, of course. That was after my father died, and my mother and my auntie were living together.'

'I don't know that we have the right,' said Ruth.

'It's your duty,' Nathan pronounced. He turned to Edward, appealing: 'In my mother's case it wasn't a duty, although she said it was. But in your case it's definitely a duty to steam open that letter. It might be dynamite you've been carrying.'

Edward said, 'He should have left it open. It might be really offensive or something. It was ill-mannered of Harvey. I noticed it at the time, in fact.'

'You should have objected,' Nathan said. Edward was now delighted that Nathan was there with them that evening.

'It's difficult to object,' Ruth said. 'But I think we have a right to know what's in it. At least you do, Edward, since you're the bearer.'

They steamed open the letter in the kitchen and stood reading it together.

Dear Stewart,

This letter is being brought to you by Edward Jansen, an old friend of mine from university days. I don't know if you've met him. He's a sort of actor but that is by the way. My wife Effie is his sister-in-law. He came to see me about Effie's divorce. As you know I'm not contesting it. She wants a settlement. Let her go on wanting, let her sue.

The object of this letter is to tell you that I agree the date of *Job* is post-exile, that is, about 500 BC, but it could be the middle of the 5th century. It could easily be contemporaneous with the *Prometheus Bound* of Aeschylus. (The *Philoctetes* of Sophocles, another *Job*-style work, is dated I think about 409.)

Yours,
Harvey

'I won't deliver it,' Edward said.

'Oh, you must,' said Nathan. 'You mustn't let him think you've opened it.'

'There's something fishy about it,' Edward said. He was greatly annoyed.

'Calling you a sort of actor,' Ruth said, in a soothing voice that made him nearly choleric.

'It's Effie's fault,' said Ruth. 'She's brought out this quality in Harvey.'

'Well, I'm too busy tomorrow to go in person to Gray's Inn,' Edward said.

'I'll deliver it,' said Nathan.

III

IT WAS OCTOBER. HARVEY SAT at his writing-table, set against the wall of the main room in his little house.

'*Job* 37, 5,' he wrote, 'God thundereth marvellously with his voice . . . '

'I think we'll have to send to England for some more cretonne fabric,' said Ruth, looking over his shoulder.

It was at the end of August that Ruth had moved in, bringing with her Effie's baby, a girl. The baby was now asleep for a merciful moment, upstairs.

Harvey looked up from his work. 'I try to exude goodwill,' he said.

'You positively try to sweat it,' Ruth said, kindly. And she wondered how it was that she had disliked and resented Harvey for so many years. It still amazed her to find herself here with him. That he was perfectly complacent about the arrangement, even cheerful and happy, did not surprise her so much; everything around him, she knew – all the comings and goings – were really peripheral to his preoccupation with the *Book of Job*. But her being there, with Effie's baby, astonished her sometimes to the point of vertigo. This was not at all what she had planned when she decided to turn up at the cottage with Effie's baby daughter.

Once, after she had settled in, she said to Harvey, 'I didn't plan this.'

'It wasn't a plan,' said Harvey, 'it was a plot.'

'I suppose it looks like that from the outside,' Ruth said. To her, what she had wanted was justice. Given Effie's character, it was not to be expected that she would continue to live with Ernie Howe on his pay in a small house. Ruth had offered to take the baby when Effie decided she wasn't in love with Ernie any more. Harvey's money would perhaps not have made much difference to Effie's decision. At any rate, Ruth had known that, somehow, in the end, she would have to take on Effie's baby. It rather pleased her.

Effie was trying to sue Harvey for alimony, so far without success. 'The lawyers are always on the side of the money,' she said. Harvey continued to ignore her letters.

The baby, named Clara, had been born toward the end of June. Effie went back to her job in advertising for a short while after she had left Ernie Howe. Then she took a job with an international welfare organization in Rome. Ernie wasn't at all happy, at first, with Ruth's plan to take the baby Clara to visit Harvey. They sat in the flat in Pimlico where Ernie often came, now, for consolation, as much as to see his daughter.

'He doesn't sound the sort of man to have any *sent-y-ments*,' Ernie said.

Edward wanted very much to give Ernie some elocution lessons to restore his voice to the plain tones of his origins. 'He hasn't any sentimentality, but of course he has sentiments,' said Edward.

'Especially about his wife's baby by a, well, a lover.'

'As to that,' said Edward, 'he won't care who the father is. He just won't have any sentimental feelings, full stop.'

'It's a matter of justice,' Ruth said.

'How do you work that out?' said Nathan.

'Well, if it hadn't been for Harvey leaving Effie she would never have had a baby by Ernie,' Ruth said. 'Harvey should have given her a child. So Harvey's responsible for Clara; it's a question of justice, and with all his riches it would be the best thing if he could take responsibility, pay Effie her alimony. He might even take Effie back.'

'Effie doesn't want to go back to Harvey Gotham,' said Ernie.

'Harvey won't take her back,' Edward said. 'He believes that Effie boils down to money.'

'Alas, he's right,' said Ernie.

'Why can't Clara go on living with us?' said Nathan, who already knew how to prepare the feeds and bath the baby.

'I'm only taking her for a visit,' Ruth said. 'What's wrong with that? You went to see Harvey, Edward. Now I'll have a try.'

'Be sure to bring her back, Ree-uth,' said Ernie. 'The legal position – '

'Do you still want to marry Effie?' Edward asked him.

'No, quite frankly, I don't.'

'Effie's so beautiful,' Nathan said. He got up to replenish the drinks. 'What a beautiful girl she is!'

'A matter of justice. A balancing of accounts.' This was how Ruth put it to Harvey. 'I'm passionate about justice,' she said.

'People who want justice,' Harvey said, 'generally want so little when it comes to the actuality. There is more to be had from the world than a balancing of accounts.'

She supposed he was thinking of his character Job, as in fact he was. She was used to men answering her with one part of their mind on religion. That was one of the reasons why Edward had become so unsatisfactory after he had ceased to be a curate and become an actor.

Ruth and Effie grew up in a country rectory that today is converted into four commodious flats. The shabbiness of the war still hung over it in the late fifties, but they were only aware of the general decay by the testimony of their elders as to how things were 'in the old days', and the evidence of pre-war photographs of garden parties where servants and trees stood about, well-tended, and the drawing room chintzes were well-fitted and new. Otherwise, they simply accepted that life was a muddle of broken barrows, tin buckets in the garden sheds, overgrown gardens, neglected trees. They had an oak of immense girth; a mulberry tree older than the house, to judge from early sketches of the place. The graveyard had a yew the circumference and shape of their oval dining-table; the tree was hollow inside and the bark had formed itself into the shape of organ pipes. Yews were planted in graveyards, originally, because they poisoned cattle, and as they were needed for long-bows they were planted in a place where cattle didn't go. All this Ruth picked up from God knows where; the air she breathed informed her. Housemartins nested under the eaves outside Ruth's room and used to make a dark-and-white flash almost up to the open window as they came and fled in the morning.

There was a worn carpet on the staircase up to the first landing. After that, bare wood. Most of the rooms were simply shut for ever. They had been civil servants' bedrooms in war-time before Ruth was born, and she never knew what it was like to see the houseful of people that the rectory was made for.

For most of Ruth's life, up to the time Edward became an actor, religion was her bread and butter. Her father was what Edward at one time called a career-Christian; she assumed he was a believer too, as was her mother; but she never got the impression that either had time to think about it.

Effie was three years younger than Ruth. The sisters were very close to each other all their schooldays and in their early twenties. Ruth often wondered when exactly they had separated in their attitude to life. It was probably after Ruth's return from Paris where she had spent a year with a family. Shortly afterwards Effie, too, went off to be an *au pair* in France.

If you are the child of a doctor or a butcher you don't have to believe in your father's occupation. But, in their childhood, they had to believe in their father's job as a clergyman in a special way. Matins and Sunday services and Evensong were part of the job; the family was officially poor, which was to say they were not the poor in the streets and cottages, but poor by the standards of a country rector. Ruth's mother was a freelance typist and always had some work in hand. She could do seventy words a minute on her old pre-war typewriter. Before her marriage she had done a hundred and thirty words a minute at Pitman's shorthand. Ruth used to go to sleep on a summer night hearing the tap-tapping of the typewriter below, and wake to the almost identical sound of the woodpecker in the tree outside her window. Ruth supposed this was Effie's experience too, but when she reminded her sister of it many years later Effie couldn't recall any sound effects.

Effie went to a university on her return from France and left after her first year about the time that Ruth graduated and married Edward. Ruth worked with and for Edward and the parish, organising a live crib at Christmas with a real baby, a real cow and a real virgin; she wrote special prayers to the Holy Spirit and the Trinity for the parish magazine (which she described as Prayers to the HS etc.) and she arranged bring-and-pay garden lunches. She lectured and made bedspreads, and she taught child-welfare and jam preserving. Ruth was very much in the business. Effie, meanwhile, went off the rails, and when this was pointed out to her in so many words, she said, 'What rails?

Whose rails?' It was Effie who first called Edward an actor more than a man of God, and she probably put the idea in his mind.

Effie was doing social work when Ruth got married. The sisters looked very much alike in their separate features; it was one of those cases where the sum total of each came out with a difference, to the effect that Effie was extremely beautiful and Ruth was nothing remarkable; perhaps it was a question of colouring and complexion. Whatever the reason, everyone looked at Effie in a special way. Both sisters were fair with the fair-lashed look and faint eyebrows of some Dutch portraits.

It was Edward who introduced Effie to Harvey Gotham. Effie was in the habit of despising the rich, but she married him. They had a small house in Chelsea and at first they travelled everywhere together.

When Edward became an actor Ruth got a job in a university, teaching twentieth-century history. Edward had a television part which came to an end about the time Ruth discerned that Effie and Harvey were not getting on. Effie's young men-friends from her days of welfare-work were always in her house, discussing their social conscience. Harvey was often away.

'You're sleeping around,' Ruth said to Effie.

'What do you mean?' she said.

'I know,' Ruth said.

'What do you know?'

Ruth said, 'I know all about it.' What she meant was that she knew Effie.

'You must be guessing,' said Effie, very shaken.

'I know,' Ruth said, 'that you're having affairs. Not one only. Plural.'

Edward was still out of a job. They hadn't any prospect of a holiday that year, but Effie and Harvey had planned a motoring trip in Italy.

Ruth said, 'Why don't you get Harvey to invite us to join you on your holiday in Italy?'

'He wouldn't like that,' she said. 'Four in the car.'

'It's a big car.'

'You couldn't afford your share,' said Effie, 'could you?'

'No, not all of it.'

'What all this has to do with my love affairs, real or imagined,' said Effie, 'I really do not know.'

'Don't you?' said Ruth.

'Ruth,' she said, 'you're a blackmailer, aren't you?'

'Only in your eyes. In my eyes it is simply that we're going to come to Italy with you. Harvey won't mind the money.'

'Oh, God,' she said, 'I'd rather you went ahead and told him all you know. Think of all the suffering in the world, the starving multitudes. Can't you sacrifice a pleasure? Go ahead and tell Harvey what you know. Your sordid self-interest, your – '

'You shock me,' Ruth said. 'Stick to the point. Is it likely that I would go to your husband and say . . . ?'

They went on holiday with Effie and Harvey, and they took Ruth's student, Nathan, as well. Effie stole two bars of chocolate from the supermarket on the *autostrada* and Harvey left them abruptly. It was the end of their marriage. Fortunately Effie had enough money on her to pay for the rest of the trip. It was a holiday of great beauty. Effie tried to appreciate the pictures in the art galleries, the fountains in the squares, the ancient monuments and the Mediterranean abundance, but even basking on the beach she was uneasy.

Harvey saw Effie's features in Ruth; it struck him frequently that she was what Effie should have been. It had been that situation where the visitor who came to stay remained to live. (Harvey had heard of an author who had reluctantly granted an interview to a young critic, who then remained with him for life.) The arrangement was not as uncomfortable as it might have been, for Ruth had claimed and cleared one of the shacks outside the house, where she spent most of the daytime with the baby. She was careful to make the changes unobtrusively. Delivery vans drove up with rugs or with an extra stove, but it was all done in a morning. Harvey paid for the things. When the baby cried it upset him, but that was seldom, for Ruth drove off frequently with the child, no doubt to let it cry elsewhere. She took it with her when she went shopping.

It was three weeks after she had arrived that Ruth said, 'I'm going to write to Edward.'

'I have written,' said Harvey.

'I know,' she said, and he wondered how she knew, since he had posted the letter himself. 'But I'll write myself. I couldn't be the wife of an actor again.'

'If he was a famous actor?'

'Well, he isn't a famous actor. A part here, a part there, and sometimes a film. So full of himself when he has a part. It was a much better life for me when he was a curate.'

But she had no nostalgia even for those days of church fêtes, evening lectures and sewing classes. She already had a grip of her new life, dominated as it was by the *Book of Job*.

'You feel safer when you're living with someone who's in the God-business,' Harvey said. 'More at home.'

'Perhaps that's it,' she said.

'And a steadier income.'

'Such as it is,' she said, for she asked little for herself. 'But,' she said, 'I was bored. He always agreed with me, and you don't.'

'That's because you're one of my comforters,' Harvey said. 'Job had his comforters to contend with; why shouldn't I?'

'Do you think of yourself as Job?'

365

'Not exactly, but one can't help sympathizing with the man.'

'I don't know about that,' said Ruth. 'Job was a very rich man. He lost all his goods, and all his sons and daughters, and took it all very philosophically. He said, "The Lord gave, the Lord taketh away, blessed be the name of the Lord." Then he gets covered with boils; and it's only then that his nerve gives way, he's touched personally. He starts his complaint against God at that point only. No question of why his sons should have lost their lives, no enquiries of God about the cause of their fate. It's his skin disease that sets him off.'

'Maybe it was shingles,' Harvey said. 'A nervous disease. Anyway, it got on his nerves.'

Ruth said, 'He had to be touched himself before he would react. Touched in his own body. Utterly selfish. He doesn't seem to have suffered much or he wouldn't have been able to go into all that long argument. He couldn't have had a temperature.'

'I don't agree. I think he had a high temperature all through the argument,' Harvey said. 'Because it's high poetry. Or else, maybe you're right; maybe it was the author who had the temperature. Job himself just sat there with a long face arguing against the theories of his friends.'

'Make a note of that,' Ruth commanded.

'I'll make a note.' He did so.

'Someone must have fed him,' said Ruth. 'Someone must have brought him meals to eat as he sat on the dung-hill outside the town.'

'I'm not sure he sat on a dung-hill outside the town. That is an assumption based on an unverified Greek version of the text. He is merely said to have sat in the ashes on the ground. Presumably at his own hearth. And his good wife, no doubt, brought him his meals.'

Ruth had proved to be an excellent cook, cramped in the kitchen with that weird three-tiered kerosene stove of hers.

'What to you mean, "his good wife"?' Ruth said. 'She told him, "Curse God and die."'

'That was a way of expressing her exasperation. She was tired of his griping and she merely wanted him to get it off his chest quickly, and finish.'

'I suppose the wife suffered,' said Ruth. 'But whoever wrote the book made nothing of her. Job deserved all he got.'

'That was the point that his three friends tried to get across to him,' Harvey said. 'But Job made the point that he didn't deserve it. Suffering isn't in proportion to what the sufferer deserves.'

Ruth wrote in September:

Dear Edward,

I suppose you have gathered by now that I've changed my mind about Harvey. I don't know what he's written to you.

He really is a most interesting man. I believe I can help Harvey.

I can't return to face the life we had together, ever again. My dear, I don't know how I could have thought I would. My plan was, as you know, entirely different. I feel Harvey needs me. I am playing a role in his life. He is serious. Don't imagine I'm living in luxury. He never mentions his wealth. But of course I am aware that if there is anything I require for myself or Clara, I can have it.

You may have heard from Ernie Howe that he is corning to visit Clara. She's well and pretty, and full of life.

I'm sure you have heard from Harvey how things are between him and me. It's too soon to talk of the future.

This has been a difficult letter to write. I know that you'll agree with what I say. You always do.

Ruth

She gave Harvey the letter to read, watching him while he read it. He looked younger than Edward, probably because of Edward's beard, although he was a little older. Harvey was lean and dark, tall, stringy.

'It's a bit dry,' Harvey said.

'It's all I can do. Edward knows what I'm like.'

'I suppose,' said Harvey, 'he'll be hurt.'

'He doesn't love me,' Ruth said.

'How do you know?'

'How does one know?'

'Still, he won't want to lose his property.'

'That's something else.'

Now, in October, Ruth was talking about sending to England for cretonne fabric. 'One can't get exactly what I want in France,' she said.

Harvey wrote:

Dear Edward,

Thanks for yours.

The infant is cutting a tooth and makes a din at night. Ruth has very disturbed nights. So do I. It's been raining steadily for three days. Ernie Howe came. We had a chat. He seems to feel fraternal towards me because we both had to do with Effie. He wants to talk about Effie. I don't. Afterwards, in the place next door that Ruth has fixed up for herself and Clara, Ernie asked her if she would go home and live with him and bring the baby. Ruth said no. I think he's after Ruth because she reminds him of Effie. He said he wouldn't take the child away from Ruth if she doesn't want to part with it, which she doesn't.

I'm sorry to hear that you don't miss Ruth. You ought to.

Cheque enclosed. I know you're not 'selling your wife'. Why should I think you are? You took money before I was sleeping with Ruth, so where's the difference?

I don't agree the comforters just came to gloat. They relieved Job's suffering by arguing with him, keeping him talking. In different ways they keep insinuating that Job 'deserved' his misfortunes; he must have done something wrong. While Job insists that he hasn't, that the massed calamities that came on him haven't any relation to his own actions. He upsets all their theology. Those three friends of his are very patient and considerate, given their historical position. But Job is having a nervous crisis. He can't sleep. See 7, 13–16.

When I say, My bed shall comfort me, my couch shall ease my complaint;

Then thou scarest me with dreams, and terrifiest me through visions:

So that my soul chooseth strangling, and death rather than my life.

I loathe it; I would not live alway: let me alone . . .

So I say, at least the three comforters kept him company. And they took turns as analyst. Job was like the patient on the couch.

Ruth doesn't sympathize with Job. She sees the male pig in him. That's a point of view.

The baby has started to squawk. I don't know what I'm going to do about the noise.

Yours,
Harvey

Ruth came in, jogging in her arms the baby Clara who had a whole fist in her mouth and who made noises of half-laughing, half-crying. Soon, she would start to bawl. Ruth's hair fell over her face, no longer like that of a curate's wife.

'Did you know that they want to sell the château?' she said.

The château was half a mile up the grassy pathway which led away from the cottage. Harvey knew the owner and had seen the house; that was when he first rented the cottage. He knew it was up for sale, and had been for some years.

'It's falling to bits,' he said to Ruth.

'What a pity to neglect it like that!' Ruth said. 'It's a charming house. It reminds me of something from my childhood, I don't know quite what. Perhaps somewhere we visited. I think something could be done to it.'

She brought the fretful child close to Harvey so that he could make an ugly face. He showed his teeth and growled, whereupon Clara temporarily forgot her woes. She smelt of sour milk.

IV

UP AT THE CHÂTEAU WHERE THE neglected lawns were greener than the patch round Harvey's house, and where the shrubberies were thick and very dark evergreen, the workmen were putting in the daylight hours of the last few days before the Christmas holidays. She had already reclaimed one wing for habitation. The roof had been secured in that part, but most of the rooms were cold. Ruth had arranged one sitting room, however, with a fire, and two bedrooms with oil stoves. A good start.

What a business it had been to persuade Harvey to buy the château! And now he was enchanted. Once he agreed to buy – and that was the uphill work – it was simple. Harvey sent for his London lawyer, Stewart Cowper, and for his French lawyer, Martin Deschamps, to meet in Nancy and discuss the deal with the family who owned the château. Ruth had gone with Harvey to this meeting, in October, with Clara in her folding pram. When the hotel room got too boring for the baby, Ruth hushed her, put her in her pram and took her for a walk in Place Stanislas. It was not long before Ruth saw through the splendid gilt gates the whole business group, with Harvey, trooping out to take the sun and continue the deal in the glittering square. Harvey, his two lawyers, and the three members of the de Remiremont family, which comprised a middle-aged man, his daughter and his nephew, came and joined Ruth. The

371

daughter put her hand on the handle of the pram. They all ambled round in a very unprofessional way, talking of notaries and tax and the laws governing foreigners' property in France. You could see that this was only a preliminary.

Harvey said, 'We have to leave you. I'm writing a book on the *Book of Job*.'

It was difficult to get across to them what the *Book of Job* was. Harvey's French wasn't at fault, it was their knowledge of the Bible of which, like most good Catholics, they had scant knowledge. They stood around, the father in his old tweed coat and trousers, the daughter and nephew in their woollen jumpers and blue jeans, puzzling out what was *Job*. Finally, the father remembered. It all came back to him. 'You shouldn't be in a hurry, then,' he said. 'Job had patience, isn't that right? One says, "the patience of Job".'

'In fact,' said Harvey, 'Job was the most impatient of men.'

'Well, it's good to know what it is you're writing in that wretched little cottage,' said the elder man. 'I often wondered.'

'I hope we'll soon have the house,' said Ruth.

'So do we,' said the owner. 'We'll be glad to get rid of it.' The young man and the girl laughed. The lawyers looked a little worried about the frankness and the freedom, suspecting, no doubt, some façade covering a cunning intention.

Ruth and Harvey left them then. It was all settled within a month except for the final bureaucracy, which might drag on for years. Anyhow, Harvey had paid, and Ruth was free to order her workmen to move in.

'Instead of disabusing myself of worldly goods in order to enter the spirit of *Job* I seem to acquire more, ever more and more,' was all that Harvey said.

Ruth wrote to Effie with her letter-pad on her knee, beside the only fireplace, while the workmen hammered away, a few days before Christmas.

Dear Effie,

I really am in love with Harvey and you have no reason
to say I am not. The lovely way he bought the house – so
casual – we just walked round the *Place* with Clara and
the family who used to own the château—and Harvey
shook hands and that was all. The lawyers are working it
out, but the house is ours.

I can't make out your letter. You don't want Clara, at
least not the bother of her. You despise Harvey. What do
you mean, that I have stolen your husband and your child?
Be civilized.

Ruth stopped, read what she had written, and tore it up. Why
should I reply to Effie? What do I owe her? She stole a bit of
chocolate, on principle. I stole her husband, not on principle.
As for her child, I haven't stolen her, she has abandoned her
baby. All right, Effie is young and beautiful, and now has to
work for her living. Possibly she's broke.

Dear Effie,

What attracted me most about the château was the woodpecker in the tree outside the bedroom window. Why don't
you come and visit Clara?

Love,

Ruth

She sealed it up and put it on the big plate in the hall to be
posted, for all the world as if the château was already a going
concern. The big plate on a table by the door was all there
was in the huge dusty hall, but it was a beginning.

Now she took sleeping Clara in her carry-cot and set her
beside the driver's seat in the car. She put a basket in the back
containing bread, pâté, a roast bantam hen and a bottle of

Côte du Rhône, and she set off down the drive to Harvey's house for lunch. The tired patch of withered shrubbery round Harvey's cottage was still noticeably different from the rest of the château's foliage, although Ruth had dug around a few bushes to improve them, and planted some bulbs. As soon as she pushed open the door she saw he had a visitor. She dumped the food basket and went back for the baby, having glimpsed the outline of a student, a young man, any student, with those blue jeans of such a tight fit, they were reminiscent of Elizabethan women's breasts, in that you wondered, looking at their portraits, where they put their natural flesh. The student followed her out to the car. It was Nathan. 'Nathan! It's you – you here. I didn't recognise . . . ' He woke Clara with his big kiss, and the child wailed. He picked her up and pranced up and down with the wakened child. Harvey's studious cottage was a carnival. Harvey said to Ruth, 'I've told Nathan there will be room for him up at the house.'

Nathan had brought some food, too. He had been skilful as ever in finding the glasses, the plates; everything was set for lunch. Ruth got Clara back to sleep again, but precariously, clutching a ragged crust.

Harvey said very little. He had closed the notebook he was working on, and unnaturally tidied his papers; his pens were arranged neatly, and everything on his writing-table looked put-away. He sat looking at the floor between his feet.

Nathan announced, 'I just had to come. I had nothing else to do. It's a long time since I had a holiday.'

'And Edward, how's Edward?' Ruth said.

'Don't you hear from Edward?'

'Yes, of course,' said Ruth, and Harvey said the same.

Nathan opened his big travel pack and brought out yet more food purchases that he had picked up on the way: cheese, wine, pâté and a bottle of Framboise. He left the pack open while he took them to the table. Inside was a muddle of clothes and spare shoes, but Harvey noticed the edges of Christmas-wrapped parcels sticking up from the bottom of the pack. My God, he has come for Christmas. Harvey looked at Ruth: did she invite him? Ruth fluttered about with her thanks and her chatter.

'Are you off to Paris for Christmas?' Harvey enquired. This was his first meeting with Nathan since the holiday in Italy when Harvey had abandoned his party on the *autostrada*; he felt he could be distant and impersonal without offence.

'I've come mainly to visit Clara for Christmas,' said Nathan. He was lifting the baby out of the carry-cot.

'Let her sleep,' Harvey said.

'Oh, Nathan must stay over Christmas,' Ruth said. 'Paris will be crowded. And dreadfully expensive.' She added, 'Nathan is a marvellous cook.'

'So I have heard.'

Ruth didn't notice, or affected not to notice, a look of empty desperation on Harvey's face; a pallor, a cornered look; his lips were parted, his eyes were focusing only on some anguished thought. And he was, in fact, suddenly aghast: What am I doing with these people around me? Who asked this fool to come and join us for Christmas? What do I need with Christmas, and Ruth, and a baby and a bloody little youth who needs a holiday? Why did I buy that château if not for Ruth and the baby to get out of my way? He looked at his writing-table, and panicked.

'I'm going out, I'll just fetch my coat,' he said, thumping upstairs two at a time.

'Harvey, what's the matter?' said Ruth when he appeared again with his sheepskin jacket, his woollen hat. Rain had started to splash down with foul eagerness.

'Don't you want lunch?' she said.

375

'Excuse me. I'm studious,' said Harvey, as he left the cottage. The car door slammed. The starter wouldn't work at first try. The sound of Harvey working and working at the starter became ever more furious until finally he was off.

When he came back in the evening the little house was deserted, all cleaned up. He poured himself a whisky, sat down and started to think of Effie. She was different from Ruth, almost a race apart. Ruth was kind, or comparatively so. Effie wasn't comparatively anything, certainly not kind. She was absolutely fascinating. Harvey remembered Effie at parties, her beauty, part of which was a quick-witted merriment. How could two sisters be so physically alike and yet so totally different? At any moment Ruth might come in and reproach him for not having the Christmas spirit. Effie would never do that. Ruth was thoroughly bourgeois by nature; Effie, anarchistic, aristocratic. I miss Effie, I miss her a lot, Harvey told himself. The sound of Ruth's little car coming down the drive, slowly in the mist, chimed with his thought as would the stroke of eight if there was a clock in the room. He looked at his watch; eight o'clock precisely. She had come to fetch him for dinner; three dinner-places set out on the table of the elegant room in the château, and the baby swinging in a hammock set up in a corner.

Ruth came in. 'You know, Harvey,' she said, 'I think you might be nicer to Nathan. After all, it's Christmas time. He's come all this way, and one should have the Christmas spirit.'

Nathan was there, at the château, settled in for Christmas. Harvey thought: I should have told him to go. I should have said I wanted Ruth and the baby to myself for Christmas. Why didn't I? – Because I don't want them to myself. I don't want them enough; not basically.

Ruth looked happy, having said her say. No need to say any more. I can't hold these women, Harvey thought. Neither Effie nor Ruth. My mind isn't on them enough, and they resent it, just as I resent it when they put something else before me, a person, an idea. Yes, it's understandable.

He swallowed down a drink and put on his coat.

'Nathan thinks it was marvellous of you to buy the château just to make me comfortable with Clara,' said Ruth.

'I bought it for myself, too, you know. I always thought I might acquire it.'

'Nathan has been reading the *Book of Job*, he has some ideas.'

'He did his homework, you mean. He must think I'm some sort of monster. In return for hospitality he thinks he has to discuss my subject.'

'He's polite. Besides, it's my subject too, now,' said Ruth.

'Why?' said Harvey. 'Because I've put you in the château?'

He thought, on the way through the misty trees that lined the long drive, They think I'm such a bore that I have to bribe them to come and play the part of comforters.

He made himself cheerful at the château; he poured drinks. In his anxiety to avoid the subject of *Job*, to be normal, to make general conversation, Harvey blurted out the other thing he had on his mind: 'Any news of Effie?'

God, I've said the wrong thing. Both Nathan and Ruth looked, for a moment, startled, uncomfortable; both, discernibly, for different reasons. Nathan, Harvey supposed, had been told to avoid the subject of Effie. Ruth didn't want to bring Effie into focus; it was enough that she was still Harvey's wife, out there vaguely somewhere else, out of sight.

'Effie?' said Ruth.

'I heard from her,' said Nathan. 'Only a postcard, after she got out.'

'Out from where?'

'From prison in Trieste. Didn't you hear about it?'

'Harvey never discusses Effie,' said Ruth. 'I've only just heard about it. She wrote to me last week from London, but she didn't mention prison.'

'What happened?' said Harvey.

'She was caught shop-lifting in a supermarket in Trieste. She said she did it to obtain an opportunity to study a women's prison at first-hand. She got out after three days. There was a small paragraph about it in the *Telegraph*, nothing in the other papers; it was about a month ago,' Ruth said. 'Nathan just told me.'

'All she said on the card was that she was going to Munich,' said Nathan.

'I wish her well of Munich,' said Harvey.

'I thought it was a beautiful town,' Ruth said.

'You thought strangely. There is a carillon clock with dancers coming out of the clock-tower twice a day. That's all there is in Munich.'

'She has friends there,' Nathan said. 'She said on the card she was joining friends in Munich. She seems to be getting around.'

'Well, I'm glad, for Effie, there is something else in Munich besides the carillon clock. Who made this soup?'

'Nathan did,' said Ruth.

'It's great.' He wondered why Stewart Cowper hadn't told him about Effie being arrested. He felt over-protected. How can you deal with the problem of suffering if everybody conspires to estrange you from suffering? He felt like the rich man in the parable: it is easier for a camel to go through the eye of a needle than for him to enter the Kingdom of Heaven.

'One must approach these things with balanced thought,' Ruth was saying, alarmingly. Harvey bent his mind to take in what they were discussing. It emerged that they were talking about the huge price Nathan had paid for the taxi from the airport to the château.

'There's a train service,' Harvey said.

'I've just been telling him that,' said Ruth. 'Spending all that money, as much as the air fare. He could have phoned me from the airport.'

'I don't have the number,' said Nathan.

'Oh, yes, I forgot,' said Ruth. 'No one gets the number. Harvey has to be protected; in his position everyone wants him for something. He's here to study an important subject, write a thesis, get away from it all. You have to realise that, Nathan.'

Nathan turned to Harvey. 'Maybe I shouldn't have told you about Effie.'

'Oh, that's all right. I asked you about her, after all.'

'Yes, you did,' said Ruth. She had served veal, delicately cooked in white wine. 'You did bring up the subject, Harvey.'

'A beautiful girl, Effie,' said Nathan. 'What a lovely girl she is!'

Harvey wondered how much he knew about how beautiful Effie was. He looked at Nathan and thought, He has barged into my peace, he's taking his place for Christmas, he's discussing my wife as if she was everybody's girl (which she is), and he's going to get together again with Ruth; they will conspire how to protect me. Finally, he will ask me for a loan.

'Will you be all right up here alone in the château tonight?' Harvey said with determination. 'Ruth and I always shack down in my cottage; Ruth brings the baby back here immediately after early breakfast so that I can start on my work at about seven-thirty.'

'If you'll leave Clara with me I won't feel lonely,' said Nathan.

'Not at all,' said Harvey. 'We have a place for her. She's teething.'

'Nathan's used to Clara,' said Ruth. 'He's known her and looked after her since she was born.'

'I don't think we need ask our guests to baby-sit for us.' Don't think, Harvey said within himself, that you are one of the family here; you are one of 'our guests' in this house.

'Well, as she's teething,' said Ruth, 'I'd better take her with me. I really do think so, Nathan.'

'We'll move up here to the château for Christmas,' Harvey said, now that Ruth was winding up the feast with a cheese *soufflé* as light as could be. He fetched the brandy glasses.

V

Dear Edward,

Happy New Year. Thanks for yours.

The day before Christmas Eve he turned up. After dinner he sat up late discussing his ideas on *Job* – he'd done some reading (for my benefit, which I suppose is a compliment). I don't agree with you that he seems 'positively calculating', I don't agree at all. I think he wanted to spend Christmas with Ruth and the baby. He would have preferred to spend Christmas with Effie. He didn't want to spend Christmas alone with you; that's why you're sour. You should get a lot of friends and some of your colleagues, pretty young actresses, have parties. Nathan would like that.

We went to Midnight Mass at the local church. Nathan carried Clara in a sling on his back and she slept throughout. There was a great crowd.

He hasn't left yet. He shows no sign of leaving.

I agree that Job endlessly discusses morals but there is nothing moral about the *Book of Job*. In fact it is shockingly amoral.

God has a wager with Satan that Job will not lose faith, however much he is afflicted. Job never knows about this wager, neither do his friends. But the reader knows. Satan finally makes the explicit challenge (2,5):

381

But put forth thy hand now, and touch his bone and
his flesh, and he will curse thee to thy face.

And God says, Go ahead ('Behold, he is in thine hand; but
save his life.')

Consequently Job, having lost his sons and his goods, is
now covered with sores. He is visited by his bureaucratic
friends who tell him he must have deserved it. The result
is that Job has a sort of nervous breakdown. He demands
an explanation and he never gets it.

Do you know that verse of Kipling's?

The toad beneath the harrow knows
Exactly where each tooth-point goes;
The butterfly upon the road
Preaches contentment to that toad.

I think this expresses Job's plight. The boils are personal,
they loosen his tongue, they set him off. He doesn't reproach God in so many words, but he does by implication.

I must tell you that early in the New Year we started to be bothered by people hanging around the house.
Some 'tourists' (at this time of year!) went to the château
and asked if they could see round the house – a couple of
young men. Nathan got rid of them. Ruth says she heard
there were 'strangers' in the village shop asking questions
about me the other day. A suspicious-looking workman
came to my cottage, saying he'd been sent to test the electricity (not to read the meter, but to test). He showed me
his card, it looked all right. But the electricity department
hadn't heard of him. We suspect that Effie is putting in
some private detectives. I've written to Stewart Cowper.
Where would she get the money?

Why didn't you tell me that Effie had been arrested for shop-lifting in Trieste?

I hope you get that part in the play you write about in your letter. You must know by now.

Yours,
Harvey

Please check the crocodiles for me at the London Zoo. Their eyelids are vertical, are they not? Leviathan in *Job* is generally supposed to be the crocodile. It is written of Leviathan, 'his eyes are like the eyelids of the morning.' None of the commentaries is as yet satisfactory on this. You may remember they never were.

PART II

VI

THE VILLAGE SHOP, ABOUT TWO kilometres from Harvey's cottage, was normally busy when, about nine in the morning, Harvey stopped to buy a newspaper and cigarettes. He remembered this clearly later, when the day had developed and in the later profusion of events he set about to decipher them, starting from this, the beginning of his day.

The shop was divided into two parts, one leading into the other. The owner, a large man in his forties, wearing a dark grey working apron the colour of his hair, looked after the part which sold groceries, detergents, ham, pâté, sausage, cheese, fruit, vegetables, all well laid-out; and also a large stock of very good Vosges wines stacked in rows and arranged according to types and prices. The other part of the shop was presided over by the wife, plump, ruddy-cheeked, with short black curly hair, in her mid-thirties. She looked after the coffee machine, the liquor bar, the pre-wrapped buns and sweets, the newspapers and cigarettes, some stationery and other conveniently saleable goods.

That morning Harvey took an espresso coffee, his packet of cigarettes and the Vosges local paper which he scarcely glanced at. He looked around as he drank his coffee; the suspect people were not there today; it was not to be expected that they would always be at the bar, it would have been too obvious had they been hanging around all day and every day: two young Belgians, touring forests and caves, students, campers, the shopkeepers had said. It seemed unlikely; they were too old for students. There had been another man and woman, older still, in their forties; they looked like a couple of *concierges* from Paris. Harvey was convinced these were Effie's detectives, getting enough evidence for Effie's huge alimonial scoop. The owners of the shop had seemed to take them for granted as they walked up and down in the road. The so-called Belgians had a dormobile with a Lyons registration number – that meant nothing, they had probably hired it. The middle-aged couple, both of them large and solid, came and went in a sad green Citroën Dyane 6. Harvey, having got such a brisk reply to his casual enquiries about the Belgians, had not ventured to enquire about the second couple. Maybe the shopkeepers were in their pay.

This morning, the strangers were not in sight. Only two local youths were at the bar; some countrywomen queued up at the counter on the grocery side. Harvey drank his coffee, paid, took up his paper and cigarettes and left. As he went out he heard behind him the chatter of the women, just a little more excited and scandalised than usual. '*Les supermarchés, les supermarchés . . .*' was the phrase he took in most, and assumed there was a discussion in progress about prices and food.

He put down the paper beside him and as he drove off his eye caught a picture on the front page. It was a group of three identikits, wanted people, two men and a girl. The outlines of the girl's face struck him as being rather like Ruth's. He must remember to let her see it. He turned at the end of the road towards Epinal, the town he was bound for.

After about two kilometres he ran into a road-block; two police motor cycles, three police cars, quite a lot. It was probably to do with the identikits. Harvey produced his papers and sat patiently while the policeman studied them, gave a glance at the car, and waved him on. While waiting, Harvey looked again at the newspaper on the seat by his side. The feature with the identikits was headed 'Armed Robberies in the Vosges'. Undoubtedly the police were looking for the gang. At Epinal he noticed a lot of police actively outside the commissariat on the banks of the Moselle, and, above that, at the grand prefecture. There, among the fountains and flags, he could see in the distance flashes of blue and white uniforms, blue, red and white police cars, a considerable display. He noticed, and yet took no notice. He had come to look once more, as he had often done before, at the sublime painting, *Job Visited by His Wife* at the *Musée* of Epinal. He parked his car and went in.

He was well known to the receptionist who gave him a sunny greeting as he passed the desk.

'No schoolchildren today,' she said. Sometimes when there were school-groups or art-college students in the gallery Harvey would turn away, not even attempting to see the picture. But very often there were only one or two visitors. Sometimes, he had the museum to himself; he was already half-way up the stairs when the receptionist told him so; she watched him approvingly, even admiringly, as he ran up the staircase, as if even his long legs, when they reached the first turning of the stairs, had brought a touch of pleasure into her morning. The dark-blue custodian with his hands behind his back as he made his stately round, nodded familiarly as Harvey reached the second floor; as usual the man went to sit patiently on a chair at the other end of the room as Harvey took his usual place on a small bench in front of the picture.

The painting was made in the first part of the seventeenth century by Georges de La Tour, a native of Lorraine. It bears a resemblance to the Dutch candlelight pictures of the time. Its colours and organisation are superb. It is extremely simple, and like so much great art of the past, surprisingly modern.

Job visité par sa femme: To Harvey's mind there was much more in the painting to illuminate the subject of Job than in many of the lengthy commentaries that he knew so well. It was eloquent of a new idea, and yet, where had the painter found justification for his treatment of the subject?

Job's wife, tall, sweet-faced, with the intimation of a beautiful body inside the large tent-like case of her firm clothes, bending, long-necked, solicitous over Job. In her hand is a lighted candle. It is night, it is winter; Job's wife wears a glorious red tunic over her dress. Job sits on a plain cube-shaped block. He might be in front of a fire, for the light of the candle alone cannot explain the amount of light that is cast on the two figures. Job is naked except for a loin-cloth. He clasps his hands above his knees. His body seems to shrink, but it is the shrunkenness of pathos rather than want. Beside him is the piece of broken pottery that he has taken to scrape his wounds. His beard is thick. He is not an old man. Both are in their early prime, a couple in their thirties. (Indeed, their recently-dead children were not yet married.) His face looks up at his wife, sensitive, imploring some favour, urging some cause. What is his wife trying to tell him as she bends her sweet face towards him? What does he beg, this stricken man, so serene in his faith, so accomplished in argument?

The scene here seemed to Harvey so altogether different from that suggested by the text of *Job*, and yet so deliberately and intelligently contemplated that it was impossible not to wonder what the artist actually meant. Harvey stared at the picture and recalled the verses that followed the account of Job's affliction with boils:

And he took him a potsherd to scrape himself withal; and he sat down among the ashes.

Then said his wife unto him, Dost thou still retain thine integrity? curse God, and die.

But he said unto her, Thou speakest as one of the foolish women speaketh. What? shall we receive good at the hand of God, and shall we not receive evil? In all this did not Job sin with his lips.

But what is she saying to him, Job's wife, in the serious, simple and tender portrait of Georges de La Tour? The text of the poem is full of impatience, anger; it is as if she is possessed by Satan. 'Dost thou still retain thine integrity?' She seems to gloat, 'curse God and die.' Harvey recalled that one of the standard commentators has suggested a special interpretation, something to the effect, 'Are you still going to be so righteous? If you're going to die, curse God and get it off your chest first. It will do you good.' But even this, perhaps homely, advice doesn't fit in with the painting. Of course, the painter was idealising some notion of his own; in his dream, Job and his wife are deeply in love.

Some people had just arrived in the museum; Harvey could hear voices downstairs and footsteps mounting. He continued to regard the picture, developing his thoughts: Here, she is by no means the carrier of Satan's message. She comes to comfort Job, reduced as he is to a mental and physical wreck. 'You speak,' he tells her, 'as one of the foolish women;' that is to say, he doesn't call her a foolish woman, he rather implies that she isn't speaking as her normal self. And he puts it to her, 'Shall we receive good at the hand of God, and shall we not receive evil?' That domestic 'we' is worth noticing, thought Harvey; he doesn't mean to abandon his wife, he has none of the hostility towards her that he has, later, for his friends. In order to have a better look at Job's wife's face, Harvey put his head to one side. Right from the first he had been struck by her resemblance to Effie in profile. She was like Ruth, too, but more like Effie, especially about the upper part of her face. Oh, Effie, Effie, Effie.

There were people behind Harvey. He glanced round and was amazed to see four men facing towards him, not looking at the other pictures as he had expected. Nor were they looking at the painting of Job. They were looking at him, approaching him. At the top of the staircase two other men in police uniform appeared. The keeper looked embarrassed, bewildered. Harvey got up to face them. He realised that, unconsciously, he had been hearing police sirens for some time. With the picture of Job still in his mind's eye, Harvey had time only to form an abrupt impression before they moved in on him, frisked him, and invited him to descend to the waiting police cars.

Harvey had time to go over again all the details of the morning, later, in between interrogations. He found it difficult to get the rest of his life into focus; everything seemed to turn on the morning: the time he had stopped at the village shop; the drive to Epinal; the thoughts that had gone through his mind in front of the painting, *Job visité par sa femme*, at the museum; the moment he was taken to the police car, and driven over the bridge to the commissariat for questioning.

He answered the questions with lucidity so long as they lasted. On and off, he was interrogated for the rest of the day and half the night.

'No, I've never heard of the FLE.'

'*Fronte de la Libération de l'Europe*. You haven't heard of it?'

'No, I haven't heard of it.'

'You know that your wife belongs to this organization?'

'I don't know anything about it.'

'There was an armed robbery in a supermarket outside Epinal this morning. You were waiting here to join your wife.'

'I'm separated from my wife. I haven't seen her for nearly two years.'

'It was a coincidence that you were in Epinal this morning visiting a museum while your estranged wife was also in Epinal engaged in an armed robbery?'

'If my wife was in Epinal, yes, it was a coincidence.'

'Is that your English sense of humour?'

'I'm a Canadian.'

'Is it a coincidence that other supermarkets and a jeweller's shop in the Vosges have been robbed by this gang in the last two weeks? Gérardmer, La Bresse, Baccarat; this morning, Epinal.'

'I don't read the papers.'

'You bought one this morning.'

'I give no weight to local crimes.' If Effie's involved, thought Harvey, plainly she's in this district to embarrass me. It was essential that he shouldn't suggest this, for at the same time it would point to Effie's having directive authority over the gang.

'I still can't believe that my wife's involved,' said Harvey. He partly meant it.

'Three of them, perhaps four. Where are they?'

'I don't know. You'd better look.'

'You recently bought the château. Why?'

'I thought I might as well. It was convenient.'

'You've been a year at the cottage?'

'About a year and a half.'

'How did you find it?'

'I've already explained –'

'Explain again.'

'I found the cottage,' recited Harvey, 'because I was in the Vosges at that time. I had come here to Epinal expressly to look at the painting *Job Visited by His Wife* by Georges de La Tour. I had heard through some friends that the château was for sale. I went to look it over. I said I'd think about it, but I was struck by the suitability of the cottage to my needs, and took that on in the meantime. The owner, Claude de Remiremont, let me have it.'

'How much rent do you pay?'

'I have no idea,' Harvey said. 'Very little. My lawyer attends to that.'

(The rich!)

This interrogator was a man of about Harvey's age, not more than forty, black hair, blue eyes, a good strong face, tall. A chief-inspector, special branch; no fool. His tone of voice varied. Sometimes he put his questions with the frank lilt of a query at the end; at other times he simply made a statement as if enunciating a proved fact. At the end of the table where they sat facing each other was a hefty policeman in uniform, older, with sandy hair growing thin and faded. The door of the room opened occasionally, and other men in uniform and ordinary clothes came and went.

'Where did you learn French?'

'I have always spoken French.'

'You have taken part in the French-Canadian liberation movement.'

'No.'

'You don't believe in it?'

'I don't know anything about it,' said Harvey. 'I haven't lived in Canada since I was eighteen.'

'You say that your wife's sister has been living with you since last October.'

'That's right.'

'With a baby.'

'Yes. My wife's baby daughter.'

'But there was a woman with a baby in your house for a year before that.'

'Not at all. The baby was only born at the end of June last year.'

'There was another infant in your house. We have evidence, M. Gotham, that there was a small child's washing on the line outside your house at least from April of last year.'

'That is so. But there wasn't any baby, there wasn't any woman.'

'Look, M. Gotham, it is a simple trick for terrorists to take the precaution, in the case of discovery, to keep a woman and a child in the house in order to avoid a shoot-out. Rather a low and dangerous trick, using a baby as a cover, but people of that nature – '

'There was no baby at all in my house, nobody but myself,' Harvey explained patiently. 'It was a joke – for the benefit of my brother-in-law who came to visit me. I brought some baby clothes and put them out on the line. He obviously thought I had a girl living with me. I only put them out a few times after that. I told my brother-in-law that I did it to keep women from bothering me with offers of domestic care. As they do. They would assume, you see, that there was a woman. I suppose I'm an eccentric. It was a gesture.'

'A gesture.'

'Well, you might say,' said Harvey, thinking fast how to say it, 'that it was a surrealistic gesture.'

The inspector looked at Harvey for rather a long time. Then he left the room and came back with a photograph in his hand. Effie, in half-profile, three years ago, with her hair blowing around.

'Is that your wife?'

'Yes,' said Harvey. 'Where did you get this photograph?'

'And the woman you are living with, Ruth, is her sister?'

'Mme Jansen is her sister. Where did you get this photograph of my wife? Have you been ransacking through my papers?'

The inspector took up the photograph and looked at it. 'She resembles her sister,' he said.

'Did you have a search warrant?' said Harvey.

'You will be free to contact a lawyer as soon as you have answered our questions. I presume you have a lawyer in Paris? He will explain the law to you.'

'I have, of course, a French lawyer,' Harvey said. 'But I don't need him at the moment. Waste of money.'

Just then a thought struck him: Oh, God, will they shoot Ruth in mistake for Effie?

'My sister-in-law, Ruth Jansen, is, as you say, very like her sister. She's caring for the baby of nine months. Be very careful not to confuse them should you come to a confrontation. She has the baby there in the château.'

'We have the baby.'

'What?'

'We are taking care of the baby.'

'Where is she?'

The sandy-faced policeman spoke up. He had a perfectly human smile: 'I believe she is taking the air in the courtyard. Come and see out of the window.'

Down in the courtyard among the police cars and motor-bicycles, a large policeman in uniform, but without his hat, whom Harvey recognised as one of those who had escorted him from the museum, was holding Clara in his arms, wrapped up in her woollies; he was jogging her up and down while a young policewoman was talking to her. Another, younger policeman, in civilian clothes, was also attempting to curry favour with her. Clara had her chubby arms round the large man's neck, enjoying the attention, fraternizing with the police all round.

'Is she getting her feeds?' said Harvey. 'I believe she has some special regular feeds that have to be – '

'Mme Jansen is seeing to all that, don't worry. Let's proceed.'

'I want to know where Ruth Jansen is,' said Harvey.

'She's downstairs, answering some questions. The sooner we proceed with the job the sooner you will be able to join her. Why did you explain your baby clothes to your brother-in-law Edward Jansen in the words, "The police won't shoot if there's a baby in the house"?'

'Did I say that?' said Harvey.

'Mme Jansen has admitted it,' said the inspector.

Admitted it. What had Edward told Ruth, what was Ruth telling them downstairs? But 'admitted' was not the same as 'volunteered' the information.

'You probably suggested the phrase to her,' said Harvey. The old police trick: Is it true that he said 'The police won't shoot . . . ?

'Did you or did you not say those words last April when M. Jansen came to see you?'

'If I did it was a joke.'

'Surrealism?'

'Yes, call it that.'

'You are a man of means?'

'Oh, yes.'

'Somebody is financing the FLE,' said the inspector.

'But I am not financing it.'

'Why do you live in that shack?'

'It doesn't matter to me where I work. I've told you. All I want is peace of mind. I'm studious.'

'Scholarly,' said the inspector dreamily.

'No, studious. I can afford to study and speculate without achieving results.'

The inspector raised his shoulders and exchanged a glance with the sandy-haired policeman. Then he said, 'Studious, scholarly . . . Why did you buy the château?'

'It was convenient for me to do so. Mme Jansen thought it desirable for her to have a home for herself and the baby.'

'It isn't your child.'

It was Harvey's turn to shrug. 'It's my wife's child. It makes no difference to me who the father is.'

'The resemblance between your wife and her sister might be very convenient,' said the inspector.

'I find them quite distinct. The resemblance is superficial. What do you mean – "convenient"?' Harvey, not quite knowing what the man was getting at, assumed he was implying that an exchange of lovers would be easy for him, the two sisters being, as it were, interchangeable. 'They are very different,' said Harvey.

'It would be convenient,' said the inspector, 'for two women who resemble each other to be involved in the same criminal organization. I am just hypothesizing, you understand. A question of one being able to provide an alibi for the other; it's not unknown . . . '

'My papers are in order,' Harvey said now, for no reason that was apparent, even to himself.

The inspector was very polite. 'You maintain your wife financially, of course.'

'I've given her no money since I left her. But if I had, that wouldn't signify that I was financing a terrorist organization.'

'Then you know that your wife is an active member of the FLE, and consequently have refused to supply money.'

'I never knew of the existence of the FLE until now. I don't at all know that my wife is a member of the group.'

'And you give your wife no money,' the policeman said.

'No money.'

'You knew that she was arrested in Trieste.'

'I didn't know until the other day. Nobody told me.'

'Nobody told you,' stated the inspector.

'That's right. Nobody told me. I'm studious, you see. I have arranged for people not to bother me, and they don't; rather to excess. I think someone should have told me. Not that it would have made any difference.'

'Your wife knows where you live?'

'Yes.'

'You have written to her?'

'No. I left her two years ago. Eventually she found out where I lived.'

'How did she find out?'

'I suppose she got it out of someone. She's an intelligent woman. I doubt very much she's mixed up with a terrorist group.'

'You must have had some reason to abandon her. Why are you so eager to protect her?'

'Look, I just want to be fair, to answer your questions.'

'We know she's an activist in the FLE.'

'Well, what exactly have they done?'

'Armed robbery and insurrection in various places. Of recent weeks they've been operating in the Vosges. Where are their headquarters?'

'Not in my house. And if my wife is involved in these incidents – which I don't admit she is – isn't it possible she has been kidnapped and forced to join this FLE? It's happened before. The Hearst case in the United States . . . '

'Do you have reason to believe she has been kidnapped?'

'I don't know. I have no idea. Has anyone been killed, injured, by this group?'

'Injured? But they are armed. They've collected a good deal of money, wounded twelve, damaged many millions of francs' worth of property. They are dangerous. Three men and a girl. The girl is your wife. Who are the others?'

'How should I know? I've never heard of the – '

'Nobody told you.'

'Correct.'

'It's time for lunch,' said the inspector, looking at his watch; and, as he got up, he said, 'Can you explain why Nathan Fox disappeared from the château last night?'

'Nathan Fox. Disappeared?'

'Nobody told you.'

'No. I left my cottage at nine this morning.'

'Where is Nathan Fox?' said the inspector, still standing.

'I have no idea. He's free to come and go . . . I don't really know.'

'Well, think it over.' The inspector left the room.

Harvey's cottage was in darkness when he drove back at four in the morning. He was tempted to go in and see what had happened to his papers, his work; had they been careful or had they turned everything upside down? Later, he found everything more or less intact with hardly a sign of a search; he had suspected that at least half the time he was kept for questioning had been for the purpose of giving the police leisure to continue their search at the cottage and the château; much good it had done them.

He didn't stop at the cottage that early morning, but drove up to the château. A police car was parked at a bend in the drive. Harvey tooted twice, softly and quickly, as he passed it. Friendly gesture. The light was on in the porch. He let himself in. Ruth came out of the living room in her dressing gown; she had been sleeping on a sofa, waiting for him. 'They brought us back at half-past six,' she said. She came to hug him, to kiss him. 'Are you all right?' they both said at the same time. Clara was sleeping in her carry-cot.

The first thing that struck him was the colour in the room. There was nothing new, but after the grey and neutral offices, hour after hour, at the police headquarters, the blue of Ruth's dressing gown, the flower-patterned yellow sofa, green foliage arranged in a vase, the bright red tartan rug folded over Clara's cot, made a special impact on his senses. He smiled, almost laughed.

'Do you want to go to bed? Aren't you tired?' Ruth said.

'No. I'm wide awake.'

'Me, too.'

They poured whiskies and sodas. 'I simply told them the truth,' Ruth said. She decided she couldn't face her whisky and took orange juice.

'Me, too. What else could one say?'

'Oh, I know you told them everything,' Ruth said, 'I could guess by the questions.'

Harvey quoted, ' "The police won't shoot if there's a baby in the house." '

'Yes, why did you bring that up?' said Ruth. 'Was it necessary? They're suspicious enough – '

'I didn't suggest it to them.'

'Well, neither did I,' said Ruth. 'The inspector asked me if it was true you'd made that remark. I said I believed so. Edward told me, of course – '

'They're quite clever,' Harvey said. 'How did they treat you?'

'Very polite. They were patient about my *au pair* French.'

'How many?'

'Two plain-clothes men and a glamorous policewoman. Did you see the policewoman?' said Ruth.

'I saw one, from the window, playing with Clara.'

'They were very decent about Clara.'

Harvey's interrogators had been three, one after the other, then starting in the late afternoon with the first again.

Ruth and Harvey described and identified their respective policemen, and in a euphoric way compared a great many of their experiences of the day, questions and answers. Finally Ruth said, 'Do you really think Effie's in it?'

'Up to the neck,' said Harvey.

'Can you blame them for suspecting us?'

'No. I think, in fact, that Effie has chosen this district specifically to embarrass me.'

'So do I.'

He sat on the sofa beside her, relaxed, with his arm round her. She said, 'You know, I'm more afraid of Effie than the police.'

'Did you tell them that?'

'No.'

'Did they come and look round the château while you were at the headquarters?'

'I don't think so, because when they brought me back they asked if they might have a look round. I said, of course. They went all over, attics, cellars, and both towers. Actually, I was quite relieved that they didn't find anything, or rather anyone. It would be easy to hide in this house, you know.'

'Did you tell them you were relieved?'

'No.'

'Now tell me about Nathan.'

'It's a long story,' said Ruth. 'He's in love with Effie. He'd do anything she asked him.' Her voice had changed to a mumble.

Harvey said, 'But when did you know – ' Then he stopped. 'My God,' he said, 'I'm becoming another interrogator. I expect you've had enough.'

'Quite enough.'

It was he who had the idea to go and make breakfast, which he brought in on a tray. 'I had a lousy pizza for supper,' he said.

She said, 'Nathan must have left last night. He didn't sleep here. He wasn't here when I came up from the cottage this morning. His bed wasn't slept in.'

'Did Anne-Marie see him?' Anne-Marie was a local woman who had been coming daily to help in the house for the past two weeks.

'No, he wasn't here when she arrived at eight. He'd taken nothing special that I could see. But he had a phone call yesterday. He said it was from London. I was annoyed at the time, because I'd told him not to give anyone your number.'

The telephone at the château operated through an exchange for long distance. 'One could easily find out if it came from London,' Harvey said.

'The police say there was no call from London,' Ruth said.

'Then it might have been a national call. He could have been in touch with Effie.'

'Exactly,' she said.

'How much did you tell them about Nathan?'

'Everything I know.'

'Quite right.'

'And another thing,' Ruth said, 'I told them – '

'Let's forget it and go to bed.'

Clara woke up just then. They shoved a piece of toast into her hand, which seemed to please her mightily.

It was nine-fifteen when the telephone rang. This time it was from London. At the same time the doorbell rang. Harvey had been dreaming that his interrogator was one of those electric typewriters where the typeface can be changed by easy manipulation; the voice of the interrogator changed like the type, and in fact was one and the same, now roman, now élite, now italics. In the end, bells on the typewriter rang to wake him up to the phone and the doorbell.

He looked out of the window while Ruth went to answer the phone. Reporters, at least eight, some with cameras, some with open umbrellas or raincoats over their heads to shield them from the pouring rain. Up the drive came a television van. Behind him, through the door of the room, Ruth called to him, 'Harvey, it's urgent for you, from London.'

'Get dressed,' Harvey said. 'Don't open the door. Those are reporters out there. Keep them in the rain for a while, at least.'

Clara began to wail. The doorbell pealed on. From round the side of the château someone was banging at another door.

On the phone was Stewart Cowper from London.

'What's going on there?' said Stewart.

Harvey thought he meant the noise.

'There's been a bit of trouble. Reporters are at the doors of the house and the baby's crying.'

'There are headlines in all the English papers. Are you coming back to England?'

'Not at the moment,' Harvey said. 'I don't know about Ruth and the child; but we haven't discussed it. What are the headlines?'

'Headlines and paras, Harvey. Hold on, I'll read you a bit:

Millionaire's religious sect possibly involved in French terrorist activities. Wife of English actor involved . . .

And here's another:

Playboy Harvey Gotham, 35, with his arsenal of money from Gotham's Canadian Salmon, whose uncles made a fortune in the years before and during the Second World War, has been questioned by the *gendarmes d'enquêtes* of the Vosges, France, in connection with hold-ups and bombings of supermarkets and post offices in that area. It is believed that his wife, Mrs Effie Gotham, 25, is a leading member of FLE, an extreme leftist terrorist movement. Mr Gotham, who has recently acquired a base in that area, denies having in any way financed the group or having been in touch with his estranged wife. He claims to be occupied with religious studies. Among his circle are his sister-in-law, Ruth, 28, sister of the suspected terrorist, and Nathan Fox, 25, who disappeared from the Gotham château on the eve of the latest armed robbery at Epinal, capital of the Vosges.

There's a lot more,' said Stewart. 'If you're not coming back to England I'd better come there. Have you got hold of Martin Deschamps?'

'Who the hell is he?'

'Your Paris lawyer.'

'Oh, him. No. I don't need lawyers. I'm not a criminal. Look, I've got to get rid of these reporters. By the way,' Harvey continued, partly for the benefit of the police who had undoubtedly tapped the phone, and partly because he meant it, 'I must tell you that the more I look at La Tour's *Job* the more I'm impressed by the simplicity, the lack of sentimentality above all. It's a magnificent – '

'Don't get on the wrong side of the press,' shouted Stewart.

'Oh, I don't intend to see them. Ruth and I have had very little sleep.'

'Make an appointment for a press conference, late afternoon, say five o'clock,' said Stewart. 'I'll send you Deschamps.'

'No need,' said Harvey, and hung up.

None the less, he managed to mollify the soaking pressmen outside his house, speaking to them from an upstairs window, by making an appointment with them for five o'clock that afternoon. They didn't all go away, but they stopped battering at the doors.

Then, to Ruth's amazement their newly-engaged, brisk domestic help, Anne-Marie, arrived, with a bag of provisions.

It was her second week on the job. She managed to throw off the reporters who crowded round her with questions, by upbraiding them for disturbing the baby, and by pushing her way through. Inside the front door, Harvey stood ready to open it quickly, admitting her and nobody else.

'The police,' Anne-Marie said, 'were at my house yesterday for hours. Questions, questions.' But she seemed remarkably cheerful about the questions.

VII

A LONG RING AT THE FRONT DOORBELL. Outside in the pouring rain a police car waited. From the upper window Harvey saw the interrogator he had left less than twelve hours ago in the headquarters at Epinal.

'Ah,' said Harvey from the window. 'I've been missing you dreadfully.'

'Look,' said the man, 'I'm not enjoying this, am I? Just one or two small questions to clarify – '

'I'll let you in.'

The policeman glanced through the open door at the living room as he passed. Harvey conducted him to a small room at the back of this part of the château. The room had a desk and a few chairs; it hadn't been furnished or re-painted; it was less smart and new than the police station at Epinal, but it was the next best thing.

'You have no clue, absolutely no idea, where your wife is?'

'No. Where do you yourselves think she is?'

'Hiding out in the woods. Or gone across into Germany. Or hiding in Paris. These people have an organization,' said the inspector.

'If she's in the woods she would be wet,' said Harvey, glaring at the sheet rain outside the window.

'Is she a strong woman? Any health complications?'

'Well, she's slim, rather fragile. Her health's all right so far as I know,' Harvey said.

'If she contacts you, it would be obliging if you would invite her to the house. The same applies to Nathan Fox.'

'But I don't want my wife in the house. I don't want to oblige her. I don't need Nathan Fox,' Harvey said.

'When things quieten down she might try to contact you. You might oblige us by offering her a refuge.'

'I should have thought you had the house surrounded.'

'We do. We mean to keep it surrounded. You know, these people are heavily armed, they have sophisticated weapons. It might occur to them to take you hostages, you and the baby. Of course, they would be caught before they could get near you. But you might help us by issuing an invitation.'

'It's all a supposition,' Harvey said. 'I'm not convinced that this woman-terrorist is my wife, nor that my wife is a terrorist. As for Nathan Fox, he's a mystery to me, but I wouldn't have thought he'd draw attention to himself by going off and joining an armed band at the very moment when they were active.'

'If your wife is a fascinating woman –'

'I hope,' said Harvey, 'that you're taking special precautions to protect the baby.'

'You admit that the baby might be in danger?'

'With an armed gang around, any baby might be in danger.'

'But you admit that your wife's baby might be an object of special interest to your wife.'

'She has taken no interest in the child.'

'Then why are you suggesting that we specially protect this child?'

'I hope you have made arrangements to do so,' said Harvey.

'We have your house and grounds surrounded.'

'The baby,' said Harvey, 'must be sent back to England. My sister-in-law will take her.'

'A good idea. We can arrange for them to leave, quietly, with every protection. But it would be advisable for you to keep the move as secret as possible. I mean the press. We don't want this gang to know every move. I warn you to be careful what you say to the press. The examining magistrate – '

'The press! They've already – '

The man spread his hands helplessly. 'This wasn't my fault. These things leak out. After all, it's a matter of national concern. But not a word about your plans to send the child away.'

'The maid will know. They talk – '

'Anne-Marie is one of our people,' said the inspector.

'You don't say! We rather liked her.'

'She'd better stay on with you, then. And hang out baby clothes on the line, as you always want to do. I might look in again soon.'

'Don't stand on ceremony.'

'How is it possible,' Ruth said, 'that the police think the gang might turn up here, now that this story's all over the papers, on the radio, the television? It's the last place they would come to. Clara's safer here than anywhere. How can they think – '

'The police don't think so, they only say they think so.'

'Why?'

'How do I know? They suspect me strongly. They want the baby out of France. Maybe it's got something to do with their public image.'

'I don't want to go,' said Ruth.

'I don't want you to go,' said Harvey, 'but I think you should. It's only for a while. I think you must.'

'Are you free to come, too? Harvey, let's both get away.'

'On paper, I'm free to go. In fact, they might detain me. The truth is, I don't want to leave just at this moment. Just bloody-mindedness on my part.'

'I can be stubborn, too,' said Ruth; but she spoke with a fluidity that implied she was giving way. 'But, after all,' she went on, 'I suppose you didn't ask me to come here in the first place.'

Harvey thought, I don't love her, I'm not in the least in love with her. Much of the time I don't even like her very much.

Anne-Marie had put some soup on the table. Harvey and Ruth were silent before her, now that she wasn't a maid but a police auxiliary. When she had left, Ruth said, 'I don't know if I'll be able to keep this down. I'm pregnant.'

'How did that happen?' Harvey said.

'The same as it always happens.'

'How long have you known?'

'Three weeks.'

'Nobody tells me anything,' Harvey said.

'You don't want to know anything.'

Had Ruth stopped taking the pill? Was it his child or Nathan's? She didn't guess his first thought, but she did his second. 'I never slept with Nathan, ever,' she said. 'His mind's on Effie – That's one thing I didn't mention to the police.'

'Take some bread with your soup. You'll keep it down better.'

'You know, I'd rather not go back to England. Now that Edward's having this amazing success – '

'What success?'

'He's having an astonishing success on the West End. That play – '

'Well, how long have you known about this?'

'Three weeks. It's been in the papers, and he wrote – '

'Nobody tells me anything.'

'I think it funny Edward hasn't rung us up today. He must have seen the papers,' Ruth said. 'Maybe it scared him. A scandal.'

'Where would you like to go?' Harvey said.

'Have you got anyone in Canada I could take Clara to?'

'I have an aunt and I have an uncle in Toronto. They're married but they live in separate houses. You could go to either. I'll ring up.'

'I'll go to the uncle,' said Ruth. She started to smile happily, but she was crying at the same time.

'There's nothing to worry about,' Harvey said.

'Yes there is. There's Effie. There's Edward.'

'What about Edward?'

'He's a shit. He might have wanted to know if I was all right. He's been writing all the time I've been here, and phoning every day since we got the telephone put in. Up to now.'

Anne-Marie came in with a splendid salad, a tray of cheeses.

'Shall I help Madame to pack after lunch?' she said.

'How did she know I was leaving?' Ruth said when the maid had gone out.

'Somebody told her. Everyone knows everything,' said Harvey, 'except me.'

Ruth was in the bedroom, packing, and Harvey was pushing the furniture here and there to make a distance between the place where he intended to sit to receive the reporters, and the part of the room reserved for them. Ruth, Harvey thought as he did so, has been crying a lot over the past few weeks, crying and laughing. I noticed, but I didn't notice. I wonder if she cried under the interrogation, and laughed? Anyway, it isn't this quite unlooked-for event that's caused her to cry and laugh, it started earlier. Did she tell the police she was pregnant? Probably. Maybe that's why they want to get rid of her. Is she really pregnant? Harvey plumped up a few cushions. Yellow chintzes, lots of yellow; at least, the chintzes had a basis of yellow, so that you saw yellow when you came into the room. New chintzes: all right, order new chintzes. Curtains and cushions and cosiness: all right, order them; have them mail my lawyer the bill. You say you need a château: all right, have the château, my lawyers will fix it. Harvey kicked an armchair. It moved smoothly on its castors into place. Ruth, he thought, is fond of the baby. She adores Clara. Who wouldn't? But Clara belongs to me, that is, to my wife, Effie. No, Clara belongs to Ruth and depends on Ruth. It's good-bye, good-bye, to Clara. He looked at his watch. Time to telephone Toronto, it's about ten in the morning there. The story of playboy Harvey Gotham and his terrorist connections is certainly featured in the Canadian press, on the radio, the television.

Anne-Marie had come in, shiny black short hair, shiny black eyes, clear face. She had a small waist, stout hips. She carried a transistor radio playing rock music softly enough not to justify complaint.

'Do you know how to get a number on the telephone, long-distance to Toronto?' Harvey said.

'Of course,' said the policewoman.

He thought, as he gave her the number, She doesn't look like a police official, she looks like a maid. Bedworthy and married. She's somebody's wife. Every woman I have to do with is somebody's wife. Ruth, Job's wife, and Effie who is still my wife, and who is shooting up the supermarkets. Twelve people hurt and millions of francs' theft and damage. If the police don't soon get the gang there will be deaths; housewives, policemen, children murdered. Am I responsible for my wife's debts? Her wounded, her dead?

Anne-Marie had left the transistor while she went to telephone; the music had been interrupted and the low murmur of an announcement drew Harvey's attention; he caught the phrases: terrorist organization . . . errors of justice . . .; he

turned the volume up. It was a bulletin from FLE issued to a
Paris news agency, vindicating its latest activities. The gang
was going to liberate Europe from its errors. 'Errors of society, errors of the system.' Most of all, liberation from the
diabolical institution of the *gendarmerie* and the brutality of
the *Brigade Criminelle*. It was much the same as every other
terrorist announcement Harvey had ever read. 'The multi-
nationals and the forces of the reactionary imperialist powers
. . .' It was like an alarm clock that ceases to wake the sleeper
who, having heard it morning after morning, simply puts out
a hand and switches it off without even opening his eyes.

The bulletin was followed by an announcement that fifty
inspectors of the *Brigade Criminelle* were now investigating
FLE's activities in the Vosges where the terrorists were still
believed to be hiding out. End of announcement: on with the
music.

'Your call to Toronto,' said Anne-Marie.

Ruth was to go to Paris and leave next morning, with
Clara, for Canada. A Volvo pulled up at the door. When he
had finished his call, Harvey saw two suitcases already packed
in the hall. Those people work fast. 'Not so fast,' Harvey
said to Anne-Marie. 'The child's father might not agree to her
going to Canada. We must get his permission.'

'We have his permission. Mr Howe will call you tonight.
He has agreed with Scotland Yard.'

'The press will be here any minute,' said Harvey. 'They'll
see Madame and the baby driving off.'

'No, the police have the road cordoned off. Madame and
the child will leave by a back door, anyway.' She went out
and gave instructions to the driver of the Volvo, who took
off, round to the back of the house. Anne-Marie lifted one
of the suitcases and gestured to Harvey to take the other. He
followed her, unfamiliar with all the passages of his château,

through a maze of grey kitchens, dairies and wash-houses as yet unrestored. By a door leading to a vast and sad old plantation which must have once been a kitchen garden, Ruth stood, huddled in her sheepskin coat, crying, cuddling the baby.

'Is it to be Toronto?' she said.

'Oh, yes, you'll be met. Do you have the money with you?' Harvey had given her charge of a quantity of cash long before the trouble started.

'I've taken most of it.'

'You'll be all right once you're at my uncle Joe's.'

'Who did you say I was?' she said.

'My sister-in-law.'

'And Clara?'

'Your niece. Ernie Howe has given his permission—'

'Oh, I know. I spoke to him myself,' she said.

'Nobody tells me anything,' Harvey said.

'Will I like your uncle Joe?'

'I hope so. If not, you can go to my auntie Pet.'

'What is "Pet" short for?' said Ruth.

'I really don't know.' He could see she wanted to delay the parting. 'Ring me tonight from Paris,' he said. He kissed Ruth and he kissed Clara, and practically pushed them towards Anne-Marie who had already seen the suitcases into the car, and was waiting for Ruth, almost taking her under arrest. With a hand under Ruth's arm she led her along the little path towards the wider path where the car waited. They were off, Ruth and Clara in the front seat beside the driver. They were like an affluent married couple and child. Anne-Marie came back to the house, closed and locked the back door. Harvey said, 'You lead the way back. I'll follow you. I don't know my way about this place.' She laughed.

Twenty minutes later the press were let in. 'Quiet!' said Anne-Marie. 'We have a baby in the house. You mustn't wake her.'

Harvey, freshly and acutely aware of Clara's innocent departure, was startled for an instant, then remembered quickly that Ruth and Clara were gone in secret.

'Madame is resting, too,' announced Anne-Marie, 'please, gentlemen, ladies, no noise.'

There were eighteen men, five women; the rest were at the road-block outside the house arguing vainly with the police. This, Harvey learned from the reporters themselves, who crowded into the living room. There was a predominance of French, British and Americans among them. Harvey scrutinized them, as best he could trying to guess which one of them was a police agent. A wiry woman of about fifty with a red face, broken-veined, and thin grey hair fluffed out and falling all over her face as if to make the most of it, seemed to him a possible *flic*, if only for the reason that unlike the others she seemed to have no one to talk to.

'Mr Gotham, when did you last see – '

'I will answer no questions,' Harvey said, 'until you stop these flash-photographs.' He sat back in his chair with folded arms. 'Stop,' he said, 'just stop. I'll answer questions first, if they're reasonable. Then you can take some photos. But not all at once. Kindly keep your voices down; as you've heard, there's a baby sleeping upstairs and a lady who needs a lot of rest.' One of the reporters, slouching by the door, a large fair middle-aged man, was already taking notes. What of? The man's face seemed familiar to Harvey but he couldn't place it.

The French journalists were the most vociferous. 'Do you know where your wife is?' – 'How long has she been a member – ?' – 'Your wife Effie's terrorist activities, do you ascribe them to a reaction against her wealthy matrimonial experience, with all the luxury and boredom that capitalism produces?' – 'What exactly are the creed and aims of your religious group, Mr Gotham?'

Harvey said, 'One at a time, please.'

'With all your prospects and holdings, you still believe in God, is that right?' – 'Are you asking us to believe that you have come to this château to study the Bible?' – 'Isn't it so that you originally lived in that little lodge at the end of the drive?'

'Yes,' said Harvey, 'I went to work down there.'

'Where does your wife get the money for her terrorist activities?'

'I don't know that my wife is engaged in terrorist activities.'

'But the police have identified her. Look, Mr Gotham, those people of the FLE get their money from someplace.' This came from a fat young American who spoke like a machine-gun.

'Would you mind speaking French so that we all know where we are?' said Harvey. A Frenchman swiftly came to his American colleague's aid, and repeated the question in French.

'Apparently they bomb supermarkets and rob the cash. Haven't you read the papers?' Harvey said.

'If your wife came in here with a sub-machine-gun right now – ?'

'That is a hypothetical question,' Harvey said. The question was asked by a timid young Asiatic type with fine features and a sad pallor, who had evidently been let in to the conference on a quota system. He looked puzzled. 'Your question is all theory,' Harvey said, to help him. The young man nodded wisely and made some notes. What notes? – God knows.

'Didn't you hear a registration in the police station of your wife's voice on a loudspeaker warning the people to leave the supermarket before the bombing? – Surely you recognized your wife's voice?' said an American.

'I heard no registration. But if my wife should happen to give a warning to anyone in danger at any time, that would be very right of her, I think,' Harvey said.

Most of the reporters were younger than Harvey. One, a bearded Swede, was old, paunchy. He alone seemed to know what the *Book of Job* was. He asked Harvey, 'Would you say that you yourself are in the position of Job, in so far as you are a suspicious character in the eyes of the world, yet feel yourself to be perfectly innocent?'

Harvey saw his chance and took it: 'I am hardly in the position of Job. He was covered with boils, for one thing, which I am not. And his friends, merely on the basis of his suffering, accused him of having sinned in some way. What Job underwent was tantamount to an interrogation by the Elders of his community. I intend no personal analogy. But I am delighted to get down at last to the subject of this conference: what was the answer to Job's question? Job's question was, why does God cause me to suffer when I've done nothing to deserve it? Now, Job was in no doubt whatsoever that his sufferings came from God and from no other source. The very rapidity with which one calamity followed upon another, shattering Job's world, leaving him destitute, bereft and sick all in a short space of time, gave dramatic evidence that the cause was not natural, but supernatural. The supernatural, with power to act so strongly and disastrously, could only, in Job's mind, be God. And we know he was right in the context of the book, because in the Prologue you read specifically that it was God who brought up the subject of job to Satan; it was God, in fact, who tempted Satan to torment Job, not Satan who tempted God. I'm afraid my French version of the scriptures isn't to hand, it's down in my study in the cottage, or I'd quote you the precise passage. But – '

'Mr Gotham,' said a young Englishwoman dressed entirely in dark grey leather, 'I'm sorry to interrupt but I have to file my story at six. Is it true that Nathan Fox is your wife's lover?'

'Please stick to French if you can. Anyway, I am addressing this gentleman,' said Harvey, indicating the elderly Swede, 'on a very important subject and – '

'Oh, no, Mr Gotham. Oh, no.' This was a tough pressman, indeterminately British or American, who spoke with a loud, fierce voice. 'Oh, no, Mr Gotham. You're here to answer our questions.'

'Keep your voice down, please. The fact is that I am here because it is my home. You are here to listen to me. The subject is the *Book of Job* to which I have dedicated many years of my life. This gentleman,' said Harvey, nodding to the grave and rather flattered Swede, 'has asked me an interesting question on the subject. I have answered his question and I am elaborating on it. Your chance, and that of your colleagues, to put further questions will come in due course. As I was about to remark, Job's problem was partly a lack of knowledge. He was without access to any system of study which would point to the reason for his afflictions. He said specifically, "I desire to reason with God," and expected God to come out like a man and state his case.'

'Mr Gotham – '

'Mr Gotham, can you state if you would side with your wife in any sense if she came up for trial? Do you yourself feel politically that the FLE have something to offer the young generation?' – This was from a lanky French journalist with bright eyes and a wide smile. He was rather a sympathetic type, Harvey thought, probably new to his trade.

'I'm really sorry to disappoint you,' said Harvey with some charm, 'but I'm giving you a seminar on *Job* without pay.'

A hubbub had now started to break out. Protests and questions came battering in on Harvey from every side.

'Quiet!' bawled Harvey. 'Either you listen to me in silence or you all go. Job's problem, as I was saying, was partly a lack of knowledge. Everybody talked but nobody told him anything about the reason for his sufferings. Not even God when he appeared. Our limitations of knowledge make us puzzle over the cause of suffering, maybe it is the cause of suffering itself. Quiet, over there! The baby's asleep. And I said, no photographs at present. As I say, we are plonked here in the world and nobody but our own kind can tell us anything. It isn't enough. As for the rest, God doesn't tell. No, I've already told you that I don't know where my wife is. How the *Book of Job* got into the holy scriptures I really do not know. That's the greatest mystery of all. For it doesn't – '

'Mr Gotham,' said the tough pressman, 'the FLE have held up supermarkets, jewellers and banks at Gérardmer, La Bresse, Rambervillers, Mirecourt and Baccarat. Your wife is – '

'You've left out Epinal,' said Harvey. Cameras flashed. 'Will you allow me to continue to answer the question put to me, or will you go?'

'Your wife – ' . . . 'Your background, Mr Gotham – ' . . . 'Your wife's sister – '

'Conference over,' said Harvey.

'Oh, no.' – 'No, Mr Gotham.' – 'Wait a minute.'

Some were swearing and cursing; some were laughing.

But Harvey got up and made for the door. Most of the reporters were on their feet, very rowdy. The wiry red-faced woman, the possible police agent, sat holding her tape-recorder modestly on her lap. The large fair man at the door had grabbed a belt as if from nowhere and was fastening it rapidly round his waist. Harvey saw that it was packed neatly with cartridges and that a revolver hung from a holster, with the man's hand on it. He recognized him now as the sandy-haired policeman who, in uniform, had sat at the table throughout his interrogation at Epinal.

Harvey said, 'I must tell you that there is a policeman in the room.'

'What police? *La Brigade antigang*?'

'I have no idea what variety. Kindly leave quietly and in order, and don't wake the baby.'

They left without order or quietness.

'Why don't you get out while you can? Get back to Canada,' said a girl. – 'We'll be seeing you in the courtroom,' said another. Some joked as they left, some overturned chairs as they went. From everywhere came the last-minute flashes of the cameras recording the policeman, the overturned chairs, and recording Harvey standing in the middle of it, an image to be reproduced in one of next morning's papers under the title, 'Don't Wake the Baby'. But at last they had gone. The wiry red-faced woman said sadly to Harvey as she passed him, 'I'm afraid you'll get a very bad press.'

The policeman followed them out and chivied them down the drive from his car. Before he shut the door Harvey noticed something new in the light cast from the hall: a washing-line had been slung well in evidence of the front portico. Anne-Marie had just finished taking baby clothes from it, had evidently been photographed doing so. She came towards him.

'Not very convincing,' Harvey said. 'Nobody hangs washing within sight of the approach to a château.'

'Nobody used to,' Anne-Marie said. 'They do now. We, for example, are doing it. Nobody will find it in the least suspect.'

'Didn't she tell you the hotel where she was going to in Paris?' Harvey said.

'Not me,' said Anne-Marie. 'I think she'll ring you if she said she would. In any case, the inspector is sure to know where she's staying.'

It was nine-thirty, and Anne-Marie was leaving for the night, anxious about being extraordinarily late in returning home; she lived several miles away. A car driven by a plain-clothes policeman was waiting at the door. She hurried away, banged the car door, and was off.

Stewart Cowper had arrived about an hour before, full of travel-exasperation and police-harassment; he had been frisked and questioned at the entrance to the house; he had been travelling most of the day and he was cold. At present he was having a shower.

Harvey and Anne-Marie had together put the living room to rights. Ruth had not yet rung him from Paris as she had promised. Where was she? Harvey then noticed something new in the room, a large bowl of early spring flowers, professionally arranged, beautiful. Irises, jonquils, lilies, daffodils; all too advanced to be local products; they must have come from an expensive shop in Nancy. Anne-Marie must have put them there at some time between the clearing up of the mess and her leaving, but Harvey hadn't noticed them. They stood on a low round table, practically covering it as the outward leaves of the arrangement bent gracefully over the edge of the bowl. Harvey hadn't noticed them, either, while he was sitting having a drink with Stewart, trying to calm him down, nor while Anne-Marie, anxious about the time, laid out a cold supper that was still sitting on the small dining-table, waiting for Stewart to wash and change. Where did those flowers come from? Who brought them, who sent them? Anne-Marie hadn't left the house. And why should she order flowers?

Stewart came in and went to get himself another drink. He was a man of medium height, in his mid-forties with a

421

school-boy's round face and round blue eyes; but this imma-
ture look was counteracted by a deep and expressive quality
in his voice, so that as soon as he spoke the total effect was
of a certain maturity and intelligence, cancelling that silly
round-eyed look.

'Did you bring these flowers?' said Harvey.

'Did I bring what?'

'These flowers – I don't know where they've come from.
The maid – and by the way she's a policewoman – must have
put them there some time this evening. But why?'

Stewart brought his drink to the sofa and sat sipping it.

Harvey's mind was working fast, and faster. 'I think I
know why they're there. Have you ever heard of a vase of
flowers being bugged?'

'Rather an obvious way to plant a bug if the flowers wer-
en't there already,' said Stewart.

But Harvey was already pulling the flower-arrangement to
bits. He shook each lily, each daffodil; he tore at the petals of
the irises. Stewart drank his drink and told Harvey to calm
down; he watched Harvey with his big blue eyes and then
took another sip. Harvey splashed the water from the bowl
all over the table and the floor. 'I don't see anything,' he said.

'From what I understand the police have had every opportunity to plant bugs elsewhere in the house; they need not
introduce a bunch of flowers for the purpose,' Stewart said.
'What a mess you've made of a lovely bunch of flowers.'

'I'd take you out to dinner,' said Harvey. He sat on the
sofa with his dejected head in his hands. He looked up. 'I'd
take you out to eat but I've got to wait in for a call from
Ruth. She's in Paris but I don't know where. I've got to let
my uncle in Toronto know the time of her arrival and her
flight number. Did I tell you that she's taking the baby to my
Uncle Joe's?'

'No,' said Stewart.

'Well, she is. I've got to arrange for her to be met, and get through to Toronto and give them reasonable notice. And I've got to have a call from Ernie Howe, I think. At least he said he'd ring.'

'How many other things have you got to do?'

'I don't know.'

'Why don't you relax? You're in a hell of a state.'

'I know. What are you supposed to be doing here?'

'Giving you some advice,' Stewart said. 'Of course, I can't act for you here in France.'

'I don't need anyone. I've got what's-his-name in Paris if necessary.'

'Martin Deschamps? – I've been in touch with him. He can't act for you in a case like this. No one in his firm can, either. That means they won't. Terrorism is too unladylike for those fancy lawyers. I'm hungry.'

'Let's sit down, then,' said Harvey; they sat at the table to eat the cold supper. Harvey's hand shook as he started to pour the wine. He stopped and looked at his hand. 'I'm shaking,' he said. 'I wonder why Ruth hasn't rung?'

Stewart took the bottle from him and poured out the wine. 'Your nerves,' he said.

'She must have had her dinner and put the baby to bed by now,' Harvey said. 'I'll give it another hour, then I'm going to ring the police and find out where she is. Ernie Howe should have rung, too.'

'Maybe she didn't stop over in Paris. Perhaps she went straight to the airport.'

'She should have rung. She could have been taken ill. She's pregnant.'

'Is she?'

'So she says.'

423

The telephone rang. An inspector of police. 'M. Gotham? – I want to let you know that Mme. Ruth Jansen has arrived in London.'

'In London? I thought she was going to stop overnight in Paris. I've arranged for her to go to Canada to my – '

'She changed her mind.'

'Where is she in London?'

'I can't tell you. Good night.'

'If she didn't ring you as promised,' said Stewart the next morning, 'and Ernie Howe didn't ring you as promised, and if, in addition, it transpires she went to London, I should have thought you would suspect that the two were together.'

'You think she has gone to Ernie Howe? Why should she go to him? She is pregnant by me.'

'She has Ernie Howe's baby in her arms. It would be natural to take her to the father. You can't possess everything, Harvey.'

'Do you know more than you say?' said Harvey.

'No, it's only a supposition.'

'I'll ring Ernie Howe's flat as soon as my call to Canada has come through. It's hard on my uncle, mucking him about like this. He's not so young. I've just put through a call.'

'It's the middle of the night in Toronto,' said Stewart.

'I don't care.'

Anne-Marie arrived in her thick coat, scarves and boots. 'Good morning,' she said, and then gave a pained wail. Her eyes were on the flowers that she had left in such a formal display the night before, now all pulled to pieces, even the petals torn to bits.

'I was looking for an electronic bug,' Harvey said.

'I think you are not human,' said Anne-Marie. She was now in tears, aimlessly lifting a daffodil, putting it down, then a blue, torn iris.

424

'Who ordered them, who sent them?' said Harvey.

Stewart said, 'I'll help to clear the mess. Leave it to me.'

'I had them sent myself,' said Anne-Marie. 'To give you some joy after your ordeal with the press and your loss of the baby. My sister-in-law has a flower shop and I made a special-messenger arrangement with her for the most beautiful flowers; a personal present. I thought that with the loss of Madame and Clara you would enjoy those lovely spring flowers.'

Stewart had his arm round the police agent's shoulders. 'His nerves gave way,' said Stewart. 'That's all.'

The telephone rang; Harvey's call to Canada. It was a sleepy manservant who answered, as Harvey had counted on. He was able to explain, without having to actually talk to his uncle, that Ruth and the baby were probably not coming after all, and that any references to him in the newspapers and on the television were probably false.

He put down the receiver. The telephone rang: 'Hallo, Harvey!' The telephone rang off. Again it rang: 'Harvey, it's Ruth.' She was speaking in a funny way. She was calling herself Ree-uth, although definitely the voice was hers. It must be the London influence, Harvey registered all in a moment. But she was going on. 'I changed my mind, Harvey. I had to bring Clara (pronounced Clah-rah) to her father (pronounced fah-thar).'

'What are you saying?' said Harvey. 'You mean you're not going to my uncle Joe in Toronto. You've decided to shack down with Ernie Howe, is that it?'

'That's it,' said Ruth.

'Then I think you might have had enough consideration for my uncle Joe – he's seventy-eight – to let me know.'

'Oh, I was busy with Clah-rah.'

'Pass me Ernie,' said Harvey.

425

'Ernie, do you mind?' said Ruth's voice, apart.

'Hallo,' said the other voice.

'Ernie Howe?'

'That's me.'

'What are you doing with Ruth?'

'We've just had a tunah-fish salad. We fed Clah-rah.'

Harvey then remembered Ernie's voice (that's where Ruth got the Clah-rah).

'I make a good fah-thah,' said Ernie; 'and I don't like your tone of superiority.'

After a great many more hot words, Harvey began to recollect, at the back of his mind, that he really had no rights in the matter; not much to complain of at all. He said good night, hung up, and returned to the sitting-room hoping for some consolation from his friend.

His friend was sitting on the sofa holding hands with Anne-Marie. Harvey was in time to hear him say, 'May I fall in love with you?'

'She's married,' said Harvey in English.

'Not at all,' said Anne-Marie in her most matter-of-fact voice. 'I live with my married brother.'

'Well, I thought you were married,' said Harvey.

'That's when you thought I was a maid.'

'If you're not a maid then what are you doing here?' said Harvey.

'He's exasperated,' said Stewart. 'Don't mind him.'

Anne-Marie took a long glance at the disorderly table of ruined flowers and said, 'I have to remain here on duty. I'm going to make the coffee.'

When she had left, Harvey said, 'You're behaving like an undergraduate who's just put foot on the Continent for the first time, meeting his first Frenchwoman.'

'What was the news from England?'

426

'Ruth is with Ernie Howe.'
'What do the newspapers say?'
'I don't know. Find out; it's your job.'
'Is it?' said Stewart.
'If it isn't, what are you doing here?'
'I suppose I'm just a comforter,' Stewart said.
'I suppose you are.'

VIII

'IS IT POSSIBLE,' SAID HARVEY, 'for anyone to do something perfectly innocent but altogether unusual, without giving rise to suspicion?'

Stewart said, 'Not if his wife is a terrorist.'

'Assume that she is not.'

'All right, I assume. But here you were in a small hamlet in France, a rich man living in primitive conditions. Well, nobody bothered you until the police began to suspect a link between you and the FLE a certain time ago, and even then they only had you under surveillance, from a distance; they didn't haul you in immediately or harass you so that your life was uncomfortable. You weren't even aware of their presence till lately. And now you've been questioned, grilled; it's only natural. It might have been worse. Much worse. You don't know the police.'

'My papers have been scrutinized, all my work, my private things – '

'I can't sympathize too much, Harvey. I can't say you've really suffered. These police obviously are going carefully with you. They're protecting you from the mob, the phone calls. They probably believe you; they know by now, I should think, that you have no contact with Effie. I think they're right to watch out in case she has any contact with you.'

'You are wrong,' said Harvey, 'to say that I haven't suffered. Did you hear the press round-up on the radio this morning? – My name's worse than Effie's in the eyes of the press.'

The local newspaper, the only one so far to arrive in his hands, was on the coffee-table in front of them, with the front page uppermost. The headline 'The Guru of the Vosges' stretched above a picture of Harvey, distraught, in his sitting-room of final disorder at the press conference. Under the picture was the title-paragraph of the subsequent article:

Harvey Gotham, the American 'prophet', inveighing against God, who he claims has unjustly condemned the world to suffering. *God is a Shit* was one of the blasphemies preached at an international press conference held yesterday in his 40-roomed château recently acquired by this multimillionaire husband of the gangster-terrorist Effie Gotham, leading activist of FLE.

In the article, the writer of it reflected on the influence of Harvey on a girl like Effie 'from the poorer classes of London', and on her sister and an infant, Clara, still under his control at the château.

Harvey said to Stewart, 'I never once said "*Dieu est merde*."'

'Maybe you implied it.'

'Perhaps I did. But I did not speak as a prophet; I discussed some aspects of *Job* in an academic sense.'

'For a man of your intelligence, you are remarkably stupid,' said Stewart. 'It's Effie they wanted news of. Failing that, they made the best of what they got. You should have let Effie divorce you with a huge settlement a long time ago. She can get a divorce any time; it's the money she wanted.'

'To finance FLE?'

'You asked me to assume she isn't involved.'

'I don't want to divorce Effie. I don't want a divorce.'

'Are you still in love with Effie?'

'Yes.'

'Then you're an unhappy man. Why did you leave her?'

'I couldn't stand her sociological clap-trap. If she wanted to do some good in the world she had plenty of opportunity. There was nothing to stop her taking up charities and causes; she could have had money for them, and she always had plenty of time. But she has to rob supermarkets and banks and sleep with people like *that*.' He pointed to a row of photographs in the paper. Three young men and Effie. The photograph of Effie was that which the police had found among his papers. Harvey told Stewart this, and said, 'They don't seem to have any other picture of Effie. I wonder how they got photos of her friends.'

'In the same way that they got Effie's, I expect. Through rummaging in the homes of their families, their girl-friends.'

'What can she see in them?' Harvey said. Stewart turned the paper round to see it better. One of the men was dressed in a very padded-shouldered coat, a spotted bow tie and hair falling down past the point where the picture ended, which was just above his elbow; the second man was a blond, blank-faced boy with thick lips; the third seemed to be positively posing as the criminal he was alleged to be, being sneery, narrow-eyed and double-chinned, and bearing a two-day stubble beard. There was Effie amongst them, looking like Effie. The men were identified by French names, Effie by the name of Effie Gotham, wife of the millionaire guru.

'What does she see in them?' demanded Harvey. 'It's not so much that I'm jealous as that I'm intellectually insulted by the whole thing. I always have been by Effie's attitude to life. I thought she'd grow out of it.'

'I am to assume that Effie is not involved,' said Stewart.

'Well, there's her picture along with the others. It's difficult for me to keep up the fiction,' Harvey said.

'Do you mean that the photograph convinces you?' Stewart said. 'You know where the police got the photograph. Out of a drawer in your desk.'

'It wasn't exactly out of a drawer in a desk,' Harvey said. 'It was out of a box. I keep things in boxes down there in my working cottage. I'll take you to see it. I haven't been back to the cottage since I was arrested in Epinal three days ago.'

'Were you really arrested?'

'Perhaps not technically. I was definitely invited to come along to the commissariat. I went.'

'I wonder,' said Stewart, 'why there's been so little in the press about Nathan Fox. I only heard on the radio that he'd disappeared suddenly from your house. And they don't include him in the gang. Maybe they couldn't find a photograph of him. A photo makes a gangster real.'

'There was an identikit of Effie in the papers the day I was hauled in,' said Harvey.

'Did it look like Effie?'

'I'm afraid so. In fact it looked like Ruth. But it would pass for Effie. It looked like Job's wife, too. You know, it was a most remarkable thing, Stewart, I was sitting in the museum at Epinal reflecting on that extraordinary painting of Job and his wife by Georges de La Tour, when suddenly the police – '

'You told me that last night,' said Stewart.

'I know. I want to talk about it.'

'Don't you think,' said Stewart, 'that it would be odd if Effie wanted alimony from you simply to finance the FLE, when she could have sold her jewellery?'

'Hasn't she done that?'

'No, it's still in the safety-box at the bank. I hold the second key. There's still enough money in her bank to meet the standing orders for insurances and charities. Nothing's changed.'

'Well, why did she want to fleece me?'

'I don't see why she shouldn't have tried to get maintenance of some sort from you. It's true that her child by Ernie Howe damaged her case. But you walked out on her. She behaved like a normal woman married to a man in your position.'

'Effie is not a normal woman,' said Harvey.

'Oh, if you're talking in a basic sense, what woman is?'

'Women who don't get arrested in Trieste for shop-lifting are normal,' said Harvey. 'Especially women with her kind of jewellery in the bank. Whose side are you on, anyway, mine or Effie's?'

'In a divorce case, that is the usual question that the client puts, sooner or later. It's inevitable,' said the lawyer.

'But this is something different from a divorce case. Don't you realize what's happened?'

'I'm afraid I do,' said Stewart.

Next day was a Saturday. They sat in Harvey's cottage, huddling over the stove because the windows had been opened to air the place. There had been a feeling of spring in the early March morning, but this had gone by eleven o'clock; it was now winter again, bleak, with a slanting rain. As Harvey unlocked the door of his little house Stewart said, 'Lousy soil you've got here. Nothing much growing.'

'I haven't bothered to cultivate it.'

'It's better up at the château.'

'Oh, yes, it's had more attention.'

This was Harvey's first visit to the cottage since the police had pounced. He looked round carefully, opening the windows upstairs and downstairs, while Stewart lit the stove. 'They haven't changed the décor,' Harvey said. 'But a few bundles of papers are not in the places I left them in. Shifted, a matter of inches – but I know, I know.'

'Have they taken any of your papers, letters, business documents?'

'What letters and business papers? You have the letters and the business papers. All I have are my notes, and the manuscript of my little book, so far as it goes – it's to be a monograph, you know. I don't know if they've subtracted the few files, but they could have photographed them; much good might it do them. Files of notes on the *Book of Job*. They did take the photograph of Effie; that, they did take. I want it back.'

'You're entitled to ask for it,' said Stewart.

From the window, a grey family Citroën could be seen parked round a bend in the path, out of sight of the road; in it were two men in civilian clothes occupying the front seats. The rain plopped lazily on to the roof of the car and splashed the windscreen. 'Poor bastards,' Harvey said. 'They do it in three- or four-hour shifts.'

'Well, it's a protection for you, anyway. From the press if not from the terrorists.'

'I wish I was without the need for protection, and I wish you were in your office in London.'

'I don't go to the office on Saturday,' Stewart said.

'What do you do at the weekends?'

'Fuck,' said Stewart.

'Do you mean, fuck the question or that on Saturdays and Sundays you fuck?'

'Both.'

'Don't you ever go to a concert or a film on Sundays? Never go to Church?'

'Sometimes I go to a concert. I go away for the weekends, often. I do the usual things.'

'Well, you're wasting your time here,' Harvey said.

'No, because first you're my most valuable client. That's from a practical point of view. And secondly, I'm interested in your *Book of Job*; it just beats me how a man of your scope should choose to hide himself away in this hole. And thirdly, of course, I'm a friend; I want to see you out of this mess. I strongly advise you to come back to London here and now. Do you have your passport?'

'Yes, they gave me back my passport.'

'Oh, they took it away?'

'Yes, they took the stuff out of my pockets,' Harvey said. 'They gave it all back. I'm not leaving.'

'Why?'

'Well, all my books and things are here. I don't see why I should run away. I intend to go on as usual. Besides, I'm anxious about Effie.'

'Maybe Effie would move to another field of action if you weren't in the Vosges,' said Stewart. 'You see, I don't want you to become an unwilling accomplice.'

'Effie follows the gang,' said Harvey.

'Doesn't she lead it?'

'Oh, I don't know. I don't even know for certain that she's in it. It's all mere allegation on the part of the police.'

Stewart walked about the little room, with his scarf wound round his neck. 'It's chilly,' he said. He was looking at the books. 'Does Anne-Marie cook for you?' he said.

'Yes, indifferently. She's a police agent by profession.'

'Oh, that doesn't mean much,' said Stewart, 'when you know that she is.'

'I used to love mealtimes with Effie,' said Harvey. 'I enjoyed the mealtimes more than the meals.'

'Let's go out somewhere for lunch,' said Stewart.

'We can go in to Nancy. Undoubtedly we'd be followed.'

'That doesn't mean much if you know you are being followed,' said Stewart.

Harvey stood in the middle of the room watching with an irritated air while Stewart fingered his books.

'There's nothing of interest,' said Harvey, 'unless you're interested in the subject.'

'Well, you know I am. I still don't see why you can't write your essay elsewhere.'

'I've got used to it here.'

'Would you like to have Ruth back?' said Stewart.

'Not particularly. I would like to have Clara back.'

'With Effie?'

'No, Effie isn't a motherly type.'

'Ruth is a mother?'

'She is a born children's nurse.'

'But you would like to have Effie back?' Stewart said, and he made light of this, as of all his questions, by putting them simultaneously with a flicking-through of the pages of Harvey's books.

'Yes, I would; in theory,' said Harvey. 'That is the *New English Bible*. The translation is godforsaken.'

'Then you'd be willing to take Ruth back if she brought Clara. But you'd prefer to have Effie to make love to?'

'That is the unattainable ideal. The *New English Bible*'s version of *Job* makes no distinction between Behemoth and Leviathan. They translate the two as "the crocodile", which has of course some possibility as a theory, but it simply doesn't hold in the context.'

'I thought Behemoth was the hippopotamus,' said Stewart.

'Well, that's the general view, not necessarily correct. However, the author of *Job* turns God into a poet at that point, proclaiming wonderful hymns to his own creation, the buffalo, the ostrich, the wild ass, the horse, the eagle; then there's the sparrow-hawk. And God says, Consider this, look at that, reflect on their ways, how they live and survive; I did it all; where were you when I did it? Finally come Behemoth and Leviathan. Well, if you are going to translate both Behemoth and Leviathan as the crocodile, it makes far too long a passage, it gives far more weight to the crocodile as one of God's marvels than is obviously intended. As for the features of Behemoth, they fit in with the hippopotamus or some large and similar creature equally as well as with the crocodile. Why should God be so proud of his crocodile that he devotes thirty-eight verses to it, and to the horse only seven?'

'There must be some good arguments in favour of Behemoth and Leviathan both being the crocodile, though,' Stewart said.

'Of course there are arguments. The scholars try to rationalize *Job* by rearranging the verses where there is obviously no sense in them. Sometimes, of course, the textual evidence irresistibly calls for a passage to be moved from the traditional place to another. But moving passages about for no other reason than that they are more logical is no good for the *Book of Job*. It doesn't make it come clear. *The Book of Job* will never come clear. It doesn't matter; it's a poem. As for Leviathan and Behemoth, Lévêque who is the best modern scholar on *Job* distinguishes between the two.' Harvey was apparently back in his element. He seemed to have forgotten about the police outside his house, and that Effie was a criminal at large.

Stewart said, 'You amaze me.'

'Why?'

'Don't you want to know the facts about Effie?'

'Oh, Effie.'

Harvey had in his hands one of Lévêque's volumes. 'He accepts Leviathan as the crocodile and Behemoth as the hippopotamus. He takes Behemoth to be a hippopotamus or at least a large beast.'

'What about these other new Bibles?' said Stewart, pointing to a couple of new translations. He wondered if perhaps Harvey was not so guileless as he seemed. Stewart thought perhaps Harvey might really be involved with Effie and her liberation movement. There was something not very convincing about Harvey's cool-headedness.

'Messy,' said Harvey. 'They all try to reach everybody and end by saying nothing to anybody. There are no good new Bibles. The 1945 *Knox* wasn't bad but still obscure – it's a Vulgate translation, of course; the *Jerusalem Bible* and this *Good News Bible* are not much improvement on the old *Moffat*."

'You stick to the *Authorised* then?'

'For my purpose, it's the best English basis. One can get to know the obvious mistakes and annotate accordingly.'

Harvey poured drinks and handed one to Stewart.

'I think I can see,' said Stewart, 'that you're happy here. I didn't realize how much this work meant to you. It has puzzled me slightly; I knew you were dedicated to the subject but didn't understand how much, until I came here. You shouldn't think of marriage.'

'I don't. I think of Effie.'

'Only when you're not thinking *of Job*?'

'Yes. What can I do for her by thinking?'

'Your work here would make a good cover if you were in with Effie,' said the lawyer.

'A very bad cover. The police aren't really convinced by my story. Why should you be?'

'Oh, Harvey, I didn't mean – '

Anne-Marie arrived with a grind of brakes in the little Renault. She left the car with a bang of the door and began to proclaim an urgency before she had opened the cottage gate.

'Mr Gotham, a phone call from Canada.'

Harvey went to open the door to her. 'What is it from Canada?' he said.

'Your aunt on the telephone. She'll ring you back in ten minutes.'

'I'll come up to the house right away.'

To Stewart, he said, 'Wait for me. I'll be back shortly and we'll go out to lunch. You know, there could have been an influence of *Prometheus* on *Job*; the dates could quite possibly coincide. But I find vast differences. Prometheus wasn't innocent, for one thing. He stole fire from Heaven. Job was innocent.'

'Out to lunch!' said Anne-Marie. 'I'm preparing lunch at the château.'

'We'll have it cold for dinner,' thundered Harvey as he got into the car. Anne-Marie followed him; looking back at Stewart who gave her a long smile full of what looked like meaning, but decidedly so unspecific as to mean nothing.

As they whizzed up the drive to the château Anne-Marie said, 'You think because you are rich you can do anything with people. I planned a lunch.'

'You should first have enquired whether we would be in for lunch,' said Harvey.

'Oh, no,' she said, with some point. 'It was for you to say you would be out.'

'I apologize.'

'The apologies of the rich. They are cheap.'

Half an hour went by before the telephone rang again. The police were vetting the calls, turning away half the world's reporters and others who wanted to speak to the terrorist's guru husband. Harvey therefore made no complaint. He sat in patience reading all about himself once more in the local morning newspaper, until the telephone rang.

'Oh, it's you, Auntie Pet. It must be the middle of the night with you; how are you?'

'How are *you*?'

'All right.'

'I saw you on the television and it's all in the paper. How could you blaspheme in that terrible way, saying those things about your Creator?'

'Auntie Pet, you've got to understand that I said nothing whatsoever about God, I mean our Creator. What I was talking about was a fictional character in the *Book of Job*, called God. I don't know what you've seen or read, but it's not yet proved finally that Effie, my wife, is a terrorist.'

'Oh, Effie isn't involved, it goes without saying. I never said Effie was a terrorist, I know she isn't, in fact. What I'm calling about is this far more serious thing, it's a disgrace to the family. I mean, this is to blaspheme when you say that God is what you said he was.'

'I never said what they said I said he was,' said Harvey. 'How are you, Auntie Pet? How is Uncle Joe?'

'Uncle Joe, I never hear from. But I get to know.'

'And yourself? I haven't heard from you for ages.'

'Well, I don't write much. The prohibitive price of stamps. My health is everything that can be expected by a woman who does right and fears the Lord. Your uncle Joe just lives on there with old Collier who is very much to blame, too. Neither of them has darkened the door of the church for as long as I can remember. They are unbelievers like you.'

'On the contrary, I have abounding faith.'

'You shouldn't question the Bible. Job was a good man. There is a Christian message in the *Book of Job*.'

'But Job didn't know that.'

'How do you know? We have a lovely Bible, there. Why do you want to change it? You should look after your wife and have a family, and be a good husband, with all your advantages, and the business doing so well. Your uncle Joe refused the merger.'

'Well, Auntie Pet, it's been a pleasure to talk to you. I have to go out with my lawyer for lunch, now. I'm glad you managed to get my number so you could put your mind at rest.'

'I got your number with the utmost difficulty.'

'Yes, I was wondering how you got it, Auntie Pet.'

'Money,' said Auntie Pet.

'Ah,' said Harvey.

'I'll be in touch again.'

'Keep well. Don't take the slightest notice of what the newspapers and the television say.'

'What about the radio?'

'Also, the radio.'

'Are you starting a new religion, Harvey?'

'No.'

Stewart and Harvey crossed the Place Stanislas at Nancy. The rain had stopped and a silvery light touched the gilded gates at the corners of the square, it glittered on the lamp-posts with their golden garlands and crown-topped heads, and on the bright and lacy iron-work of all the balconies of the *hôtel de ville*.

'The square always looks lovely out of season,' said Stewart.

'It's supposed to have crowds,' Harvey said. 'That's what it was evidently made for.'

Two police cars turned into the square and followed them at a crawl.

'The bistro I had in mind is down a narrow street,' said Harvey. 'Let them follow us there. The police have to eat, too.'

But they had a snack-lunch in the police station at Nancy, two policemen having got out of their car and invited Harvey and Stewart to join them.

'What's the matter, now?' Harvey had said when the police approached them.

Stewart said, 'I require an explanation.'

The explanation was not forthcoming until they were taken later in the afternoon to the police headquarters in Epinal.

'A policeman has been killed in Paris.'

A policeman has been killed in Paris.

IX

STEWART COWPER, HAVING INVOKED the British Consul, was allowed to leave the police headquarters the same afternoon that he was detained with Harvey. He refused to answer any questions at all, and his parting advice to Harvey was to do likewise. They were alone in a corridor.

'The least I can do,' said Harvey, 'is to defend Effie.'

'Understandable,' said Stewart, and left to collect his luggage from the château and get a hired car to Paris, and a plane to London.

Harvey got home later that night, having failed to elicit, from the questions he was asked by an officer who had come to Epinal for the purpose – the same old questions – what had exactly happened in Paris that morning, and where Effie was supposed to fit into the murder of the policeman.

'Did you hear about the killing on the radio, M. Gotham?'

'No. I've only just learned of it from you. I wasn't in the château this morning. I was in the cottage with my English lawyer, Stewart Cowper.'

'What did you discuss with your lawyer?'

'The different versions of the *Book of Job* in various recent English translations of the Bible.'

Harvey's interrogator looked at him with real rage. 'One of our policemen has been killed,' he said.

'I'm sorry to hear it,' said Harvey.

They escorted him to pick up his car at Nancy, and followed him home.

Next day the Sunday papers had the same photograph of Effie. There was also a photograph of the policeman, lying in the street beside a police car, covered by a sheet, with some police standing by. Effie had been recognized by eye-witnesses at the scene of the killing, in the eighteenth *arrondissement*. A blonde, long-haired girl with a gun. She was the killer. Her hair was drawn back in a pony-tail at the time of the commando-raid; she was wearing blue jeans and a grey pull-over. The Paris security police and the *gendarmerie* were now operating jointly in the search for FLE and its supporters, and especially for the Montmartre killers.

That was the whole of the news, though it filled several pages of the newspapers. The volume of printed words was to be explained by the length of the many paragraphs ending with a question mark, by numerous interpolations about Harvey and his Bible-sect, his wealth, his château, and by details of the unfortunate policeman's family life.

It was not till after lunch on Monday that he was invited to the commissariat at Epinal once more. Two security men from Paris had arrived to interrogate him. Two tall men, one of them in his late forties, robust, with silvering sideburns, the other fair and skinny, not much over thirty, with gilt-rimmed glasses, an intellectual. Harvey thought, if he had seen them together in a restaurant, he would have taken the older man for a business-man, the younger for a priest.

Later, when he chewed over their questions, he was to find it difficult to distinguish between this second interrogation and the first one of a few days ago. This was partly because the older man, who introduced himself by the name of Chatelain, spent a lot of time going over Harvey's previous deposition.

'My house is surrounded by your men,' said Harvey. 'You have your young woman auxiliary in my house. What are you accusing me of?' (Stewart Cowper had advised him: If they question you again, ask them what they have against you, demand to know what is the charge.)

'We are not accusing, Mr Gotham, we are questioning.'

'Questions can sound like accusations.'

'A policeman has been shot dead.'

And their continual probe into why he had settled in France: Harvey recalled later.

'I liked the house,' said Harvey, 'I got my permit to stay in France. I'm regular with the police.'

'Your wife has been in trouble before.'

'I know,' said Harvey.

'Do you love your wife?'

'That's rather a personal question.'

'It was a personal question for the policeman who was killed.'

'I wonder,' said Harvey, conversationally. He was suddenly indignant and determined to be himself, thoughtfully in charge of his reasoning mind, not any sort of victim. 'I wonder . . . I'm not sure that death is personal in the sense of being in love. So far as we know, we don't feel death. We know the fear of death, we know the process of dying. From the outside it looks the most personal of phenomena. But isn't death the very negation of the personal, therefore strictly speaking impersonal? A dead body is the most impersonal thing I can think of. Unless one believes in the continuity of personality in its terrestrially recognizable form, as opposed to life-after-death which is something else. Many disbelieve in life after death, of course, but – '

'Pardon? Are you trying to tell me that the death of one of our men is trivial?'

'No. I was reflecting on a remark of yours. Philosophizing, I'm afraid. I meant – '

'Kindly don't philosophize,' said Chatelain. 'This is not the place. I want to know where your wife is. Where is Effie?'

'I don't know where Mme Gotham is.'

And again:

'A policeman has been killed by the FLE gang. Two men and a girl, all armed. In the eighteenth *arrondissement* in Paris.'

'I'm sorry that a policeman has been shot,' said Harvey. 'Why in the eighteenth *arrondissement*?'

'That's what we're *asking* you,' said Chatelain.

'I have no idea. I thought these terrorists acted mainly in popular suburbs.'

'Was your wife ever before in the eighteenth *arrondissement*, do you know?'

'Of course,' said Harvey. 'Who hasn't been in the eighteenth? It's Montmartre.'

'Have you and your wife any friends there?'

'I have friends there and I suppose my wife has, too.'

'Who are your friends?'

'You should know. Your colleagues here went through my address book last week and checked all my friends.'

In the middle of the afternoon Chatelain became more confidential. He began to melt, but only in resemblance to a refrigerator which thaws when the current is turned off. True warmth, thought Harvey at the time, doesn't drip, drip, drip. And later, in his cottage, when he reconstituted the scene he thought: And I ask myself, why was he a refrigerator in the first place?

'Don't think I don't sympathize with you, Mr Gotham,' said Chatelain, on the defreeze. 'Not to know where one's wife is can not be a pleasant experience.'

'Don't think I don't sympathize with you,' said Harvey. 'I know you've lost one of your men. That's serious. And I sympathize, as everyone should, with his family. But you offer no proof that my wife, Effie, is involved. You offer only a photograph that you confiscated from a box on my table.'

'We confiscated . . . ?' The man consulted Harvey's thick file which lay on the desk. 'Ah, yes. You are right. The Vosges police obtained that photograph from your house. Witnesses have identified that photograph as the girl in the gang. And look – the identikit, constructed with the help of eye-witnesses to a bank robbery and supermarket bombings, some days prior to our obtaining the photograph. Look at it – isn't that your wife?'

Harvey looked at the drawing.

'When I first saw it in the paper I thought it resembled my wife's sister, Ruth, rather than my wife,' he said. 'Since it couldn't possibly refer to Ruth it seems to me even more unlikely that it refers to Effie.'

'Mme Gotham was arrested in Trieste.'

Harvey was still looking at the identikit. It reminded him, now, of Job's wife in La Tour's painting even though the drawing was full-face and the painting showed a profile.

'She was arrested for shop-lifting,' said Harvey.

'Why did she do that?'

Harvey put down the identikit and gave Chatelain his attention. 'I don't know that she did it. If she did, it does not follow that she bombs supermarkets and kills policemen.'

'If I was in your place,' said Chatelain, 'I would probably speak as you do. But if you were in my place, you would press for some indication, any indication, any guess, as to where she is. I don't blame you for trying to protect your wife. You see,' he said, leaning back in his chair and looking away from Harvey, towards the window, 'a policeman has been shot dead. His wife is in a shop on the outskirts of Paris where they live, a popular quarter, with her twelve-year-old daughter who has a transistor radio. The lady is waiting her turn at the cash-desk. The child draws her mother's atten-tion to a flash item of news that has interrupted the music. A policeman has been shot and killed in the eighteenth *ar-rondissement*; the name is being withheld until the family can be informed. The assassins, two men and a girl, have escaped. The terrorist gang FLE have immediately telephoned the press to claim the crime. The main points of the news flash are repeated: a policeman killed, leaving a wife and two daughters aged fourteen and twelve respectively. Now this lady, the policeman's wife, is always worried when she hears of the death or wounding of a policeman. In this case the de-scription is alarmingly close. The eighteenth *arrondissement* where her husband is on duty; the ages of their daughters. She hurries home and finds a police car outside her block of flats. It is indeed her husband who has been killed. Did she deserve this?'

'No,' said Harvey. 'Neither did the policeman. We do not get what we merit. The one thing has nothing to do with the other. Your only course is to prevent it happening again.'

'Depend on us,' said the policeman.

'If I may say so,' said Harvey, 'you are wasting efforts on me which might profitably be directed to that end.'

'Any clue, any suggestion . . . ' said Chatelain, with great patience. He almost pleaded. 'Are there any houses in Paris that you know of, where they might be found?'

'None,' said Harvey.

'No friends?'

'The few people I know with establishments in Paris are occupied with business affairs in rather a large, multinational way. I don't believe they would like the FLE.'

447

'Nathan Fox is a good housekeeper?'

'I believe he can be useful in a domestic way.'

'He could be keeping a safe house for the gang in Paris.'

'I don't see him as the gangster type. Honestly, you know, I don't think he's in it.'

'But your wife . . . She is different?'

'I didn't say so.'

'And yourself?'

'What about myself? What are you asking?' Harvey said.

'You have a connection with the gang?'

'No.'

'Why did you hang baby clothes on the line outside your cottage as early as last spring?' said Chatelain next.

Harvey was given a break at about seven in the evening. He was accompanied to a café for a meal by the tall young Parisian inspector with metal-rimmed glasses, Louis Pomfret by name.

Pomfret spoke what could be described as 'perfect English', that awful type of perfect English that comes over Radio Moscow. He said something apologetic, in semi-disparagement of the police. Harvey couldn't now remember the exact words. But he recalled Pomfret remarking, too, on the way to the café, 'You must understand that one of their men has been killed.' ('Their' men, not 'our' men, Harvey noted.)

At the café table the policeman told Harvey, 'A Canadian lady arrived in Paris who attempted to reach you on the telephone, and we intercepted her. She's your aunt. We've escorted her safely to the château where she desired to go.'

'God, it's my aunt Pet. Don't give her any trouble.'

'But, no.'

If you think you'll make me grateful for all this courtesy, thought Harvey, you are mistaken. He said, 'I should hope not.'

The policeman said, 'I'm afraid the food here is ghastly.'

'They make a good omelette. I've eaten here before,' said Harvey.

Ham omelettes and wine from the Vosges.

'It's unfortunate for you, Gotham,' said Pomfret, 'but you appreciate, I hope, our position.'

'You want to capture these members of the FLE before they do more damage.'

'Yes, we do. And of course, we will. Now that a member of the police has been killed . . . You appreciate, his wife was shopping in a supermarket with her son of twelve, who had a transistor radio. She was taking no interest in the programme. At one point the boy said – '

'Are you sure it was a boy?' Harvey said.

'It was a girl. How do you know?'

'The scene has been described to me by your colleague.'

'You're very observant,' Pomfret smiled, quite nicely.

'Well, of course I'm observant in a case like this,' said Harvey. 'I'm hanging on your lips.'

'Why?'

'To hear if you have any evidence that my wife is involved with a terrorist gang.'

'We have a warrant for her arrest,' said Pomfret.

'That's not evidence.'

'I know. But we don't put out warrants without reason. Your wife was arrested in Trieste. She was definitely lodging there with a group which has since been identified as members of the FLE gang. When the police photograph from the incident at Trieste noticeably resembled the photograph we obtained from you, and also resembled the identikit made up from eye-witnesses of the bombings and incursions here in France, we call that sufficient evidence to regard your wife as a suspect.'

'I would like to see the photograph from Trieste,' said Harvey. 'Why haven't I been shown it?'

'You are not investigating the case. We are.'

'But I'm interested in her whereabouts,' Harvey said. 'What does this photograph from the police at Trieste look like?'

'It's an ordinary routine photograph that's taken of all people under arrest. Plain and flat, like a passport photograph. It looks like your wife. It's of no account to you.'

'Why wasn't I shown it, told about it?'

'I think you can see it if you want.'

'Your people at the commissariat evidently don't believe me when I say I don't know where Effie is.'

'Well, I suppose that's why you've been questioned. You've never been officially convoked.'

'The English word is summoned.'

'Summoned; I apologize.'

'Lousy wine,' said Harvey.

'It's what you get in a cheap café,' said Pomfret.

'They had better when I ate here before,' said Harvey. 'Look, all you've got to go on is an identikit made in France which resembles two photographs of my wife.'

'And the address she was residing at in Trieste. That's most important of all.'

'She is inclined to take up with unconventional people,' said Harvey.

'Evidently, since she married yourself.'

'Do you know,' said Harvey, 'I'm very conventional, believe it or not.'

'I don't believe it, of course.'

'Why?'

'Your mode of life in France. For an affluent man to establish himself in a cottage and study the *Book of Job* is not conventional.'

'Job was an affluent man. He sat among the ashes. Some say, on a dung-heap outside the city. He was very convention-al. So much so that God was bored with him.'

'Is that in the scriptures?' said the policeman.

'No, it's in my mind.'

'You've actually written it down. They took photocopies of some of your pages.'

'I object to that. They had no right.'

'It's possible they had no right. Why have you never brought in a lawyer?'

'What for?'

'Exactly. But it would be the conventional thing to do.'

'I hope you're impressed,' said Harvey. 'You see, if I were writing a film-script or a pornographic novel, you wouldn't find it so strange that I came to an out-of-the-way place to work. It's the subject of *Job* you can't understand my giving my time to.'

'More or less. I think, perhaps, you've been trying to put yourself in the conditions of Job. Is that right?'

'One can't write an essay on *Job* sitting round a swimming pool in a ten-acre park, with all that goes with it. But I could just as well study the subject in a quiet apartment in some city. I came to these parts because I happened to find the cot-tage. There is a painting of Job and his wife here in Epinal which attracts me. You should see it.'

'I should,' said Pomfret. 'I shall.'

'Job's wife looks remarkably like my wife. It was painted about the middle of the seventeenth century so it can't be Effie, if that's what you're thinking.'

'We were discussing Job, not Mme Effie.'

'Then what am I doing here,' said Harvey, 'being interro-gated by you?'

Pomfret remained good-natured. He said something about their having a supper and a talk, not an interrogation. 'I am

451

genuinely interested,' said Pomfret, 'speaking for myself. You are isolated like Job. But you haven't lost your goods and fortune. Any possibility of that?'

'No, but I'm as good as without them here. More so before I took the château.'

'Oh, I was forgetting the château. I've only seen your cottage, from the outside. It looks impoverished enough.'

'It was the boils that worried Job.'

'*Pardon*? The boils?'

'Boils. Skin-sores. He was covered with them.'

'Ah, yes, that is correct. Don't you, like Job, feel the need of friends to talk to in your present troubles?'

'One thing that the *Book of Job* teaches us,' Harvey said, 'is the futility of friendship in times of trouble. That is perhaps not a reflection on friends but on friendship. Friends mean well, or make as if they do. But friendship itself is made for happiness, not trouble.'

'Is your aunt a friend?'

'My aunt Pet, who you tell me has arrived at the château? – I suppose she thinks of herself as a friend. She's a bore, coming at this moment. At any moment. – You don't suppose this is anything but an interrogation, do you? Any more questions?'

'Would you like some cheese?'

Harvey couldn't help liking the young man, within his reservation that the police had, no doubt, sent him precisely to be liked. Soften me up as much as you please, Harvey thought, but it doesn't help you; it only serves to release my own love, my nostalgia, for Effie. And he opened his mouth and spoke in praise of Effie, almost to his own surprise describing how she was merry at parties, explaining that she danced well and was fun to talk to. 'She's an interesting woman, Effie.'

'Intellectual?'

'We are all more intellectual than we know. She doesn't think of herself as an intellectual type. But under a certain stimulus, she is.'

They were walking back to the commissariat. Harvey had half a mind to go home and let them come for him with an official summons, if they wanted. But it was only half a mind; the other half, mesmerized and now worked up about Effie, propelled him on to the police station with his companion.

'She tried some drugs, I suppose,' said Pomfret.

'You shouldn't suppose so,' said Harvey. 'Effie is entirely anti-drug. It would be extraordinary if she's taken to drugs in the last two years.'

'You must recognize,' said Pomfret, 'that she is lively and vital enough to be a member of a terrorist gang.'

'Lively and vital,' said Harvey, 'lively and vital – one of those words is redundant.'

Pomfret laughed.

'However,' said Harvey, 'it's out of the question that she could be a terrorist.' He had a suspicion that Pomfret was now genuinely fascinated by the images of Effie that Harvey was able to produce, Effie at a party, Effie an interesting talker, a rich man's wife; his imagination was involved, beyond his investigator's role, in the rich man's mechanism, his free intellectual will, his casual purchase of the château; Pomfret was fascinated by both Effie and Harvey.

'A terrorist,' said Pomfret. 'She obviously has an idealistic motive. Why did you leave her?'

The thought that Effie was a member of a terrorist band now excited Harvey sexually.

'Terrorist is out of the question,' he said. 'I left her because she seemed to want to go her own way. The marriage broke up, that's all. Marriages do.'

453

'But on a hypothesis, how would you feel if you knew she was a terrorist?'

Harvey thought, I would feel I had failed her in action. Which I have. He said, 'I can't imagine.'

At the police station Pomfret left him in a waiting-room. Patiently sitting there was a lean-faced man with a dark skin gone to a muddy grey, bright small eyes and fine features. He seemed to be a Balkan. What was he doing there? It was after nine in the evening. Surely it was in the morning that he would come about his papers. Perhaps he had been picked up without papers? What sort of work was he doing in Epinal? He wore a black suit, shiny with wear; a very white shirt open at the neck; brown, very pointed shoes; and he had with him a brown cardboard brief-case with tinny locks, materials such as Harvey had only seen before in the form of a suitcase on a train in a remote part of Sicily. The object in Sicily had been old and battered, but his present companion's brief-case had a new-bought look. It was not the first time Harvey had noticed that poor people from Eastern Europe resembled, not only in their possessions and clothes, but in their build and expression, the poor of Western Europe years ago. Who he was, where he came from and why, Harvey was never to know, for he was just about to say something when the door opened and a policeman in uniform beckoned the man away. He followed with nervous alacrity and the door closed again on Harvey. Patience, pallor and deep anxiety: there goes suffering, Harvey reflected. And I found him interesting. Is it only by recognizing how flat would be the world without the sufferings of others that we know how desperately becalmed our own lives would be without suffering? Do I suffer on Effie's account? Yes, and perhaps I can live by that experience. We all need something to suffer about. But *Job*, my work on *Job*, all interrupted and neglected, probed into and interfered with: that is experience, too; real experience, not vicarious, as is often assumed. To study, to think, is to live and suffer painfully.

Did Effie really kill or help to kill the policeman in Paris whose wife was shopping in the suburbs at the time? Since he had left the police station on Saturday night he had recurrently put himself to imagine the scene. An irruption at a department store. The police arrive. Shots fired. Effie and her men friends fighting their way back to their waiting car (with Nathan at the wheel?). Effie, lithe and long-legged, a most desirable girl, and quick-witted, unmoved, aiming her gun with a good aim. She pulls the trigger and is away all in one moment. Yes, he could imagine Effie in the scene; she was capable of that, capable of anything.

'Will you come this way, please, Mr Gotham?'

There was a stack of files on Chatelain's desk.

The rest of that night Harvey remembered as a sort of roll-call of his visitors over the past months; it seemed to him like the effect of an old-fashioned village policeman going his rounds, shining his torch on name-plates and door-knobs; one by one, each name surrounded by a nimbus of agitated suspicion as his friends' simple actions, their ordinary comings and goings came up for questioning. It was strange how guilty everything looked under the policeman's torch, how it sounded here in the police headquarters. Chatelain asked Harvey if he would object to the conversation being tape-recorded.

'No, it's a good thing. I was going to suggest it. Then you won't have to waste time asking me the same questions over and over again.'

Chatelain smiled sadly. 'We have to check.' Then he selected one of the files and placed it before him.

'Edward Jansen,' he said, 'came to visit you.'

'Yes, he's the husband of my wife's sister, Ruth, now separated. He came to see me last April.'

Chatelain gave a weak smile and said, 'Your neighbours
seem to remember a suspicious-looking character who visited
you last spring.'

'Yes, I daresay that was Edward Jansen. He has red hair
down to his shoulders. Or had. He's an actor and he's now
famous. He is my brother-in-law through his marriage to my
wife's sister, but he's now separated from his wife. A lot can
happen in less than a year.'

'He asked you why there were baby clothes on the line?'

'I don't remember if he actually asked, but he made some
remark about them because I answered, as you know, "The
police won't shoot if there's a baby in the house."'

'Why did you say that?'

'I can't answer precisely. I didn't foresee any involvement
with the police, or I wouldn't have said it.'

'It was a joke?'

'That sort of thing.'

'Do you still hear from Edward Jansen?' Chatelain opened
one of the files.

'I haven't heard for some time.'

Chatelain flicked through the file.

'There's a letter from him waiting for you at your house.'

'Thanks. I expect you can tell me the contents.'

'No, we can't.'

'That could be taken in two senses,' Harvey said.

'Well, you can take it in one sense: we haven't opened
it. The name and address of the sender is on the outside
of the envelope. As it happens, we know quite a lot about
Mr Jansen, and he doesn't interest us at the moment. He's
also been questioned.' Chatelain closed the file, evidently
Edward's dossier; it was rather thin compared with some of

the others. Chatelain took up another and opened it, as if starting on a new subject. Then, 'What did you discuss with Edward Jansen last April?'

'I can't recall. I know his wife, Ruth, was anxious for me to make a settlement on her sister and facilitate a divorce. I am sure we didn't discuss that very much, for I had no intention of co-operating with my wife to that end. I know we discussed the *Book of Job*.'

'And about Ruth Jansen. Did you invite her to stay?'

'No, she came unexpectedly with her sister's baby, about the end of August.'

'Why did she do that?'

'August is a very boring month for everybody.'

'You really must be serious, Mr Gotham.'

'It's as good a reason as any. I can't analyze the motives of a woman who probably can't analyze them herself.'

Chatelain tapped the file. 'She says here that she brought the baby, hoping to win you over to her view that the child would benefit if you made over a substantial sum of money to its mother, that is, to your wife Effie.'

'If that's what Ruth says, I suppose it is so.'

'She greatly resembles your wife.'

'Yes, feature by feature. But of course, to anyone who knows them they are very different. Effie is more beautiful, really. Less practical than Ruth.'

Pomfret came in and sat down. He was less free of manner in the presence of the other officer. He peered at the tape-recording machine as if to make sure everything was all right with it.

'So you had a relation with Mrs Jansen.'

'Yes.'

'Your sister-in-law and wife of your friend.'

'Yes, I grew fond of Ruth. I was particularly taken by the baby. Of course, by this time Ruth and Edward had parted.'

'Things happen fast in your set.'

'Well, I suppose the parting had been working up for a long time. Is there any point in all these questions?'

'Not much. We want to check, you see, against the statements made in England by the people concerned. Did Ruth seem surprised when she heard that Effie was involved in the terrorist attacks?'

What were these statements of Ruth, of Edward, of others? Harvey said firmly, even as he felt his way, 'She was very much afraid of the police, coming into our lives as they did. It was quite unforeseen. She could no more blame her sister for it than she could blame her for an earthquake. I feel the same, myself.'

'She did not defend her sister?'

'She had no need to defend Effie to me. It isn't I who accuse Effie of being a terrorist. I say there is a mistake.'

'Now, Nathan Fox,' said the officer, reaching for a new file. 'What do you know about him?'

'Not very much. He made himself useful to Ruth and Edward when they were living in London. He's a graduate but can't find a job. He came to my house, here, to visit Ruth and the baby for Christmas.'

'He is a friend of your wife?'

'Well, he knows her, of course.'

'He is a weak character?'

'No, in fact I think it shows a certain strength of character in him to have turned his hand to domestic work since he can't find anything else to do. He graduated at an English university, I have no idea which one.'

'What about his friends? Girls or boys?'

'I know nothing about that.'

'Why did he disappear from your house?'

'I don't know. He just left. Young people do.'

'He had a telephone call and left overnight without saying good-bye.'

'I believe so,' said Harvey.

'He said the telephone call was from London. It wasn't.'

'So I understand. I was working in my cottage that night. You must understand I'm very occupied, and all these questions of yours, and all these files, have nothing whatever to do with me. I've agreed to come here simply to help you to eliminate a suspect, my wife.'

'But you have no idea why he should say he got a phone call from London, when he didn't. It must have been an internal call.'

'Perhaps some girl of his turned up in France; maybe in Paris, and called him. And he skipped.'

'Some girl or some boy?'

'Your question is beyond me. If I hear from him I'll ask him to get in touch with you. Perhaps he's come down with influenza.'

Pomfret now spoke: 'Why do you suggest that?' He was decidedly less friendly in French.

'Because people do come down with 'flu. They stay in bed. This time of year is rather the time for colds. Perhaps he's gone back to England to start a window-cleaning business. I believe I heard him speculating on the idea. There's always a need for window-cleaners.'

'Anything else?' said Chatelain.

'The possibilities of Nathan Fox's whereabouts are such that I could go on all night and still not exhaust them.'

'Would he go to join your wife if she asked him?'

Harvey considered. 'That's also a possibility; one among millions.'

'What are his political views?'

'I don't know. He never spoke of politics to me.'

459

'Did he ask you for money?'

'After Christmas he asked me for his pay. I told him that Ruth had the housekeeping money, and kept the accounts.'

'Then Mrs Jansen did give him money?'

'I only suppose,' said Harvey, 'that she paid him for his help. I really don't know.'

'Do you think Ruth Jansen is a calculating woman? She left her husband, came to join you with the baby, induced you to buy the château – '

'She wanted the château because of a tree outside the house with a certain bird – how do you say "woodpecker"?' – Harvey put the word to Pomfret in English.

Pomfret didn't recognize the word.

'It makes a sound like a typewriter. It pecks at the wood of the tree.'

'*Pic*', said Pomfret.

'Well, she liked the sound of it,' said Harvey.

'Are you saying that is why you bought the château?'

'I'd already thought of buying it. And now, with Ruth and the baby, it was convenient to me.'

'Ernest L. Howe,' said Chatelain. 'He came to see you, didn't he?'

'Yes, some time last autumn. He came to see his baby daughter. He wanted Ruth to go back to London with the baby and live with him. Which, in fact, she has now done. You see, he doesn't think of what's best for the child; he thinks of what's most pleasant for himself. To console his hurt pride that Effie walked out on him – and I don't blame her – he's persuaded her sister to go and live with him, using the child as an excuse. It's contemptible.'

Harvey was aware that the two men were conscious of a change in his tone, that he was loosening up. Harvey didn't care. He had nothing, Effie had nothing, to lose by his expressing himself freely on the subject of Ernie Howe. He was tired of being what was so often called civilized about his wife's lover. He was tired of the questioning. He was tired, anyway, and wanted a night's sleep. He deliberately gave himself and his questioners the luxury of his true opinion of Ernie.

'Would you care for a drink?' said Pomfret.

'A double scotch,' said Harvey, 'with a glass of water on the side. I like to put in the water myself.'

Chatelain said he would have the same. Pomfret disappeared to place the orders. Chatelain put a new tape in the recording machine while Harvey talked on about Ernie.

'He sounds like a shit,' said Chatelain. 'Let me tell you in confidence that even from his statement which I have in front of me here, he sounds like a shit. He stated categorically that he wasn't at all surprised that Effie was a terrorist, and further, he says that you know it.'

'He's furious that Effie left him,' Harvey said. 'He thought she would get a huge alimony from me to keep him in comfort for the rest of his life. I'm sure she came to realize what he was up to, and that's why she left him.'

Pomfret returned, followed by a policeman with a tray of drinks. It was quite a party. Harvey felt easier.

'I'm convinced of it,' he said, and for the benefit of Pomfret repeated his last remarks.

'It's altogether in keeping with the character of the man, but he was useful,' said Chatelain. He said to Pomfret, 'I have revealed to M. Gotham what Ernest Howe stated about Effie Gotham.'

And what Chatelain claimed Ernie had said was evidently true, for Pomfret quite spontaneously confirmed it: 'Yes, I'm afraid he was hardly gallant about her. He is convinced she's a terrorist and that you know it.'

'When did you get these statements?' said Harvey.

'Recently. Ernest Howe's came through from Scotland Yard on Sunday.'

'You've got Scotland Yard to help you?'

'To a certain degree,' said Chatelain, waving his right hand lightly, palm-upward.

Was he softening up these men, Harvey wondered, or they him?

'It would interest me,' said Harvey, 'to see the photograph of my wife that was taken of her by the police in Trieste, when she was arrested for shop-lifting.'

'You may see it, of course. But it isn't being handed out to the newspapers. It has been useful for close identification purposes by eye-witnesses. You will see it looks too rigid – like all police photos – to be shown to the public as the girl we are actually looking for. She is quite different in terrorist action, as they all are.' He turned to Pomfret. 'Can you find the Trieste photograph?'

Pomfret found it. The girl in the photo was looking straight ahead of her, head uplifted, eyes staring, against a plain light background. Her hair was darker than Effie's in real life, but that might be an effect of the flash-photography. It looked like Effie, under strain, rather frightened.

'It looks like a young shop-lifter who's been hauled in by the police,' said Harvey.

'Do you mean to say it isn't your wife?' said Pomfret. 'She gave her name as Signora Effie Gotham. Isn't it her?'

'I think it is my wife. I don't think it looks like the picture of a hardened killer.'

'A lot can happen in a few months,' said Chatelain. 'A lot has happened to that young woman. Her battle-name isn't Effie Gotham, naturally. It is Marion.'

In the meantime Pomfret had extracted from his papers the photograph of Effie that the police had found in Harvey's cottage. 'You should have this back,' said Pomfret. 'It is yours.'

'Thank you. You've made copies. I see this photo in every newspaper I open.'

'It is the girl we are looking for. There is movement and life in that photograph.'

'I think you should publish the police-photo from Trieste,' said Harvey. 'To be perfectly fair. They are both Effie. The public might not then be prejudiced.'

'Oh, the public is not so subtle as to make these nice distinctions.'

'Then why don't you publish the Trieste photograph?'

'It is the property of the Italian police. For them, the girl in their photograph is a kleptomaniac, and in need of treatment. They had put the treatment in hand, but she skipped off, as they all do.'

'I thought she went to prison.'

'She had a two weeks' sentence. That is a different thing from imprisonment. It was not her first offence, but she was no more than three days in prison. She agreed to treatment. She was supposed to register with the police every day, but of course – '

'Look,' said Harvey. 'My wife is suffering from an illness, kleptomania. She needs treatment. You are hounding her down as a terrorist, which she isn't. Effie couldn't kill anyone.'

'Why did you leave her on the motorway in Italy?' said Pomfret. 'Was it because she stole a bar of chocolate? If so, why didn't you stand by her and see that she had treatment?'

'She has probably told Ernie Howe that story, and he has told you.'

'Correct,' said Chatelain.

'Well, if I'd given weight to a bar of chocolate, I would have stood by her. I didn't leave her over a bar of chocolate. To be precise, it was two bars.'

463

'Why did you leave her?'

'Private reasons. Incompatibility, mounting up. A bar of chocolate isn't a dead policeman.'

'We know,' said Chatelain. 'We know that only too well. We are not such fools as to confuse a shop-lifter with a dangerous assassin.'

'But why,' said Pomfret, 'did you leave her? We think we know the answer. She isn't a kleptomaniac at all. Not at all. She stole, made the easy gesture, on ideological grounds. They call it proletarian re-appropriation. You must already have perceived the incipient terrorist in your wife; and on this silly occasion, suddenly, you couldn't take it. Things often happen that way.'

'Let me tell you something,' said Harvey. 'If I'd thought she was a terrorist in the making, I would not have left her. I would have tried to reason her out of it. I know Effie well. She isn't a terrorist. She's a simple shop-lifter. Many rich girls are.'

'Is she rich?'

'She was when she was with me.'

'But afterwards?'

'Look, if she needed money, she could have sold her jewellery. But she hasn't. It's still in the bank. My lawyer told me.'

'Didn't you say – I think you said – ' said Pomfret, 'that you only discussed the recent English translations of the Bible with your lawyer?'

'I said that was what we were discussing on Saturday morning, instead of listening to the news on the radio. I haven't said that I discussed nothing else with him. You see, I, too, am anxious to trace the whereabouts of my wife. She isn't your killer in Paris. She's somewhere else.'

'Now, let us consider,' said Chatelain, 'her relations with Ernest Howe. He has stated that he knows her character. She is the very person, according to him, who would take up with a terrorist group. The Irish terrorists had her sympathy. She was writing a treatise on child-labour in England in the nineteenth century. She often – '

'Oh, I know all that,' Harvey said. 'The only difficulty is that none of her sympathies makes her a terrorist. She shares these sympathies with thousands of people, especially young people. The young are very generous. Effie is generous in spirit, I can say that.'

'But she has been trying to get money out of you, a divorce settlement.'

'That's understandable. I'm rich. But quite honestly, I hoped she'd come back. That's why I refused the money. She could have got it through the courts, but I thought she'd get tired of fighting for it.'

'What do you mean, "come back"?' said Pomfret. 'It was you who left her.'

'In cases of desertion in marriage, it is always difficult to say who is the deserter. There is a kind of constructional desertion, you know. Technically, yes, I left her. She also had left me. These things have to be understood.'

'I understand,' said Chatelain. 'Yes, I understand your point.'

Pomfret said, 'But where is she getting the money from?'

'I suppose that the girl who calls herself Marion has funds from the terrorist supporters,' said Harvey. 'They are never short of funds. It has nothing whatsoever to do with my wife, Effie.'

'Well, let us get back to your visitors, M. Gotham,' said Chatelain. 'Has there been anyone else besides those we have mentioned?'

'The police, and Anne-Marie.'

'No one else?'

'Clara,' said Harvey. 'Don't you want to hear about Clara?'

'Clara?'

'Clara is the niece of my wife's sister.'

Chatelain was getting tired. He took a long moment to work out Harvey's representation, and was still puzzling while Pomfret was smiling. 'The niece?' said Chatelain. 'Whose daughter is she?'

'My wife's.'

'You mean the infant?'

'That's right. Don't you have a dossier on Clara?' Harvey asked the security men.

'M. Gotham, this is serious. A man has been fatally shot. More deaths may follow. We are looking for a political fanatic, not a bar of chocolate. Can you not give us an idea, a single clue, as to where your wife can be hiding? It might help us to eliminate her from the inquiry.'

'I wish I could find her, myself.'

X

'I BROUGHT YOU SOME English mustard,' said Auntie Pet. 'They say English mustard in France is a prohibitive price even compared to Canadian prices.'

Harvey had slept badly after his late return from the session with the security police at Epinal. He hadn't shaved.

'You got home late,' said Auntie Pet. Already, the château was her domain.

'I was with the police,' said Harvey.

'What were you doing with them?' she said.

'Oh, talking and drinking.'

'I shouldn't hob-nob too close with them,' she said, 'if I were you. Keep them in their place. I must say those plain-clothes officers who escorted me here were very polite. They were useful with the suitcases, too. But I kept them in their place.'

'I should imagine you would,' Harvey said.

They were having breakfast in the living room which the presence of Auntie Pet somehow caused to look very shabby. She was large-built, with a masculine, military face; grey eyes which generally conveyed a warning; heavy, black brows and a head of strong, wavy, grey hair. She was sewing a piece of stuff; some kind of embroidery.

'When I arrived,' she said, 'there was a crowd of reporters and photographers on the road outside the house. But the police soon got rid of them with their cars and motor-cycles. No problem.' Her eyes rose from her sewing. 'Harvey, you have let your house go into a state of dilapidation.'

'I haven't had time to put it straight yet. Only moved in a few months ago. It takes time.'

'I think it absurd that your maid brings her baby's washing to do in your house every day. Hasn't she got a house of her own? Why are you taking a glass of scotch with your breakfast?'

'I need it after spending half the night with the police.'

'They were all right to me. I was glad of the ride. The prohibitive price of fares,' said his aunt, as one multi-millionaire to another.

'I can well believe they were civil to you. I should hope they would be. Why shouldn't they be?' He looked at her solid, irreproachable shape, her admonishing face; she appeared to be quite sane; he wondered if indeed the police had been half-afraid of her. Anne-Marie was already tip-toeing around in a decidedly subdued way. Harvey added, 'You haven't committed any offence.'

'Have you?' she said.

'No.'

'Well, I should have said you have. It's certainly an offence if you're going to attack the Bible in a foreign country.'

'The French police don't care a damn about the Bible. It's Effie. One of their policemen has been shot, killed, and they think she's involved.'

'Oh, no, not Effie,' said Auntie Pet. 'Effie is your wife. She is a Gotham as of now, unfortunately, whatever she was before. No Gotham would stoop to harm a policeman. The police have always respected and looked up to us. And you're letting yourself go, Harvey. Just because your wife is not at home, there isn't any reason to neglect to shave.'

468

Harvey escaped to go and shave, leaving Auntie Pet to quarrel with Anne-Marie, and walk about the grounds giving orders to the plain-clothes police, whom she took for gardeners and woodsmen, for the better upkeep of shrubs and flower-beds, for the cultivation of vegetables and the felling of over-shady trees. From his bathroom window Harvey saw her finding cigarette ends on the gravel path, and chiding the men in full spate of Canadian French. Prompted by Anne-Marie, they took it fairly well; and it did actually seem to Harvey, as he found it did to Anne-Marie, that they were genuinely frightened of her, armed though they were to the full capacity of their leather jackets.

When Harvey came down he found in the living-room a batch of press-cuttings which he at first presumed to be about himself and Effie; Stewart Cowper had left them behind. But a glance at the top of the bundle showed him Edward's face, now beardless. The cuttings were, in reality, all reviews of the play Edward had made such an amazing success in; they were apparently full of lavish praise of the new star, but Harvey put them aside for a more serene moment. Amongst some new mail, a letter from Edward was lying on the table. Edward's name and address was written on the back of the envelope. Maybe the police hadn't read it; maybe they had. Harvey left this aside, too, as Auntie Pet came back into the room.

'I have something to tell you,' she said. 'I have come all the way from Toronto to say it. I know it is going to hurt you considerably. After all, you are a Gotham, and must feel things of a personal nature, a question of your honour. But say it I had to. Not on the telephone. Not through the mail. But face to face. Your wife, Effie, is consorting with a young man in a commune, as they call it, in the mountains of California, east of Santa Barbara if I recall rightly. I saw her myself on the television in a documentary news-supplement about communes. They live by Nature and they have a sort of religion. They sleep in bags. They – '

'When did you see this?'

'Last week.'

'Was it an old film – was it live?'

'I guess it was live. As I say, it was a news item, about a drug-investigation by the police, and they had taken this commune by surprise at dawn. The young people were all scrambling out of their bags and into their clothes. And I am truly sorry to tell you this, Harvey, but I hope you'll take it like a man: Effie was sleeping in a double bag, a double sleeping-bag, do you understand; there was a young man right in there with her, and they got out of that bag sheer, stark naked.'

'Are you sure it was Effie? Are you sure?'

'I remember her well from the time she came when you were engaged, and then from the wedding, and I have the wedding-photo of you both on my piano, right there in the sitting room where I go every day. I ought to recognize Effie when I see her. She was naked, with her hair hanging down her shoulders, and laughing, and then pulling her consort after her out of the extra-marital bag, without shame; I am truly sorry, Harvey, to be the bearer of this news. To a Gotham. Better she killed a policeman. It's a question of honour. Mind you, I always suspected she was unvirtuous.'

'You always suspected?'

'Yes, I did. All along I feared the worst.'

'Are you sure,' said Harvey, very carefully, 'that perhaps your suspicions have not disposed you to imagine that the girl you saw on the television was Effie, when in fact it was someone who resembled her?'

'Effie is not like anybody else,' said Auntie Pet.

'She resembles her sister,' said Harvey.

'How could it be Ruth? Ruth is not missing, is she?'

'No. I don't say it could have been Ruth. I only say that there is one case where Effie looks like somebody else. I know of another.'

'Who is that?'

'Job's wife, in a painting.'

'Job's wife it could not be. She was a foolish woman but she never committed adultery in a sack. You should read your Bible, Harvey, before you presume to criticize it.'

Harvey poured himself a drink.

'Don't get over-excited,' said Auntie Pet. 'I know this is a blow.'

'Look, Auntie Pet, I must know the details, every detail. I have to know if you're absolutely sure, if you're right. Would you mind describing the man to me?'

'I hope you're not going to cite him as co-respondent, Harvey. You would have to re-play that news item in court. It would bring ridicule on our heads. You've had enough publicity.'

'Just describe the young man she was with, please.'

'Well, this seems like an interrogation. The young man looked like a Latin-Mediterranean type, maybe Spanish, young, thin. I didn't look closely, I was looking at Effie. She had nothing on.'

Auntie Pet had not improved with the years. Harvey had never known her so awful. He thought, She is mistaken but, at least, sincere. He said, 'I must tell the police.'

'Why?' said Auntie Pet.

'For many reasons. Not the least of which is that, if Effie and her friend are in California and decide to leave – they might come here, for instance, here to France, or here to see me; if they do that, they could be shot at sight.'

'That's out of the question. Effie wouldn't dare come to your house, now. But if you tell the police how I saw them, the story will go round the world. And the television picture, too. Think of your name.'

Harvey got through to the commissariat. 'My wife has been seen in California within the last few days.'

'Who saw her?'

'My aunt.'

'Ah, the aunt,' said the police inspector.

'She says she saw her in a youth-documentary on the television.'

'We had better come and talk to your aunt.'

'It isn't necessary.'

'Do you believe your aunt?'

'She's truthful. But she might be mistaken. That's all I have to say.'

'I would like to have a word with her.'

'All right,' said Harvey. 'You'll find her alone because I'm going down to my cottage to work.'

He then rang Stewart Cowper in London but found he was out of the office. 'Tell him,' said Harvey to the secretary, 'that I might want him to go to the United States for me.'

He had been in his cottage half-an-hour when he saw the police car going up the drive, with the two security men from Paris. He wished them well of Auntie Pet.

Harvey had brought his mail with him, including Edward's letter.

In his old environment, almost smiling to himself with relief at being alone again, he sat for a while sorting out his thoughts.

Effie and Nathan in a commune in California: it was quite likely. Effie and Nathan in Paris, part of a band of killers: not unlikely.

He began to feel uneasy about Auntie Pet, up there at the house, being questioned by the security men. He was just getting ready to go and join them, and give his aunt a show of support, when the police car with the two men inside returned, passed his cottage, and made off. Either they had made short work of Auntie Pet or she of them. Harvey suspected the latter. Auntie Pet had been separated from Uncle Joe for as long as Harvey could remember. They lived in separate houses. There was no question of a divorce, no third parties, no lovers and mistresses. 'I had to make a separate arrangement,' Uncle Joe had once confided to Harvey. 'She would have made short work of me if I'd stayed.'

Harvey himself had never felt in danger of being made short work of by his aunt. Probably there was something in his nature, a self-sufficiency, that matched her own.

He wondered how much to believe of what she had told him. He began to wonder such things as why a news supplement from California should be shown on a main network in Toronto. Auntie Pet wasn't likely to tune in to anything but a main network. He wondered why she had felt it necessary to come to France to give him these details; and at the same time he knew that it was quite reasonable that she should do so. It would certainly be, for her, a frightful tale to tell a husband and a Gotham.

And to his own amazement, Harvey found himself half-hoping she was wrong. Only half-hoping; but still, the thought was there: he would rather think of Effie as a terrorist than laughing with Nathan, naked, in a mountain commune in California. But really, thought Harvey, I don't wish it so. In fact, I wish she wasn't a terrorist; and in fact, I think she is. Pomfret was right; I saw the terrorist in Effie long ago. Even if she isn't the killer they're looking for, but the girl in California, I won't live with her again.

He decided to get hold of Stewart Cowper later in the day, when he was expected back at his office. Stewart would go

to California and arrange to see a re-play of the programme
Auntie Pet had seen. Stewart would find out if Effie was there.
Or he would go himself; that would be the decent thing to do.
But he knew he wouldn't go himself. He was waiting here for
news of Effie. He was writing his monograph on the *Book of
Job* as he had set himself to do. ('Live? – Our servants can do
it for us.') He wouldn't even fight with Ernie Howe himself;
if necessary, Stewart would do it for him.

He opened Edward's letter.

Dear Harvey,
The crocs at the zoo have rather lack-lustre eyes, as can be
expected. Perhaps in their native habitat their eyes are 'like
the eyelids of the dawn' as we find in *Job*, especially when
they're gleefully devouring their prey. Yes, their eyes are
vertical. Perhaps Leviathan is not the crocodile. The zoo
bores me to a degree.

I wish you could come over and see the play before it
closes. My life has changed, of course. I don't feel that
my acting in this play, which has brought me so much
success, is really any different from my previous performances in films, plays, tv. I think the psychic forces, the
influences around me have changed. Ruth wasn't good
for me. She made me into a sort of desert. And now I'm
fertile. (We are the best of friends, still. I saw her the other
day. I don't think she's happy with Ernie Howe. She's only
sticking to him because of Clara, and as you know she's
pregnant herself at long last. She claims, and of course I
believe her, that she's preg by you. – Congratulations!)
Looking back – and it seems a long time to look back
although it's not even a year – I feel my past life had a
drabness that I wasn't fully aware of at the time. It lies
like a shabby old pair of trousers that I've let fall on the

bedroom floor: I'll never want to wear *those* again. It isn't
only the success and the money, although I don't overlook
that aspect of things – I don't want to crow about them,
esp to you. It's simply a new sense of possibility. One
thing I do know is when I'm playing a part and when I'm
not. I used to 'play a part' most of the time. Now I only
do it when I'm onstage. You should come over and see
the play. But I suspect that possibly you can't. The police
quizzed me and I made a statement. What could I say?
Very little. Fortunately the public is sympathetic towards
my position – brother-in-law, virtually *ex*-brother-in-law
of a terrorist. (Our divorce is going through.) It isn't a
close tie.

I've almost rung you up on several occasions. But then
I supposed your phone was bugged, and felt it better not
to get involved. Reading the papers – of course you can't
trust them – it seems you're standing by Effie, denying that
she's the wanted girl, and so on. Now, comes this ghastly
murder of the policeman. I admire your stance, but do
you feel it morally necessary to protect her? I must say, I
find it odd that having left her as you did, you now refuse
to see (or admit?) how she developed. To me (and Ruth
agrees with me) she has always had this criminal streak in
her. I know she is a beautiful girl, but there are plenty of
lovely girls like Effie. You can't have been so desperately
in love with her. Quite honestly, when you were together,
I never thought you were really crazy about her. I don't
like giving advice, but you should realise that something
tragic has happened to Effie. She is a fanatic – she always
had that violent, reckless streak. There is nothing, Harvey,
nothing at all that anyone can do for her. You shouldn't
try. Conclude your work on *Job*, then get away and start
a new life. If your new château is as romantic and grand

as Ruth says it is, I'd love to see it. I'll come, if you're still there, when the play closes. It'll be good to see you.

Affectionately,
Edward

Harvey's reply:

Dear Edward,

That was good of you to go to the zoo for me. You say the zoo bores you to a degree. What degree?

I congratulate you on your success. It was always in you, so I'm not surprised. No, I can't leave here at present. Ruth would be here still if it were not that the place is bristling with the police – no place for Clara whom I miss terribly.

As to your advice, do you remember how Prometheus says, 'It's easy for the one who keeps his foot on the outside of suffering to counsel and preach to the one who's inside'? I will just say that I'm not taking up Effie's defence. I hold that there's no proof that the girl whom the police are looking for is Effie. A few people have 'identified' her from a photograph.

Auntie Pet has arrived from Toronto wearing those remarkable clothes that so curiously bely her puritanical principles. This morning she was wearing what appeared to be the wallpaper. Incidentally, she recognized Effie in a recent television documentary about a police-raid on a mountain commune in California. She was with a man whose description could fit Nathan Fox.

I've been interrogated several times. What they can't make out is why I'm here in France, isolated, studying *Job*. The last time it went something like this:

> *Interrogator* – You say you're interested in the problem of suffering?
> *Myself* – Yes.
> *Interrogator* – Are you interested in violence?
> *Myself* – Yes, oh, yes. A fascinating subject.
> *Interrogator* – Fascinating?

Almost anything you answer is suspect. At the same time, supermarkets have been bombed, banks robbed, people terrorized and a policeman killed. They are naturally on edge.

There is a warrant of arrest out for my wife. The girl in the gang, whoever she is, could be killed.

But 'no one pities men who cling wilfully to their sufferings.' (*Philoctetes* – speech of Neoptolemus). I'm not even sure that I suffer, I only endure distress. But why should I analyze myself? I am analyzing the God of *Job*.

I hope the mystery of Effie can be cleared up and when your show's over you can come and see Château Gotham. Ruth will undoubtedly come.

I'm analyzing the God of *Job*, as I say. We are back to the Inscrutable. If the answers are valid then it is the questions that are all cock-eyed.

> *Job* 38, 2–3: Who is this that darkeneth counsel by words without knowledge?
> Gird up now thy loins like a man; for I will demand of thee, and answer thou me.

It is God who asks the questions in Job's book.

Now I hope you'll tell Ruth she can come here with Clara when the trouble's over, and have her baby. I'm quite willing to take on your old trousers, Edward, and you know I wish you well in your new pair, your new life.

Yours,

Harvey

PART III

PART III

XI

'SO THE LORD BLESSED the latter end of Job more than his beginning.' It was five days since Stewart Cowper had left for California. He had telephoned once, to say he had difficulty in getting the feature identified which Auntie Pet had seen, but he felt he was on the track of it now. There definitely had been a news item of that nature.

'Ring me as soon as you know,' said Harvey.

Meantime, since he was near the end of his monograph on Job, he finished it. The essay had taken him over three years to complete. He was sad to see his duty all ended, his notes in the little room of the cottage now neatly stacked, and his manuscript, all checked and revised, ready to be photocopied and mailed to the typist in London (Stewart Cowper's pretty secretary).

The work was finished and the Lord had blessed the latter end of *Job* with precisely double the number of sheep, camels, oxen and she-asses that he had started out with. Job now had seven sons and three daughters, as before. The daughters were the most beautiful in the land. They were called Jemima, Kezia and Kerenhappuch, which means Box of Eye-Paint. Job lived another hundred and forty years. And Harvey wondered again if in real life Job would be satisfied with this plump reward, and doubted it. His tragedy was that of the happy ending.

He took his manuscript to St Dié, had it photocopied and sent one copy off to London to be typed. He was anxious to get back to the château in case Stewart should ring with news. He hadn't told Auntie Pet of Stewart's mission, but somehow she had found out, as was her way, and had mildly lamented that her story should be questioned.

'You're just like the police,' she said. 'They didn't actually say they didn't believe me, but I could see they didn't.'

He got back to the château just in time to hear the telephone. It was from the police at Epinal.

'You have no doubt heard the news, M. Gotham.'

'No. What now?'

'The FLE gang were surrounded and surprised an hour ago in an apartment in Paris. They opened fire on our men. I regret to say your wife has been killed. You will come to Paris to identify the body.'

'I think my wife is in California.'

'We take into account your state of mind, Monsieur, but we should be obliged if – '

Anne-Marie was standing in the doorway with her head buried in her hands.

L'Institut Médico-Légal in Paris. Her head was bound up, turban-wise, so that she looked more than ever like Job's wife. Her mouth was drawn slightly to the side.

'You recognize your wife, Effie Gotham?'

'Yes, but this isn't my wife. Where is she? Bring me my wife's body.'

'M. Gotham, you are overwrought. It displeases us all very much. You must know that this is your wife.'

'Yes, it's my wife, Effie.'

'She opened fire. One of our men was wounded.'

'The boy?'

'Nathan Fox. We have him. He was caught while trying to escape.'

Harvey felt suddenly relieved at the thought that Nathan wasn't in California with Effie.

The telephone rang when, finally, he got back to the château. It was from Stewart. 'I've seen a re-play of the feature, Harvey,' he said. 'It looks like Effie but it isn't.'

'I know,' said Harvey.

He said to Auntie Pet, 'Did you really think it was Effie in that mountain commune? How could you have thought so?'

'I did think so,' said Auntie Pet. 'And I still think so. That's the sort of person Effie is.'

Anne-Marie said, 'I'll be saying good-bye, now.'

XII

EDWARD DRIVES ALONG THE ROAD between Nancy and
St Dié. It is the end of April. All along the way the cherry trees
are in flower. He comes to the grass track that he took last
year. But this time he passes by the cottage, bleak in its little
wilderness, and takes the wider path through a better-tended
border of foliage, to the château. Ruth is there, already showing her pregnancy. Clara staggers around her play-pen. Auntie
Pet, wrapped in orange and mauve woollens, sits upright on
the edge of the sofa, which forms a background of bright yellow and green English fabrics for her. Harvey is there, too.

'You've cut your hair,' says Harvey.

'I had to,' says Edward, 'for the part.'

It is later, when Clara has gone to bed, that Edward gives
Harvey a message he has brought from Ernie Howe.

'He says if you want to adopt Clara, you can. He doesn't
want the daughter of a terrorist.'

'How much does he want for the deal?'

'Nothing. That amazed me.'

'It doesn't amaze me. He's a swine. Better he wanted money than for the reason he gives.'

'I quite agree,' says Edward. 'What will you do now that
you've finished *Job*?'

'Live another hundred and forty years. I'll have three
daughters, Clara, Jemima and Eye-Paint.'

Muriel Spark (1918–2006) was born in Edinburgh in 1918 and educated in Scotland. A poet, essayist and novelist, she is most well-known for *The Prime of Miss Jean Brodie* and her writing is widely celebrated for its biting wit and satire. Muriel Spark has garnered international praise and many awards, including the David Cohen Prize for Literature, the Ingersoll T.S. Eliot Award, the James Tait Black Memorial Prize, the Boccaccio Prize for European Literature and the Golden PEN Award for a Lifetime's Service to Literature. She became an Officer of the Order of the British Empire in 1967 and Dame Commander of the Order of the British Empire in 1993, in recognition of her services to literature. *The Times* placed her eighth in its list of the '50 greatest British writers since 1945'. She died in 2006.

SPARK'S SATIRE

Anarchic, irreverent and razor-sharp, this new collection of Muriel Spark's satires confirms its creator as the mistress of British wit

From a fraudulent psychiatrist grappling with two equally fraudulent clients in *Aiding and Abetting*, to the dirty dealings of *The Abbess of Crewe*'s band of corrupt nuns, to the three plane crash survivors of *Robinson* eking out an existence on an Atlantic island after its resident mystic disappears, these three satires probe the recesses of human fallibility with formidable precision.

Spanning five decades, the glittering, sharp and sinister works of *Spark's Satire* confirm their author as one of our most incisive and wickedly funny satirists.

'Muriel Spark's novels linger in the mind as brilliant shards, decisive as smashed glass' John Updike, *New Yorker*

'Enchanting, devastating, genius' Helen Dunmore

www.canongate.tv

THE FINISHING SCHOOL

In *The Finishing School* Muriel Spark is once again at her biting, satirical best. On the edge of Lake Geneva in Switzerland, a would-be novelist and his wife run a finishing school of questionable reputation to keep the funds flowing. When a seventeen-year-old student's writing career begins to show great promise, jealousy and tensions run high.

A keen portrait of devouring regret, psychological unravelling and the glittering promise of youth, *The Finishing School* is the perfect partner to Muriel Spark's most famous novel *The Prime of Miss Jean Brodie*.

'One of her funniest novels . . . Spark at her sharpest, her purest and her most merciful' Ali Smith

'An eloquent, subtle, poetic exploration of what words are and what they do to us. Enchanting, devastiting, genius' Helen Dunmore, *The Times*

www.canongate.tv

THE BACHELORS

'I am dazzled by *The Bachelors*. It is the cleverest and most elegant of all Spark's clever and elegant books' Evelyn Waugh

The Bachelors displays the best of Sparkian satire, placing her at the heart of a great literary tradition alongside Waugh and Trollope, Wilde and Wodehouse. It demands rediscovery.

'It's easy to see why Waugh admired *The Bachelors*. On one level, it is a blithely carnivorous satire in the Waugh mould. The bachelors of the title – almost the only men we meet in the narrative – are the thirty-something male barristers, teachers, journalists and museum attendants of a small patch of West London. They lead inturned, doddery, superannuated lives, pottering between grocers, coffee-houses, bedsits and the houses of their mothers and aunts. But the comedy here is serious in a way that Waugh's satanically energetic comedies of misery rarely are . . . comedies of English manners have seldom been darker' *Daily Telegraph*

'My admiration for Spark's contribution to world literature knows no bounds. She was peerless, sparkling, inventive and intelligent – the crème de la crème' Ian Rankin

www.canongate.tv

THE PRIME OF
MISS JEAN BRODIE

The Prime of Miss Jean Brodie is Muriel Spark's most significant
and celebrated novel, and remains as dazzling as when
it was first published in 1961. Now available as an ebook.

Miss Jean Brodie is a teacher unlike any other, proud and cultured,
enigmatic and free-thinking; a romantic, with progressive, sometimes
shocking ideas and aspirations for the girls in her charge. At the
Marcia Blaine Academy she takes a select group of girls under her
wing. Spellbound by Miss Brodie's unconventional teaching, these
devoted pupils form the Brodie set. But as the girls enter their teenage
years and they become increasingly drawn in by Miss Brodie's
personal life, her ambitions for them take a startling and dark turn
with devastating consequences.

'Muriel Spark's most celebrated novel . . . This ruthlessly
and destructively romantic school ma'am is one of the
giants of post-war fiction' *Independent*

'A brilliantly psychological fugue' *Observer*

www.canongate.tv